The Whisper of Leaves

CRAIG SMITH

The Whisper of Leaves

SOUTHERN ILLINOIS UNIVERSITY PRESS

Carbondale and Edwardsville

05 04 03 02   4 3 2 1

Library of Congress Cataloging-in-Publication Data

Smith, Craig, 1950–
    [Silent she sleeps]
    The whisper of leaves / Craig Smith.
        p. cm.
    1. Murder victims' families—Fiction. 2. Mothers—Death—Fiction.
    3. College teachers—Fiction. 4. Women teachers—Fiction.
    5. Illinois—Fiction. I. Title.

PS3569.M51678 S55 2002
813'.54—dc21
ISBN 0-8093-2480-6 (alk. paper)   2002018760

Printed on recycled paper. ♻

The paper used in this publication meets the minimum requirements of
American National Standard for Information Sciences—Permanence of Paper
for Printed Library Materials, ANSI Z39.48-1992. ♾

For Martha

When a husband and wife have a single heart,
they bring ruin to their enemies and joy to their friends.

—Homer, *Odyssey*

Acknowledgments

Novels begin in the solitude of one's imagination and end with a community of friends and associates. For this reason, it is one of the great pleasures of writers to name those individuals whose support along the way has meant so much. First, I want to thank my wife, Martha, who believes in what I am doing. My mother, Shirley, and her husband, Marion Underwood, my brother Doug and his wife, Maria, have always supported my endeavors as well, and there are no words to describe what that has meant to me over the years. My father, Stanley, taught me tenacity, which more than anything gets a manuscript to press, and through the years my friends who read my fiction gave me courage to keep after the dream.

I owe a special debt of gratitude to Professor Don Jennermann of Indiana State University, who first introduced me to the poetry of the ancients, and to Professor Rick Williams of Southern Illinois University Carbondale, who ably took over in my education and read Plato and Homer and Sophocles with me, phrase by phrase. The two finest teachers I have ever encountered, I am lucky to have studied with them. For Professor Williams, I also have a special thanks. He not only believed in this novel after he read it, but he made the phone call that brought it to the attention of the staff of Southern Illinois University Press. To Matthew Jockers of Stanford University, I am indebted for his brilliant insights on the riddle of the word known to all men that appears in *Ulysses*. I have shamelessly borrowed his work and given it to Josie Fortune as her own.

Finally, I wish to thank Rick Stetter, who directs Southern Illinois University Press, and Elizabeth Brymer, my sponsoring editor, as well as Carol Burns, Kristine Priddy, Jonathan Haupt, and all the people at the Press who worked so hard on this project. Without them, *The Whisper of Leaves* would have remained only a dream stuck away in the solitude of my imagination.

Part One

Lues Creek

L UES CREEK *comes out of the wooded hills of southern Illinois. Surrounding it is once prosperous mining country full of crossroads with names like Gallows Hill, Pilatesburg, Clems Hollow, Prophets Grove, Carbine Ridge, Codswallop, and Huree. The creek tunes up fast on its run to a place called Campus Falls, then spews out over a polished stone ledge in the way that only wild things can. A few hundred feet below, the water crashes into Lues Creek Canyon and breaks apart on the wet stones so that the lower canyon walls are hidden in mist. From there, it gathers itself up and meanders lazily through civilization, such as it is. A couple of miles or so beyond the falls, well past Lues State University and the town of Lues itself, it joins its lonesome, crooked sister, West Lues Creek. From there to the Ohio River at Pauper Bluff, it carves a crooked path through a silent woods.*

Here the roads are unpaved and uncommon. It is a hill-locked land full of deer, timber rattlers, and folks who are solitary and cautious to a fault. There are no fences and no farms. What cabins you see you know to avoid. The locals survive on pure stubbornness. It has always been this way and remains so today. It is a place where every turn affords a haunting vision of a primeval time and every story, if someone bothers to tell it, comes down as legend.

Campus Falls

It was a gray Thursday afternoon, and the students were skipping a class in World History for a hike in the woods. They had been out for about half an hour, taking it slowly. They wore their fraternity and sorority sweat shirts, jeans, and either boots or tennis shoes. The two young men had blue nylon day packs slung across their backs. One of the packs was already empty, the other was mostly flattened. They all carried a beer can. They were laughing. The woods about them were alive with springtime. There were flowers on the forest floor, tender green leaves budding in the tress. The earth was black, the air moist and cool. There was a faint haze to the air, an old quiet to things. Last up the trail was Melody Mason, who was smoking a Lucky Strike filterless cigarette and shouting to the others that she needed to pee. She was a city girl and the thought of pulling her jeans down in the woods was more a fear of bugs and weeds than of mixed company. Still, Melody didn't really have a choice. She was a girl who liked her beer. When her companions ignored her first complaints, she called out again, "I'm going behind this tree. Nobody look! You guys! Don't look!" Bob Tanner, who was in the lead, called back that he was going to look, even though he kept pushing forward up the trail. Tossing her beer can into a patch of wild flowers, Melody slipped her jeans over her ample hips and screamed back that he had better not. She heard their distant laughter, then nothing more.

Melody was a plump, pretty girl. She had dark hair and there was a certain sparkle in her eye. She was a girl with a reputation, but it was mostly exaggerated. At least that was what she told herself. She had a problem with alcohol, that was all, and boys took advantage of it sometimes. Melody had been at Lues State almost a full year without indulging in these woods. There was plenty to do in her sorority house, lots of college bars to go to in Lues, even if it wasn't quite legal. She was only in the woods today because her suitemates, Cat and Susie, had talked her into it and because Bob Tanner was with them. They were taking Melody to Campus Falls. Still squatting beside her tree trunk, Melody rolled her eyes. Campus Falls was some kind of slew heaven and she had told them so, like that meant something. Melody took a drag on her Lucky, keeping it in her lips, and stood up. She didn't recognize the poison sumac she had squatted in. She pulled her jeans over her hips with some effort and looked out across the greening forest. She sucked it in and bounced a couple of times as she snapped her jeans to, then stepped back into the path. For the first time, Melody was struck with a chill of fear. Her friends had ditched her, and she was suddenly alone. She looked at the trail ahead of her, then back the way they had come. A palpable threat, the silence of the woods went on for miles. As she considered her situation, Melody felt sure someone was on the trail behind her, watching. Nervously, she dropped her cigarette on the path, leaving it to burn out, and started running in the direction she had last seen the others heading, then stopped herself almost immediately, gasping for breath. She listened for her friends, but all she could hear was the dull, muffled roar of the waterfall somewhere off in the distance.

Her voice squeaked when she called out to her friends. "You guys?" She repeated herself and looked behind her again. The trail was empty, but she was certain someone was back there. She swore with a whisper and decided to start on. That was when the hand grabbed her. Melody screamed and spun around into the face of Bob Tanner. He was shouting too.

It was a joke. The others came out from behind the trees, laughing at her. Melody knew it was because she was city and they were all from places like Raccoon Holler and Frog Pile Junction. "You guys scared the pee out of me!" she confessed, now laughing as hard as they were.

Mocking her, Jim Burkeshire squeaked, "scared the pee out of me." He was like that, really smart but not always nice. He was Bob Tanner's frat brother, and she didn't care if he took a flying leap into the frigging canyon they were hiking to.

Bob Tanner gave her a smile, "Come on, you've got to see the falls, Mel. This place is great." He had not let go of her yet. His hand was hot. The touch of it was nice, and Melody wished he would get up the nerve to ask her out. He had only been thinking about it since October.

Melody asked for a beer, and Cat Sommerville pulled the last can from Jim Burkeshire's pack. "You guys! We drank all twenty-four!" Cat announced. They all laughed and accused each other of being alcoholics.

As soon as they started up the rocks that guarded the falls, the footing grew treacherous. Melody downed her beer in two final gulps, threw her can back into the woods, and belched prettily. The five of them scrambled across the rocks, with Bob Tanner and Jim Burkeshire racing ahead of the others to the crest. That left Susie and Melody last in line, staring up at Cat's tight little virgin butt.

"You guys!" whispered Susie Hill for only Melody to hear, "we drank all twenty-four!"

Melody smiled up at Cat evilly and whispered a bit more loudly than she intended, "Slip, bitch."

Cat's black glossy hair swung freely over her shoulders as she looked back toward them. She was smiling, but she had heard Melody even if she pretended otherwise.

Embarrassed, Melody tried to changed the subject and asked Susie, "So is this place like . . . *safe?*"

Susie laughed, "Fuck no! That's why we're drunk." She scampered up the rocks, then stepped over the crest. Like the others, she passed out of sight. Melody heard Susie screaming as if she had gone over the cliff. Her voice echoed off the rock walls of the canyon.

Melody looked behind her as she started up the last incline. This time she wasn't disappointed. A couple of hundred feet below her, a man was standing beside a tree staring at her. Melody couldn't say exactly how old he was. She saw very little of him actually, since he pulled back out of sight immediately. He was probably in his twenties. He was average height. He had dark features, but at that distance, Melody could get no distinct impression of him, other than her certainty that he was a slew. The denim jacket and feed-store hat were the giveaways. He looked like one of those Georgia hicks in *Deliverance*.

Melody shivered at the thought and climbed the rocks quickly. She looked over her shoulder once and fought the impulse to shout out something stupid. She just wanted to get with the others. At the top of the hill, Melody saw her friends already out on the ledge overlooking the canyon. When she looked back, the slew was still hiding. She was safe. He wasn't coming after her, he knew better with Bob and Jim so close by. Before going on, Melody took a moment to look at the canyon. It was nearly a quarter of a mile long but only two hundred feet across at its widest point. On all four sides, bloodred sandstone walls, glistening with the mist of the falls, descended perpendicularly to the stream below, and despite Melody Mason's determination to be unimpressed with the place, she was excited by it, a little. Okay, she thought, the place was incredible. She hadn't expected anything like this. She had seen pictures, of course, but this wasn't like the pictures. This was like amazing! She urged herself toward the edge of the rocks, where she could get a better look. On her end of the canyon, the water poured over a rock that was still above her. Thirty or forty feet below her was a natural stone ledge that crossed behind the falls. About the width of a country road on this side, it narrowed to a couple of feet close to the other side. A wooden guardrail ran along it for protection. As Melody took all this in, Bob and Jim were running back and forth behind the falls. They were soaked and laughing. This side of the falls, Susie and Cat huddled in a niche well back from the railing. They too were soaked and laughing. Melody decided they had already run behind the falls.

All afternoon Melody had heard about the height of the falls and the kids who had jumped to their death or fallen there, but it had been meaningless until she had seen it. Even from here, well back of any sort of precipice, the sight of such a descent made her knees quiver and her heart pound uncontrollably. She looked down anyway. Hundreds of boulders were strewn so thickly in the stream bed that the water trickled in various channels along the canyon floor with no ground visible.

Before she started down to join the others, Melody glanced behind her to make sure the slew wasn't coming any closer. He was still hiding. They were always hiding in *Deliverance,* too. They just never went away.

Bob Tanner came out from under the falls and waved for Melody to join them. He shouted something, but his voice was lost in the thunder of the falls. Melody looked down into the canyon again, then shook herself out of her trance and stepped carefully over the rocks. She ducked under a hanging slab of moss-covered stone and breathed in the moisture. Fifteen feet below, she came out into the misty air at the very edge of the world. To her left, the canyon opened under her. To her right, a vertical wall of red sandstone soared up toward the source of the falls. Directly before her, Cat and Susie were wet, shivering and grinning as they watched Bob and Jim running senselessly behind the falls.

"I think someone is following us," Melody told Cat and Susie. By now the slew was simply a perverse curiosity. Cat asked her what she meant. Melody pointed back toward the woods. "There was a slew back there in the woods." Melody added with a wince, "I think he watched me pee."

Susie's lip curled, "He probably sniffed it after you left."

Cat gagged, "You guys! That's gross!"

Susie shouted up toward the rocks, "I hate slews!"

Melody joined her, "Go home, Slew!" Their voices echoed inside the canyon.

Cat tried to shush them. "You guys, what if he hears you?"

At their backs, there were screams. All three turned in time to see Bob Tanner and Jim Burkeshire coming at them with their arms flinging about like a couple of lunatic slews. They ran together. Bob, at the very lip of the rock, was coming right for Melody. Jim grabbed Susie, pushing her back along the ledge. Bob took Melody by the shoulders and turned her out toward the canyon, so she was leaning back against the railing. Over her own screams, Bob was shouting maniacally, "Don't jump, Mel! Don't do it!" His damp hands held Melody tightly, but the force of her weight, coupled with his pushing and tugging against her, snapped the water-rotted board supporting her.

As it did, Melody's weight pulled her out into space. Bob's grip was not as good as it should have been, and when the board broke, he had no chance to adjust his hold. Melody could feel herself sliding out of his hands, as a piece of the fence dropped away. The sudden panic in Bob's broad face was obvious. Melody's arms slipped entirely out of his fingers. Bob still held her sweatshirt, but that was all he held. The cotton sleeves stretched out as she went back farther, and Melody's screams ceased in the next desperate second. The only sign of their struggle was written in their stunned expressions, a mix of surprise, panic, and helpless fear. Melody didn't even know if the others saw what was happening. She could see nothing but the face of Bob Tanner, feel nothing but space under her. The sweat shirt pulled up gently over her belly. It inched up across her back.

Certain she was about to fall, Melody whispered to the others, "A little help, here." It was all the breath she had to offer.

She saw Bob's red face. She saw the red stone wall, then the gray sky above. Vaguely, she heard both Susie and Cat scream something. Her shoulders pulled away, and in panic, she looked below her. It was the wrong thing to do! She looked once more at Bob Tanner and to her terror saw him leaning toward her, his balance uncertain. His eyes shifted their focus to the canyon, and Melody was certain he was about to let go of her. Melody clawed at his forearms before he could do it. It was her only chance. Her sweatshirt slipped up as high as her shoulders. Her fingers slipped over the wet cloth of his sweatshirt, then her fingernails caught the thick cotton and tore into his flesh like talons. He was coming with her, she thought wildly. They were going over together!

Jim Burkeshire stepped up beside Bob and slipped his fingers between Melody's bare belly and her jeans. He jerked her toward him easily. Melody caught her balance, then pushed passed both Bob and Jim as she scrambled for safety. Looking back, she saw Bob wind-milling his arms, almost going over. At the last moment, Jim caught his shirt and pulled him back.

Melody stumbled into the niche in the rock beside Susie and Cat. She heard Susie and Cat screaming. She heard Bob answer all of them loudly, "I had her!" He walked toward Melody, who shivered as he got closer, "I had you, Mel! I was teasing!" Melody curled away from him. When he came closer still, she staggered past him, making her way toward the broken railing, screaming at him to leave her alone. She was certain she was about to vomit. At the edge, holding on to a steel pipe, she got down on her hands and knees and looked straight below. Her gut somersaulted as she realized she would *still* be falling if Jim hadn't caught hold of her. Fascinated by what had almost occurred, she studied the mist as it shifted slightly amid the rocks below. Still falling, she thought. She almost passed out at the idea, then blinked and suck at the air, a long, deep gasp.

That was when she saw something on the rocks below. Even as Melody tried to understand what it was, the mist covered it again. She kept watching, though, and soon she could see it again. Almost an illusion, it was utterly still, tiny, distant . . . the color of flesh.

A nude body, she thought, but then she could see nothing. She squinted. It was just beside the falls, on one of the large stones. As she continued staring down at it, a hand touched the small of her back. "Are you okay?" It was Jim Burkeshire. His hand gave her the creeps, but she didn't say anything about that. "There's someone down there!" she told him.

Jim Burkeshire knelt beside her. The others came closer and leaned over the railing to look as well.

"I think it's a body," Melody whispered.

Susie was the first to respond, straightening up. "Oh, God. Someone jumped."

"You see it?" Melody asked.

"Oh, God," Susie repeated. She saw it.

Bob came between them, "Where!" They all stared straight down into the abyss without seeing anything. "I don't see it," he said.

Melody saw it again and shouted, "There! Right below us!"

"I see it!" Jim shouted, pointing.

Cat, standing over him, jumped excitedly at the same moment, "There! There! I see it too!"

Melody screamed urgently, certain now she was right. "You see it?"

"It's a body!" Jim cried. "It has to be!"

Bob stared dumbly, "What is it?"

"Someone jumped," Jim answered him. "That's got to be it."

Bob stared, but he didn't see it. None of them did now. The mist seemed to swallow the image, rolling up over the boulders. Finally, Cat said they had better check to be sure. Then she laughed nervously. "I mean I don't want to call the police if it's like a sheet of plastic or something."

Susie giggled, "Maybe it's a blow up doll. Melody's slew was probably up here poking his squeeze and pop! There she goes, folks!" Susie made a wavy line of flight with her hand and arm, indicating a swirling, drifting descent. They all laughed nervously at the image. Then, almost in a single motion, they all looked back down into the canyon.

Lues Creek Canyon

They went back the way they had come. It was a long, circuitous descent. Melody watched for the slew, but he was gone. They took nearly thirty minutes before they came to Greek Circle. Once out of the woods, Bob wanted to forget it. He was sure it was nothing. The others convinced him that they had to go look and be sure. If it was a body, they couldn't just act like they hadn't seen it! Reluctantly, he agreed, and together the five them followed the trail until they were forced into the creek, then waded upstream into the rocky vaults at the mouth of the canyon. They swam a short way, and finally, waist deep in cold water, they entered the tight confines of the canyon. They couldn't see the ledge they had stood on—only the guardrail was visible. The falls dropped in a long heavy stream, a shower of white against the red walls. Even at the distance of almost a quarter of a mile away, the air was thick with mist.

All five of them pushed toward the falls, but because of the heavy rocks, they soon took separate routes. Melody found she was walking in water no more than knee deep, then suddenly she was into it as high as her chest. Slowly, she worked her way into the canyon. It was cold work. Overhead, the sky was stone gray. The light of day seemed to be fading, although that was only an illusion. It was still mid-afternoon. Melody saw Cat moving ahead of her well to her left as Jim Burkeshire, close on Melody's right, emerged from behind a small set of boulders. Momentarily, she lost sight of Susie and Bob. "You guys okay?" she called.

Bob appeared suddenly as he came out of the water and stood on one of the boulders, looking toward the falls. "This is crazy!" he shouted.

Without looking at him, Jim pushed forward, "So go back," he said. Bob Tanner leapt into the water again and pushed on. If they were teasing him, at least they were all getting wet.

Melody imagined seeing the slew waiting for her and felt a tremor of fear. He had just been out in the woods, she told herself reasonably. He wasn't following them. Then she decided the slew had tossed someone off the ledge. That was why he had been out here in the first place. And she was the only one who saw him! She looked for the others. Cat was standing on one of the bigger rocks now. She was totally soaked. Her black hair was flat against her scalp. She was trembling. Melody could not see the others. Maybe, she thought, the slew had heard them saying they had better check it out and had come into the canyon to wait for them. Maybe Cat and she were the only ones left. "You guys see anything?" Melody called. She knew they hadn't or they would have said something. She just wanted to hear their voices, something besides the roar of the falls.

Nobody answered.

Cat looked down at her sickly, then jumped back into the water. They were getting closer to the falls. Melody thought the guys were in front of her on her right, but then she saw a man's dark lean figure moving closer to Cat. Tensely, Melody watched. The two figures glided beside each other now, and Melody realized it was Jim Burkeshire.

Susie came up beside Melody. Bob climbed up on another stone. He looked directly into the falls. "To your right!" Melody called.

He jumped down again and angled right. Melody saw that Susie was staring ahead vacantly.

"Come on!" Melody commanded. "We're almost there."

Susie answered, "Fuck it!" and plunged forward. They all wandered among the heavy stones just in front of the falls, trying to find a way through. It was a labyrinth of narrow, watery passageways, the boulders sometimes as high as fifteen feet. Jim Burkeshire stood up on a rock and stared about. Melody had lost sight of the rest of them. The falls were almost directly overhead. A heavy mist poured over her face. "You guys?" she shouted.

Jim Burkeshire answered from his rock, "Still here!"

Bob's voice cut through the roar of the falls from well off to the right, "You guys really saw something?"

Up to her waist in the cold water, Melody waded around a rock that was twice as tall as she was. She found two more and climbed up into the crack between them, only to come face to face with more rocks. Melody was soaked, discouraged, and now convinced that what they had seen was just some reflection or, like Cat had thought, a sheet of plastic.

Susie Hill called to them from behind Melody, her voice shaking with cold, "Let's go home. It was nothing."

Jim Burkeshire answered from far to the right, "Another minute!"

Cat screamed.

Two-Bit

Dressed in his waders and slicker, a plastic cap slipped over his felt Stetson, Sheriff Pat Bitts splashed back into Lues Creek Canyon along with two uniformed Lues city police officers, a team of city detectives, and four county deputies. Bitts, who had known Lues Creek Canyon since he was a boy and was now fifty-seven years old, picked his way carefully along the east edge of the creek in order to avoid the deep center. Jason Morgan, his second in command, led the deputies well behind the sheriff. The city took the shortest route, straight up the center of the canyon. When Bitts got to the base of the falls, he looked back to see the dimly reflected lights coming through the twilight within the labyrinth of enormous boulders. Bitts cast the light of his Coleman about but didn't see the corpse. The campus security officer who had held the scene until the city police arrived gave the location as a pool in front of the falls. Bitts shook his head. There were a lot of pools in front of the falls. He pointed his light and saw three of them but no corpse.

Bitts had to shout to be heard when he called to Jason Morgan. "That boy said she was in *front* of the falls?" Morgan nodded, and the two of them shined their lights fruitlessly into the flashing sheet of water. Their lights searched behind several boulders, then into the white water directly before them. Finally, Morgan's light fell on a particularly violent hole and he shouted that he saw something. Bitts aimed his light at it also. Fifteen feet in diameter, the hole was rimmed by boulders. The water swirled and foamed. Something was in there all right. He saw what appeared to be hair, then the white lump of a human shoulder pressing up through the froth. He watched it spin, then slam against the rock.

At Morgan's signal, one of the county deputies got his camera out and began photographing the scene. The city detectives and one of the uniforms with his own camera came in and photographed the area. Finally, Bitts moved around behind the pool to a ledge that afforded the best access to reach in and grab at the body. Morgan followed. Morgan was short, maybe 5'7" in his thick socks, but he could deadlift a big man with a single hand. Bitts had seen him do it in too many fights to count. Bitts himself was six-and-a-half-feet tall. Before he got *sense*, Bitts had backed down from nothing but God. Bitts braced himself on the rock and, holding Morgan in an interlocking wrist grip, let the younger man lean out to snatch the corpse. On his second try, Morgan caught hold of the long hair. Two of the deputies and one of the city patrolmen came next to Bitts and Morgan, catching arms and legs. Slowly they lifted the body up from the churning waters, then waded back toward a huge flat rock just beside the falls, laying the victim across it. The torso had been eviscerated. Pulling his attention away from this, Bitts noticed a thin, gray mark encircling the neck. The ligature ran under each jaw, as if she had been hanged. Below this were two thumb size bruises at the center of the throat as well as bruises to each side of the neck. At the wrists and ankles, there were deep indentations. She had been tied up for several hours before she had died, apparently. The wonder was that she could have even walked in. Then again, maybe she hadn't.

Happy Harpin, the younger of the two city detectives, a man only a couple of years older than Jason Morgan, stepped up next to Bitts while he was looking at the corpse. He pointed at the woman's chest. Just over her heart were the letters *h-o-r,* the *r* capitalized. It was the work of a razor, Bitts decided, a day or two old, the wounds healed, then broken apart again. The sheriff looked overhead. As he did, the falls sent a heavy spray over his face. He had assumed, when the call first came in, the victim had fallen. Bitts's theory had been that his anonymous callers had been with the woman on the ledge above. She had gone through the railing somehow and dropped to her death. They had telephoned his office without identifying themselves because they didn't want to get involved. That, he had decided, or the call was a prank. Both were good theories until they got into a head-on with the facts. This woman hadn't fallen, and this sure wasn't a prank. He pointed his

Coleman through the gray light toward various rocks close by. He was looking for clothes, but there were none. Finally, Bitts stepped back, letting the older detective, Kyle Raider, study the victim. Raider was close to retirement. They had worked homicides together for more than twenty years when Raider was a state policeman with the Criminal Investigation Division and, later, after he had joined the Lues city police as a homicide detective. That Kyle hadn't become chief of detectives was a mystery to most people, but not Bitts. He was good at what he did, but he had no fire in his guts when it came to politics—unlike Colt Fellows, who had taken over the position.

Raider and Harpin stepped back at nearly the same moment, and Bitts nodded to his men. They lay a body bag next to the corpse, then lifted the shoulders into it. Next they brought the sack under the hips. Finally they brought the legs in and zipped it closed.

Four men took the body, while Raider joined Bitts on the walk out. "You figure she's a student?" Raider asked.

"Could be an older student," Bitts answered. "My guess is mid-twenties or so."

Raider nodded. "Whoever did it, Two-Bit, he was one mean son of a bitch."

Bitts allowed himself a thin, cold smile. "Hanged, strangled, and cut open." He shook his head, "Old boy just couldn't kill her enough, Kyle."

The detective nodded solemnly, "And that's only the half of it." He was talking about the rape with what looked like a knife. They walked for a while without talking. Bitts was pretty sure now that they had a murder with some profile to it Colt Fellows would be taking it for his own. He had done it before with a case involving the murder of a prominent attorney in town. Kyle Raider's sad old face carried the same conviction, though neither man mentioned it. At the end of the canyon, they came to the tight channel leading out and waded into the deep water. Bitts managed to keep it out of his waders, as he had going in, by walking along a submerged ledge. He had first found the footing when he was a boy. Back then, he had used the ledge to keep his nose out of the water, since in those days he couldn't yet swim. He let that memory, his first time into Lues Creek Canyon, wash over him as they left the serpentine passage and reached the trailhead where they had all parked their vehicles. Greeting them were four uniformed campus security officers. All dry. The one who had gone into the canyon earlier in the evening was gone on home—soaking wet and seven-eighths of the way to a jim-dandy cold.

Beyond this group, a small clutch of reporters had stationed themselves. In the distance, not two-hundred-yards southeast, the fraternities and sorority houses were lit up. Several hundred kids were milling about on the circle and edging closer to watch the police and sheriff's deputies as they loaded the body in the sheriff's van and taped off the area. The university would post a guard overnight, Detective Harpin told Bitts. Harpin was on Colt's fast track, as dirty as his boss, just not as smart about it. When he spoke to Bitts, the old sheriff kept his eyes on the trees.

After they had loaded the body, Bitts stripped off his waders, his slicker and the plastic raincover for his Stetson. He was perfectly dry, right down to his thick silver hair. Jason Morgan, his uniform plastered against his body, his boots squishing with water, watched enviously. Bitts enjoyed the moment. Age has few rewards the equal of besting a man in his prime, even if it is only tending to the creature comforts with the superior forethought of a man practiced in the field. Bitts reached into the back of his sedan, grabbed a sheriff's jacket to keep the evening chill off, then looked at his deputy. "You want to get the body on to the university medical center, Jason?" he asked.

It was an order, not a question, but his deputy was curious. "Sure. What are you going to do, Two-Bit?"

Bitts's old face creased with flinty humor as his gray eyes glittered brightly from under his Stetson. "Me? I figured since I'm on campus, I'd go looking for some babes."

Calls

Bitts spoke briefly to the reporters. An unidentified female. Homicide. When the questions started, he told them it would be the city's case. He answered a few more questions, then walked toward Harpin and Raider. Pointing toward Greek Circle, where the crowd of kids watching the excitement still milled about, Bitts told the two detectives, "Thought I might walk around over there and see if I can't find out who called us about that body. You two want to come along?"

Raider looked at the houses, then back toward his partner. "Love to, Two-Bit, but Colt just called us. He wants to see us before we do anything else."

Bitts gave the man half of a smile. They both knew what it meant. What bothered Bitts was Raider just seemed to take it in stride. Somewhere along the line, all the fight just got kicked out of him. That came, Bitts figured, from working for Colt Fellows.

"Well, been good almost working with you again, Kyle."

"Pleasure as always, Two-Bit."

As Bitts started away, Detective Harpin called to him. "You find anything, Sheriff, you let us know!"

Bitts turned and studied the young detective for a long, angry moment. No one, absolutely no one, told a county sheriff what his business was, and Bitts was half-inclined to say just that. Instead, he smiled. "You do the same, Detective."

At Greek Circle, Pat Bitts turned off the road and watched his deputies, the city vehicles, and media vans push on through campus. Bitts used the pay phone in the parking lot. Polly answered on the second ring.

"How you doing?" he asked.

"My husband's out, why don't you come on by?"

"That old bear is a mean one is the way I hear it. I don't think I want to risk it, even for a country beauty like you."

"Was it a bad one, Two-Bit?"

"They're all bad, Pol."

"You come on home now. There's nothing there that can't wait until tomorrow."

"The call we got this afternoon was from some kids. I thought I might try to see if I could find who it was."

"And it can't wait 'til morning?"

He wanted this one before Colt Fellows got into it. "Well, they're all mostly home now." He looked at his watch. It was just after nine o'clock on a Thursday night. They would all be home inside three or four hours. "It's kind of important," he added.

"I'll be up."

"No, you get some sleep! I'm looking at midnight if I don't have any luck. If I find them, it'll be later."

"I'll be waiting," Polly answered.

When they broke off, Bitts checked the telephone directory in the dim light and found two Yeagers. Calvin Yeager was the head of security at Lues

State. Yeager had been Colt Fellows's supervisor when Colt was a patrolman up in Peoria years ago. A couple three years back, right after Colt's promotion, if Bitts remembered it correctly, the job of director of campus security had come open, and Yeager had slipped into the job without much resistance. Bitts didn't hold that against the man, everyone was entitled to a friend with some pull, but he had heard rumors that Yeager coveted a bit more than just being a glorified supervisor of parking lots. He had heard, in fact, Yeager was toying with the idea of running for sheriff. Right now, Bitts was running unopposed, as he had the last two elections, but if Yeager wanted to try his luck, Bitts was ready. Win or lose, that was just fine with him. Once his lawman days were finished, he was aiming for a long tenure on the Ohio River with a fishing pole, plenty of cold beer, and Polly there beside him to make life worth living.

"Cal?" he said into the phone. "Listen, I'm sorry to bother you at home, but we've brought out the body. The reason I called, I want to find the kids who telephoned us."

Bitts had called Yeager personally that afternoon and asked him to send someone into the canyon to check out the report of a body in the canyon before he contacted the city and they all went marching in on one great big frat-style hoax.

"That could be tough, Two-Bit. It's a big campus."

Bitts glanced toward the houses. They were still lit up. Most of the dark swarming masses who had spilled out to watch the excitement were still there. "I thought I could nose around Greek Circle here and find out something. You know they pretty much lay claim to the falls and canyon."

"Yeah, we've had some problems with that. Listen, I'll come on out and run interference for you, if you don't mind. I've had a lot of contact with the frats this last year or so. Fact is, my son's a Tau Lambda pledge this semester. I might be able to help, I guess is what I'm trying to say."

It was a nice speech, as far as it went, but Bitts knew the university was fiercely resistant to unescorted members of law enforcement agencies on campus. It was a policy that kept the reportable consumption of drugs and alcohol at near zero and that made the moms and pops of the great Midwest happy with Lues State. "I'm at the west end of the Circle."

"I'll find you," Yeager answered.

Ruminations

Hanging up, Bitts studied the crowd of kids again, then headed back to his cruiser. He started the car, then hit his lights. When he didn't drive away, he could almost feel their reaction. They grew quiet first, then suspicious. Then the smart ones went inside. Finally, even the slow learners found refuge, and Bitts, settling back to wait for Yeager, called in his position to his second-shift dispatcher.

Besides being the sheriff of Lues County, Bitts performed the role of coroner for all suspicious deaths, city or county. That meant he was responsible for determining the manner, cause, and time of death. That was usually a fairly straightforward medical issue, but there were always variables that had nothing to do with medical science. In a case like this, with the body temperature compromised by the water and with the contents of the stomach, like the stomach itself, eliminated from the equation, they wouldn't have much direct medical evidence. Rigor mortis could give them a good idea about the time, but witnesses could narrow it down. If the case ever got to trial, that just might prove to be critical.

Bitts snapped on the lamp on his console, taking a pen and a fresh notepad, he muttered fondly, the way his uncle had always done it when he had been the sheriff and Bitts was his deputy, "What are the observable facts here, Two-Bit?"

To start with, the call, which should have gone to the city, had come to the sheriff's office at 4:41. Jerri, his second-shift dispatcher, had said the caller was a male—calm, intelligent, and cautious. That alone was a curious piece of information, Bitts decided. Most people finding a dead body lost about twenty IQ points. Jerri had told Bitts there were voices in the background. She was fairly sure she had heard one male and two females. Bitts calculated thirty minutes from the base of the falls to the first public telephone, the one he had just used. It was maybe five or ten minutes quicker if you knew to use the east edge of the canyon, where the footing was level and the water rarely rose over your knees. With the call occurring at a nice round 4:40, that put the death as late as twenty-five minutes before the call, about 4:15. Assuming the callers were *not* the murderers, there were other factors to consider, of course. Had the killer still been inside the canyon when the kids started in?

Had they interrupted him or maybe walked right by him as he left? With the boulders scattered about, it was possible to conceal yourself. Maybe he had been inside the canyon when they entered, then followed them out. On the west wall of the canyon, the water was deep and still and the big boulders provided good cover if you wanted to hide.

Bitts had seen the body at 8:20. Typically, rigor mortis began to set in between two and six hours after the death. Assuming a typical situation, at least until he could get the autopsy report from Waldis, the death probably could not have occurred earlier than 2:20. Neatly on the left side of the pad, he wrote TIME OF DEATH—2:20–4:15.

"Working hypothesis," he whispered, "kids go into the canyon, leaving the trailhead no later than 3:40."

His brow creased, as he drew a rectangle, roughly duplicating the general shape of the canyon. By the falls, he placed an X. At the entrance, he wrote 3:40. It was maybe too much to hope for that the kids had seen the killer, but it was possible. Certainly, it would have been beyond the killer's control if he met someone as he left the canyon. It was a chance, anyway, and given the condition of the body, the lack of any rigor around the neck or in the fingers or toes, Bitts was inclined to put the death as close to 4:15 as reason and circumstance could afford. Truth was even that seemed a bit early.

He looked out at the parking lot, at the flash of headlights, but saw it wasn't Cal Yeager. The kids were all inside. He was sure they were keeping an eye on him. He looked at his numbers again, bounced the tip of his pen on the pad several times, then wrote "Clothes." He underlined it. Her clothes were carried out or they were left somewhere in the canyon. Or she didn't have any. Bitts had worked one like that a few months earlier and never did find the clothes. Be easy enough to find out tomorrow, he told himself. He tapped his pen on the pad again. Then he wrote, "Carries body in?" It seemed like he would have to, but he couldn't imagine packing a woman over your shoulder and hiking back into the canyon, not with anyone on Greek Circle able to watch! He shook his head at the idea, then smiled serenely recalling one of the first things his uncle had taught him. The simple ones never were. The crazy ones, what looked like a real mystery at the start, just had a way of solving themselves.

Crazy as this thing was, Bitts thought, even Colt Fellows would probably have it worked out by happy hour tomorrow. Assuming, of course, the sheriff of Lues County didn't beat him to it.

A Few Anomalies

There were a total of thirteen fraternities and nine sororities on Greek Circle. The houses were set to either side of a wooded circular drive, with most of the houses pushing back into the forest. The houses were large, three-tiered structures, sufficient for forty to sixty kids, all university owned, rented by the various chapters of different national orders. The complex was marked by a distinctive architectural design, but the various buildings were pretty much interchangeable.

When Cal Yeager showed up, it was just after 9:30. They hit the first door at 9:40. Yeager did the talking. His son, Vincent, actually answered the door at their second stop. Yeager explained that they were looking for some kids who had found a body. The kids weren't suspects, and they weren't in trouble. It was just important that Sheriff Bitts talk to them. As witnesses, they could help clear up a few anomalies in the investigation—he actually said *anomalies*. After the initial questions, Yeager would finally step back and let the sheriff try a couple. Did anyone see any hikers this afternoon, anything unusual? Bitts asked. A young woman with long reddish blonde hair? Maybe between one o'clock and four o'clock? To this, some of the young men said they would ask around and left it at that. Others sent someone through the house, while Yeager and Bitts waited. Vincent Yeager's fraternity was no different from the rest. The law did not cross the threshold without a warrant. A little smirk on his face, too, when he refused them, and his dad just took it, the way he took it from all of them, smiling, friendly, good ol' Cal Yeager, the sap. After an hour-and-a-half, the two men had nothing for their trouble but unspoken insults and, for Bitts, the mother lode of indigestion.

When they started on the sororities, they found a different attitude immediately. Bitts reflected, maybe a bit too sarcastically, they had already been notified of his presence and had had enough time to get their marijuana flushed. In each house, he and Yeager were able to enter the formal lounge and call the women into their presence. Bitts made his plea without Yeager's help this time. He was running out of chances, and he wanted those witnesses. Two women had been with his male caller. He needed them. He had a coed who had been raped and murdered, he told the women. He didn't know if she was a coed or not, but he wanted them thinking about their own skins.

He told them the witnesses who had called his office could be of enormous help and might not even realize it. Having said this, he turned the screws down a little, the way Yeager never would. "A man like this won't stop until he's caught. He waits until one of you gets alone, then he grabs you, like he grabbed that poor girl this afternoon!" He let this settle over them, before he added the rest, "Now a lot of times, ladies, these kind of men will find themselves what we call a *hunting ground*. . . ."

At the third house, as Bitts said these words, a lone hand went up. "I think we'd better talk," the girl announced. The girls to either side of her flushed and looked at her. She looked at them, and the three of them stood, all about nineteen or twenty, all pretty much worried. When the others had gone, Cal Yeager and Sheriff Pat Bitts faced them. The one who had first announced her involvement was a beautiful young woman, thin with dark glossy hair nearly to her waist. She dressed well and had the look of a conscientious student. She seemed to be a girl unused to deception. The other two were cut from different cloth. They were nervous, but Bitts saw immediately they weren't at all relieved to have come forward. They had an edginess about them that Bitts couldn't entirely trust. In fact, he was fairly certain they hadn't hardly a neighborly acquaintance with the truth.

"A young man called us this afternoon," Bitts said to them.

Conspirators, the three of them looked at one another. "There were two others with us," the pretty one answered. "They're both in Tau Lambda Kappa."

"Their names?"

She looked at the other two again, then answered him, "Jim Burkeshire and Bob Tanner. Jim made the call to you."

Bitts turned to Yeager, "Can you get them?"

Yeager nodded. It was his son's house.

When the young men arrived, Bitts pointed toward two empty seats, then told Cal Yeager, "I want to talk to each one in turn, and I don't want these people comparing notes. They can study or they can sleep, but I don't want any talk among them." To the kids, he added, "If one of you wants to get some blankets and pillows or maybe some school books, that will be okay with me." Fiercely now, Bitts looked at them in turn, daring them to lie again.

The thin, intelligent young man answered, "We're okay." He hadn't lied to Bitts. It was the other one, the big, dumb one, but Bitts had seen this one, Jim Burkeshire, in the background at the Tau Lambda Kappa house, while his buddy Bob Tanner stood next to Cal's kid and lied six ways to Sunday. He had almost called this Burkeshire kid out to ask him some questions, just gut instinct. Well, he thought, trust the gut next time, Two-Bit! Cal had been handling them all with his kid gloves on, and Bitts had minded his manners. Enough of that!

Bitts pointed at Cat Sommerville, not an entirely friendly gesture, "I'll start with you, Catherine."

When they had settled into a study room, Bitts asked the girl about that afternoon. As she started to explain where they had gone, he stopped her. "You went up to the falls?"

She nodded. Her look seemed to ask him what he had expected.

"What time was that?"

"I don't know what time we started exactly, but I checked my watch when the last beer was gone. I was thinking we were drinking too fast, you know?" Bitts nodded agreeably to keep her talking. "It was ten minutes before three then."

"Where were you at that point?"

"We were on the trail just below the falls. I got to the falls about three o'clock, I guess, maybe a couple of minutes before that."

Bitts looked at her watch. "Was that the watch?" Cat Sommerville nodded. "Have you set it since you got back or wound it?" She shook her head, and he gestured with his fingers to see it. She took it off and handed it to him. The hands indicated it was 11:57, the same as his own. He gave her the watch back.

"We didn't actually go to the top. We went out on the ledge just under the falls." Bitts nodded to let her know he knew the area. "We were going to hike across, then go to the top, but Melody saw the body."

Bitts smiled angrily. "Are you telling me you could see the body from up there?"

"We saw something. We thought it might be a body." Bitts shook his head. It didn't seem possible, but he didn't say it. "That's why we went down to check," she added.

"Now wait a minute. You were on the ledge just under the falls at three o'clock, then went down into the canyon?"

"That's what I said." Cat Sommerville gave him a look of obvious resentment. Her expression seemed to say she was telling the truth, and she couldn't understand why he wouldn't accept that.

"Go on," Bitts told her irritably.

"I was the first to find her. I'll never forget it."

Bitts nodded impatiently. He was pretty sure now they had all worked up the same story, and he was going get five statements nearly identical in their details. He just couldn't figure out why, unless these kids had actually killed the woman.

"What time was this?"

"I don't know. I didn't look at my watch."

"How did you know it was a woman?"

"Excuse me?" The look Bitts got was something beyond astonishment. She thought he was crazy.

"Did you assume it was a woman because you saw long hair?"

Cat looked trapped, nervous, as though she imagined he was making some kind of come-on. Noticing the effect, Bitts walked entirely away from her. He looked out one of the windows into the dark night. "Tell me exactly what you saw, Catherine."

"I saw the body of a woman lying on a rock. She didn't have any clothes on. I know what a woman looks like, you know!" This was supposed to be dripping with irony. Instead, the effect was shrill, odd, even panicked. Bitts felt a warm rage boiling up in him. First the boys, when Yeager had talked to them, now this girl. What was going on here? "It was almost like she was asleep, except her eyes were open. They were rolled back in her head. The face was swollen, but she was beautiful. She was so beautiful, and we just all stared at her for the longest time."

"Why didn't you people stick around after you called my office. Why didn't you identify yourselves?"

"We voted. The majority wanted to stay out of it. They were afraid."

"How did you vote, Catherine?"

"I said we should call and identify ourselves. So did Jim."

"What time did you call my office?"

"I don't know. As soon as we came out. I know we came back, made the call. I took a shower, changed clothes. Dinner was at 5:15. We just made it. I did, anyway. Melody and Susie didn't show for dinner. They stayed in their room, I guess."

"Did you know the dead woman?"

"No. I'd never seen her."

Still at the window, Bitts studied her angrily. "We'll have an ID by tomorrow, I expect. I don't want to find out she was a friend of yours, maybe a classmate or one of your sorority friends."

"What is your problem?" Cat Sommerville had become progressively angrier as they talked. This was pure aggressiveness, and it bothered him. It could have been an act, but if so, it was a good one.

"I'll tell you my problem, Catherine. My problem is I found a woman who had been gutted. You know how a hunter guts what he kills, Catherine? That's what I saw! Gutted and then tossed into a whirlpool like so much trash! The water was running so fast and white I could hardly see her when I was standing right over her, and you tell me you could see her from the falls!" Cat Sommerville's face was expressionless but washed entirely of color. "Is that what you saw too, Catherine?"

"I told you what I saw."

The two of them stared at each other in a cold rage. "Well, I don't believe you."

"I can't help that. I'm telling the truth."

"On a rock?"

"That's what I said."

"Okay. You see any marks? Bruises? Anything like that?"

"Something on her chest, some kind of letters, I don't remember what."

Bitts looked at her in surprise. "Anything else?"

"I think there was something on her wrists. Oh! Like on her neck . . . something on her neck, like a band, I guess. I don't remember exactly." She shook her head, frustrated at her failure to recall everything.

"You see bruises on her neck?"

"I don't think so. I don't know."

"Think, girl!"

"I am. I don't know. I can't remember. There was something here." She pointed just under her jaw. "Is that what you mean?"

"Here," he answered, pointing to his own neck, "like she had been grabbed and throttled."

"I'm sorry."

Bitts stayed with the young woman several more minutes, but he couldn't really push it. She had given him all she was going to. When he asked her to go through it all again, to let her hang herself with the details, she didn't make any mistakes. Maybe one of the others would scare into the truth, especially if he could catch one of them in a contradiction. This one, not likely.

"Good enough," he said finally. "Is there anything else you can think of that I ought to know?"

"Only about the man."

Bitts felt his pulse kick up. Here it was, the thing falling into his lap. He hadn't even remembered to ask, he had been so upset about the lying!

"What man? Talk to me."

"I didn't see him. I don't know if anyone else did, either. I mean besides Melody. She thought he was following us."

"Into the canyon or out of it?"

"Above the falls. It was before we saw the body. She said she thought he had watched her . . . she had to pee, and she thought he watched her. Anyway, Susie said he probably sniffed it. Something like that. I said they were gross, and they started screaming and calling him . . . something."

"Calling him what?"

"A slew. That's what the kids call the locals." She gave Bitts a look, as if to say, You're a slew. You know all about slews.

Josie Hazard

Bitts was at the trailhead to Lues Creek Canyon at 7:15 the next morning. There were already more than a half-dozen city and university police vehicles in the clearing and a WKTV van parked on the trail. As Bitts came out of his cruiser, he saw Colt Fellows walking around the van, apparently coming down from the top of the falls or maybe just from behind a tree. Bitts was hardly surprised to see Colt was dry.

"Two-Bit! Glad you could make the party. I went ahead and started without you." In his mid-thirties, Colt was a big man, overweight and flushed. He had a thick, short neck and a round, mean face that one or two ill-advised men had tried to adjust—to their sorrow. The first time he met Colt, Bitts had been impressed. He was agreeable, even friendly. Partly, it was the pure mass of the man. He was hard to ignore. Partly, it was the way he took you into his confidence. It hadn't been long, though, before Bitts changed his mind about the man. Colt Fellows was a lot of bark and not much more. To put it plainly, he was lazy—always ready for the shortcut. Not that Colt didn't have his strengths. He was a fairly good administrator, or at least he always knew what was going on, and when it came to interrogation, especially getting confessions, Colt Fellows was the best. It was hard to admit, because Bitts disliked the man so much, but the truth was Bitts had never seen a lawman to equal Colt when it came to getting a suspect to give it up. It had to do with an innate sense of timing. He never missed his chances when they presented themselves. He had a nose for a man's weaknesses, knew instinctively what he valued and what he wanted. He never pushed a thing when it wasn't ready to give way, so when he did push, walls came crashing down.

"How you doing, old man?" There was a touch of affection in this, if not sincerity, as Colt reached to take Bitts's hand.

"I've had longer nights."

"I heard you got Cal Yeager out of bed! That there takes some doing!"

Bitts smiled ingenuously. "Nothing too serious. We just kicked around Greek Circle talking to the kids."

"You get anything from your witnesses, Two-Bit?"

Bitts shook his head, very happy he had told Cal Yeager as little as possible. "Five different versions of absolutely nothing."

"Well, I wouldn't worry about it. After we got our body to the med center last night, one of the orderlies recognized her as one of the strippers out at the Hurry On Up."

"Paper said the name was Hazard," Bitts answered.

Colt grinned. "As in 'I married a lunatic.' The worst of them, Two-Bit: John Christian. You remember Jack Hazard, don't you?"

"I've arrested him a couple of times, but it's been a few years back. Quite a few, actually."

"Murder, wasn't it?"

"They were both homicides."

"Whatever. Soon as I knew what I had, I had one of my people called Jack and get him down to the med center. He shows up with his daughter, makes it official, and I proceed to get his movements for all of yesterday. He tells me he went out to your office Wednesday to make a missing person's report. You hear about it?"

"Missing person? No."

"She was apparently on campus sometime Tuesday afternoon but then never made it home."

"Must be some comfort to Kyle Raider to have his chief of detectives assisting him," Bitts offered pleasantly.

"Kyle's off the case, Two-Bit. I made the decision as soon as I heard what we had! In his day, Kyle was a hell of a cop, but the last couple of years . . . seems he's just marking time 'til retirement."

"We can all rest easy now you're running things."

Colt smiled at this like he thought Bitts meant it. "Well, there's still work to do, but at least we know who did it."

Bitts started to answer but stopped when he heard a car pulling up. Both men watched Jason Morgan climb out of his patrol car, two large cups of coffee balanced delicately in his hands. He juggled the cups briefly, closed the door with his foot, then started for Bitts and Fellows.

Colt Fellows laughed and shouted loudly enough for Morgan to hear him, "Damn! Two-Bit, how do you get your people trained like that? I don't get a cupcake on my birthday."

Morgan came toward them and grinned at Fellows, not entirely un-friendly, "If you'd quit acting like a horse's ass, they'd bring you coffee! I'd bring you coffee if you did something about that bad breath." He handed a cup to the sheriff, "There you go, sir. Cream 'til Thursday, like you like it." To Fellows, "How's it going, big guy?"

"Keep grinning, Jason. You're the one going out to arrest Jack Hazard this morning."

Morgan started to sip his coffee but looked up at this. "What are you talking about? Have you got something?"

"Your body last night. It was Jack Hazard's wife."

Morgan made a face. It didn't register.

"She's a stripper at the Hurry On Up. Blows half the town for drinks. And Jack don't give a damn, long as he gets the money."

"You some kind of expert on the strippers out there?" Jason asked him.

"All I know is the old whore flunked her swimming lessons last night. One less frigging Hazard, am I right?"

Jason grinned coldly, "I don't know about that, but you're plenty stupid."

"What time is Waldis cutting, Jason?" Bitts asked.

Morgan shook his head, "I was just talking to him. He's teaching a class this morning. Doesn't know when he can get to her, but he's scheduled it for eleven o'clock. They're supposed to give us a call in time for us to get there."

"Like to get the time of death fixed," Bitts muttered.

"Late," Colt answered. Bitts looked at him surprised. "Figure, half hour after six, maybe seven o'clock, somewhere in there. Be my guess."

Bitts nodded thoughtfully. "It's food for thought," he said. "Still, be nice to get a medical opinion."

"Only thing Waldis is going to tell you is how, Two-Bit. We get that, and I go for the warrant, which I'm going to have to ask you guys to execute, much as I envy you the pleasure."

Morgan smiled easily, sipping his coffee. "Got any proof it was Jack Hazard, Colt?"

"Motive, means, and opportunity, Jason. Not to mention a lawman's instincts."

"Gee, that's good enough for me." Morgan turned to Bitts, "Why don't we just go on out and get him now?"

"We go when I say," Bitts answered. There was no humor in this, and Morgan's face went blank. He turned on his heels and made a quick exit from the two men. At the car, he pulled out waders and a heavy raincoat. The young man was prepared this morning, not that it was going to do him any good.

Bitts called to him, "We're going up the trail, Jason. You won't need that stuff today. Just a camera for now."

"What's up there?" Colt Fellows asked.

Bitts smiled mystically, "Woods, Colt. A detective of your stature, I thought you could figure that out."

Not Your Typical Domestic

Bitts and his deputy had not gone far when they began sighting empty beer cans. "What's this, a beer blast?" Morgan asked.

"How fresh, Jason?"

Morgan was twenty-four, a connoisseur of the hops when his wife would let him out, which wasn't very often on his salary. He picked up one of the cans with a twig and smelled it. "Day old, Two-Bit. Still got a little bite in it."

Bitts pulled a plastic trash sack from his pocket. "Take it into evidence, will you?"

Morgan's eyebrows raised slightly, but he did as he was told. As they walked up the hill, Bitts laid out what he had. "I found our callers last night, Jason. They said our corpse was lying in one piece on a rock beside the falls."

Morgan stopped walking and look at Bitts incredulously. "They said *what?*"

Bitts shrugged philosophically. He hadn't any better idea than before what it all meant. "The five of them said our victim was stretched out over a rock like Sleeping Beauty. All in one piece."

"What do you make of it, Two-Bit?"

"I don't know what to tell you, Jason. I'm not even sure it's true."

Morgan thought about this for a while, then he shook his head. He had no theories either.

"I need to confirm what the kids told me," Bitts explained, as they started on. "Good news is one of them saw a man up here at the falls. Could have been the killer. Possible, anyway."

"You don't think it was Jack Hazard, I take it?"

"No."

Morgan laughed. "The husband is always a suspect, Two-Bit. You taught me that yourself."

Bitts shook his head. "She was tied up for a while, Jason. That's not your typical domestic."

"Happens though. Those things happen all sorts of ways, and they're always bad."

"They're bad, but they're quick. What happened to that poor woman we found last night . . . that wasn't quick. You saw the letters carved on her chest, *h-o-r*? One the kids last night called it slew-spelling for *prostitute*."

Morgan, like Bitts, was a local, a slew. He said nothing in response to this, but his jaw flexed, a nerve twitched, and his eyes went cold.

"Jason, this guy brings her on campus in the middle of the afternoon, not more than two hundred-some yards away from Greek Circle. Kids are likely to show up at the falls or even inside the canyon. That just doesn't make sense! There are better places to do what he did. Fact is, almost anywhere would be better. We got woods for miles around here, not a soul in sight. Not even a road. We're filthy with woods! Why march in here and risk being seen?"

"Like it not, that's exactly what he did! What's your point?"

"I'm going to ask you something, and I don't want you to get mad."

Morgan got a curious look on his face. "Okay."

"What do you suppose you would do if Charli was playing around and you found out, by and by? By that I mean, you don't walk in on it, but you *know* about it."

"Who's she screwing around with?" The young man's humor was gone.

"Hypothetically."

"Hypothetically, who's she screwing around with?" Jason looked ready to ignite.

Bitts grinned. "What's it matter?"

"Well, I'm going to kill him! That's what it matters!"

"What about Charli? You going to *kill* her?"

"I'll see how I feel about *her* after I kill *him!*"

"You don't think you'd tie her up and carve *whore* on her chest, assuming you knew how to spell a word with that many letters?"

"No, that's not the first thing to cross my mind, Two-Bit!"

Bitts tipped his head and looked up at the trees thoughtfully. "I know Jack Hazard, Jason. I've had business with him. None of it pleasant. But I'll tell you something. I don't think that's the first thing that would cross his mind either. Just a lawman's instincts, mind you."

"You just don't want to come to the same conclusion as Colt Fellows," Morgan said finally.

Bitts smiled at this and shook his head sorrowfully. "You might have something there, young man. To tell you the truth, that thought keeps me awake nights!"

Country Stupid

Ten minutes later, Bitts stared out into the canyon with his deputy beside him. They were standing next to the broken railing the kids had told the sheriff about. They had twenty-four cans in evidence. They had collected trash by the bushel.

Below them, Colt's crime scene people were combing the area. "I got a woman dead at three o'clock, Jason. Five kids claim they were looking straight down on her, and she was stretched out on that rock down there in the mist. One of them sees a man back in the woods. He's acting suspiciously. They're sure he's the killer. If they're right, that puts the time of death at two or a quarter after."

"Or the man in the woods isn't the killer."

"Either way," Bitts offered, "they go down, look at the body, then come out and call us at 4:40. By the time campus security gets here, she's been cut open and tossed in that pool where we found her."

"He went back in?"

"Or he never left."

"Or the kids are lying."

"I like that one. I just can't figure why." He worked through it quietly again, then shook his head.

"They're all in on it maybe," Jason answered. "They killed her in some kind of hazing, then covered it up with all this, just to confuse things."

"It crossed my mind, but if that's the case, they're good actors. All of them."

"What about this time of death Colt was trotting out, Two-Bit? Six or seven o'clock? Why didn't you say anything?"

"What I like best about our friend Colt Fellows is he has never let the facts get in the way of a good theory. Right now, I think the best thing to do is just let him blow hot air. Do him a little good to get the rug pulled out from under him on this one."

"He's right about the rigor. We got the first signs of it after we got her out last night. A little in the neck and toes. The doc I talked to thought two—two and half hours. That was after nine. Body temperature was a couple of degrees under the norm, but with the cold water, he thought it was about right."

"Half past six to seven?"

"That's what he told me."

"He talk to Colt?"

"I don't know. Probably. Colt wasn't there when I showed up. I took care of receipting the body and got on home."

Bitts nodded. "Normally, I'm not one to argue with science, but this . . . I don't know. Rigor's not always reliable."

"Which leaves us with body temperature."

"At least until we get an autopsy," Bitts answered.

"But three o'clock . . ."

"*Before* three o'clock. I know. It doesn't accord with nature."

"Maybe Waldis can figure it out," Morgan said finally.

"That's what I'm hoping. He's the expert."

Twenty-three minutes later, Bitts and his deputy arrived at the trailhead. Colt Fellows, still dry, came toward them grinning excitedly. "We got him, Two-Bit!"

"What are you talking about?" Bitts asked.

Percolating with his own importance, Colt held up a plastic evidence bag. Inside was a wristwatch. "Laying right on top of one of the boulders back close to the falls! The band is broke, so you figure some hiker lost it, right? Now look on the back." He held the thing up and read the name aloud for them. "*John C. Hazard!* Is that boy country stupid or what?"

"Who found it?" Bitts asked.

"Happy Harpin did. He brought it out about ten minutes ago."

"Lucky break," Bitts remarked dryly.

Colt met his gaze, his grin going icy, "Ain't it, though?"

"You said something about getting Jack Hazard's movements yesterday, Colt. You got him for this?"

"He's locked in with an alibi 'til around two, when he's opening that bar of his with his brother Virgil, a half-dozen strippers, and about fifteen or twenty customers. The rest of the afternoon, though, he's out in the woods with his brother Louis. Just the two of them. Which is to say, no alibi at all, Two-Bit."

"Two o'clock then?"

"Give or take. Just enough time to leave the bar, get the little woman, and get her in here so he can do his thing."

"You're probably right, but just to be on the safe side, you might want to wait for Waldis to give you a time of death, before you go off and ask Don Stackman to get you a warrant. You wouldn't want any surprises popping up."

"Between six and seven, Two-Bit. You can take it to the bank."

"As I understand it, Colt, the banks aren't handing out the warrants. Judges do that, and they don't like to get egg on their face when a cop gets ahead of himself."

Colt got cautious suddenly. "So what are you saying, Two-Bit?"

"Just some friendly advice. I've been at this game a little longer than you have, and the one thing I've learned is you move too fast, you can embarrass a whole lot of people. You do that to a man like your pal Stackman and he'll never forget it. All I'm telling you is slow it down and be certain. Jack Hazard isn't going anywhere and neither is our victim."

"What do I need here, Two-Bit! A written confession on the canyon wall? This is it!" Colt shook the plastic bag with the watch at Bitts, laughing. "It doesn't get any better than this, Two-Bit! You got a man who's killed twice, that we know of. He rides herd on a whorehouse, and he's married to the queen bee herself! She starts screwing around with the receipts, maybe, or, maybe, just screwing around, and Jack gets his pocketknife out!"

"It's your case, Colt. You do what you have to do, and I'll do what I have to." Bitts gave the big man a wink. "We'll still be friends in the morning."

Fellows looked at Morgan theatrically. "Help me out here, Jason. Tell me what I'm missing!"

"Brains, Colt."

Miscuing

After Bitts had left, Morgan made a hard run up the hill to the falls, then came down at full throttle. Carefully, he recorded the times, then, hardly recovered, he threw himself into the creek and started back into the canyon. Less than half an hour later, he came back out, staggering in exhaustion and soaking wet.

It was at that point that Colt chose to approach him, offering him a cup of coffee from his thermos.

"What are you doing?"

"Getting times."

Colt shook his head in sympathy. "The old drunk works you too hard, Jason. You come into the city, I'll make you a detective. Coffee and dough-nuts 'til nine."

Taking a sip, Jason grinned up at him, "Trouble is, Colt, I'd have to look at your ugly face all day long."

Colt took the insult in stride. He liked Morgan, liked his style. There wasn't another man in Lues County had the guts he did, and it wasn't just talk. Colt had seen the kid in a fist fight once, and he was good! "Offer's open any time you want it, Jason. I'm not kidding. I could use a man with your abilities. I got all the yes-men I can stomach. I need a real cop, especially if I leave the detectives."

"Where you going?"

"Up to the big man's office. When that happens, I got to have someone in the field I can trust. Happy's a good man, but I don't think he's quite ready to run things. A year or two working with me out here on cases, I got no doubt you'll be the second-best cop in southern Illinois."

Morgan looked at him curiously, for the first time taking the offer seri-ously. "I like it where I am, Colt. Two-Bit's taught me a lot."

"Two-Bit's best days are past him, Jason. This here proves it. Got the case wrapped and he won't stand with me on it. Acting like there's some great mystery I can't see. Now why in the hell would he do that?"

"He's got his reasons."

Colt moved in closer, his voice dropping almost to a whisper. "What are they? Huh? What's the old fox up to that I don't know about? He's holding something back, isn't he?"

"You talk to the sheriff about what he knows and what he doesn't. I don't talk for him unless he tells me to."

Morgan walked away and went to his patrol car. Colt watched him call-ing in, then jotting down some kind of message. When he had finished the call, he got out of the car with the look of a kid who's just put it over on his old man.

"What do you have?" Colt asked him.

Morgan's pale eyes flashed as he came toward the detective. "Chalk your stick, Colt. You're miscuing. The woman was Jack Hazard's ex. Her name's *Fortune*, not Hazard, never went by Hazard. Two-Bit's at her apartment on campus right now and wants me there five minutes ago. You want to come along? We can go from there to the autopsy." He checked his watch. "Waldis is doing it in about forty minutes."

Colt looked around for Harpin, then remembered Happy was rounding up the witnesses Bitts had found the night before. Everyone else was inside the canyon. "Give me the address, I'll send Happy over later to check it out."

Morgan went back to his cruiser to get the address and copy it out for Colt. Colt waited for the information, leaning against Morgan's driver's side back door, picking his moment.

"How about the kid," Colt asked him casually. "Is she Jack's daughter or just hers?"

"I don't know."

"Two-Bit's sure taking his time about the kid, isn't he?"

"She's okay. You told us she's with Jack."

"Well, yeah, but if they're divorced and she's not even Jack's kid ... I don't how safe she is. You know what I mean?"

Morgan looked at him curiously.

"That kid doesn't belong with her mother's ex, Jason, especially if he just killed her mother!"

"I guess not, if you put it that way."

"That's the only way to put it, buddy! Listen, you work for the old drunk. No one's blaming you. But I got a different boss. My boss don't like to see children in danger—city, county, whatever."

Morgan looked up at him uncomfortably. "What do you want me to do about it?"

"I don't want you do anything. I just want you to understand my concern here."

"Okay. I understand it. I'll say something to Two-Bit about it. Here's the address on the campus apartment. Now, I've got to go."

Morgan started to shut his door, but Colt reached out to hold it open a moment. "I'm thinking about the kid, Jason. You're with me on that?"

Morgan shrugged agreeably.

"If that little girl isn't Jack Hazard's kid, she could be in danger? You agree with me on that?"

"Sure."

Colt watched the young deputy drive off, sauntered over to his Chevy, and dropped into the driver's seat with a deep sigh of a satisfaction. There was no need now to ask for an arrest warrant. Colt had it from the sheriff's own man, Josie Fortune's kid was in danger! Reaching for his handset, Colt assured himself it was no longer his prerogative to act. With a hostage situation in progress, it was his duty!

Part Two

Odysseus in Disguise

COMING SOUTH into Lues, Josie Darling had strange flashes of recognition. Certain turns in the road, certain smells set her heart pounding with a sense of nostalgia, a shadow smile on her heart. It was nothing she could place exactly. It was the spirit of the countryside, the way the unpaved roads now and then twisted away into the forest. Josie saw a gravel road coming up at some distance, so she had a chance to slow down and contemplate it. She was nearly to the town of Lues and tired from her second long day of driving, but this road held promise and she turned off the highway excitedly. She thought this was the way home, but before she found it, the road came up against Lues Creek and stopped.

There was a little parking area, but no one was in sight. She was now a mile off the highway, in deep country, and the stillness of the place gave her chills. The only sound was water rushing over stones. An errant wind stirred the high branches of the trees. She got out of her VW and walked along the creek, checking the wooded ridges just to be sure she was alone.

She had a no idea where home was. She only knew she was close. Upstream or down? She remembered Lues Creek had cut behind their property. West Lues Creek had meandered through a field less than a quarter of a mile from their front door. There was a covered bridge over it, a long gravel road leading up to their property. This wasn't the place, but the sand beside the creek reminded her of her last and only real memory of Lues. It was a memory that was nearly twenty years old.

Josie had watched five dark sedans coming up the road to Jack Hazard's and her mother's trailer. They came fast and kicked up big funnels of dust behind them. As the cars got closer, she saw they belonged to the state police. Behind her, the door of the trailer creaked open. Jack stood next to her.

She knew it was Jack, but she couldn't remember his face. She remembered the great bending curve of the road as it collided with their property, the dust, the cars, and even how the cars pulled off the road and came across the front yard, sliding broadside to a stop. More than a half-dozen state troopers took up positions behind the sedans, their shotguns like black pipes against the gray sky. One of them called out something on a bullhorn. His voice echoed in the trees. Three troopers ran at them hard, their weapons silent in their hands. Two of them took Jack down to the ground. The third took Josie's wrist. She twisted away under his grip and broke loose. As soon as she was free, she ran for the woods. Behind her, one of them shouted, "Get the kid!"

Leaves slapped Josie's face as she ran. She was certain they meant to kill her. She heard the trooper following her, his heavy breath, the crunch of leaves, the cracking of sticks. As they came to the creek, the man took Josie's arm. He lifted her into the air. "I'm not going to hurt you!" he shouted.

For answer, Josie kicked him. He was still carrying his shotgun, and his face was red from the effort of running. He set his gun down in the grass and knelt before her, so she could see his face. "Now listen to me!" he said. He held her by her elbows, pinning them behind her back, shaking her angrily. She stopped struggling. They were both breathing heavily. She saw his shotgun. She remembered that she had kept staring at it, as he said something Josie couldn't understand. His big face was nearly against hers. She smelled the stink of tobacco on his breath and wrestled against his hold.

At the trailer, she saw Jack cuffed and being pushed into one of the sedans. Jack looked back toward her, his face bloody with a fine scarlet sheen. It was the only face of Jack Hazard Josie could remember. She shouted to him: "JAAACK!" Inside the car, Jack looked down between his knees, ashamed.

The trooper holding her said in the calmest voice imaginable, "You don't want to talk to him, honey. That man there is the one that killed your mamma."

For years after that, Josie told herself her mother was not really dead, that there had been a terrible mistake. She was certain, as only a child can be, her mother was alive and waiting for Josie to come back. She thought if she could just get home, she would find her, and everything would make sense. Eventually, Josie had given up the idea and with it, gradually, whatever vestiges of the memories she had carried out of Lues. For a time, the faces of her past were like shadows. Then, without photographs, without stories, without those accidental collisions with history that most of us encounter, even those faded. Now almost nothing of the first years of her life remained. Least of all, her memory of the road home.

She knew the reason, of course. It wasn't just that she had left and never went back. It was because her new parents had always hated Lues and Josie's life in it. The Darlings had many virtues. They were fine, good people who took Josie out of the foster care system shortly after her removal from Lues. They had loved her as their own, and all they ever asked in return, besides her natural affection for them, was that she forget the past, that she not talk about Lues or Jack Hazard or how her mother had lived and died. They told her that *that time* in her life was over. She could be anything she wanted, they said. She could make any life she cared to, but first she had to leave *those things* from Lues behind her. They told her to forget the past in many ways. They were gentle and persuasive, and Josie learned to honor their fears as her own. She forgot her first childhood so long and so hard that it came back as something else, something unrecognizable and terrible. She let it get out of hand, and even then she kept her silence. She did not look back. As a teenager, she had told no one that Jack Hazard had begun to come out from under her bed, his face a bloody mask of rage, his killing only half done. She never spoke of the woman's wailing voice that would sometimes call across the threshold of dawn, *"Josie!,"* a haunting lament or summoning or warning. Like the town of Lues itself, that voice held terrible secrets, and she had always found reason to resist its seductions.

There was a point in Josie's life when things made sense, and Josie's memories became like other people's: splotchy and embarrassing, random as a roulette wheel, neurotically normal, desperately ordinary. That was the childhood Josie Darling claimed. She had made her revolutions and compromises. She did some of the things we all shouldn't. She missed some of the other things. She was a bright, fearless scholar, a fumbling young girl with a few mistakes under her belt. She was guilty of her share but innocent of most things. There were some poignant memories of this time, her second childhood, some things she would have liked to do over. Josie had long ago come to terms with that life, if we can ever really say we have made our peace with the child we were. She grew up in her adoptive home a perfectly middle-class, suburban girl. She had hated as much as the next teenager the prefabricated life of the Midwestern small town. Unlike most of her friends, Josie got out as soon as she could. She headed east to where the ivy grows. Like most revolutionaries, she came back home because she missed it. A year later, Josie got her courage back, and this time she left for good. She went off determined to make her own way.

This was the life Josie could trace. There were records of her immodest achievements, official and otherwise. There were memories and stories and friendships and losses. That girl was Josie Darling. But there had always been the other childhood, the yawning emptiness of losing what she could not remember, the whispering of some distant voice which told her that Josie Fortune was not entirely the same person as Josie Darling.

And so she had come home. It wasn't exactly the triumphant return to Lues she had fantasized so many times when she was still a child, but it wasn't a bad return either. She had gotten a job teaching at the university without ever mentioning in her letter of application or in the subsequent phone interview that Lues was her first home. Josie liked coming back in secret. Not a soul in all the town imagined that Deborah Josephine Darling was really Josie Fortune come back. She was a kind of Odysseus, gone twenty years and slipping home in another disguise, the perfect disguise, in fact. She was no longer seven years old!

She looked back along the creek bed, then checked her watch. She needed to get back to the highway. The moment she turned, Josie heard a sound of rushing leaves behind her. Instinctively crouching down, ready for attack, she turned and saw it was only a fat doe walking into the stream. It had not been more than fifteen feet from her, and she had missed it. It was moving through the water now. Step, step. Suddenly it leapt out of the creek and up the steep bank. It bounded over the broad, flat forest floor heading for the ridge. She saw the white tail, the jagged path it took, then nothing more. That fast and it was gone. Josie was still breathing hard, still fighting down the fear that had grabbed her. Her heart thumped with adrenaline. She was thinking it could have been worse. It could have been anything. Or anyone. Out here, it wasn't always nice, what you found. She was in the middle of the woods, and no one knew where she was. If something had happened...

She did not finish the thought. Josie Darling knew only too well how things sometimes happened.

Faculty Apartments

Less than an hour later, Josie entered the town of Lues, population 26,000. Unless the university was in session, then it was almost double. The main road stirred no memories. Even the depressed real-estate close to the heart of the old town was only vaguely familiar. She wasn't sure if she remembered it or if she had only seen too many towns like it when she lived upstate. It had the generic look of the Midwest. Lots of dirty brick facades with aluminum trim. Lots of empty buildings, blacked out or broken windows, rutted gravel lots, and all the embarrassing splotches of small-town pride: Go, Lancers! Baptist Faith Revival, Lions Auxiliary Bake Sale, Welcome Back Lues State Students. There were fast-food restaurants, gas stations with enormous American flags, bars by the dozen for the college kids, and cheap apartments advertised roadside. None of it was quite what she remembered. Even the university was not especially remarkable. The sign out front, like the road, was newly constructed, three, maybe five years old. Something like that. The football stadium was probably ten or fifteen years old. There was something reassuring about a couple of the administrative buildings once she was actually on campus.

She knew she had been here before, but she could not have said what waited beyond the next curve in the road. A bit discouraged that no deep memory had revived, nor any instinctive sense of direction beckoned her to go one place or another, Josie consulted her campus map. Housing was located in Harrison Hall which was, as it turned out, around the next curve.

Josie spent the next hour getting processed for her faculty apartment. When she climbed back into her VW with her new key and yet another round of paperwork, she was no longer thinking about her lost past. Suddenly, she was in a new life, and the excitement, which had been building for several weeks, seemed finally to bloom within her. The campus was enormous. The woods edged its northern perimeter, and long fingers of it reached in elsewhere with thick shady groves of trees. The buildings came in clusters, all of them turned out in concrete, but the old trees everywhere gave shade and even a bit of character to the otherwise sterile architecture. She passed the university medical center, then saw a small sign that pointed her to faculty apartments. At the top of a fairly steep hill, Josie found two housing units facing one another.

Each building had ten apartments, all of them on a single level. The buildings were institutional, making her feel like she had joined some kind of ascetic commune instead of a modern campus, and they were made of concrete, of course, like everything at Lues State, except the very oldest buildings at the center of campus. The buildings shared a common parking lot, which at the moment was filled with young, mostly unmarried professor types, all of them busily unpacking, like so many gypsies setting up camp. Both buildings, she noticed, managed to butt back against the forest, though Josie's was set up over a fairly substantial ravine with Lues Creek running through it. She would be paying twenty-five dollars extra a month to hear the stream off her back balcony, but she was sure it would be the best money she had ever spent.

Josie toured her apartment before she began unloading her car. For anyone accustomed to real life, the two-bedroom apartment would have been disappointing. For Josie, weaned on a decade of collegiate impoverishment, with a twenty-month hiatus as an unhappy faculty wife, the place was great, sprawling even. At least by Boston standards of genteel poverty. It was relatively clean if not bright and, the reason she had picked it, fully equipped. As Josie had requested on the forms she had filled out in May, she had a master bedroom with a double bed. The mattress and box springs were firm, the sheets starched. The matching headboard and side table were done in some kind of macabre Spanish style. The second bedroom was set up as an office, everything in scratched, gunmetal gray: bookshelves, computer console, a writing table, and an office chair. These had seen too many wars, but they functioned. The kitchen was a disappointment, and Josie regretted that she had left almost her entire domestic life in a storage shed outside of Boston. The pots and pans were beat and dented, the plates were chipped and shabby, the glasses were foggy.

The main room offered a six-foot couch and two chairs in a scotch plaid just this side of nausea. The lamps were rickety and complemented in a vague way the bedroom motif, something for the last son of a bankrupt Spanish hidalgo. There was a tiny fireplace, a print of Picasso's *Don Quixote* complete with a bullet hole in it, and a telephone out of another era, the sort that used to double as a murder weapon in the Miss Marple mysteries.

Out of curiosity, Josie snapped the television on and waited. A black-and-white picture of an electrical snow storm finally presented itself. She flipped the knob and found three stations, only one of which had good reception, the only thing good about it, as it turned out. She turned the set off, opened a sliding glass door, and went out on the small balcony. About four feet by ten feet, it jutted out over the ravine. Lues Creek was some fifty feet below. Despite the public feel of the balconies, pressed up against one another as they were, Josie liked the effect. The creek was tight and quick. The air over it was noticeably cooler. The forest just beyond had a consoling effect as well.

She nodded happily, then went back to her car and began unloading it.

Orientation

The following morning, Friday, Josie appeared at Harrison Hall along with the other new faculty. There were more forms to fill out and procedures to learn. After lunch with the president and a tour of the campus, new faculty were sent off to find their individual departments. The Department of English was located in Brand Hall. Josie was one of five new faculty. One of the secretaries shuffled them off to wait in a small conference room. Only one of the new people, Deb Rainy of Kentucky, had been hired for a tenure-track position. She was therefore the star, Ph.D., *real* faculty. The others, like Josie, were on one-year contracts, all given the old fashioned tag of lecturer. Each one of them had been told if things worked out, there might be a permanent position waiting for them next year or the one following, but no promises. That made everyone in the room, except Rainy, the competition. Despite this, after a morning with the bureaucrats, followed by a hokey bus tour of campus, they were like old friends meeting up again. They shared quick embarrassed smiles and waited for the arrival of Dr. Case, the department chair.

Everett Case, as it turned out, was an affable, overweight, white-haired Chaucerian scholar who had a tendency to ramble a bit, especially prior to delivering his choicest tidbits. It was humor as British as the accent he nursed, kicking in like an afterthought. Josie liked the man immensely, but she understood almost at first glance he was the kind of academic leader who settles into power precisely because he does not care for it. Someone else in the department most assuredly ran things. After a few statistical observations about the number of books the department's faculty had produced and a bit of gentle prodding for the new folks to take up the torch and carry forward, Dr. Case finally handed each of them a thick notebook entitled *English Department Policies and Procedures*. This was nearly as thick as the *University Policies and Procedures*. Holding up his dog-eared copy for their inspection, Dr. Case told them gravely, "You can all read, I assume. We'll have a quiz over the pertinent points on Monday." Deb Rainy jotted a note to herself as Professor Case watched her without expression. When she looked up again, everyone was smiling except Case and her. Rainy blinked, then flushed, then scratched out her note. Dr. Case finally allowed himself a bit of a smile and said he wanted to welcome Dr. Rainy to *the other side*. They were teachers now, he explained, which meant they were about to learn firsthand that it was indeed better to give than to receive, especially in the matter of quizzes.

After the meeting, the department's head secretary issued keys and a map of Brand Hall. Josie's office was not far from the department's main office. She noticed that she had been placed among the senior faculty and was trying to decide if this might turn out to be a problem when she happened to notice the name Richard Ferrington on one of the doors. She could see a light on behind the curtain and knocked before she had a chance for second thoughts. The man who opened the door was around forty and, to her delight, amazingly handsome. Tall and trim with an athlete's broad shoulders, Ferrington had dark hair just beginning to gray at the temples. His eyes were dark brown, vibrant, full of passion. He was clearly busy and stared at Josie impatiently.

"Dr. Ferrington?"

"Look, I'm not letting anyone into a closed class no matter how good the story is, so you can just save it."

"I'm not a student. I'm Josie Darling."

Dick Ferrington's face registered an awkward moment of confusion, then lit up in delight. "Josie! Our new Joycean!" His body lost its tension. "I tell you, I must have had about thirty kids come by this morning trying to get into an advanced composition course I'm teaching. I just assumed . . . well, you know what they say about the word *assume*."

Josie nodded, hoping he would not spell it out for her. "Come in! Have a seat," he said. "Tell me about the drive out. Did you just get in?"

Dick Ferrington had been Josie's only contact with the department before she had arrived. He had chaired the hiring committee for her position, had conducted the phone interview last April, and had even called her when the time came for an offer. In a half-dozen phone conversations, they had gotten familiar with one another, and she was anxious to meet him, especially as she had liked the sound of his voice. So far, she like everything she saw. A lot. He moved back to his desk with the grace of an athlete. A nice smile, no wedding ring, what more could she ask for?

"I came in yesterday afternoon," she answered, taking a seat before his desk, unconsciously feeling like a student and hating herself for it. "We had new faculty orientation meetings this morning."

"Those things! Tell me, are they still trying to bore our new people to death before they even start?" As he said this, Dick Ferrington slipped his sports jacket off, revealing a surprisingly broad chest. His forearms were thick, his biceps powerful. Very nice arms, she thought, but to give him his due, Dick Ferrington didn't flex too much.

"Not so bad, really," Josie answered, crossing her legs under her short skirt and flexing a little herself. "Pick an insurance plan, settle on retirement program, meet the president, see all the trees. I've had worst days."

Ferrington seemed dubious. "Get paid for it?"

Josie flashed a pretty smile. "Got a free lunch."

Ferrington laughed easily as he rocked back in his chair. "Hasn't anyone ever told you, Josie, there are no free lunches?"

"Sure there are. It's just that they only happen when someone is trying to sell you something."

"The brass does like to sell us! If you listen to them for very long, you could start to believe we're the center of the academic universe!"

Josie notched down her smile to a coy grin, but she didn't dare answer the remark. When she had first talked to Dick Ferrington on the telephone the previous winter, he had made quite a pitch for Lues State himself. Great library, strong young faculty, a growing, dynamic graduate program. And not a word about all the trees.

"Of course we just might become that if we can snatch a few more scholars of your caliber! What do they have you teaching anyway?"

Josie told him she had two composition courses, an introduction to lit, and an American lit survey. A good assignment, he said, but it was a shame she wasn't teaching a graduate class in Joyce. "Well," she answered diplomatically, "if I'm asked to stick around for a year or two, maybe I'll get the chance. Besides, if I have any spare time, which I seriously doubt, I can use it to finish my dissertation."

"'*Ulysses* and the Word Known to all Men?'" She nodded, smiling at him. Dick Ferrington had spent ten minutes during their official telephone interview trying to bait her into telling him *the word*, the riddle of *Ulysses* that no one had yet properly answered. Now that he had her in front of him, he had to come back to it, just human nature, especially from a fellow Joycean. "You know, we lost two committee meetings trying to figure out what it is. I think a couple of people voted for you just to see if we could pry the answer out of you once we got you here."

"I guess I'm going to have to disappoint them."

He laughed. "I'll give you this, Josie, you sure play your cards close to your chest. If I had a theory like that, you couldn't keep me quiet for a minute!"

"It's not a theory, Dick. I've solved the puzzle. Joyce uses the word explicitly at one point, then implicitly confirms it on two other occasions. Once you see it, the only question that remains is why everyone else missed it."

"And no one but Josie Darling has seen this?" His tone had an edge of mockery disguised as awe.

"They've seen it. Everyone who has read the book has *seen* it. They just didn't *recognize* it."

"I'm sure you'll make an interesting argument, but my theory, and its just a theory, mind you, is this: there are some riddles in the *Ulysses* we'll never know the answer to, because there are no answers. Chalk it up to Irish humor. The word known to all men: Let them figure this one out!"

Josie knew better than to answer Ferrington. He was baiting her again, trying to get a rise out of her, a hint, maybe, if not the word itself. The only real answer she could offer was the full argument, and *that* she would make in writing in her dissertation and not before. Then the idea would be forever hers, and no else's. The scholar's pinch of immortality. Anything else was just selling cheap.

"There's something in what you say," she responded, "but I don't think every riddle is unanswerable just because no one has figured it out. After all, sometimes the truth just needs the right nudge."

"Truth, Josie, is the lie we all agree to tell. You get a little older, you'll find that out."

"And what if we all don't agree to tell it?"

"In the old days, we burned the heretics at the stake. Nowadays, we let them have their own web site. It amounts to the same thing."

This provided enough humor to take the edge off her irritation, but just barely. Josie smiled, told him he was right. Ferrington was the kind of man who needed that, she decided and fought the disappointment at his hair-trigger condescension. She knew the type a dozen times over, had married one, in fact.

They bounced a couple of jokes back and forth about various lunatics in cyberspace, and Josie finally stood up. She apologized for dropping in on him unexpectedly. "I don't want to take up your afternoon, I expect you're as busy as I am." This scored as Josie had hoped it would, and Dick Ferrington gave the obligatory groan. Summers were getting shorter and shorter as time went on. "I was just going down to my office and saw your light on and thought I'd introduce myself. It's nice to put a face with a voice."

A dark line of curiosity creased between Ferrington's eyebrows. "Which office did they put you in?"

"I don't know." She hesitated, then dug a slip of blue paper out of her briefcase. "One-thirty-one."

Ferrington gave her a look of commiseration. "So they stuck *you* in the office across from Henry Valentine."

"Is that a problem?" She could imagine the department Lothario or maybe a fossil with a case of incurable sexism. Cute penis jokes and paternal pats on the fanny.

Ferrington saw the look and laughed. "It's not what you think," he answered. "Val is . . . a wonderful man!" Ferrington's enthusiasm could not have been more tepid. The classic academic, he had mastered the quotable insult: the words kind, the meaning all in the tone. "He's certainly not going to give you any trouble personally. Val is Old South, Josie. Very proper. I don't believe he's capable of an off-color remark. Quite a writer, as a matter of fact. Wrote a hell of a novel when the world was young. What I meant was he's too damn popular for his own good. He has more students coming through his office than the rest of the department put together. The unfortunate result is that it can get crowded in the hallway, maybe a little noisy at times."

"That's it? That's the problem? He's good?"

"When Henry Valentine walks into the classroom, Josie, his students stand up and cheer."

"That's a joke, right?"

Ferrington shook his head. "It's a tradition at Lues State. Every class, every time. I don't think Val would know what to do if he ever walked into a classroom and they didn't do it." A sly grin, a bit of genuine emotion, "Naturally, we all hate him passionately for it."

Josie laughed. "Maybe I can learn his secret."

"The secret is Henry Valentine made a pact with the devil, and if I knew exactly what the bargain was, I'd make the same deal myself. We all would."

Footnotes in the Nightmare

Three doors down from Dick Ferrington's office, directly across from Henry Valentine's office, Josie found room 131 with her name and title already on the door, Josie Darling, Lecturer.

She studied the letters on the tag almost reverently, then finally laughed at herself for making a big deal out of it. Just another job. Like waiting tables or tending bar, only here you got to take the work home with you. But she knew it wasn't. This was her first step into the profession. What she did here would affect her for years to come—it was every bit as important as her promising career as a scholar. So she was excited, a bit scared, and definitely ready. Opening the door, she discovered to her delight the office itself was as large as Dick Ferrington's. It was freshly painted. The bookshelves were clean and plentiful and in good condition. All she needed to do was haul in the few books she had brought. There was a big government-issue desk, a computer, and a comfortable chair. She liked that. She planned to spend a lot of hours in that chair. Facing the desk was a straight back wooden chair for students. She had a phone with a private and personal account, e-mail, even a fax on her computer. She needed no one's permission to make a call or go on-line or work past midnight. Best of all, there were no office mates.

She dropped off the materials that the various administrators had handed out during the morning and afternoon meetings, deciding it was the beginning of a stack that would probably keep building until she cleared her desk and went off to her next job. Assuming, of course, there was a next job. Maybe this was the best job she could ask for. The only one she would ever need. With that pleasant thought to tease her, Josie spent the remainder of the afternoon moving books into her office and getting settled. Later, she began writing e-mails to friends in Boston, reminding them in the last paragraph that under no circumstances should they tell Dan Scholari where she was. She didn't expect any problems, of course, but it did not pay to be careless with an ex-husband who was taking divorce as an affront to his manhood. It had been a bad marriage, all the compromises coming from her side, but she had endured it hoping for better times, and then one afternoon, she had walked into their apartment unexpectedly. Twenty months of marriage gone in an instant. "Josie! I thought you were at the library!"

Dr. Scholari expected forgiveness or more exactly acquiescence. The eternal rights of the male. Mrs. Scholari expected nothing but a clean break. That was when the real problems started, but she was past it now, free of the bastard. A thousand miles away and finally safe.

And she was *safe* here, she assured herself. She had not felt safe for the better part of a year. Quietly, she confirmed the feeling that evening as she observed her lack of panic at watching the sunset. The failure of darkness to stir her fears said it best. She nodded happily. She felt strong, at long last. Ready, even, to chase the nightmare, which in her case meant looking into the history of Lues County.

At noon the next day, Josie drove to the parking lot before the Liberal Arts Plaza and then followed a thin ribbon of concrete past Varner and Brand Halls on her way toward Worley, the university's library. A few weeks before she had seen the advertisement for the job at Lues State, Josie had gone on-line to learn what she could about her past. The on-line archives of the *Rapids*, the local paper, however, did not go back to 1983. She knew, of course, that she could have ordered the microfilm for the paper, but, somehow, as much as she wanted to know about the death of her mother, something had kept her from taking the next logical step. Before she got around to it, Josie had seen the Lues State job advertised, and she decided almost spontaneously that maybe it was time to go back home for a closer look at things. The home of Josie Fortune, that is. She was convinced Dan Scholari was not simply her bad luck. She believed she had seen in him some kind of signal, a predisposition for violence, and she chose him because her mother had chosen such a man—everything of her first childhood forgotten but the essentials: how to get yourself killed. The only way to avoid repeating that mistake in the future was to get to the bottom of her past. Annie Wilde, her dissertation director and best friend, called it chasing the nightmare.

The entry of Worley was a long narrow vault, almost fifty feet high and twenty-feet across. It was constructed of raw concrete forms, giving it the same monolithic effect she saw everywhere on campus. Along both sides of the entryway, the portraits of several past presidents were screwed to the walls, like so many ill-starred moths. At the security desk, Josie checked a plan of the building. Her search for Jack Hazard and her mother began on the sixth floor, journalism. She had some help with the procedures, which turned out to be a bit easier than what she was used to, then spent several minutes rolling through the local and national cataclysms of late 1982 and early 1983. Holding out high hopes that she would stumble into the headlines of murder, Josie's optimism lasted about twenty minutes, into the month of August 1983, in fact. She knew that by August of that year, she had been taken upstate to live with the Darlings. August, because she had started third grade with the rest of her classmates. Somewhat dejected by yet another failure to find some public record of the violence that had forever changed her life, Josie cranked back a full twelve months and started through again, this time peeking into the corners. Her mother's death had not made headlines. Hard to admit, but true. A back-page affair. Even in the chronicles of a back-page town.

As she rolled through the year again, her eye fell invariably to the same headlines she had seen before. She was still missing the little things, she told herself, and consciously sought them this time: the honor society students at Rensselaer Junior High School, the salesman of the month at Dempsey's Auto Fair, the centennial birthdays of lives too stubborn to quit. Still, she found her attention constantly drifting. She was a student of a world that held no interest for her, except for one particular fact. She really didn't care about the other lives and bodies, and so she could not find what she was looking for. Then she noticed a "Police Bulletin" that was usually on page six but sometimes stuck back on page ten. It came out once a week, but not always on the same day. Sometimes it was apparently not included. She skimmed these bulletins looking for Hazards and finally scored. In January of 1983 alone, Josie found six Hazards on the honor roll: drunk, drunk and disorderly, drunk driving, assault (at a tavern), drunk, and drunk again. Now she was on the road to Jack Hazard! Josie began looking at these bulletins systematically, and shortly, the name John Christian Hazard appeared. Age thirty-three, he was taken into custody for assaulting four members of the Lues State football team at a tavern called the Hurry On Up. The Hurry On Up featured topless dancers. Home Sweet Home.

Josie made a detailed note of the proud moment and rolled on. She found this, dated February 10:

MYSTERIOUS DEATH

Sheriff's deputies, responding to an anonymous call, discovered the nude body of a female on Stop 16 Road early yesterday morning. Sheriff Pat Bitts reported the woman was struck by an automobile sometime during the previous night. No identification has been made.

Josie looked up and took a deep breath. Was this it? In vain, Josie searched for a follow-up article about the woman. It might well have been her mother, she realized with a strange sense of nausea. There was nothing to tell her if it was or wasn't. She read the next two city arrest-reports, but there was no mention of a vehicular homicide, although another Hazard was arrested for drunk and disorderly. His name was Virgil. She read the obituaries for several days, but there was nothing to finish the report. Jane Doe. Nude in rural Lues, struck by a car. There were hardly enough facts to notice what hadn't been included. Were her clothes found close by or did they just vanish? Had she come out into the road unexpectedly, or was she walking naked at the side of the road in the middle of the night? Were there any houses near by? Was her car found? What did her blood show—alcohol, drugs, diabetes? Josie looked up the temperature on February 10, fifty-three degrees was the high, thirty-eight degrees the low. A cold night for streaking in rural Lues. Josie cranked the handle of her machine and again searched everything in the next few days. Now she was worried that she had found her mother. The utter anonymity was the worst of it.

When she could find nothing more, Josie screwed her concentration down and pushed on. There were more Hazards drunk in March, their names like some kind of alcoholic's epic catalog. Then she found it. The article was placed beside an advertisement for ballet classes to begin in May, classes for all ages. She saw at once why she had missed it the first time through. It looked like part of the advertisement. Her mother, she learned, had been a dancer, of sorts.

Dated Friday, April 8, the first notice of her mother's murder read in full:

DANCER DISCOVERED

Chief of Detectives, Lt. Colt Fellows, announced late last night that an anonymous call to the sheriff's office yesterday sent local investigators from the county and city to the Lues State University campus late last evening, where they discovered inside Lues Creek Canyon the nude body of Josephine Hazard, 27, a topless dancer at the Hurry On Up in Lues. Fellows told reporters the sheriff has ordered an autopsy for this morning, while Fellows plans to lead a team of officers into the canyon.

Josie looked up from the article in a perfect daze. Something like ice formed in the pit of her stomach. Her name was Josephine. *Josie.* And Josie Hazard had taken her clothes off for a living. Wonderful. Anyone could look for the price of a drink. Josie understood now why they had taken her upstate, why the Darlings had done her the service of burying her past. And buried it should have stayed, she told herself sickly.

She rolled the plastic scroll to the next day with less enthusiasm. She had what she had come for. Only a morbid curiosity drove her forward now. This time the mention of a bar owner in the title alerted her, and she looked at the text closely:

BAR OWNER CHARGED

State Police arrested John Christian Hazard, 33, of rural Lues early yesterday afternoon for the murder of his ex-wife, Josephine Fortune, 27. The arrest was ordered shortly after city homicide investigators discovered Hazard's broken wristwatch near the site of the murder in Lues Creek Canyon. According to investigators, the death occurred sometime after six o'clock, Thursday, the result of strangulation. Chief of Detectives, Lt. Colt Fellows, spearheading the investigation, sought state police assistance after Sheriff Pat Bitts could not be located. "We were looking at a hostage situation with the victim's daughter, and we had to move fast," Fellows explained. Hazard was handed over to city authorities for interrogation after his apprehension. Fortune's daughter, a minor, is expected to be turned over to county welfare officials sometime today. Hazard will be arraigned in circuit court early next week on the charge of first-degree murder and kid-napping, according to sources close to the state's attorney's office.

Josie copied the story and cranked the handle, searching for more. It did not come until the following Friday.

STACKMAN OK's PLEA

State's Attorney for Lues County, Don Stackman announced yesterday that John Christian Hazard, 33, has agreed to plead guilty to charges of second-degree murder in the death of his ex-wife Josephine Fortune, 27. Fortune's body was discovered last Thursday on Lues State Campus inside Lues Creek Canyon. Authorities report that she was stranged.

strangled

Stranged? Josie cranked the film through for several more minutes, but there was nothing else to find. Josie had all of it, there being, apparently, no obituary. She rewound the film finally and boxed it. She left the room and returned the material to the librarian as if in a trance. Outside, the heat drained what little energy she had, and she went home. The great project she had set for herself had turned out to be something she didn't care to pursue, even if she could. The death of the woman who had given her life had nothing to do with her. It was simply another story of a murdered prostitute.

Suddenly Josie could think of a number of things she needed to do before school started. She drove out to the mall and wandered miserably through the stores, listening to the grating twang which was neither Midwestern nor quite fully of the South, a kind of whining cross of the two that exited through the nose. It was considerably different from the mid-state dialect she had spoken as a child, and she hated it passionately. The people seemed friendly enough, but there was a slowness she couldn't get used to. It was enough to fill her with regret at her coming here. What had she expected though? She had always hated home. None of this was much different from what she had left years ago, except that this was just a deeper, more lonesome brand of country. Down here misery added an extra twist, that was all.

And it seemed to her she was doomed to run fast and far until she had landed no more than a few inches on a map from where she had started. Josie heard her own voice slip into the cadences of the clerks who waited on her. She felt her metabolism changing even as they punched in the price of her purchases. Five different clerks asked her, "Is it hot enough for you?"

Annie Wilde

Josie phoned Annie Wilde at her home in Boston and got her answering machine on the third ring. Annie's voice was a fog horn in minor key, an old woman with an adolescent's enthusiasm, "I'm at the firing range with my Uzi so I can't answer this call in person, but if you would like to leave a message, I'll call you after my karate lesson." Annie had been confined to a wheelchair for the past forty years.

After the tone, Josie started talking. She just wanted to check in, she said. She had been to the library and found some things. She was promising to call back later when Annie picked up. "You want to come home. You've made a terrible mistake, and you're flying back to Boston first thing tomorrow." Josie told her she was right, even wished it were true. "I'm teaching that *Magnificent Metaphors* course, Josie. I just saw the latest class roster on that thing. Four hundred. I can use another grader if you want to come back."

"Don't tempt me. Listen, Annie," she began, "I found some things in the library today."

"I hear that happens sometimes." Best friend or not, Annie rarely missed a chance at plugging the joys of scholarship.

"My mother's name was Josephine, Josie Fortune."

"Not Hazard?"

"She was divorced. I'm not sure if her name was Hazard or Fortune when she was married. The paper was a little confusing on that point. Anyway, she was twenty-seven when it happened." Josie's age. Somehow, she had imagined her mother had been much older. Of course, that was just the seven-year-old doing the math.

"*How* did it happen, Josie?"

"The murder? I don't have much. All I know is she was strangled." *Stranged.* "Jack took her into the canyon on campus and did it there. A few days later, they let him plead to second-degree murder."

"But it was premeditated?"

"It doesn't sound real spontaneous to me, Annie. I mean, the first report is they found a nude body."

"You need to talk the police or the district attorney, Josie. Get the whole thing. They can probably help you find Jack, too. You need to talk to him about it. I assume he's out on parole or something, if it was second-degree."

"I think I already know more than I care to."

"What are you talking about?"

"Are you ready for this?"

"I'm sitting down, if that's what you mean."

Annie's wheelchair humor never failed to jolt Josie's composure, but at present, it hardly registered. She was thinking about her mother's profession. "She was an exotic dancer, Annie!"

"I knew you came from good stock!"

"Annie, it's not a joke! Jack owned this bar called the Hurry On Up, and she danced for him. I mean his own wife . . . can you believe this?"

With acidity, "So you've got her whole life figured out?"

"I figured out some of it! For starters, he manipulated her, degraded her, probably beat her, all of it foreplay to the last act."

Annie cut in, "Listen, did I ever tell you about my night in jail?"

"Once or twice."

"I'm a jailbird! Do you have the story of my life from that little tidbit?" Josie didn't answer. "It means nothing, Josie. So I attacked a United States Senator!"

"It's not the same thing, Annie."

"The man said the handicapped weren't his problem. I changed that, Sister! I turned out to be the biggest problem he ever had! People found out he pressed assault charges against me, and he was done! I went around Vermont in my wheelchair and got on every television station in the state. He couldn't get elected dogcatcher after that!"

"You went to jail for principles, Annie! This is just sordid. A woman who strips her clothes off for men for a living is—."

"Broke."

"There are other ways to make money."

"Sure there are! But pretty ones get to dance a few years first."

"It's humiliating. God, I'm so glad I didn't tell anyone I used to live here. I would be a laughingstock."

"You need to find out more, Josie. We always have reasons for what we do, even if we don't understand them ourselves. Find your stepfather. Start with him."

"Do you really think I'll get the truth from a man like that, Annie?"

"So help me with this, Josie. Are you afraid of his truth or his lies?"

"I'm not afraid of him, Annie."

"Of course, you're not. Your voice always quivers when you're not afraid."

"What's he going to tell me, that his Josie was sure one humdinger of a wage earner? The guys all loved it when Josie came on stage? What do I want to hear from the guy?"

"You took a year of your life to go find out what happened, Josie."

"I got a job, a good one. And I got out of Boston for a while."

"You promised yourself you'd chase this thing down."

"Well, I chased it down, and now I'm finished with it. I understand exactly what was going on."

"If that woman you read about today was anyone but your mother and you decided to do a biography of her, you would research her life completely. You'd see the world as she saw it, and you wouldn't dare jump to a bunch of stupid conclusions based on nothing but simple prejudice." She hesitated. "I'm sorry, Josie, but it's the truth, and I think you'd better hear it."

"It's not *your* mother, Annie. I don't think you quite understand what it feels like."

"What did you think, your mother was a saint, maybe a virgin?" Her voice had its lilt again. "You started something here. Now finish it!"

Josie had put her mother's life away as quickly and easily as the microfilm she had boxed up. What was more, she had no intention of going back no matter what Annie said. "It makes me sick at my stomach, Annie. The whole thing."

"You knew it would."

"No. I thought it might scare me, but this . . . it disgusts me."

"That means you have to go look at it, Josie. You run now, you run forever. Any names in the articles you found? Any people quoted?"

"A few. Lawyers and cops."

"Find everyone who's mentioned, talk to them about it. You need to go about this thing systematically, Josie, like a researcher. You remember research, don't you?" Josie said she wasn't sure. Annie let the joke go unacknowledged, "The newspapers always get something mixed up. Remember our campus rag? The profile on me? I'm a marathon runner."

"You told that boy that's what you were."

"He was looking at me, staring right at my wheelchair, Josie, and he said, 'So do you have any hobbies, Dr. Wilde?,' and I said, 'I run the Boston Marathon every day.' Talk about dumb, he didn't even blink. The next thing I know, people are sending me entry blanks for their races."

They talked a while longer after that. Annie finally got around to the gossip at Bandolier, which led naturally to the ever popular subject of Professor Dan Scholari. Annie said he had been asking people why Josie wasn't scheduled to teach this fall. Proving, she said, that not all the slow learners at Bandolier were to be found in the student body.

"Did he talk to you about it, Annie?"

"He knows better than that, Josie."

"I wrote a couple of e-mails yesterday, telling everyone where I had gone and what I was doing, but I made sure to tell them not to mention it to Dan."

"He's going to find out eventually, Josie. You'll publish a paper or go to a conference, and he'll hear about it. It's just a matter of time."

"I know. But time is on my side. I mean eventually he'll get over it."

"You mean eventually he'll find somebody else to hurt."

It was a familiar conversation, marked by fear and wishful thinking. There had been two attacks. After the first, Josie had filed charges. After the second, she simply made every effort to avoid running into her ex-husband. She had moved from one friend's place to another's during the last weeks of the spring semester, then went to Provincetown to hide for the summer. At that point, she had been certain Dan was finished with her, so long as she did not go to the police and report the attack, but her certainty had not extended to living alone or making her place of residence common knowledge. Even here, a thousand miles from Boston, Josie did not completely trust him to let it go, because if he knew where she was, it was just possible that he could show up—for old time's sake.

Fresh Meat for the Tigers

On Monday morning, Josie drove to Harrison Hall for the university faculty meeting. As she came up the walk, Josie watched her reflection in the black glass that fronted the building. Her blond hair was pulled back and tied together loosely. Though she was not a tall woman, her stride was long and loose and natural. With the trees behind her in the reflection, she seemed to be something less than the urban sophisticate she had imagined herself these past few years. Or was it something more? A touch of the wild in her step, she thought. Not such a bad thing, really. Like Annie in her dreams: a woman who rolled with the wolves. Closer to the glass, the illusion faded. Josie was nothing more or less than the person she had always known. She was twenty-seven and still trying to be a woman instead of a girl. Some days it worked, some days it didn't. She had a small oval face, a tiny round mouth, cool green eyes. The nose was wrong, but that was Dan Scholari's gift, her abiding mark of character.

She was pretty, she decided with a reasonable amount of objectivity, not beautiful. But that was fine. The closer she got to thirty, the more she realized beauty was not a matter of form. It had more to do with style and attitude and the great terror of adolescence—originality! Those things, on a good day, she had in abundance. And today *was* a good day. Nothing at all betrayed her excitement, not a twitch of her small mouth, not a flicker of her cool greens. She was a scholar! A woman with enough experience to know what to expect this morning and how to handle it. Coffee, doughnuts, chitchat. No problem. Everything was going to be fine, as long as she remembered she belonged here. "You belong here," she whispered to herself. "You've earned the right!" With such exhortations, she got through the front door easily enough.

But once inside the hall she hesitated. She had met quite a few of the administrators and new faculty during her orientation on Friday, but she saw none of those faces now. The hall was crowded with strangers, professors with time on their hands and lots of new faculty around for a bit of fun. Fresh meat for the tigers. Josie made her way toward the serving table trying not to slink and definitely trying to forget all the things she had heard different professors say over the years about the new faculty at Bandolier. Too formal or too casual, sexual preferences and habits a matter of playful speculation, and always the point of origin, She got her degree . . . *where?* Too good, so what is she doing *here?* Or too ordinary, couldn't we do better than *that?* No middle ground to any of it, because new faculty were always suspect.

When she had taken a cup of coffee and turned out of line, she heard a familiar voice at her back. "Did you find a place?"

Dick Ferrington stepped toward her, and she turned toward him, smiling with relief at seeing a friendly face. Actually, she wanted to reach out and touch him, she was so relieved. She told him she had arranged to rent one of the furnished apartments on campus before she had even come to town.

Simple, easy, and less to move, since they were completely furnished, right down to the bedding. A gypsy scholar's dream, she told him. Ferrington grimaced at the joke. "My wife Cathy and I and our three kids rented one of those my first year at Lues State. That was . . . just about the dawn of time, fall of 1989, to be precise. I was tenure-track, with a brand new degree and not a spare dime for the move or to get set up. The five of us in a two-bedroom apartment . . . tough times! I suppose it's different if you're single. Now that my kids are off at school and I'm alone . . . one of those apartments would probably be just the thing for me." He smiled agreeably, "At least, I'd be out from under the yard work."

"You have kids off at school? You're not old enough for kids in college!" What she wanted to say was, Where's the wife? He'd get to that eventually. Divorced men always did. It was the married ones who sometimes stayed obstinately silent on the subject of wives.

"My oldest is a freshmen at Chapel Hill, which is where I went for my undergrad and grad studies. My twin girls are in a private school in Vermont. They love it. Come home to see dad about two weeks a year, and even that's a chore."

Josie started to answer about the kids. Actually, she meant to say something about how she rarely got home, that Ferrington shouldn't take it personally, but just at that moment, a heavyset man came up behind Ferrington and grabbed his shoulders with good natured roughness. Ferrington's coffee splashed over Josie's skirt, but Ferrington turned too quickly to notice. "Bill!" he said happily.

The man named Bill wagged his head at Josie. "I wouldn't believe a word he says, Missy. Dick sees a pretty face, and he can't help himself, he just lies to stay in practice! I'm Bill Waters, by the way," his eyes cut playfully toward Ferrington, "since no one is making the introductions."

"Josie Darling." They shook hands, a rather horrifying experience as it turned out. Bill Waters' flesh was hot and clammy and rough, and his hand was enormous. Nor was he eager to let go once he had her.

"Josie is one our new hires in English," Ferrington answered. "Bill is in forestry."

Bill Waters dropped her hand finally, so he could gesture toward one of the windows looking out over the forest. "I've got my lab out back." The smile and wink suggested this was an old joke and about as clever as he ever got.

"The forestry service won't make a move without consulting Bill first," Ferrington explained.

Bill Waters laughed at this. The USDA Forest Service consulted him sometimes, he said, but then they went out and did exactly what they wanted to do in the first place. He gave a weary shrugged of his heavy shoulders. It was an old fight, apparently. Then he turned to Ferrington, "I want to ask you something, buddy."

What he wanted to ask was obviously something that needed privacy, and the two men excused themselves. "Faculty senate stuff," Waters explained, with a wicked flutter of his eyebrows.

"Assassinations to plan," Ferrington answered in his best *I, Claudius.*

As they departed, Josie heard a woman at her back say to her, "You've met Dick Ferrington, I see."

Josie turned and found herself looking at a tall, lean, middle-aged woman. She had a small square face and tiny, thin lips. Her eyes were dark and flat and serious, but there was something mischievous about her expression, especially as she considered Dick Ferrington and Bill Waters. "The thing to do is to burn that skirt now," she said, pointing at the coffee stain. "If it ever comes out that Dick Ferrington stained your skirt, the affirmative action office will want it for DNA testing. I'm Clarissa Holt, by the way. Communications."

Josie looked down at the coffee stain and managed to laugh, despite her irritation at probably losing a good skirt. "Josie Darling. English."

"My condolences. You're stuck with the guy on a daily basis."

At least she wasn't in forestry. "I take it you're not a member of the Dick Ferrington Fan Club?"

Both women watched Ferrington now. "Dick was bad *before* he lost his wife. He's like a kid a candy store these days. It's a bit much."

"Lost his wife?"

Holt cocked one eyebrow. "Give him half a chance, he'll tell you all about it. I understand it's one his better approaches." Clarissa Holt nodded toward a tall man just then entering the lecture hall. "Also one of yours, I'm afraid. The most popular man on campus, assuming you're under the age of twenty-two. Henry Valentine. 'Val' to his friends, as if he had any."

"Valentine? His office is right across from mine."

"Lucky girl."

Henry Valentine was maybe fifty or fifty-five years old. Josie noted, with some satisfaction, that he wore hiking boots, jeans, and a blue denim work shirt that he buttoned to the neck. His one nod to custom was a pale green silk sports jacket that was probably quite expensive a dozen years ago. His skin was dark and leathery, his head bald except for a fringe of white hair that he kept cropped close to his skull. He had large, hooded eyes and a broad mouth that seemed to be set crookedly into something of a crocodile grin. He was not a handsome man like Dick Ferrington, but there was a glorious vitality about his ugliness. He moved with the swaggering grace, she thought, of an uncaged lion. But that was not all of it, and for a moment, Josie could not understand her reaction to the man. Then it hit her. Clarissa Holt and she were not the only ones to notice Henry Valentine. Almost everyone in the room had stopped talking and took a moment to watch him. If he knew the effect he had, Valentine certainly didn't give a damn. And that, Josie decided, was his best trait.

A heavyset woman slipped next to Clarissa Holt before Josie could respond. "I see Val is looking very healthy." Her voice was cool, vaguely disappointed.

Clarissa Holt's eyebrows quivered expressively. "And I worked so hard on those voodoo spells."

"You know," the woman answered brightly, "they say heart attack victims sometimes look extremely flush and healthy just before the 'Big One.'"

"Has he had problems?" Josie asked.

The woman looked squarely into her eyes with an almost childlike innocence, "Not that I know of," she answered, "but we can always hope, can't we?"

The Medusa Principle

The faculty had more cooking on their grill than Henry Valentine. They were professors after all, and so they passed their time in a complex and meaningless game of trench warfare, tossing canisters of mustard gas to fall as they may, but it was curious to see how frequently the subject of Henry Valentine came up once he had appeared. One professor thought it could not be long before Val started thinking about retirement. There was a wistful look in his expression as he said this. Another regretted that tenure was so absolutely irrevocable. A third remarked that popularity had come to be synonymous with a complete lack of standards.

There was never a truly critical observation about him. In the case of the comment about popularity, the professor did nothing more than look in Valentine's direction, but in every case, something between envy and fear motivated them. Valentine was something other, something powerful, the quintessential bad boy all grown-up—a perfect terror to mere mortals. All of which made him all the more interesting to Josie, since she always nursed an abiding affection for bad boys, those all grown-up and those still fighting the "Great Fight."

She tried to catch up with Valentine after the meeting, but a woman in blue sweats caught her arm, announcing with fabulous excitement, "You're new!"

That, Josie was, and introductions were made. Gerty Dowell was in English, as it turned out, and so Josie felt obliged to leave Henry Valentine for another occasion. Josie had not talked long with the old woman before realizing she was eccentric, if not completely out of her mind. As a colleague, it would not do to show impatience, so Josie gave the woman her undivided attention as she skittered from students' spelling problems and comma splices to their sexual mores. When the old professor's manic blues landed on Dick Ferrington suddenly, a thought seemed to overtake her, and she whispered to Josie, "You've been warned about *him,* I suppose?"

Josie cocked her head innocently. "Warned?"

"Richard Ferrington, *Dick.* Be careful of him!"

"Careful?"

"He's very international, you know? Roman hands and Russian fingers!" With only a slight smile to indicate she had gotten the joke, such as it was, Josie thanked her new colleague and made her apologies. Lesson plans to write.

When she got back to Brand Hall, Valentine had already gone on. Well, he couldn't hide forever. This was one bad boy Josie wanted to meet, especially after she realized that Dick Ferrington had not exaggerated his popularity. Throughout the rest of the day, students came by individually and in small groups, knocking at his door despite the fact that the office was dark. She had never seen such popularity, except at Annie Wilde's office.

Josie had her own stream of visitors as well, all her new colleagues.

Names and faces flashing before her, she was certain she would never remember them all, and everyone she forgot would have hurt feelings, and
naturally would never forget the insult. Then she had an idea and went into
the university web site, where she found the English department. Names,
faces, academic rank, degrees, and concentrations were all listed. She was
scanning the list and kicking herself for not thinking of checking the page
sooner, when Dick Ferrington knocked at her door.

"You look busy," he said.

"Trying to get a handle on everyone. She gestured toward her computer.
Just found our web site. I'm trying to put names and faces together."

"I've got just the thing for you then, though it's a little old-fashioned. A
bunch of us are going out for drinks at Cokey's. Good chance to meet the
department informally."

"Sounds like a required meeting for the new kids."

"I wouldn't say *required,* Josie, but I expect you'd be crazy not to
show up."

"Count me in."

Cokey's was just off Colson Avenue at the city limits. It was owned by
an ex-football player who had been a star in his college days at Lues State,
then joined the pros for a brief and disappointing season as a tackle dummy,
or so Ferrington explained it. It was a big splashy bar that catered to the
college, especially its faculty and administration. Besides a large dining room
and lounge, Cokey's offered a number of small private rooms. It was into
such a room that Josie was directed when she arrived shortly after 4:30
that afternoon.

She found about fifteen of her colleagues sitting on either side of a
long rectangular table. The department's rising stars, Stephan Pierce and
Jan Horner, sat at either end of the table. Pierce had his first book out,
something about the beat generation. Horner, a Shakespearean, had had
her manuscript recently accepted for publication. They were freshly tenured, newly promoted, obviously flushed with success, and clearly the
shining examples for the new people. To either side of them, the length
and breadth of the table away from each other, sat Dick Ferrington and
Henry Valentine.

Without even thinking about it, Josie passed the empty chair next to
Ferrington and sat across from the Old Rebel. If Ferrington was broken-

hearted about it, he wasn't for long. Soon after Josie's arrival, Deb Rainy showed up and seemed more than happy to endure the very international Dr. Ferrington. Because Rainy was tenure-track, she had been on campus the previous spring for interviews and seemed to know everyone already. She had a pretty face with a cherubic smile, a bit heavy in the hips and thighs, Josie thought, but sexy and outspoken and not one to play at good manners if there was a good time to be had without them. A couple of beers into it, she actually got a bit bawdy, at least considering her lowly status. Ferrington, however, took no offense.

After Josie sat down, Valentine waited while she spoke to those she had already met, then caught her eye and said, "I'm Henry Valentine. Val, to my friends." He said this as if it were a magnificent fact that bore repeating often, and Josie understood why Clarissa Holt had made such a deal about "'Val' to his friends." It was an invitation to intimacy but given in such a way that you weren't quite sure if you were supposed to call him Val or Dr. Valentine. He was a tall man, with big hulking shoulders, much uglier than he had seemed at a distance. His eyes were hooded and fearsome and keenly bright, oddly disenfranchised, though, from the smile he offered. The face was tanned to a deep brown, weathered almost to the point of ruin. The hands were huge and slow moving, but he clearly still possessed the strength of a much younger man. He still wore the same soft, shapeless, long sleeve blue denim cotton shirt and the wrinkled silk sports jacket from the morning faculty meeting. It was the look of a tramp in his Sunday Best.

"Josie Darling. I'm new. I don't have any friends."

This brought a sudden mock-assault of pity from everyone, and neither Valentine nor Josie was able to speak to each other for a while. When Mary Benedict arrived, she settled her cheerful, portly self comfortably into the group, telling everyone in her best classroom pitch that Ev Case had caught her just before she left. "Sends his regrets," she said. She shrugged and gave a hearty cigarette cough. "Business with the dean."

Ferrington answered grandly, "Better Ev than one of us!"

They all laughed. Poor Ev, Ellen Marshall sighed. The work of Sisyphus, Stephan Pierce clucked. It's the nature of the chair, Peter Nugent, the eighteenth-century specialist sniffed in his best coffeehouse manner, always to sit between a rock and a department full of hard-asses. "If any of us any of us had a heart," he added, "we would offer to take our turn."

Nell McGraw cocked a lone eyebrow, "Ev's had the job forever, poor bastard." Then she laughed.

Henry Valentine leaned forward to catch McGraw's attention. "I took my turn in the hot seat seventeen years ago, Nellie. I've done my duty."

"One summer!" Ferrington chuckled from across the expanse of the table separating the two. He seemed almost to scoff at the insignificance of it.

"Maybe that doesn't sound like much to someone who has never tried it," Valentine countered, without quite looking at Ferrington, "but I can tell you this, I started that summer with a full head of hair." He rubbed his bald head for effect, "And I finished it just as I am today!"

The only one forgetting to laugh, Dick Ferrington looked at Rainy. "Maybe our new tenure-track professor will volunteer."

Nell McGraw answered for her, "Do it if they give you tenure, Deb, that's what I say!"

Deb Rainy's angelic smile twisted ever-so slightly, "For tenure, . . . I'm *available*." This, with its implicit undertow of sexuality, got the expected hoots of laughter.

As the talk swirled around the table, Henry Valentine caught Josie with his large, calm eyes. "You studied at Bandolier, I understand?" he asked. Josie nodded cautiously. She was wondering what sly insults the man might heap upon the institution. "Have you had a chance to study with Annie Wilde?"

"She's my dissertation director! Do you know her?"

Henry Valentine shook his head slowly, his eyes unblinking. "Not personally," he answered, "but I've read three of her books. My humble opinion, her *Medusa Principle* is pure genius."

Josie started to respond enthusiastically, when Ellen Marshall leaned toward her in mock confidence. "Pure genius for a woman, he means."

Josie looked first at Professor Marshall, then at Henry Valentine. Valentine's eyes lit up at the insult, but he showed no other reaction. "Have you read Annie Wilde, Ellen?"

Ellen Marshall blanched. "I just meant . . ."

"I know what you meant. I asked if you had read Annie Wilde. Easy enough question, isn't it?"

Ellen Marshall had the look of a student forced to admit she had not read her assignment. "No," she answered uncomfortably.

Valentine nodded sagely. "You should," he said. "I think you would enjoy her."

Dr. Marshall seemed to scramble. "Well, I'll try. But there's so much to read in the field and papers to grade. . . ."

Valentine clucked his lips sympathetically, ". . . and a new season of TV almost upon us."

Marshall's eyes flashed. An old wound, that. Peter Nugent leaned forward earnestly, looking at Josie as if he thought she had written the book, "I like the title, *The Medusa Principle,* but what does it mean?"

Josie glanced at Henry Valentine, who seemed more than ready to answer. "Dr. Wilde argues the value of looking directly at the things we'd rather not admit existed, Peter."

Nell McGraw snatched a fresh onion ring from the basket inopportunely set before her, "I thought if you looked at Medusa directly you turned to stone. Snakes for hair, isn't it?"

At the other end of the table, Deb Rainy rolled her eyes, "God, I've had mornings like that!"

Ellen Marshall said, to no one in particular, "I thought it was Medea with the hair."

"Dr. Wilde's argument," Valentine continued, his voice rising ever so slightly, as if to stifle a rowdy class of freshmen without breaking their spirits, "is that there is nothing at all wrong with turning to stone. In fact, she sees the image as a perfect metaphor for discovering one's inner strength. To see the truth without apology or excuses, to look at it and not blink is to become impervious to what we fear the most. Thus, to turn to stone. If we look at only the reflection of it, as Perseus did when he chopped off Medusa's head, we go away, according to Dr. Wilde, as we came, 'second rate heroes who can't keep a relationship.'"

Pan

Josie hesitated before the glass doors as she looked out across parking lot. The darkness had settled in while she had eaten and drunk and talked. She had been having such a good time, had been feeling so safe and secure, she hadn't even thought about it. But now she was alone. And the parking lot was not especially well lit.

The second time Dan Scholari attacked her, Josie was coming out of the library. It was a late winter's evening, a cold mist in the air. And dark. She had been hurrying to get out of the rain and so had not seen him by her car, until it was too late. He had been crouching in the shadows at her driver-side door. Waiting. She was fumbling with her keys when she looked up in time to see his fist coming at her face.

She went down hard but still conscious. Exactly what he intended, apparently, because he talked while he kick her. He called her baby. Four broken ribs, a fractured ankle, and, of course, her nose. "You like that, baby?" It was over pretty quickly considering the damage he did. And that was it. He straightened up, adjusted his coat a bit and walked away like a man who had simply delivered a message. Someone found Josie lying almost under her own car. Josie heard his voice, but she couldn't respond. The man screamed at someone to call an ambulance, then knelt beside her until the ambulance came. Josie didn't remember any of the things the stranger said, but it helped to try to focus on the sound of his voice. She slipped in and out of consciousness. She felt nauseous and thought she was going to die. She even heard someone ask if she was dead. Josie thought about her mother lying on the cold ground somewhere about to die. Even then her mother had no face or form. She had no name. She was only the great abstract Mother she had always been. Only suddenly not so frightening and distant—more like a fellow sufferer, actually. For the next hour, it was the sole thought that held Josie to life: she had to find her.

The detective who had interviewed Josie when she had pressed charges after the first attack came to the hospital to take her statement. He told her she couldn't let her ex-husband get away with this. Josie told him she didn't know who her attacker was. She didn't recognize the man. Description? She really didn't see anything at all. Annie had raged that she *must* charge him, but Josie couldn't. She had reasons, hours of self-justification, but the truth was she knew Dan had come back for revenge because she had filed assault charges before. She was also quite certain that if she charged him again, he would kill her.

The trouble was her silence had bought her no guarantees. She could not step into the darkness again without thinking about that night. She could not forget how easy it had been for him to catch her alone and vulnerable. She knew this, too, though she only now realized it: she had come to Lues to hide from Dan Scholari, not just to find her past. It was the last place on earth he would think to look for her. It was a place that had terrified her once, just as Dan Scholari now terrified her. So it was the perfect hiding place, except that she was still as scared of the dark as ever.

A movement beside her made her jump in surprise, but it was only Henry Valentine, jiggling his keys and looking out at the darkness. There was a faint, goatish scent about him, she realized. It wasn't entirely unpleasant. A bit . . . *Panish,* she thought. Cloven hooves, cute little horns, flute-playing, wild meadows and, of course, the insatiable appetites of the ever-ready bad-boy Pan.

"I've often thought hell must be very much like school lessons from our colleagues, Josie." His eyes stayed on the parking lot meditatively, while a crocodile smile flickered around his fangs.

Josie glanced at him, then behind them to make sure they were alone. "You think?" she asked, giving a slight conspirator's smile.

"I've never bought the theory of a lake of fire for everyone. I'm with Dante on this. *If* it exists, I'm quite sure it will be customized to fit the sinner: Ellen Marshall treating me to one of her lectures for all eternity would be about right for all the wickedness I've caused." He shook his head sadly, "I tell you, the very thought of it is nearly enough to make me a Christian. How about you? What hell do you dread, Josie?"

"Riddles without answers."

He smiled, but he was clearly disappointed. He wanted something better or crueler or more clever. "Spoken as a true Joycean," he told her with mechanical indifference. "May I walk you to your car?"

Josie smiled at the man, trying to cover her fears with exaggerated humor, "And I thought chivalry was dead."

She felt the first drops of sweat slipping over her ribs, as they stepped out into the night. She fought against the quickening of her breath. She tightened her grip on Valentine's arm, letting his body give her some small measure of comfort. He was a large man with strong arms. Like Dan, only without the flabbiness and tired gray skin. Older, but more vigorous. And as they walked, he talked so casually, with such ease. Something about nights like these keeping him here all of these years. She purred agreement. It was all he needed to keep talking, and so keep her devils at bay. Because hell was here, all around her suddenly, and Dan Scholari was its architect.

At her car, they stopped, and she did not quite know what Valentine wanted. A moment of awkwardness, the mutual reckoning of potential, despite the difference in their ages, and then pulling herself back, her quiet thanks, a smile that promised *maybe*... when they knew each other better. He took it as his dismissal. Ferrington was right. Old South. But not old-fashioned. Very nice, really. The wonder was that everyone hated him. But that was life at any university. Grudges ran deep. Sometimes, as with a family, people couldn't even say what started it. Hatred was a habit, and like all habits, it gave people some small measure of comfort.

When she was alone again, the shaking returned. Simple darkness, she told herself, willing the courage to look up into the night sky. Dan could not find her. She had taken precautions against that. And even if he knew, he was a thousand miles away! How many times did she have to tell herself that before she would believe it? It was over. It had been over for months. She was being a child by letting her fears get to her. "Stare down Medusa," she whispered, but as she tried it, she trembled. She trembled, in fact, all the way back to campus.

Only when she was home, the door closed and locked and chained behind her, did she draw a decent breath. Then she noticed that something was wrong. The doors to her office, her bedroom and the bathroom were all shut, and she knew she hadn't left them that way. She remembered that she had wanted the air to circulate. Was Dan waiting? Get it together! she told herself angrily, but her knees were weak, despite what logic told her. She had closed the doors without thinking, or someone in maintenance or housing had come by to check on the apartment. That was possible. Or a lunatic was waiting. That was possible, too. Any lunatic would do. Just not Dan Scholari!

Josie went down the hall, opened the door to her office, and walked in. The room was grim, hot, ugly. Just as she had left it. It was also empty. She checked in the closet to be sure and made a joke about the bogeyman. She checked the window and the second door. Like the other, it was made of steel. The security chain was still attached. It hadn't been tampered with. Josie crossed the hall and walked into her bedroom purposefully. She went to the closet, then checked the slender window that looked out into the forest. Under the bed she saw her slippers, but Dan Scholari was missing. Josie pushed the bathroom door open finally. Just to be sure.

That was when she saw the bright red markings on her mirror. Still not in the room, she couldn't read the words, but she was sure it was written in blood. The shower curtain was pulled shut, as well. He had found her. For a moment, the certainty that Dan Scholari was behind that sheet of plastic nearly undid her, and yet, she couldn't run or scream or even cry. She began shaking, but her eyes were dry. Her breath felt like smoke. She looked at the mirror almost in a trance. From her angle, she couldn't see the words. She knew only that he had written something. And not in blood, but in lipstick. She glanced at the shower curtain again. He wasn't waiting. He had been here. "He's gone," she whispered, as if to make it real by wishing it so, and then in a combination of rage at trespass and unabashed curiosity, she stepped fully into the room. She was ready to scream, even ready to fight, but she was not ready for the words on the mirror:

WilcuM
HoM
Josie

The letters were oddly shaped, written with the crooked uncertainty of a desperately psychotic man.

She ripped the shower curtain back, but the message was the point. She looked into the mirror again and saw her face behind the letters. The blood had been driven out of her cheeks.

With the cool indifference of exhaustion, she wet one corner of a towel and wiped the mirror. The red markings smudged over the glass, smearing like blood. She pressed harder, and the wax began gathering at the edges.

Pistolas

It was after midnight in Boston when Annie picked up her phone, "This better be good."

"You're up."

"I am now. What is it? What's wrong?"

"Did you see Dan today?"

"Classes haven't started yet, Josie. He wasn't around."

"I think he was here, Annie."

"In southern Illinois? Dan? That's impossible, Josie!"

"I got back to my apartment tonight, and there was a note written in lipstick on my bathroom mirror."

Annie swore angrily.

"It said 'Welcome home, Josie.' But everything was misspelled."

"Did you call the police?"

"I've seen how the police handle these things."

"You have to call them, Josie. My God, if he's flying out there to break into your apartment, . . . he's crazy!"

"Well, we know that already."

"How did he get in?"

"I don't know. Some kind of master key . . . bribed a janitor . . . I don't know. No idea! All I can think about is he's never going to give up. He isn't, is he?"

"You don't even know if it's Dan, Josie."

"My God, Annie, how many raging lunatics do I know?"

"Including me?"

Josie laughed, more the bark of exhaustion than humor. "Annie . . . what am I going to do?"

"First thing. Make sure you're safe tonight."

"I've got the chains on both doors. I don't think he wants to try coming up out of a ravine in the middle of the night. If he does, he can probably break through the balcony door, but I've got a steel bedroom door with a lock and a telephone. Way too complicated for Dan Scholari, Annie. I mean, the man grunts when he ties his shoes."

"Sounds like you're living in a prison!"

Josie looked around at the place, "Yeah . . . well." It suddenly felt like prison.

"You need to talk to the people at housing about the security. If Dan got hold of a key, you need a new lock!"

"I plan on it, believe me."

"And a gun, Josie. You need a gun. What he's doing is irrational. You don't know what he could do next."

She had a good idea but didn't offer it. Instead, she told her friend, "I thought he was done with it, Annie. This is like . . . it's like the whole thing is starting all over again!"

"It *is* starting all over again, Josie. You need to face that and do something constructive about it."

"Like get a gun? That's constructive?"

"It's liberating, especially if maniacs are breaking into your apartment and misspelling words."

"Annie, I've never even touched a gun."

"As my first boyfriend once told me, Josie, 'There's a first time for everything, sweetheart.'"

"I'm supposed to keep a gun . . . because my ex-husband is crazy?"

"Sounds good to me. And don't just keep it, Josie. Learn how to use it! I mean it. Do it tomorrow, first thing. Can you buy a gun there without a thirty-day waiting period?"

"I think there are counties in southern Illinois where it's against the law *not* to own a handgun, Annie."

"You suppose they deliver? Maybe you can get one tonight."

Josie laughed, the tension breaking, though she found herself staring at her front door, wondering at the strength of the chain and deadbolt. "I don't think they're quite like pizzas—even here."

"It's a business idea. If you make it through this, you might want to think about it. *Just-in-time handguns! Pistolas in thirty minutes or less. Buy a gun, get your bullets free.* That sort of thing. You'll never get rich teaching, Josie!"

"I don't want to get rich. I just want . . . I want Dan to leave me alone. Maybe a can of Mace. Spray him in the face, jump up and down, and tell him to leave me alone."

"Dan is about two attacks past chemicals, Josie. What you need, what *he needs* is a .357 Magnum pointed right between his eyes. Something that will fit in your purse."

"Annie, I can't carry a gun! It's against the law to carry a concealed weapon!"

"Sure. Keep it in your bedroom. Then when you come home some night and he's gotten past your locks again, you can ask him to give you a minute while you go back to your bedroom and find your gun."

Josie thought about the darkness and the fear it had stirred. Paranoia was one thing, something she needed to learn to face, but if Dan Scholari knew how to find her anytime he wanted, it wasn't paranoia, and Annie was right. Dan needed to be stopped, not just deterred. A gun. One she could grab on short notice. She knew Dan. If he ever saw a gun, that would end it. He would run like a dog with his tail between his legs, and he would *never* come back. And if he didn't? Well, that was why you loaded the thing.

"Look, I'll see what I can do."

"Is this going to be like the research on your mother, or are you really going to get one?"

"I'll get a gun tomorrow, Annie. Promise."

"You'll keep it with you?"

"Bed, bath, and class. Loaded."

"And learn how to use it?"

"Oh, yeah." She smiled, imaging Dan's face going ash white, as he looked at his little punching bag pointing a grown-up handgun at his face. "I'm a very good student, when I put my mind to something, Annie."

Philistines

Before they hung up, Josie told her friend, "You're not going to believe this, but I've found a fan of yours!"

"In the middle of nowhere? You've got to be kidding."

"Imagine it! And he not only reads your stuff, Annie, he can quote you."

"Put him under glass, Josie! We don't want anything to happen to him."

"The thing is nobody likes this guy!"

"I do!"

"His name is Henry Valentine, and he's the most popular teacher on campus. The students love him, but every prof I talk to positively loathes him!"

"They're Philistines, Josie!"

So began a rather lengthy discussion of Dr. Henry Valentine and the way of campus politics. It left Josie feeling less panicked. This was a world she could understand. Irrational as it might seem to the uninitiated, it was at least familiar ground. And for a time, she almost forgot that Dan Scholari was back in her life, ready or not.

Before she went to bed, Josie double-checked her locks, then gave a tug at her balcony door. When it slipped open, she realized she had locked it but then failed to close it properly. She looked out at the trees and thought about the steep sides of the ravine. Had Dan climbed through the ravine to get to her balcony? She almost laughed. *Dan?* It wasn't possible, not even in daylight. Not for Dan, anyway. He hated any ground that wasn't paved.

Was she to imagine he had hiked into the creek and tracked back through the ravine, through all that water and mud, just to leave a note? Forget whether the climb was possible or impossible. Forget likely or improbable. Simply put, the thought would never even occur to him.

And just what had he meant to do when he got up to her balcony? Break the glass and come in? No. More likely, Dan had gotten a key to the front door, and this was just to make her think otherwise. Just walk into housing and get one. Dan Scholari could do that. It wasn't so hard if you understood where to go and what to say, not if you looked every inch the debauched old prof who had absentmindedly lost his key. Universities were not known for being especially vigilant about security, not when it came to faculty, at least. There was always a way to get a key. What she couldn't understand was how he had known she was here. Within days of her arrival! *Welcome home.* She shook her head. Dan knew about Lues and the fear she had always nursed for this place. Did he just guess she was here or did someone tell him? One of her friends? She thought through the e-mails she had sent out Saturday. As easy as pushing a couple of buttons and Dan would know, but they were *her* friends, not his! They knew what he had done. So maybe Annie had a point. Assuming it was Dan. Maybe it wasn't Dan. Maybe it was Jack Hazard.

Josie could hardly imagine the possibility before she began denying it. It couldn't be Jack. Dan could have guessed, or someone could have told someone else innocently and it got to him by chance, or one of her friends could have nursed a secret affection for Dan. Anything was possible in the academy. All kinds of ways, really, that he could find her. That made sense. Jack Hazard did not make sense. How would Jack even know she had come back? How would he know her name, for God's sake? And even if he did by some miracle of coincidence, why break into her house? Why *tease* her like it was some kind of sick game? Jack had no grudge against a little girl. No, this was Dan Scholari. Dan wanted her to know how clever he was, probably expected her to call the police and let them laugh at her. *Your ex-husband in Boston? You think he showed up here to write a note on your bathroom mirror?* With no break-in, no proof, they would just assume she had done it herself for the attention. Lonely teacher, eager for a man in uniform to save her from dying of boredom. That would be Dan Scholari! His idea of a good joke, the various levels of humor, right down to the skeptical local cops nudging one another as she tried to explain about her maniac husband a thousand miles away. The son of a bitch. It had to be Dan!

But that night, it wasn't Dan Scholari who came to her in her dreams. During the few moments she actually slipped away from consciousness, it was Jack Hazard who crept out from under her bed. She had not seen him since the last nightmares of adolescence, but there he was again, his face bloody as before, his killing only half done.

The Nickel

The next morning, a mile south of the city limits, Josie found the place she was looking for, Bowers's Guns and Ammo. The building was an old structure with a fairly large addition off the back of it. The paint-peeled sign at the edge of the highway had been used for target practice. The whole place needed a whitewash. Close by, there was a bait and tackle shop. Down the road a couple of hundred yards, Josie saw a small, broken-down house. Beyond that was the forest. The owner of Bowers's Guns and Ammo was a bleached-skinned, big-bellied man in his sixties. He was only an inch or so taller than Josie, who stood 5'2". Bowers had gun oil under his nails and long oily yellow-white hair.

When Josie said she needed a gun, he told her in a slow, Lues-nasal twang he couldn't help her, that she needed a license even to buy ammunition or use his range.

Josie bit her lip to keep back the tears of frustration and anger and fear. She looked out into the parking lot. She was certain Dan was waiting, laughing at her again.

"Tell you what," Bowers said after a long moment of calculation, "if you really need a gun today, we might be able to work something out. So long as we deal in cash."

Cash, Josie had. They talked briefly about the kind of money Bowers needed and the kind of revolver Josie wanted. She paid a range fee and bought a box of fifty hollow-point bullets for the .357 Magnums and a second box of bullets for a .38, which, he said, would work in both guns. Mr. Bowers took her back to his indoor firing range with a used .357 Magnum Smith & Wesson, way too much gun, he told her, and a .38 Colt, which was probably a lot more than she needed. But she wanted a gun that would get a man's attention and insisted on trying both revolvers. Her money, her choice.

Both weapons were double-action revolvers, both capable of fitting into her purse. He loaded the guns for her, showing her how to eject the casings. They put on ear protection, and Josie fired the steel blue Colt at the fresh silhouette Bowers had sent down the wires. When Josie had finished six shots, Bowers handed her the other gun. Josie liked the second gun better. It had a beautiful nickel sheen to it. With its wide bore and black rubber grips so thick she was forced to use a second hand to hold it. This gun was all business.

When Josie had finished firing six rounds, Bowers took off his ear protection and motioned for her to do the same. Bowers told Josie to load the nickel-plated revolver on her own this time. She open the box of .357s and slipped each bullet in with care. As she did this, he warned her the .357 Magnum load would give a lot more kick than the .38. Josie nodded. She liked kick. It reminded her she wasn't grading papers. What Josie didn't know was whether or not she could really point it at Dan Scholari and kill him, as much as she hated and feared him. And she had to be ready to do that . . . if he didn't back away. Her life depended on it. Josie lifted the gun and felt Bowers's hand on her shoulder. "Ears." Josie put the little green cups over her ears and pointed the gun toward the silhouette again.

As she imagined Dan's big fist rolling toward her face, she dumped six rounds into the silhouette. The shockwaves recoiled through her hands and wrists. It was a feeling like grain alcohol poured directly over adolescent hormones, and she hit two dry-fires before she realized the chambers were empty. Dropping the gun sights off the target, she smiled down the track in an orgasmic daze, then gave the old man a sly grin. "Wow," she murmured.

Mr. Bowers apparently knew the feeling and laughed, signaling her to take the ear protection off. He suggested Josie fire in groups of two and showed her a stance with a broad base and one foot forward. He placed her arms so that her wrists and elbows were locked and had her dry-fire it a few times. He had her bring the sight into the target, instead of holding steady on the bead, and told her to squeeze the trigger. "Squeeze him dead," he whispered, as if he knew what Josie feared. He held the first gun up for her to load, the Colt, but Josie shook her head. She popped the six spent shells with a single flick of the chamber's lever and loaded her "nickel" again with the heavier charged .357s. The smell of the powder wafted up to her nostrils, a sweet burning, oddly nostalgic stink, and Josie's hands still tingled with the memory of the recoil. Her fears waned. She was ready. She wanted only Dan Scholari in front of her. She snapped the cylinder shut, put the ear cups in place, and ripped the silhouette this time, three sets of two's, all somewhere on the target. Bowers nodded happily. Removing his ear protection, gesturing for her to do the same, he said, "You're a quick study! You sure you never handled a gun?"

"Never." As she said this, she suddenly wasn't sure. There was something familiar about the smell of burnt gunpowder, the essence of the freshly oiled steel, even the kick of the gun.

"Well, work with it, and see what you think. I'm going back up front."

When Josie finished both boxes of shells, with one cautious bullet left in the chamber, she brought the silhouette up along the wire and studied her work critically. She had landed about eighty percent somewhere on the silhouette from a distance of thirty feet. Not good, but good enough, since eighty percent would mean four out of every five rounds would draw blood. Josie went back into the store and said she would take the gun. Bowers said he wanted to clean it for her, and Josie told him there was one bullet left. He looked at her curiously, then smiling as gunsmiths do, which is to say with all the confidence in the world, Bowers reached back to a shelf behind the counter and moved a box with a flick of his fingers in order to show her a fearsome pistol with a barrel at least ten inches in length and a handle grip that was big enough for a minor arsenal of firepower. "No one's coming in here we don't want to come in," he said, and suddenly Josie liked Lues a little better than before. Country does have its charms, she thought.

Bowers broke her gun down and showed her how to clean it. The process was fairly easy really. It required only patience, oil, cloth and a stiff-bristled ramrod. When he finished, Bowers put the kit back together in its box and sacked it for her in a plain brown bag. Josie took two fresh boxes of .357s and loaded five in the chambers. She kept the last chamber empty for the hammer to rest against. It was the only safety the revolver offered.

Paying the man nearly all the money she had in cash, just under three-hundred dollars, Josie dumped the contents of her purse into the sack with the cleaning kit and bullets, then set the revolver into her purse. Mr. Bowers suggested that when Josie got home, she load the revolver with spent shells and dry-fire it. "You might want to work with that purse too. They're lousy, but it's all you've got unless you got a license to carry, which they won't give you in this county. You want to get quick at flipping that latch with your left hand, while you reach across and draw the gun out business-end ready. And keep in mind, the minute you flash that thing, you've already broken a half-dozen laws." Josie nodded impatiently. She had seen what breaking the law got Dan Scholari. She saw what he meant, though, about the purse and adjusted the strap so it hung lower, then moved the gun within the purse, so the handle was the first thing she touched.

In her car, the smell of burnt gunpowder on her hands was strong but not unpleasant. It was intoxicating actually, and she found herself praying that Dan Scholari would show his face soon.

Vigilance

But Dan Scholari did not come. All of Tuesday, she waited. On Wednesday, Annie called. Dan had appeared on campus in time for classes.

Josie managed to get someone out to change her locks before the end of the week, but even then she did not relax her vigil. She carried her purse with her nickel inside everywhere she went. She had no idea when Dan might decide to steal a day from classes and fly out to see her. She couldn't very well ask Annie to call her every morning to let her know he was on campus. Day followed day, the first week and weekend passed, and every hour of it, Josie knew the fear that only the imagination can sustain. A thousand miles could be covered in a handful of hours. That thought nagged at her. It overrode everything, even the joy of her first real teaching assignment, an experience that seemed to her altogether different somehow from the classes she had taught as a teaching assistant. Josie tried to set up a new pattern for her life, to think about the unexpected, to look even when she knew no one would be there. She went twice to the range the week after she had bought the gun, firing it until her hands ached. She had one organizing principle in all that she did: stay alive. Each night, Josie unloaded the gun and practiced drawing it from her purse and dry-firing it in the same motion. Josie practiced doing it while she was sitting in a chair. She practiced it while she was standing or walking across the room. She worked on it until she could do it smoothly, and each time she drew the gun out, she tried to imagine Dan coming toward her at close range. She got a license to own a handgun at the courthouse just ahead of the Labor Day weekend and even asked about a license to carry, but they wouldn't issue such a thing. And if she needed it? she asked. Home protection, the sheriff's deputy answered. Outside the home? Best thing to do, he said, was have a cell phone handy, and some kind of chemical deterrent. She took the advice for what it was, the required answer of a man who carried a gun on his hip and a cell phone and a chemical deterrent and had a whole lot of armed friends. She had a lunatic following her, and at home or in a parking lot, she meant to finish it, to do it without hesitation. No flinching, no regrets. If he didn't run when she pulled it on him, that is. She had decided she would give Dan that much of a chance, no more.

Josie saw the world differently now. She looked for dead ends, shadows. She found even the walk to a restroom was a gauntlet. Could he be waiting in that corner? Would he be inside the stall with his legs pulled up? He waited in a thousand fantasies, and maybe one day, when she had given up her fear of him, Dan would be waiting for real. Sometimes she wondered if it really was Dan Scholari who had come into her apartment. It was a curiosity only. An uncomfortable one, at that. The idea nearly maddened her. She could watch for Dan. She could see *him* coming, but if it were Jack Hazard. . .

But of course, it wasn't her stepfather. It was Dan. His game she played.

And then there was the temptation to believe Dan was gone forever, that he had come once to let her know he could have struck and chose not too, and then he had gone away forever, with only the shadows of the big trees left to frighten her. It was a fabulous temptation and urged the sort of laxness he needed for a perfect surprise. She set routines to help her remember she was under siege. She stopped herself several times each day and thought about her movements, thought about the times she did things. She looked at her vulnerabilities and did something about them if she could. If she couldn't, she stayed alert, though always for no apparent purpose. Day following day, Dan Scholari met his classes at Bandolier, seducing new conquests, no doubt. All the time knowing he could come for Josie at his leisure. Josie didn't turn a corner or step through a door without thinking of Dan Scholari's fist. Sometimes at night she heard footsteps in the parking lot in front of her apartment building. She thought, it's now, he's here now! But it wasn't. Dan Scholari slept peacefully in Boston. Josie exhausted herself with anticipation.

A Prelude to Murder

One day, during the second week of classes, Henry Valentine asked her if she had seen Campus Falls. When she told him she had been too busy, he played the wise old man and told her that life was not all work. This best reason to teach in southern Illinois, he said, was the natural beauty of the area. Besides, he said, it was a good time of year to hike into the canyon and go under the falls. If she waited until springtime, she would have take a swim to get into the canyon! She was quite certain Val would have volunteered to be her guide if she had shown the slightest interest, but when she answered that she would try if she had some time, he changed the subject. She liked that about him, liked the way he didn't force things, and she even thought she might give him a call on Sunday morning for just such an adventure. And then maybe, she decided with wicked glee, another sort of adventure afterwards! The notion of romance surprised her somehow. For well over a year, Josie had not found anyone who really tempted her, had not really even yearned for intimacy. Until Valentine.

Late Friday afternoon of that same week, Clarissa Holt called Josie as she was cleaning up the remnants of a stack of compositions. "Drinks with the Girl Scouts, four o'clock, Josie. No excuses accepted." This, without even a greeting, but Josie knew the woman's voice at once.

"I was never a Girl Scout, Clar."

"That sounds suspiciously like an excuse."

"Not at all. If they'll have me, I'll join, especially if we get to drink."

"Are you always prepared, Josie?"

"Almost always."

"That's good enough for this crew."

They met at Cokey's, seven women in all, all shapes, all ages, all sizes. Other than Clar, Josie knew only Nell McGraw, who was in her department, but almost at once, she felt certain she had found new friends. Over the first two drinks, they worked through the chairs, deans, and various VPs, the entire pecking order of good ol' boys in suits and ties, as Clar put it, then settled into the faculty at large. Along the way, there came the rather envious observation from one of the single women that Deb Rainy seemed to have something going with Dick Ferrington. This was old news, another answered. Nell McGraw caught Josie's eyes, while she blew smoke, "Thought you might be in line for those honors, Josie."

Estelle Quick from the art department answered before Josie could, "She still might be. Dick's not had a relationship that went longer than six weeks since Cathy." This brought a review of Dick Ferrington's conquests, extending all the way back to his first semester on campus. At least that was what Nell McGraw said, and she had been there to see it. Cheryl Fischer, the round-faced Baptist mathematician protested. She thought Dick and Cathy had a *perfect* marriage!

"That it was," Clar answered. "Ferrington did what he wanted, Cathy did what she was told." This observation seemed to get a universal nod from the others, though Mrs. Fischer was still reluctant to accept it. Cathy was such a beautiful woman, she said, and a Christian. Clar nodded, "And malleable right up to the day she was murdered."

"Murdered?" Josie exclaimed.

Nell McGraw tossed the ice in her empty glass, watching for the waitress, "Right before the divorce."

Josie stepped into the hot silence of accusation, "You don't think he . . . ?"

"His own kids think it," Clar answered. "The twins come back a couple of weeks a year, when they have to. The way I hear it, his son hasn't spoken to him since it happened."

There was more, naturally. A police investigation that could do nothing with the case, though there was a lot of money at stake, hard feelings about the divorce and property settlement proposals, and, almost enough to convict, a rather extensive catalogue of Ferrington's indiscretions.

"But to hear him tell it now. . . ." Nell told them, rolling her eyes.

Clar pitched in, ". . . the love of his life."

Josie went home that evening congratulating herself that nothing had happened between Dick Ferrington and her. Just exactly the wrong man to get mixed up with! She was still thinking about Ferrington when she got home, counting herself not only lucky she hadn't fallen into that pretty smile of his but stronger and better for having eluded the instinct of self-destruction. Not so much like mamma, anymore, she told herself happily. Dan Scholar's kicks had awakened some desire for self-preservation, it seemed. She had actually veered away from Dick Ferrington, sensed something she hadn't liked, the potential violence.

Her congratulatory thoughts froze the moment she opened the door to her apartment. On the glass of the balcony door, someone had written in red:

LEt MeE IN, pleEs!!!

It was done with lipstick on the outside of the door, she realized when she had walked across the room with her revolver drawn. Written backwards, so Josie could read it. Somehow, the care taken to do that was worse than the rest.

When her breath came back and she had checked the apartment completely, she called Annie, but Annie wasn't home. Not then and not later. She spent the whole night trying to sleep and failing. She was certain Dan had flown out again, and she could not stop imagining exactly what he intended . . . ultimately. This was not just play, the old Scholari sense of humor acting up. It was something far worse. This was, without a doubt, a prelude to murder. But why? Why couldn't he just let it go? There was no reason for this!

On Sunday, Josie thought about calling Henry Valentine for a hike to the falls and whatever else might come up, but then meekly decided to stay in her apartment. She graded papers, read, exercised in her front room, practiced drawing her nickel and firing it at ghosts, even took a short trip to town for shopping. On the broad streets of campus, in the light of day, she tasted the fever of paranoia burning at her throat, and that evening, while she made her dinner, her heart hammered just as it had on Friday and Saturday night. Sunset brought new tremors, and her breathing simply would not slow down.

She had a madman playing with her, and he wasn't going away.

Annie returned her call just before Josie slipped into bed. She said she had no idea if Dan had been on campus Friday. She had been in Vermont, plugging her new book on a couple of local television stations. They loved her in Vermont, criminal record or not. "I'll check, though," she said. "I'll ask around tomorrow."

Annie called her Monday night. Dan's last class on Friday finished at eleven. He had apparently taught the class and left campus. "But the guy leaves campus early every Friday, Josie."

"He could have made it here, Annie. I wasn't home until seven. That's eight hours, plus the time difference."

"Josie, you need to call the police. If Dan's flying out there, they can find out. You can charge him for this. It's not domestic anymore."

"No way, Annie. The first thing they'll do is check *me* out! I'm not going to give Dan the satisfaction. This is between us. When he's ready to face me, I'm ready for him."

More than ready. Every night, every shadow, every footstep she heard, she stirred herself into a crisis and waited with shallow, ragged breath. Was this it? The last sane moment of life? Or maybe the last moment? She prayed for it, if only to be finished with the waiting. And every time it happened it came to nothing. Innocent life passing her door, crossing her path, leaving her with a hollow feeling in her stomach that she knew was adrenaline but that was beginning to feel like some kind of tumor.

God, but she wanted him to show his face!

Josie Fortune

"Department meeting at Cokey's tonight, Josie," Dick Ferrington told her with a wink as they passed each other in the hall beyond the main office. They had seen each other almost every day but their talk had always been limited to professorly complaints about papers to grade.

Josie smiled eagerly at the invitation. She liked the group last time and had been hoping to get to know some of them a little better. Especially Henry Valentine. The group was considerably smaller than the first get-together, however. Josie had the feeling this was Ferrington's party, *his* group. As before, Ferrington sat with Deb Rainy, but this time, they took very little time confirming the rumor of their affair. With the coy looks and casual intimacies, Rainy was looking almost tenured in her happiness.

In vain, Josie waited for Henry Valentine and Nell McGraw to arrive. They clearly fell into the ranks of Old Guard, the enemy of youth and progress and academic enlightenment. There was talk about getting Ev Case to step down, this time quite seriously. Ferrington, looking at Rainy, said what they needed in the chair was new blood. Pierce and Horner nodded solemnly. No one with any sense really wanted to be chair, but if someone would actually agree to take it, they were certainly willing to see it happen. Case was obsolete, definitely Old Guard. Valentine, of course, was the problem, Horner told them. Hated women, so he would oppose any attempt to dethrone Case and put Rainy in. Nell McGraw wasn't much better, Pierce answered. She was too old school to think anyone under fifty had much to offer.

And so it went. Josie had the feeling she had turned up at the wrong party, a very dangerous thing for the new kid, and decided she ought to finish her drink and get out when Ellen Marshall told them that Valentine didn't hate women, he just expected their complete acquiescence. This stopped Josie from leaving too quickly. She wanted to hear what Marshall had to say about Val. But that was all she dared on two drinks. Horner disagreed with this assessment. In the old days, at least the way she heard it, and on very good authority, Henry Valentine always humiliated one woman per class as a warning to the rest. "Every semester, every class he taught, he wouldn't rest until he had sent someone running out of his class in tears."

Deb Rainy, her hand on Ferrington's thigh, was outraged. "He quit doing that, I hope? Because if he hasn't, I'll personally cut his balls off!"

Jan Horner smiled fondly. "He *had* to stop. Got called on the carpet about it a couple times. Tenure or no tenure, they told him he was gone if he kept it up. Did a complete turn around. Now everyone loves him. And why not? You take a class with Henry Valentine, you improve your grade point average."

Marshall nodded at this wisdom. "If you ask me," she muttered, "they should have made an example out of him. I don't know why they didn't."

Ferrington told them it was a different time. Tenure was sacred in those days, and they didn't dare go after someone without lots of warnings. Anything short of rape, he said, the administration always managed to look the other way.

Josie let things play out a few minutes more, hoping for more about Val, but when they moved on to other examples, she decided to make her excuses. Papers to grade. Just as she was setting her glass aside to do so, however, their waitress stepped into the room and said there was a call for Josie Fortune. When no one answered her, the waitress gave it one more shot. "Josie Fortune?"

"We have a *Josie*," Ferrington answered, laughing good naturedly, making sure to catch Josie's eye.

The waitress, who found her because everyone one was looking at her, suddenly said, "They said she's in here, so I guess they want *you*."

Josie had no choice but to follow the woman out of the room to the bar. The bartender nodded toward the phone, telling her to make it quick. Josie pulled her earring off as she grabbed the handset. "This is Josie," she said.

But there was no one waiting on the other end. She handed the phone back to the bartender, her anger on a short fuse. As he hung it up, Josie asked, "Did you recognize the voice?"

The bartender looked at her curiously. "What are you talking about?"

"Did you take that call?"

Her tone was challenging, and he answered in the same tenor. "I took it, yeah."

"Did you recognize the caller's voice?"

The bartender studied her, then sucking his teeth thoughtfully, he answered her, "It was a guy, a man's voice, that's all I know."

"Was it long distance?"

"Long distance? Who knows, lady? I got more on my mind than where some guy is calling from."

"A Boston accent, maybe, eastern sounding?" Josie pressed.

"How the hell would I know that?"

He was reacting to her anger, and she tried to calm herself, to make amends. "Look, it was an obscene call. I need to know what he sounded like."

"You tell me, lady. It was *your* obscene call."

"Was he from around here or did he have an accent? That's all I want to know."

"Lady, I wasn't paying attention, okay? I work here. I know you're out drinking, having fun, that's great, but I'm working. See, this is what I do for my living. Someone calls me up, I answer it. I don't pay attention where he's from. What do you want? Boston? Okay, it was Boston. Long distance? Sure. Had a Chinese operator jabbering at me for half an hour!"

They had the interest of every man sitting at the bar now, and Josie was sorry she had asked. She was embarrassed and angry. It was not just Dan this time, it was the way the men at the bar looked at her, their amusement at her discomposure. A hand took her shoulder. Without thinking, she spun around, grabbing for her purse. She had her hand inside it before she understood that Dick Ferrington was standing next to her. "What's the matter?" he asked. As he spoke, Ferrington looked down and saw Josie's revolver. His eyes squinted tightly as he stared at her, then at the gun again. Josie snapped her purse shut and breathed deeply. My God, she thought, she had almost pulled the thing on him!

"It was an obscene phone call," Josie answered. "I was trying to find out—

listen, let's just drop it." Josie saw the bartender shaking his head as he caught another customer's look and gave a wink. *Women.*

"Okay, we drop it," Ferrington answered. "Are you okay?"

"I'm fine. I need to go. Tell the others . . . just say I wasn't feeling well."

He touched her arm again. His hand felt like a jolt of electricity, and she wanted him to let go, hated his impertinence, the assumption that he had earned the right to such intimacy. "If you feel the way you look, Josie, I won't be lying. Maybe you'd better sit down for a few minutes." Ferrington couldn't quite keep from looking at Josie's purse one more time as he said this.

"No. I'm okay." Then, "Tell me something, Dick. Did anyone know we were coming here? I mean besides the people inside?"

Dick's brow knitted, "People talk, Josie. I don't know who knew we were coming here. Why?"

She shook her head. He had followed her. It had to be that.

"Who's Josie Fortune, anyway?"

Josie shook her head and looked in the direction of the bartender. "That's what I was trying to get out of the bartender."

Ferrington hesitated, confused. "What did the caller say? Can you repeat it?"

"Nothing," she answered. "He didn't say anything at all."

Annie's Call

"Annie, something happened," Josie announced.

When she had described the call at the bar, Annie responded with the obvious question. How had Dan found out she was going to a bar that afternoon?

"He followed me."

"He was around here all day, Josie. I saw him a couple of times."

"He's hired someone to watch me, then. He's just scaring me."

"He's scaring both of us, kiddo. But that doesn't mean it's Dan."

"You think it's Jack Hazard?" she asked.

"I don't know what to think, except that you had better start finding out what you're dealing with here. There's no way Dan knew where you were unless he's psychic. Psychotic, yes, psychic . . . I'm not buying it."

"Find out *what,* Annie? Just *what* exactly do you suggest I do?"

"For one thing, why don't you start by finding out where Jack Hazard is. I thought you went there to find out some things. All I hear is how you're too busy to bother. Have you been out to the place where you grew up? Have you talked to the police about your mother? What about opening a telephone book? Have you tried that?"

"I've been kind of distracted with this thing with Dan."

"Well, Dan was in Boston today, Josie."

"I still think it's Dan. Lues has nothing to do with what's going on. He hired someone to follow me and then make the call. The whole point of it is to unnerve me! It's just a sick game with him, Annie!"

"Josie, you're not dealing with the facts. Everything is a reaction, an assumption. You're better than that. Get to the bottom of this thing."

"Meaning I find Jack Hazard? Hi, Jack, long time no see, are you fucking with me, by any chance, because someone is, and I really don't think it's my *ex,* even though he put me in the hospital last year because I caught him in bed with another woman?"

"Look, I can't do it for you, Josie. You're going to have to do it on your own or just quit your job and disappear again."

Again. Her lost summer. Her lost year, to be more precise. No. Not that again. "I've got a career started here, Annie. I'm not going to run away."

"You are running away, Josie, call it what you want. You've been running away since the day you got there."

Running in Place

Josie was trying as hard as anyone could. At least, that was what she told herself when she got off the phone. She had set her life around new routines. She had gone back to the range to shoot. She had a license to own a firearm. She was ready if Dan wanted to try something. Just what did Annie want her to do, anyway? Well, she knew what she wanted her to do, she just didn't see the point of it. What was the good of seeing the little trailer they had lived in? My God, she thought, she didn't need to rub her nose in the obvious. Josie was second generation trailer trash with a bit of ambition. She knew that. As such, she had tried to marry the exact opposite of her mother's husband, but got the same guy in different skin. Dan Scholar had better diction. That was the only real difference. It was how she was raised!

Marry the kind of man you deserve. Except, she didn't plan to let it end the way it had for her mother. She was watching for the bastard, and whether he was playing tricks on the telephone or dropping by the apartment when she was out, when he wanted her, really wanted her, he had to show up in front of her, and when he did, she would give him the fight of his life! Just maybe the last fight of his life.

Despite her determination, however, she spent the rest of the week and weekend in her apartment or at Brand Hall, with only brief and essential forays into town. Every step off a familiar path, she reminded herself to be careful. She told herself frequently that she was not afraid, just ready. She graded papers, then read a couple more books on the writings of James Joyce, notching up number two hundred in the process, though it felt like a thousand. Her stack of notes was starting to look like a Thomas Wolfe manuscript. She was thoroughly and comfortably hidden away, the busy scholar who just happened to keep a gun close by.

When she had survived Dan Scholari another week, she celebrated with white wine on her balcony, watching the woods until the sun set, then staring into the dark woods, hoping the ice deep in her bowels would somehow melt. It didn't.

At least there was consolation to be had at school, a crumb of sanity to answer the general madness of her life. Students came to see her on a fairly regular basis, and when they did, they listened eagerly to what she had to say. It wasn't even about grades. There were graduate students who wanted to talk about the admission standards for schools in the East. There was an eighteen-year-old Latin major who needed eyes for his epic about his almost state-champion Huree football team, every line stitched in a perfect dactylic hexameter, and one she enjoyed enormously for some reason, a forty-eight-year-old grandmother named Harriet, who was trying to write sonnets, her first efforts at any sort of poetry. They were crude but touching poems about her divorce and the devastation of starting over so late in life. The woman had set for herself the pace of one sonnet a day and wanted Josie to read them all. Josie gave the woman all the energy she could muster, as she did all of her students. They came for help, advice, to get to know her, to ask the oddest questions. She listened and advised and spoke as honestly as tender egos could bare. In stolen hours, she raced into her work. She read hundreds of pages at a sitting.

But then she would be alone again, walking to her car, stepping along a path in the woods on her way to class, sitting at home at night, and she would have to remind herself that he would come for her when she least expected it. She knew that much from hard experience.

What knowledge could be more important than that?

Val

In those first weeks, Josie came to see exactly why everyone hated Henry Valentine. He was almost always in his office, and there was almost always someone with him. It started sometimes before eight and lasted usually until well past five. His only break seemed to be class. He kept the door to his office open, and when Josie passed, she heard the confessions of his students, by turns marked by silliness, eroticism, or tragedy. A boy had just lost his father. A girl had been raped by her boyfriend but was afraid to say anything. Another wanted to go home. She hated Lues. There were boys who had conquests to brag about or nothing at all to be proud of, mature women who worried about their teenage children and what was to become of them in a world such as this, men past thirty who were back in school and uncertain about their futures, desperate with the fear that life was passing them by while they studied. There were intimate things, terrible things, voices that droned on and on, laughter, and agonized moans. Val let them say what wore upon their hearts, and their honesty was startling. Sometimes the kids were loud, almost shouting or laughing. Sometimes they whispered. The whispers were the worst. Once, Josie heard a female voice telling him in a bedroom whisper, "I didn't want them to, I mean the three of us were just friends, but they took their penises out and started slapping the back of my head." Josie pushed into her office and closed the door quickly, never knowing the rest of what had happened, sick with knowing what little she had heard. Another time, Josie heard a woman tell him, "I didn't care after that. It just didn't matter. I stabbed him again. The blood came, and I kept stabbing him. I didn't care." That one, Josie didn't even see. She knew only the disembodied voice of a murderess, or maybe a fiction writer reading her story. When Josie did look into the office, she saw Val invariably facing the speaker, staring intently with those large, penetrating eyes of his, his sympathy like an old dog's or maybe God's.

When Josie and Val passed in the hall, they didn't always speak, but there was always a look. Twice Josie met him as they came out of their respective offices together. No one was coming in either direction. For a moment each time, they stared at one another with a peculiar intensity. Josie imagined that she had only to step back into her office and he would follow, and they would close the door. Only the thought of departmental gossip stopped her. Anyone, she thought, but Henry Valentine. And then she would ask herself why she worried about scandal. She was doing fine. Professionally, it couldn't be going better. If Deb Rainy had Ferrington, who had murdered his wife, why couldn't she have Valentine, who was simply popular?

One day Josie saw Val heading into Varner Hall. She knew he was going there to teach a class. A pile of books braced against his hip, Val was late but sauntered along like a man who knew the party would never start without him. Curious about something, Josie followed him into the building. As he stepped from the hallway into his classroom, Josie hurried forward, then stopped in front of the door. Some fifty kids rose as if on cue, their sudden cheers startling her. She even saw two of her own students in the crowd. They were quiet kids who sat patiently—all right, miserably—through her lectures. They were wildly different, she realized, in Henry Valentine's class. They loved him. They grinned and stomped and clapped as loudly as the rest. Josie understood the feeling of failure Val inspired in all of the other faculty: this couldn't be real teaching. But it *was* something, and like everyone else, she longed to know his secret. Val stood before the class perfectly at ease, his heels together, giving a slight, appreciative bow like an experienced actor on a familiar stage. As the cheering faded, he turned to close the door and saw Josie. His face registered no surprise. He seemed to know she had been following him. He even understood her envy, his expression something between abashed amusement and a good-humored apology for success. The conspiratorial friend, Val winked, then shut the door.

Virgil Hazard

Her phone hardly ever rang, so when it did, she was cautious. There had been a couple of hang ups, but never a voice or a threat. She thought it might come eventually, was almost certain it would, actually, and she did not want to be caught unprepared. Smiling or making a joke only to have Dan Scholari on the other end of the line with a vile threat. So when the phone rang, her mood always changed.

It was almost two weeks after the call at Cokey's for Josie Fortune when her phone rang at an especially late hour. Josie had been grading papers and was groggy from the work, but the moment the silence broke, she was alert. Almost midnight. No one called her that late. Cold anger came over her as she went to the phone. Dan Scholari or Jack Hazard or the devil in hell who meant to drive her mad, she was ready. "Yes." Her tone was imperious. They would just be words, nothing more. And that game could be played equally well from both sides!

"Amazing things, these computers," Annie announced. Her breezy enthusiasm was unnaturally sweet, especially given the hour. She was up to something. They hadn't talked for a couple of weeks, as it happened. Both of them pouting after their last call, angry the other couldn't see the obvious. There had been only one exchange of e-mail. Annie had written that Dan Scholari was behaving irrationally at school. She had included no other details, not even a salutation or her name at the end. In the same spirit, Josie had answered: so what's new?

"Computers?" Annie still wrote with a quill.

"I have a grader for my Magnificent Metaphors course, Josie. I told you about that course?" She had, Josie told her. "Turns out she's combining women's studies with computer programming. Great idea! Fabulous opportunities! If you don't finish your dissertation and the handgun-delivery-thing doesn't work out, you might try it. Anyway, I asked her to do a little work for me, a project I've started about an exotic dancer."

Josie groaned.

"I'm thinking about a biography of a common woman. I call it *Pawn of the Patriarchy.* Good title, huh?"

"Great title. So what kind of work did your grader do for you?"

This was Annie at her best or worst, according to your perspective. After the pep talks had failed, she did your work for you until utter shame kicked you into gear. Annie had started reading Blavatsky at the beginning of Josie's dissertation research. Josie had solved the riddle, had simply seen the answer as she read a particular passage one day. She just didn't know how it connected to anything. The wailing of an infant at birth. The word we all know before we know anything. But Annie had a hunch. When Josie didn't follow it, she started reading Blavatsky's book herself. "Eight hundred pages of metaphysical agonies," Annie had called it. She delivered daily reports until Josie had finally taken the book from her and had done the work that she should have from the start. The worst of it, of course, was that Annie had been right. Blavatsky, who was little more than a passing jest in the human comedy of *Ulysses,* was the key to the whole riddle of the word known to all men, which it turned out predated James Joyce by a few centuries. It was Blavatsky who had called the word *MAH.* Turning the sound into the newborn's cry at birth, Joyce had both mocked the mystic and solved the riddle in a literal sense—at least for those readers who happened to notice.

Such was Annie's genius for finding the true center of a thing somewhere out in the periphery, and such was her passion to nag her best students until they followed her.

"Turns out she can access the county records of Lues."

"She found Jack Hazard?" Josie had tried the phone book, but that was her limit. As far as she could see, there were no Hazards in Lues County with a telephone.

"Better than that, Josie! Listen to this. John Christian Hazard and Deborah Josephine Fortune, not Hazard, mind you, bought county lot seven-hundred-seventy-one with a building and business, called the Hurry On Up, and all the furnishings, including a liquor license, from a Louis Bonner Hazard, the Fourth, for thirty-eight-thousand dollars. This is in 1979. In August of 1982, they sold the tavern, *et al.,* to Virgil Hazard for fifty-two-thousand dollars. Virgil and Louis B. are Jack's brothers, by the way."

Josie recalled a Virgil Hazard who had been arrested for D and D or some kind of alcoholic crime and decided it had to be the same guy. "How do you know they're brothers?" she asked.

"Do you want me to fax you a copy of their birth certificates?"

"Not necessary! I'll take your word for it, Annie." Josie was smiling into the receiver, shaking her head and wondering how she could ever imagine Annie had given up on her.

"So Josie, what I want to know is how your mother managed to dance for Jack Hazard, when Virgil was the owner of record at the time of her death?"

"Excuse me?"

"I'm not talking loud enough?"

"You're saying Jack Hazard didn't own the bar when my mother was killed? Annie, the paper said 'Bar Owner Charged.'"

"They'd already sold it, Josie. County records prove it."

"But she was a dancer?"

"I'm afraid they don't put that kind of information in government records. The point is I don't know what she was doing, and I don't think you do either."

"This could be like your marathon thing, couldn't it?"

"No promises, Josie, just some interesting contradictions. You don't dance for a man if he's already sold the bar. As far as that goes, I've never heard of a former owner dancing for the man who bought the bar from her, but then I don't knows Lues that well!"

"That doesn't make much sense, does it?"

"I've got more. Jack Hazard was released May 17 of this year from the state correctional facility in Vienna. Vienna . . . sounds like a wonderful place, but probably a lot of tourists milling around all the time."

"I don't believe you!" Josie laughed. "You got all that from Boston?"

"It's not where you are that matters, these days, kiddo, it's how badly you want it."

"Annie, I'm sorry I was such a coward about this. I should have done this."

"Well, since you're volunteering, I do need you to check on something for me. I'll pay you your standard research fee."

"What's my standard research fee?"

"A shoulder to cry on. Now write this down." Annie read off a telephone number.

"What do you want me to do with it?"

"Call it, and keep calling until you get something. I've tried, but I can't get an answer. I thought I was a night owl!"

"Whose number is it?" Josie asked.

"Virgil Hazard, Codswallop. We got the number from a cyber PI, private, unlisted numbers his specialty. Cost me all of four dollars! He had a little trouble with the *Codswallop,* though. Thought I was looking for an Internet start-up selling large jockstraps."

"What should I say to this guy when I get an answer?"

"Virgil is Jack's brother, so why don't you ask him if his sister-in-law ever danced at his bar."

"Sure doesn't sound right, does it?"

"There you go again, Kierkegaard, making those leaps of faith before you've gotten all your facts nailed down."

"Okay. I'll find out what I can from him. And thanks, Annie. I thought you'd given up on me."

"If you don't chase the nightmare, kiddo, the nightmare chases you. I'm not going to let that happen to the best student I ever had, not if I can do something to stop it."

When she got off the phone, Josie tried the number Annie had given her. There was no answer, but early the following morning, she got Virgil Hazard on the line. She could hear the sleep still in his voice. Josie identified herself as D. J. Darling from Lues State University, her voice bright and professional, her purpose a bit vague. Virgil was cross about the call and said if she wanted work, she should come by the club. Josie answered that she wasn't looking for work. She wanted to talk to him about the Hurry On Up. Virgil Hazard got quiet. She heard him lighting a cigarette, the scratching of flint, the breathy exhale of smoke. Finally, he answered, "What did you say your name is?"

"D. J. Darling." It was the truth. Rather, it was *a* truth. "I'm working at Lues State University on a research project about Lues County, and I wanted to know about the Hurry On Up. You were the owner of it, weren't you?"

Virgil Hazard hung up.

Codswallop

Codswallop was close to half an hour north of the university. The countryside was hilly and wooded. Here and there, a farm struggled to make it. Codswallop had an old grocery store with a rusted-out sign and a sagging wooden porch. There were two gas stations, only one operable, and two bars. The Dew Drop Inn could never be called a club, so Josie drove into the crowded parking lot of the Bust of Country.

Across the street, she saw two men roofing an old house. The place was broken-down, hardly worth saving. She noticed them because the younger of the two stopped working and was unabashedly watching her as she walked to the front door of the Bust of Country. He was a dark-haired young man, her age, she thought. He was smiling at her, or maybe just smiling, but he said nothing. No whistle, no come-on. Just a nice country boy stopping to look at a woman—a woman, as it happened, who was obviously going into a strip club so she could take her clothes off and make money doing it. The second fellow she hardly noticed. Just an old roofer climbing a ladder and not bothering to catch the sights, such as they were.

A three-hundred-pound doorman stood at the end of the long entry hall checking the IDs of a couple of men when Josie entered the bar. All three men looked at her, and it took all her courage to keep going. The two customers went on, and the fat man rocked slightly from one foot to the other until Josie finally stood before him. The hand-printed sign on the wall beside him said it was two dollars to get in after six, free otherwise. At least she didn't have to pay the cover. The doorman took Josie in with a quick appraisal. She was wearing a dark blue business skirt, a matching jacket, and a white silk blouse underneath. The skirt was short, but that hadn't seemed a problem on campus. This was different. He was looking at her as if she was dressed up in a costume, the overworked lady executive out for a hot afternoon of fun in the country—with real country boys. Josie leveled her gaze on the man, not a bit of fun in her.

"You want work?" the fat man asked.

Flustered at the assumption, all the more so since she had anticipated it, Josie answered sharply, "I want to see Virgil Hazard."

"Mr. Hazard's busy."

So it *was* Virgil's club. Josie congratulated herself and pushed on wryly, as if the man could comprehend irony.

"So whom do I see if I want work?"

"Mr. Hazard is *whom.*"

Josie had just the thing in her purse for people who made fun of good grammar, but instead of school lessons, she smiled at him flirtatiously, "I guess we're not communicating. I wanted to see Mr. Hazard about working for him."

"You want to be a dancer?"

"It's a dream of mine, okay? Just get Mr. Hazard."

He whistled to the bartender and made a gesture. The bartender picked up the phone, and a moment later, through a set of black curtains, a short, bulky man came out toward Josie. He had on an open black shirt with thick gray hair sprouting out of the top and wore a grungy fake-gold necklace. In costume and attitude, Virgil Hazard seemed unconscious that more than twenty-five years had passed since the death of disco. As he was Jack's brother, Josie had been expecting the reflection of Jack Hazard in the man's face and figure, still not knowing what that was, but she saw nothing here besides a middle-aged man who still did too many drugs. But around the eyes, there was something familiar. "Come on!" he said automatically and turned to lead her around the bar. In the main room, which Josie could see only after she had passed the doorman, three stages were placed so that a number of tables and chairs could be set between them. Each stage was about twenty by fifteen feet and included brass poles and spotlights. At the moment, only one stage was lit up, a single dancer moving across it. The air was smoky. The track lights flashed on the dancer, and a sea of feed-store caps below her tilted up reverently. The girl was thin and pretty with dark red hair and a prominent nose. She was entirely naked except for a G-string and lone dollar-stuffed garter. Her breasts were small and pointed. Garth Brooks sang "Papa Loved Mamma" as she executed a perfect backbend, walking over with her hands until she stood upright again, her arms extended over her head in the finish, like an X-rated gymnast. Several of the men shouted and presented their dollars in the form of neat, green penises all around the edge of the stage. Josie realized she had stopped to watch and hurried to catch up with Virgil. She pushed through the dark curtains and bumped into him. Great, she thought. Not only did she want to dance naked for a bunch slews, she was desperate for the job.

The office was small and cluttered. On one of the walls, there were several unframed posters of superstar exotic dancers. On the opposite wall, there was only a large framed poster of Bogart from the movie *Casablanca*. Josie shifted her attention from the smiling dancers and a mournful Bogart to Virgil Hazard's cluttered desk. He had a huge ashtray filled with butts. The office stank of it. Next to the ashtray, she saw a stack of beer and liquor distributors' invoices with a couple of overdue notices stamped in red. Virgil took a seat behind the little black wooden desk and gestured for Josie to sit in front of the desk, where a lone straight-back chair waited. He was almost treating this like a real interview, she thought with some humor. As she sat down, he reached for a folder.

Tossing a generic application across his desk, Virgil asked, "Where have you worked, honey?" His tone was all business, but his eyes fixed on Josie's legs as she crossed them. They were good legs, as good as any in *this* club, she thought.

"Have you ever heard of the Hurry On Up?" Josie asked. Her tone insinuated she had worked there, but of course, the name of the place stopped him cold.

Not exactly happy, Virgil Hazard answered her smile with a tight, twisted grin, "Let me guess. You're the college chick with the local history project, right?" He stood up as he finished his question. It was Josie's signal to exit, but she held her ground.

"I want to know about the Hurry On Up before you owned it." This stopped him for some reason, and he stood, considering her from behind his desk, his smile creasing his gray, flabby cheeks. Josie took the expression as permission to continue. "Did they have dancing?"

"What was your name again?"

"D. J."

"You're talking girls, right? Strippers?" Josie nodded. "No, they didn't have dancers. I started that."

"What about Josie Fortune? She was one of the owners you bought it from."

"I know who I bought it from."

"Did she dance for you?"

The man laughed. "Listen, D. J., I don't know where this is going, and I don't care. They told me you said you wanted to work. Were they lying or were you?"

"I guess I was."

His eyebrows rose expressively, his intent a kind of mutual larceny. "I got an empty stage out there and a full house. I've seen auditions pull a hundred dollars inside five minutes. It's easier than a trick if you have the stuff." His eyes settled on Josie's thighs again. He made no attempt to disguise the attention. Josie was confused, then faintly irritated that she had been misread so entirely. What did he mean *trick?* Did he think she was a prostitute? Couldn't he see? Couldn't anybody *see?* She wasn't that sort of woman! Virgil became positively genial now, "Those boys out there will give their last dollar to see what's under that skirt of yours, D. J."

"Did Josie Fortune ever dance for anyone? Was she a dancer?" Josie struggled to keep her voice level and her temper in control. It was a losing battle.

Virgil tipped his head slightly. It was a look of curiosity, hardly more than a casual reflection. Was it the thought that he had seen her somewhere before? Josie couldn't remember the man at all, except the eyes, and, too, there was something in his voice, especially in his whining drawl that was both sour and familiar.

"What do you care about Josie for?" he asked.

"Can I be honest with you?"

The man's expression broke apart into a wild, cruel smile, "Naw, hell, just keep on lying. I don't want you to rupture anything!"

"I'm doing research for a woman who's writing a book on exotic dancers. It's kind of a feminist perspective thing. Anyway, I read that Josie Fortune was a dancer at the Hurry On Up."

"You read it wrong. She never danced. She was the bartender, but that was before she and Jack sold the place to me."

"Did she ever work for you after she sold the place, as a bartender, maybe?"

Warily, "Look, honey, there's not going to be an interview here. You want to know if Jose Fortune was a dancer. The answer is no. She owned the Hurry On Up with my brother Jack. She worked it. They both worked it. They sold it to me, and that's it. You want an exotic dancer, I got them coming out my ears, but Josie Fortune," he laughed again, "no way in hell." A dawning of recognition, "I get it now. This is about the murder, right? You're a reporter, aren't you?"

Josie nodded, trying to hold the man's gaze but failing.

Virgil Hazard's face tightened down angrily, "There's a door right behind you, D. J. If you're smart, you won't let it hit you on that pretty little ass of yours on the way out."

"Why did they sell the place?"

"I got things to do, bills to pay, a doorman to fire. Now do you want to take your clothes off and go to work, or do you just want to waste my time?" He came around the desk, his mood darkening, his manner aggressive and deliberate. When Josie didn't move, Virgil sat down on the edge of the desk directly before her. He looked down at Josie's legs with obvious lust now.

"Maybe you just want to show *me* what you got under that skirt. Hmm? Is that what you really want, honey? You want to show Virgil what you got?" He coaxed her meanly, the cooing of a man intent on driving her out in a hurry or getting his fondest wish, one or the other, and he didn't seem to care which. "Show it to me. I want to see it. Show me what you got, baby."

Josie hit the latch of her purse as she let her legs slowly separate for him. She brought her hand across her waist and into the purse in a single unhurried motion, her legs splaying open seductively for him. Transfixed, Virgil watched her legs, his nostrils flaring, his grin frozen. At the last moment, he looked away to see what she was doing with her purse. He didn't do anything else. He didn't have time. In a single motion, Josie lay the hammer back and put the revolver between his legs, snug up against his crotch.

"Holy Jesus!"

Still seated, Josie held the gun with both hands now, straight before her face, her arms extended, her voice tight. "Seen enough?"

Croaking, his words breaking through the phlegm of his throat, Virgil Hazard answered, "Yeah, I've seen all I want. Now can you point that somewhere else, somewhere not so important, like my brain, just not *there*? Please!"

Josie stood up, rising directly in front of him, the gun still nestled into his crotch.

"Just one more thing, okay?"

"Name it." A strained, pale smile with this.

"Do you know where I can find Jack?"

"I can get him here in five minutes if that will make you happy. All I have to do is make a phone call."

Uncle Virgil

"I'm going to back away a couple of steps, and when I do, I want you to go back behind the desk. I don't want you to do anything but sit back down. Okay?"

Josie and Virgil Hazard effected their tenuous treaty with care. Josie had no problem with the idea of shooting the man. She was certain her mother had been manipulated by Jack and his brother. She had owned her own place, and then they had changed things on her. The sale had only been a ruse to get the ownership legally out of her hands. Josie could almost imagine their blandishments, then the arguments among the three of them that followed. There would have been the promise of higher profits, dignity always takes a backseat for that, then the double cross. Well, she didn't like it! Keeping her aim on Virgil's crotch, she decided she was just damn tired of all of it!

Virgil moved behind his desk, his hands raised to about the level of his chest. Josie could see he wasn't at all sure he was going to live through the next minute. He read people pretty well, she thought. Finally, a spark of sense pulling at her, Josie shifted the sights off him and lowered the hammer on her nickel, though she kept both hands on the gun as she pointed it to the floor directly in front of her, her arms forming a V. "I want to know why the paper said Josie Fortune was an exotic dancer if she never danced."

"I can't help you there. All I know is she was my sister-in-law, right? So I knew her, okay? She didn't dance. *Ever.*"

Believe him?

Virgil Hazard read Josie's expression. He saw it mattered, that emotionally she wanted his words to be true. "What's with you, doll? What the hell does it matter to you if Josie. . . ." Something happened, and his expression brightened into a sort of amazement, then he laughed suddenly. "I'll be damned! You're Josie's kid, aren't you?"

"I'm just trying to find out—."

"I can't believe it! D. J., Deborah Josephine!" He dropped his hands, and he flopped casually into his chair. Little Josie Fortune wasn't going to shoot her Uncle Virgil, or at least that was what Josie read in the gesture. And maybe he was right.

Josie shifted her weight awkwardly, feeling like a kid. She let the gun slip to her side. She wasn't entirely taken in, but he seemed so happy about seeing her it was hard to keep pointing her gun at him. "So do I know you?" she asked.

"I'm your Uncle Virgil!" He kicked his legs up on the desk and leaned back benignly in his chair, folding his hands over his ample belly. "Where have you been, kid? Hell, Jack and I went looking for you about five, six months ago! No one would tell us where you were! Have you been here all along?"

Josie kept it simple and vague. "I've been growing up."

"I can see that. You look good. Don't shoot my nuts off or anything, but you look damn good!"

"So why were you looking for me?" she asked.

"Jack got out of prison, and he wanted to find you."

"Why? Unfinished business?" Irony without humor.

"Hey, that guy loved you. I mean, you and your mom were his whole world."

Josie took this for what it was, a probable, ugly truth. After all, men like Dan Scholari and Jack Hazard loved women to death. She opened her purse and set the gun back inside. Virgil seemed about as threatening as a trout. "So you never told me why they sold you the bar."

"Long story."

"I really am trying to find out about my mother. It's why I came to Lues."

"Running a bar is long hours, hard work, and the truth is Josie wanted to go to school. So I mean there were a lot of reasons, but I guess school was the big reason. She wanted to make something of her life." He broke off suddenly, not saying the rest of what he meant to say, whatever it was. He shrugged fatalistically, a look to suggest school had killed her.

"She went to school? To the university?" To that point, Josie had discredited everything Virgil had told her about her mother. This she believed. For one thing, she could verify it. More than that, she wanted to believe it. It was important to her that her mother had gone to college. It had a tangible worth in her own hierarchy of values.

Virgil grinned, "Loser State. You didn't know that? Hell, you hated it as much as we did."

Josie shook her head numbly. "Is that why Jack killed her?"

"Jack didn't kill Josie. He never touched her!"

"He confessed to it. Are you saying he confessed but he didn't do it?"

"Well that was all bullshit." Virgil's puffy face composed itself into an expression of old anger and resolute sincerity. Josie read it at once as the liar's protocol. Unconsciously, Josie's left hand slipped back to the latch of her purse. "He confessed, but he didn't have any choice."

"Look, it was a long time ago. It doesn't really matter if he did it or not. I just I need to see him. I don't remember much about my life here or my mother. I mean . . . I don't remember any of it, really. My whole life here is a blank. And I thought . . . I mean . . . do you think he'd talk to me?"

Virgil stared at Josie in dumb amazement. "Jesus, I've heard about things like that, but I never. . . ." Virgil had no concept of what Josie had gone through. To Virgil Hazard, *trauma* was running out of coke at the orgy.

"Things are coming back a little," Josie answered with a shrug of her shoulders. "I remember some things. I just can't always fit them into place. It's helped to come back and see things, but I thought maybe more of it would make sense if I could talk to Jack. Maybe if I see him. . . ."

Virgil checked his watch, then grabbed his phone. "I need you over here now," he said. "Got a new girl. Says she knows you from the old days. No, she's hot. Somebody's little sister or something. No. I mean . . . *real hot.* Okay? I don't know. *You* ask her why!" When he hung up, Virgil gave her a sheepish smile. "He's across the street fixing up a place I bought. He said if you're so hot, what do you want to work here for?"

"Why didn't you just tell him the truth?"

"Hey, don't worry about it. Just go on out and talk to him. The guy really wants to see you. I know that for a fact."

Josie laughed nervously, "I wasn't ready to meet Jack today. I'm not sure I'm ready for it." She took a couple of deep breaths.

"He's changed a lot. You might not recognize him . . . well, if you don't remember anything, I mean. . . ." He reached for his cigarettes and pulled one out. "You remember Jack, don't you? I mean the guy was your whole world!"

"I'd prefer you didn't smoke," Josie told him. Cigarette in his mouth, Virgil considered this request for a moment, his eyes reverting to Josie's purse. Then he threw the cigarette on the desk. "I'm sorry about the gun," Josie added genuinely. "I just don't like to be called *baby.* It's got real bad associations for me."

Virgil Hazard shrugged, "Don't worry about it. It's in the blood. Your mother kept a sawed-off 12-gauge under the bar. I saw her pull it out a couple of times. No one ever doubted she'd use it either."

"Aren't sawed-off shotguns illegal?"

"So is pulling a gun during a job interview."

"People didn't push her around, I guess?"

"Your mother?" Virgil laughed, then howled as if Josie had just made the funniest remark he had ever heard. "Your mother . . . pushed around? You did forget everything, didn't you?" He shook his head, his eyes wet with laughter and maybe something else. "No. Not Josie Fortune. Nobody pushed your mamma around, kid. Let me tell you something. Josie Fortune was as friendly and easy going as they come. She'd give you her last dime if she thought you needed it worse than her, but cross her or cross Jack ... or even look at her kid cross-eyed! Well, you just didn't do that."

"You said Jack didn't have any choice but to confess. What did you mean by that?"

"What they did was this. They got an old watch that nobody ever saw, I mean everybody knows Jack and nobody ever saw this watch, and they put his name on it, and they dropped it close by where they found your mother. The cops got hold of it, and they gave Jack a choice. All or nothing if he pleads not guilty, or twenty years if he cops to it. They had a couple of witnesses ready to put Jack at the falls, and Jack figures with twenty, he can be out in eight, nine years. That's what they said anyway. So he cops to it. Look, he's a Hazard, and there hasn't been a one of us born in six generations, maybe a hundred, that ever had any luck before a judge."

Josie pulled herself back emotionally. Just words, that's all they were. "Who planted the watch?" she asked. She thought she expressed enough sympathy in her tone to keep Virgil going, but the question itself was skeptical, even cruel.

Virgil gave a worldly shrug, though he was anything but worldly, "Maybe they just found it or maybe the cops put it there. All I know is the cops never gave it a second thought once they had that watch. They were waving it at him and saying it proved he done it."

Men like Virgil always had a story, always made everything sound reasonable and the law's version unreasonable. They were always persecuted by authority. The proof, the only thing she could trust, was the fact that Jack had jumped for twenty years instead going to trial. Would an innocent man go for something like that? Not very likely.

When the phone rang, he smiled. "You want me to tell him it's you?"

She shook her head without really considering the question. She looked away and found herself struggling to breathe. Jack was outside. Waiting.

Virgil reached for his phone, hit a single digit. "No! Tell him she's coming out. Sure she is. Just tell him to hang on a second. She's a little nervous about the audition." Virgil winked at Josie. "I'm giving her a pep talk!"

He looked at Josie as he set the receiver back in place. His gray face wrinkling in some kind of affection and understanding, "You're expected, Josie. Go talk to the guy."

Josie looked back at the door nervously. Josie had chased the nightmare to get here, but this was different. This was staring down Medusa.

Jack Hazard

Josie caught sight of Jack Hazard immediately. He was standing at the end of the bar, waiting for her, the old guy across the street she had seen on the ladder. He wasn't a big man, only a couple of inches taller than she, and physically, he was wiry, hardly enough man to assault four football players. She had expected more of him, somehow. The face was hard and solemn, but at least it wasn't especially lined or baggy. Prison had probably saved him from a drug habit like his brother's. Still, there was a certain numbness about his look. He had that prison air about him: the well-behaved, empty-souled ex-con. She had the feeling that she had liked him once. How else could she explain the sudden feeling of happiness? Virgil had said he was her whole world. Seven-years-old. At seven, you love anyone who gives you a little attention.

Jack looked toward Josie as she thought about his hands taking her own neck and strangling the life out of her, as he had her mother. The look on his face was one of feigned politeness. He did not recognize her. "I know you?" he asked.

"I'm Josie Fortune," Josie announced, reaching out to shake the man's hand.

The politeness vanished, and Jack's eyes locked into Josie's. "Say it again."

Josie dropped her hand and smiled at him. "Don't you know your own stepdaughter, Jack? I'm Josie! Virgil said you'd be glad to see me."

"Josie?" She nodded at his confusion. "Well, you're not dancing for Virgil!"

He was playing the good stepfather who is indignant at his little girl's choices, and it irritated her, especially as stripping seemed just fine for other men's daughters.

"I'll do whatever I want. I don't think you have any say in the matter," she snapped.

"The hell I don't!"

He slipped past her and was inside Virgil's office before Josie could answer. For a moment, she thought about following, explaining, apologizing. Instead, she stood there feeling stupid that she had gone along with Virgil's joke. She looked out at the stages. All three were filled now. The music was loud. One of the dancers had one of the men's caps and was fitting her breasts into it. Another did a backbend to bring up a dollar off the stage floor with her tongue. The third hung upside down, her naked legs wrapped about a brass pole. The waitress came up to the bar and picked up the drinks the bartender had pulled for her. She said something to Josie, and Josie stepped toward her, asking what she had said. "I said, 'What's your name?'" Josie could barely hear the woman, even though she shouted. The music was too loud.

"Josie!"

"You going up like that?"

"No!"

"You better get your clothes and go change then! You're up next! Use the dressing room back there!" She pointed toward one of the two rooms where the dancers came and went.

"I'm not going to change!"

The woman studied her critically. "At least ditch the pantyhose. You wear pantyhose, you'll wilt their dicks, hon!" The woman cut back across the floor toward the far corner, Josie calling after her, thinking to correct the misunderstanding. Then, in a conversational tone that no one could hear, she added, "My pantyhose are just fine, *hon.*"

Josie looked back toward the curtains where Jack had vanished. He was probably in there killing Virgil. Maybe she should go in and help.

She told the bartender she was going to wait outside. He didn't understand her. As she repeated herself, the music stopped. Suddenly, she was the only one in the room making any noise. "I SAID TELL JACK—."

The silence broke her speech, and before she could finish, a spotlight caught her and the disc jockey started crooning in a sleazy carnival style. His voice was full of the obscene huzzahs of a man among men and pussy in the air: "GIVE A HAND JOB FOR THOSE THREE LOVELIES, AND NOW, GENTLEMEN, AS ADVERTISED, WE HAVE THE BUST OF COUNTRY'S LATEST DREAM MACHINE STRUTTING HER STUFF TO SEE IF SHE'S GOT THE STUFF. . . . FOR YOUR VIEWING PLEASURE . . . MISS JOSIE*!!!*"

Josie had spun around and looked out from the bar the moment the spotlight hit her. Now, as they stood to applaud her, there was nothing to do but turn her back on them. She looked toward the dark curtains in front of Virgil Hazard's office with a kind of desperation, but Jack and Virgil did not come out. "DON'T BE BASHFUL," the voice cajoled, "WE MIGHT LICK BUT WE DON'T BITE . . . MUCH!"

A man from one of the closest tables approached Josie, still clapping his hands, like the rest of them. They were all clapping their hands, cheering. He said something to her and took her hand.

"I don't work here!" Josie shouted angrily.

"They said you're going to audition, so damn it, audition! Take it off, baby!"

"Let go of me!" Past the man, she saw the crowd waiting good naturedly. Their good nature seemed to extend so long as she *eventually* gave in to them.

"Hell, everyone's waiting to see it!"

The waitress slipped by her now, smiling coyly and offering another piece of hard-won wisdom, "Tell 'em you need fifty dollars before you do it. They'll pay it!"

Josie thought to explain, thought to shout her denial, thought to pull her revolver. The man, who had her wrist now and was suddenly a little more insistent, started pulling her in the direction of the nearest stage. The song started. The dancers were watching her, clapping like the men.

Josie started to brace herself and fight the man off, when she felt something at her shoulder and saw Jack reaching between her and the man who had her wrist. He was easily a head taller than Jack, but when Jack nudged the man, he faded away without protest, stumbling back to his table and his equally drunk companions. Jack took Josie's arm and turned her toward the exit. "Come on." The cheers at their backs mixed with good-natured boos. Josie looked around and saw Virgil slipping under the counter. Virgil made a gesture of a drink, then another sign that Josie didn't understand. As she passed the doorman and started down the hall, Jack was still holding her, his fingers pinching her muscles painfully. Josie heard the disc jockey break-in over the song: "I THINK JACK'S GOING TO KEEP HER FOR HIS-SELF, BUT RIGHT NOW WE'VE GOT TWO-FERS! TWO DRINKS FOR THE PRICE OF ONE. . . ." The music returned, another soft, crooning, country ballad by Garth Brooks, this one about friends in low places.

The bar faded from Josie's worries as they started down the long walkway toward the door, and she started thinking about going outside with Jack. She balked suddenly. The parking lot, though still bright, was menacing. "Where are we going?" she demanded. It was all the protest she could summon at the moment.

"To get a cup of coffee or a drink. Whatever. We need to talk."

Through the glass doors, Josie saw two men coming toward them across the lot. They were bearded, lanky workmen-types. They were all workmen-types at the Bust of Country. Through the glass door, they were studying Josie with interest, like the eighty or so voyeurs inside. Jack seemed irritated with their grins and happy nudges to one another.

"Look," Josie explained, "I don't feel comfortable just running out like this."

As the workmen walked through the door, one of them said Jack's name and clucked his tongue with grudging envy. "This is my stepdaughter," Jack growled at him.

The other one laughed, "That's the way, Jack, keep it in the family!"

Both of them went on, but they turned back to look at Josie when the big doorman said something and pointed toward Jack and Josie. Josie hated the feeling of their eyes on her, and she blamed Jack. With all her heart, she blamed him.

"I want to talk," Josie answered, "but I've got an appointment back at the university. A department meeting. I can't miss it. Can you meet me tomorrow?"

"What time?"

"I can be free after two."

Jack hesitated. "Sure. Where?"

"The McDonald's in Lues." He rolled his eyes. "What?" she asked.

He grinned in a way Josie recognized. She liked the effect and knew that once upon a time, she had really liked this man. "Nothing. McDonald's is great. Two o'clock." Smiling now, even looking, she thought, like a proud stepfather, he said to her. "You *really* a professor, Josie?"

She thought about correcting the mistake, explaining that she was only a lowly lecturer, then decided it made no difference to a man like Jack. "Yeah. I'm really a professor."

"Your mother would have been proud."

Josie tried not to be taken in by his act. She stared him down, thinking about the murder, with his bare hands! And then she pushed the door open.

"Hey!" he called before the door closed. Josie looked back. "Virgil says you got a .357 in your purse." The silly lopsided grin again. "That's exactly what your mother always carried."

She heard her own childish laughter echoing in her imagination. She had loved Jack Hazard when she was too young to know better. *Loved* him! She knew that suddenly. It was there in the way he looked at her, the way he smiled. He had been the center of her whole world, just like Virgil said. Because she was a stupid kid who didn't know any better. Josie's gut tightened and then twisted. *With his bare hands, he'd strangled her.* She blinked slowly, finding the proper distance in her voice. "I'll see you tomorrow, Jack."

A Lunatic's Prayer

Josie had parked close to the front of the tavern but well away from the door, almost to the woods. As she came outside, she scanned the trucks in her habitual manner and stayed off the line of vehicles a bit as she walked toward her VW. Some kind of monster truck was parked beside her VW, so she couldn't see it. Josie looked out to her right to the next line of vehicles, then drifted a step or two wider, in case there was some kind of surprise waiting. Dan did love his parking lots. Josie looked behind her and thumbed the latch of her purse. She brought her right hand to the opening as she stepped wide of the truck and looked expectantly toward the VW.

In the next instant, she had the gun out, the hammer cocked. She pointed it first toward the VW, then in a wide arc back around her, her arms and wrists locked, her legs flexed and ready for the attack. No one was there, but all the glass had been smashed. The back panel of glass and both of the windows in the front doors were broken out completely. The windshield was spidery with cracks, and in two spots, the glass was caved in. She saw two men moving parallel to her two rows over. He apparently didn't see her. There was no one else in the lot, at least no one that Josie could see. She stepped beyond her car to check beside the passenger door, then went on past two more cars, almost to the woods. She slipped toward the front of the line to be sure no one was hiding in front of the VW. She kept both hands on the gun, her arms locked, her shoulders moving with the gun, and walked back the way she had gone in, approaching the VW now from behind. Two men came out of the bar and started toward Josie without seeming to notice her. Josie reached into her jacket pocket and pulled her keys out. As she unlocked the door, she saw that the safety glass was all over the driver seat. She turned back and saw the two men coming closer, still apparently unaware of her presence. Josie hurried into the car, sitting down on the glass pellets. She turned the key. Thankfully, the car started. She let the hammer down gently on the .357, and set it on the rubble of glass in the passenger seat. Then she shifted into reverse and backed out almost directly in front of the two men. At the sight of her or the broken windows, she didn't know which, one of the men called out drunkenly, "What happened?" The other hollered out something about a show, and Josie pushed the gearshift into first. The car leapt forward.

Once she made it to the street, Josie drove a little over two hundred yards before pulling into an empty lot. Painfully, she slipped out of the car. Setting her revolver on the floor of the driver's side, she began picking the glass from the back of her skirt and ruined pantyhose. Occasionally, she looked around to be sure she was alone. The kid on the roof, who had been working with Jack, was gone. She looked for Dan. Unless he was still in the parking lot and watching her, or back in the woods somewhere, he was already gone. Probably had a flight to catch.

Finally, satisfied that she had the glass off of her, Josie began removing it from the driver seat. That was when she saw the torn slip of paper on the floor of the passenger side. Nothing seemed to be written on it, but it wasn't hers. For one thing, it lay on top of the glass, not buried beneath it. Carefully, Josie leaned across and picked it up. On the back of it, she found the hand printed words:

stil tHinkING Of u, hoR

She dropped the sheet and stood up to look around again. She was still alone, but it felt like she was being watched. She finished picking the glass out of the driver seat, and only when most of it was gone did Josie cut herself with the dust of it as she tried to sweep it out with her fingertips. Swearing bitterly, she hissed for no one but herself to hear, "Come on, Dan! Just once, show your lousy face! What are you waiting for?" The streets of Codswallop were empty.

In this great solitude, Josie's whispers sounded like a lunatic's prayer.

Problems in the Space-Time Continuum

Josie called Annie at her office, but she wasn't in. On her home answering machine, she left the message that Annie should call her immediately. Big news, she announced. Afterwards, Josie went to strip her business suit off and discovered the blood across the seat and back panel of the skirt as well as the bloodied stains on her hose and the backs of her legs. She went to the bathroom and set the dark blue skirt to soak. The white pantyhose *(wilt their dicks!)* Josie threw into the wastebasket. She took a quick shower to be sure the glass and blood was completely washed off her legs. It had been stupid to jump into the car like that, but at the time, she had just wanted to leave.

Josie shut off the flow of water and stepped out of the shower. She looked steadily now into the mirror. Like one of the dancers, her breasts were un-fettered, visible. Her eyes were proud and angry. She was fully naked but alone. No eyes to see her. *stil tHinkING Of u, hoR.* He was going to kill her, and there was nothing she could do about it. Unless she quit her job and left the profession . . . and just disappeared. Tell no one, not even Annie or the Darlings, where she was going. Drive somewhere, anywhere. Change her name. Maybe dance for a living. What the pretty ones get to do for a few years. At least she'd never be found.

No! She hadn't done anything wrong. She wasn't going to run like a fugitive or play the whore so she could hide. She wasn't going to let Dan have her life that way. He might take it, but she would never give it! It was here and now. "Fight him!" she whispered, and it was strange, but her voice was not quite her own. It was far too country to be her, and she smiled at the woman in the mirror. Dan wasn't close enough to her to see the changes. He thought it would be like before, but when he got close this time, she had a surprise for him. The same one she had given Virgil Hazard.

She patted the back of her thighs, even as her mind seethed with an equal mix of fear and courage. The scratches stung her, so she opened the cabinet and put some first-aid cream on. Then still naked, she stomped across the hall to her bedroom. She finished drying herself in front of her large mirror. To distract herself, she studied her reflection. She tried to see herself critically, the way those men had seen her or wanted to. She threw the towel over a chair and posed stupidly like one of them. Arms high, as if she had just finished a backbend and walkover. What was the point? she wondered. She saw nothing in any of it but the innate power of the men and the bad choices of the women. It was a form of worship that corrupted both sides, and she shook her head and went to the beat-up chest where she kept her underwear and dress-downs. She put on a pair of jeans and a T-shirt. She was feeling better with her nakedness covered. Less vulnerable. Something to eat and then some reading in bed, her nickel-plated .357 magnum on the table beside her. For luck. She thought about her insurance. She didn't know if they would pay if she didn't report it to the police, and she didn't want to do that. She needed more humiliation like she needed a job working for Virgil Hazard!

In the kitchen, Josie opened the refrigerator and looked at her choices. The thing was full but nothing looked good. She tried to focus her thoughts on food, on anything besides Dan Scholari with his plane flights out of Boston. It wasn't possible. All she could think about was the degree of rage and lunacy a man must have to fly here and follow her just so he could break the glass out of her car. He had to be obsessed, planning each slight degree of escalation. Absolutely, totally insane. Well, Annie had written that e-mail to say he was behaving strangely. Maybe it was a bit more than the usual. Maybe she had underestimated his deterioration over the past year.

The telephone rang, and Josie jumped in surprise. Was this it? Did he tell her now what he meant to do to her? She walked into the living room and picked up the telephone, simply waiting for him to speak, summoning the courage to answer him without fear.

"Things are crazy here, but I had to call." It was Annie.

"Hi, Annie. Did you get my message?"

"No. I'm still at school. Your ex-husband went off the deep end this afternoon, Josie."

"He *what?*"

"Sometime after lunch, he just appeared in the dean's office with a gun and said he didn't like his spring teaching assignment!"

"Annie! *Today? This afternoon?* Dan was on campus this afternoon?"

"And the psychiatric ward this evening."

"Annie!" The old woman stopped. "Annie, someone broke out all the glass in my car *this afternoon.*"

"Oh, God, Josie." Annie's voice was barely more than a whisper.

"He left a note, telling me he was still thinking about me. He called me a whore. Same weird handwriting as last time, same kinds of misspelled words. I was sure it was Dan."

"It wasn't Dan, Josie. It couldn't have been."

"It's Jack Hazard. It has to be Jack."

"You don't know that!"

"He was there, Annie. I saw him."

"You saw him?"

"I talked to him."

"And you think he's doing this?"

Jack had seen her, though he acted like he hadn't, and the moment she went inside he had gone over to her car, smashing all the glass. That had to be it. And when Virgil had called him up, he had decided to come in and act surprised. She went through the afternoon with some editorializing but covered the essentials, the meeting with Virgil, the fact that Jack and some kid had been across the street when she arrived. A long talk with Virgil, plenty of opportunity. When she had finished, Annie remained silent for a long time. Finally, though, she spoke. "Josie, what are you going to do about it?"

"I don't think I have a choice at this point, Annie. I think I have to go to the police."

Part Three

Tobias Crouch

D ESK BOUND, his ankle wrapped tightly in an Ace bandage, a cane leaning against the wall behind him, traffic patrol officer Tobias Crouch of the Lues city police looked out across the detectives' desks longingly. He had been assigned here for the next three days cleaning up files. He was thinking he wouldn't mind staying at a desk. At forty-three, he deserved a desk of his own. Across the room with their backs to him, K. C. and Jonesy were filling out reports. Loser State graduates, like Crouch, they were detectives. Their careers were going places. Toby Crouch wasn't going to be a detective at this late date in his career, but he thought he deserved to stay at a desk until he retired. Watch command would be nice. That was going to open up next month. There was plenty of speculation about the new watch commander, but Toby Crouch's name never came up. Crouch looked at his swollen foot longingly. Digging postholes for his mother, he had stepped into his own creation. It hurt like hell, but at least he could milk some good out of it with a few days off patrol. He knew if he asked Colt Fellows for a permanent desk position, Colt would laugh at him. If you wanted to get something from Colt, you gave him something he wanted. The last time Crouch had done that was almost twenty years ago, a really big favor, and that was how he got on the force. He just hadn't been able to provide the man with anything else, no fortuitous saves, no secrets he had unearthed, no special favors. Not a hell of a lot going on Colt didn't already have his finger on. Because of it, Colt had let him drift. If he needed something dirty, he always had Happy Harpin. Mr. Fix-It. Crouch shook his head. There just wasn't any way around it. He was going to have to go back to patrol.

Ruby Collins came in, stood over Jonesy's desk for a couple of minutes, then picked up a stack of papers and left the office. Seventh year, and just promoted to detective. Wonder what she gives the boss? Crouch looked at the clock. It was not quite eight. He wanted another cup of coffee and maybe a couple of doughnuts, but he didn't want to walk out and get them. Damn postholes, anyway.

K. C.'s voice brought Toby out of his reveries. "Take line three, we're busy." Crouch looked down and saw the light flashing. He hadn't even heard the phone ringing. Happened sometimes. He picked up. Woman. Complaint. Right. Yeah. Send her back. Crouch watched the glass until the woman passed. *Blonde.* She kept going. *One, two, three.* She opened the door. *Hello.* Even Jones looked up for this one, and he was dead below the waist. Called it happily married. K. C., who got anything he wanted when his wife wasn't looking, gave Crouch a you-lucky-bastard look. *Yeah, well, you were busy.*

Start with the legs: wrap those around your hips, big boy. Small pert breasts: high and dry. Toby remained seated, watching her check out K. C. hopefully. K. C. looked like Hollywood, even if he was a total fuck-up. "They sent me back." Uptight, fake-eastern accent. A bit brassy. Scared. Boyfriend. Always the boyfriend. Let a man between your legs and he thinks he owns you. *I'll be your boyfriend, sweetie.*

Both men pointed to Crouch. "Name?" he asked her.

She hesitated, then came forward, taking the chair in front of Crouch's desk. "Josie Darling. I teach at the university."

"Address?" Toby wrote the name and address down, then took down the phone number. "And what was the problem?"

It was kind of complicated. *Here we go.* Josie Darling had a briefcase, all beat-up with a broken zipper and two big loops for the handle, someone's hand-me-down. Professors. All talk, no money. "You'll get the idea from this."

Look interested. Crouch took the slip of paper she handed him. stil tHinkING Of u, hoR. *hoR?* Where had he seen that? *Thoroughly professional, college graduate.* Crouch looked up impassively, the traffic cop with a twisted ankle pulling office time. 5'8" and 280 pounds. *Do you like to do a fat man now and then, Dr. Josie?* "This is it?"

"There have been some other things."

"Tell me about them." Crouch took notes as she explained.

h-o-R. h-o-R? *Where in the hell have I seen that?* "I see," he said, interrupting her. "Why didn't you report that?" She crossed her legs nervously, as she explained, but Crouch missed it. "You were embarrassed someone had broken into your apartment?"

"Maybe I had better start at the beginning."

Sure, yeah, start at the beginning. Crouch adjusted his seat for a better view if those legs moved again and found himself wondering what it would be like just once to ride a live one, kicking and screaming all the way home. "Arrested yesterday?" he asked. "Spell that name for me." She spelled the name of her ex-husband, while Crouch forced himself to concentrate on something besides those thighs. *Blah, blah, blah.* "Who?"

"Jack Hazard."

That was it! *hoR.* How could he have forgotten Jack Hazard! Heart hammering but with the cop's impassive expression, Crouch reached for the slip of paper again, and now he smiled to himself. *stil tHinkING Of u, hoR.* Colt had told that story all the time in the old days. Dead stripper in the canyon, she's carved up with the letters *h-o-r* on her titty, and Jack Hazard in the hot seat, looking like what the cat drug in. *"Okay, Jack. I believe you. You're an innocent man! The watch ain't yours. Both my witnesses are lying. Just tell me how to spell whore and I'll let you go."* Lawyer screaming, and Jack, as dumb as the rock he crawled out from under, *"I can spell whore, h-o-r!* . . . *No!* . . . *h-o-r-e!"* Crouch looked up from his notes in surprise, "Where?"

"The Bust of Country. It's not what you think."

Nervously she uncrossed her legs. Blue! Blue panties. See her in those and nothing else. Crouch slipped his hand into his pocket and adjusted the load.

"How do you know what I'm thinking?"

"I was doing some research. Okay, I have to be honest."

Jack Hazard's stepdaughter. Real name Fortune. Toby Crouch looked back at the words on the paper again as he jotted down the pertinent details. *Watch Commander Toby Crouch.* He listened absently. *Spell whore for me, Jack.* Crouch took one last peek under her little skirt. *Gone but not forgotten!* "Are you prepared to bring charges against him?" he asked. While she thought about it, he wrote in giant letters, JACK HAZARD. He underlined the name, then put stars and stripes and a big box around it.

"What can you do to him if I press charges?" Nervous. Biting her lip.

Toby Crouch reached for the phone and dialed Colt's extension. "What?" came the growl at the other end of the line.

"Colt, I have a woman here who's received a threat. I think you'd better look at it."

Colt Fellows's voice was loud and mean now. "What the hell are talking about, Tobias!"

Crouch took a deep breath. *Washing toilets if this doesn't work.* "You'll want to see this, Colt, I guarantee it."

"There's not a damn thing I want to see right now, Tobias! Give it to Jonesy or K. C."

"It's important, Colt. Trust me."

He hung up before the wires burned out, then looked at Josie Fortune's daughter. A little like mamma, now that he got a good look at her above the shoulders, but mamma didn't wear blue panties. Mamma wasn't wearing panties at all the day Toby Crouch met her. "I just called the chief, Ms. Darling. He's coming to take a look at this note." Sanders and Jones turned around and looked at Crouch like he was crazy, then they both stood up and made for the door at the same time like it was a fire drill. Crouch felt a fine sheen of sweat covering his face. "Colt worked your mother's case. I think he'll have some information about this," he waved the scrap of paper at Josie, "which might surprise you."

"Colt Fellows?"

The door to the big office swung open with a bang. Huge, fat, gray, Colt stood for a moment and glared at Toby Crouch, then came between the desks angrily. When he finally stopped, he stood directly over Crouch and stared down at him. "What?" He made it sound like three syllables, all of them mean ones. But that was Colt. Rough as a country road. Say anything, do anything, he was the sort of guy to bend the world around to his view, and if it didn't bend, he'd break it in half. A walking war zone, when he was in a mood, and right now, he was in a dandy. Crouch knew of no one who had ever crossed him and smiled to tell about it.

"Chief Colt Fellows, Professor Darling from the university."

Colt nodded in the direction of the professor without really looking at her. "Pleased to meet you."

"Colt, I want to show you a note Professor Darling received yesterday. I think you'll recognize who wrote it."

A hard look from both of them now, but Crouch presented the slip of paper dramatically. "Ring any bells?"

Frowning, Colt slipped his reading glasses on and came around the desk. Silently, he read the message: stil tHinkING Of u, hoR. He was breathing like a foundered horse. Finally, standing straight again, taking his glasses off in a big sweeping gesture like he always did, Colt answered, "Jack Hazard." Then he looked Josie Darling square in the eye. "You know this maggot?"

Colt Fellows

Colt Fellows led as Crotch-Sniff followed him into his office. Ms. Josie Darling waited in his outer office with Peg. Crotch-Sniff on his cane. Anything for a little desk time. Closer to the doughnuts. "So what the hell is Jack Hazard up to, Tobias?"

Crotch-Sniff took a seat in front of Colt's desk. A nobody in the big man's office and feeling very pleased about some damn thing or another. "The professor is Jack's stepdaughter."

"I got that. Josie Fortune when she lived here."

"She shows up this fall teaching at Loser State going by the name of Darling, but ever since she's been in town, she's been getting threats. First day or so in town, she gets an illegal entry at her campus apartment. The guy writes 'Welcome home, Josie' on her bathroom mirror. Claims it's the same handwriting as this." He waved the slip of paper at Colt.

"She call campus security?"

"Didn't report it. Just got someone out to change the locks. Lots of problems with the ex, who's back in Boston. Figures he's playing some angle to embarrass her. He does it again, only on the outside this time. No break-in. He writes . . . something like 'Let me in!' Like that. Gives her a phone call a week or so later out at Cokey's, only he asks for *Josie Fortune*. When she comes to the phone, no one's there. She can't figure how the hell the ex-husband working it, but she's starting to get real worried."

"But won't call us?"

"She charged the bastard with assault last fall."

"Did she now?" Colt smiled.

"He put her in the hospital after he got a suspended sentence for it. She's a little gun-shy about the police after that. Anyway, yesterday, someone smashes in her car windows and leaves this little love letter." He nodded toward the slip of paper that now lay on the edge of Colt's desk. Turns out

Jack was across the street when she drove up. She still thinks it's the ex-husband until she finds out he was definitely in Boston yesterday, pulling a gun on his dean at the college."

"He sounds like a sweetheart."

"All I know is now she thinks this whole thing with the threats is Jack Hazard's doing."

"And all of a sudden the police are her friends?"

"She's scared of Jack. I mean real scared, Colt. The ex-husband . . . he kind of just pisses her off, but Jack . . . that's something else."

Colt nodded. He could understand the feeling. "Where did this happen, the thing with the windows?"

"The Bust of Country."

"Key-rye-st, Tobias! That's county! What's she doing here?"

Crouch shrugged. "A lot of the stuff happened inside the city. Everything but that, actually."

Colt thought about saying something else, but another thought began tugging at him. A chance maybe to take care of some unfinished business. "So what does she want us to do? Assuming we can actually do something."

"Make sure it's him. Talk to him. Keep an eye on him. Give her protection. Put the fear of God in him. I don't know. She wasn't even sure Jack was behind all of it until you pulled that lightning quick ID out of your hat."

Read your notes, Crotch-ity. "Pretty good, huh?" Colt smiled for Crouch's benefit and considered the woman's situation coolly. Jurisdiction was a problem, but if he worked it right, he just might turn that to his advantage. Might work out real well, actually. "So we got any evidence against Jack besides my photographic memory for a crime that's what? Fifteen, eighteen years ago?"

"Twenty years this coming April, Colt."

"Yeah, whatever."

"Just the way he spelled *whore*." Crouch shrugged, "And he was there. She saw him across the street when she went into the bar. That's about it."

Colt shook his head irritably. Not much to go on, especially if the victim wasn't even sure. "You tell her anything about the murder?"

"I saw that note, the way he spelled *whore,* and I called you. Thought you'd want to see her."

Colt leaned over his desk and picked the note up. "You couldn't get an arrest warrant on this with a bribe, Tobias."

"Jack on parole? If he's on parole, you wouldn't need a warrant."

"They cut him loose the minute he finished his sentence. He's a free man."

"So what do you want to do with the professor?"

"I want to help her, Tobias, but she's going to need to file a complaint with the county. She going to do that for me?"

"I don't imagine she will, Colt. She was wrong about the ex and all. . . ."

Colt glared angrily at the sky. "Get her in here. And get a female deputy sheriff down here on the double. Have her ready to take a complaint. I want her waiting at your desk within the next fifteen minutes, you understand? You tell the county dispatcher this is a personal favor to me, lights and sirens if they have to."

"I'll try. . . ."

"No. You'll do it. And get hold of that file on Josie Fortune. I want to look at that case again."

"That file would be downstairs in storage, Colt. They won't pull that out for us without taking a week to get around to it."

"Send Collins for it. *ASAP*, Tobias. I don't want excuses, here. I want the fucking file, and I want it ten minutes ago! Anybody doesn't like it, they're unemployed . . . *after* I nail them to the wall and rip out their throat! You got me!"

"I'll take care of it, Colt."

Colt nodded with a bit of satisfaction, then thought of one more thing. "And tell Happy I need to see him as soon as our professor leaves my office."

"You don't need him, Colt. I can take care of anything you need."

Colt glared at the patrolman angrily. "How do you know what I need, Tobias?"

"Just give me the chance. Whatever you want."

Colt considered the man for several seconds before he relented. Crotch-Sniff had his limitations, but he wasn't completely useless. No, sir. There was a streak of mean in him that went real deep. That and a bit of unhealthy ambition. "Okay, Tobias. You're my lead man on this, but I don't want to hear about what I can and cannot do again. You understand me?"

"Anything you want, Colt. I'm there for you."

"I'm going to take you at your word, Tobias. Don't make me sorry I trusted you."

"I won't, Colt."

"You take care of me, I take care of you. We understand one another?"

"Yes, sir."

"Good. Now go get our professor with the cute ass and send her in here."

h-o-R

Josie Darling, aka Josie Fortune, entered Colt's office looking uncertain.

"Have a seat," Colt said. Still by the window, hardly glancing more than a couple of times at her as he began, Colt asked her what she knew about her mother's death.

Just what she had read in the paper, she answered.

"I was there, Ms. Darling. It was my case."

"That's what I understand."

"The cause of death—strangulation. You read that?" She nodded uncomfortably. "Let me tell you something. That was the *last* thing Jack Hazard did to your mother."

"I'm not sure I understand."

"Jack got hold of your mother a couple, three days before he left her in Lues Creek Canyon for us to find. To tell you the truth, we don't know for sure what he did to her during that time. There were rope burns around her neck, where he had hanged her, and marks on her hands and feet, like she had been tied up the whole time she was missing. We're pretty sure he raped her, but we didn't get enough physical evidence to prove it."

"You mean to prove Jack did it?"

"To prove it even happened."

"I thought that was fairly easy. . . ."

"Well, it might have been if we'd have had a chance to make a proper examination. As it happened, when your stepfather finished choking the life out of your mother, he took a knife to her. Thirty-odd years of carrying a badge, I never saw anything like it."

"My God."

"We first thought it was just to mutilate the body. That kind of thing isn't completely unheard of, but the more I thought about it, the more it seemed to me Jack was worried about us connecting the thing back to him. In those days, we could usually get a blood type from semen. Nobody had ever heard of DNA, at least as far as a crime scene. But with a blood type and a little circumstantial evidence, we could usually get our killer. Without it, without a witness or anything to connect the killer to the crime, we had to go for a confession."

"Jack's brother Virgil tells me he didn't do it." Her voice was weak, skeptical.

"Jack himself told me he did. Of course, I had him dead to rights, and Jack's brother has twenty years working for him. At this point, he can pretty much tell it anyway he wants. But this is the truth. We found a wristwatch in the canyon with Jack's name on it. On top of that, I had two witnesses identify him in a lineup. Jack was watching the canyon from up at the falls and my witnesses saw him. They had no trouble picking him out."

"Why would he be doing this to me? I mean, it's like some kind of sick game. First time it was, Welcome home. Then it was, Let me in. Then a telephone call while I'm at a bar. Yesterday was the first time it got really physical. With the note, . . . it was vicious, like, I don't know . . . like I've done something to him, but the truth is I haven't seen the man for almost twenty years."

"I'm going to tell you something we didn't let out to anyone. Before she was even dead, at some point while he was still letting her hang by her neck for the hell of it, Jack cut three letters into your mother's flesh, just over her heart. You know what three letters they were, Ms. Darling?" She shook her head, her eyes wide open, her little mouth dropped into a confused *o*. "*h-o-r*. The first two letters lowercase, the last capitalized—same as that note he gave you yesterday. Now Jack's not the brightest guy in the world, but I always figured he could spell *whore* just fine. He was mocking your mother. She was going to school, making something of her life. And Jack, . . . he was working as a bouncer at his little brother's topless bar. It hurt his pride."

Josie Fortune's kid just stared at him. But Colt thought she understood.

"Virgil say anything about Jack being on parole?"

She sat up straight again, seemingly confused, shaking her head. "We didn't talk about anything like that."

"Well, I made a call to the department of corrections just now. They tell me if they get a complaint on Jack, they can send him back over to Vienna to finish out his sentence."

"I thought it was finished."

Colt shook his head, thought to add something, then just let it drop like that. A hard, cold fact.

"You think you could get him put back in prison for this?"

Colt allowed himself a slight, mean smile. "The beauty of it is we don't have to meet the standards of proof they set up for a jury. Fact is, we can use our discretion. Parole officer doesn't like what he sees, he pulls the man off the street and sends him back to finish his time, or he gets us to do it, I should say."

"I need to talk to his parole officer?"

"No. You need to file a complaint. You do that, I'll take care of the rest of it."

A long moment of calculation, then, "Who were the witnesses who saw Jack at the falls?"

Colt made no pretense of disguising his surprise at the change of subject. The last thing he wanted was to get into all that again, but if he acted coy about the case or reluctant to give her what she wanted, she wasn't going to trust him. He needed trust.

"One of the kids that found the body: she saw Jack out there in the woods. The other was a campus security officer. Saw Jack staring down at him from the rim of the canyon when he went in to check out the report the kids made."

"You don't have the names?"

"Officer Crouch was the campus security officer."

"The man I just talked to?"

"I liked the way he handled himself, and that summer, I convinced him to come over to the city. He's been a hell of a cop for us ever since."

"And the other witness?"

Colt studied the woman for a long moment, then picked up the phone. Crotch-Sniff. "You get that file, Tobias?" Coming. "When you get it, I want the name of the witness who saw Jack Hazard. . . . I know that. Besides you. . . . No. Call me. What about that other thing I asked you to do?" Coming over from the courthouse. "Good. Call me when you get the name of that witness."

Colt hung up and studied Josie Fortune's kid for a long time, pretending to come to some kind of decision. "You know about the other people Jack's killed, I take it?"

Josie shook her head, the last blush of blood draining out of her pretty cheeks. Colt allowed himself a sad smile. "When Jack was ten-years old, he shot his uncle with a hunting rifle, in his uncle's kitchen."

The woman swore quietly. Colt finally had her full attention.

Nodding, Colt told her, "After Jack's father passed away, Jack's mother moved in with her sister and, of course, the sister's husband. Jack and his brothers and sister came along. This fellow had his own family and he took another. Jack repaid him for his kindness one morning, maybe four or five months after they moved in. Not a word said, just walked into the man's kitchen, while he was eating his breakfast, leveled that rifle on him and fired away. Put the first two in his uncle's face. The man was crawling across the floor and bawling when Jack shot him point-blank through the back of his skull."

"My God." Her voice was hardly more than a squeak.

Colt shook his head. "I was a kid then myself, had just started high school. People talked about it for weeks. That was big news back forty-some years ago. Kids didn't do that kind of thing every day the way they do now." Colt smiled grimly. "Virgil was there. Virgil saw it happen. He forget to tell you about that?" Josie looked down at her folded hands. *Getting the message, lady?* "Jack wasn't but a couple or three years out of the juvenile detention center for that and what's he do but shoot a black man up in Pilatesburg. I was a rookie cop in Peoria at the time, but I heard plenty about it later," Colt smiled. "Put a gun in that poor man's throat and unloaded it. If you can believe it, they never even charged him for it. His lawyer was screaming self-defense, and the state's attorney at that time backed down and let it go. Of course, if the man Jack shot had been *white,* they might have had a different opinion."

"Last fall, I charged my husband with assault."

Colt nodded sympathetically. She was coming around. "We had just separated and he came by my apartment to talk about dividing the property. He had a sheet of paper, everything written out. Very calm, relaxed. I thought . . . well, I let him in. The minute he was through the door he punched me, and he . . . it was . . . bad. Anyway, afterwards . . . I went to the police. They arrested him. He made bail the same day. A few months later, he went to court and got a suspended sentence. A couple of weeks after that, he caught me in a parking lot. He really hurt me that time. Broken bones.

This." She pointed at her nose, like there was something wrong with it. "I didn't have the nerve to press charges after that. I knew if I did, he would kill me the next time."

Her message was clear. She was telling Colt what she needed. Everybody needed something. Josie Darling needed to feel safe.

Colt kept his gaze locked on her for a long, tense moment, letting her know he understood exactly what she was asking, then he leaned back in his chair and looked up at the ceiling. "Toby was telling me that when this thing started, you thought it was your ex-husband?"

The woman smiled, ducking her head. "I seem to be living out some kind of childhood trauma. It's all I can figure. The lunatics aren't finding me. I'm finding them."

"Well, I can't help you with your ex, unless he comes to town, but Jack Hazard I can do something about. Assuming you file a complaint."

"I just don't know how Jack could find out I was coming to Lues. It was like he knew I was coming, and that doesn't make sense."

"He's got a lot of family. If any of them found out about your coming, he'd know about it, too."

"Why is he doing this?"

Colt knew better than to plead ignorance. What he did was meet her gaze and smile. It was the sad, wise smile of a man who has seen all too much human depravity. "I expect because he enjoys it."

The last vestiges of resistance wilted away, and after she had looked at her hands, she lifted her eyes up and asked him, "So what exactly can you do?"

"Let me tell you something. When your ex-husband crossed the line, the police didn't have enough authority to do what they knew had to be done. Now I'm not going to second guess the judge. His hands are tied, same as the cops' are. This kind of thing happens all the time in domestic cases. A man with a good record and a real bad attitude can work the system. We charge him, his lawyer gets him out on bail, and the wife or ex-wife takes the brunt of it. Believe me, you're not the only woman who has gone through something like this. The point is cops can't do anything but pick up the pieces after it's over. And sometimes that means working a homicide. If a man wants to brutalize his wife, he's going to do it. Eventually he'll pay, but by the time he does, it's not going to do his victim any good. Now you can lament the system and hope it changes, and nobody wants it to change more than me, but for now, the thing to do is accept it as a fact of life. Not a very pretty one, but that's just the way it is. Fortunately, what we're dealing with here is entirely different, and I don't think I've quite made that clear. First, there's no question but that this is going to come down to life and death at some point. Jack's shown his colors on three occasions that we know about. Second, there's something the police can do to stop him. You file a complaint, and I'll have him picked up. No bail, no judge, and no jury. We put him back in Vienna, and there he stays until he finishes his twenty, which will be sometime after next summer."

"Nobody saw him do it, and I can't swear it was Jack."

"But you know it was him?"

She nodded. "It couldn't be anyone else. I mean no one in Lues knows who I am."

"How did you get that bruise?"

The professor looked at her arm in surprise. "That was . . . Jack grabbed me."

"Yesterday?"

"He was trying to get me out of the bar. I mean, he was *helping* me!"

"Pretty nasty bruise for a guy helping you out, don't you think?"

"Maybe I better explain what happened."

Colt listened patiently. When she had finished her story, he said, "So a lot of people saw him dragging you out of there?"

"The place was packed. There must have been eighty people who saw it."

"What happened after that?"

"Nothing. We got to the door, and I told him I didn't want to leave with him."

"Why?"

"I didn't know what he might do once we were alone."

"Smart woman. Now listen to me. I've got a deputy sheriff waiting with Officer Crouch. What I want you to do is file an assault charge against your stepfather. We won't even worry about the broken glass and the note—."

"But—!"

Colt held up his hand. "Give me something to work with here. That's all I need. You file the complaint, I promise you I will personally find out if Jack is behind the rest of this before I go to his parole officer."

"How?"

"I'll talk to him."

"Can't you just talk to him without a complaint?"

"This thing will never go before a judge, Ms. Darling. What it is, I need some leverage."

"I don't understand."

"You're not going to have to deal with testifying, and you're not going to have to worry about Jack making bail. I pick him up, talk to him about what's he's been doing, and once I'm convinced he's behind these threats, I'll see that his parole officer gets the whole story. What he'll do is get Jack to finish out his term for murdering your mother. That locks him up at least until next summer. You get to finish the school year in peace, and maybe at that point, before he gets out, you might want to think about your options."

"Leave town?"

"I would."

"Can you guarantee he'll be gone until summer?"

"As soon as we find him, I can."

"That's not a problem. He's going to be at the McDonald's this afternoon at two o'clock."

"Here in town?" Colt almost smiled. It was going to be easier than he thought.

She nodded.

"How did you get him to agree to come into Lues?"

"I asked him. Why?"

"I just wondered. I'll tell you what. You stay away from the McDonald's. Don't even think about going there. I'll send someone by to pick him up . . . assuming we have a complaint properly filed against him. As soon as we have him in custody, I'll talk to him. If he's behind this thing, I'll find out."

The phone rang. Crouch with the witness. "Is the deputy with you?" Waiting. "Okay. Thanks, buddy." When he got off the phone, Colt told Josie Darling, "The second eyewitness was Melody Mason, age nineteen at the time, a freshman at Lues State. The only address we had was a sorority house on campus." He grinned, "I doubt it's current. And we have a deputy sheriff here, who's ready when you are."

Her eyes cut toward the window. One last bit of reluctance. "What if he lies, convinces you he isn't doing anything?"

"Well, there are people who can work me, Ms. Darling. That's a fact. But Jack Hazard isn't one of them. I got him to confess to murder. Next to that, this will be a walk in the park."

"What if he's really innocent?"

"Ms. Darling, it's either this or we let it him go and you sit around and wait for the guy to show up some night and take you away, the same as he did your mother."

Josie Darling flinched at this, then shuffled in her briefcase for a pencil and a slip of paper. She wrote the name Melody Mason down, then slipped it back into the briefcase and looked up at Colt. "Okay," she said, "let's do it."

The Purdey

When Josie Darling shut the door to Colt's office, he called Crouch with instructions, then turned again to study the gray sky. Something in the way Miss Darling moved had reminded Colt of her mother. He had hadn't seen it when she had come into his office or sat there before him like a scared rabbit, but it was there as she left, that same cocky walk-away. Almost like Josie Fortune had come back to life. He shivered involuntarily at the thought, then shook his head like a man ridding himself of cobwebs. Josie Fortune back from the grave: now there was a nightmare!

It hadn't been long after Jack got away with shooting Hazy Mundy that he met himself the prettiest girl anyone ever saw in Lues County. Miss Josie Fortune. And she was a beauty. They got married, bought the Hurry On Up from Jack's older brother, and went into business. Paid cash or so the records indicated. Since Josie Fortune had had no money that anybody knew about and Jack Hazard shouldn't have had much, Colt had kicked around the idea that the bar was bought with money from some upstate banks, without the usual loan papers signed. Alfred Moore, one of Colt's better informants at the time, had confirmed as much. Alfred had told him that Hazy had been using Jack on some projects that nobody knew much about, meaning, it turned out, that Hazy had Jack robbing banks.

Colt had decided it was best simply to watch and see how Jack and Josie's business went, marking his time, and letting them get their feet planted good and solid, before he pulled the rug out from under them. As it happened, business was plenty good, so one evening, Colt went out to try to collect some interest on the bank loan, *as it were.* He laid it out pretty plain with the names of banks, the dates, and the amounts that were stolen. They were all old jobs dating back to Jack's association with Hazy, and all he really had was circumstantial evidence, but, hell, sometimes a good bluff will make you more than a fist full of aces.

He sat down with them after closing. It was just Jack and Josie Fortune and Colt, about three in the morning, each of them with a shot glass, a half-full bottle of Jack Daniels between them. There was an ashtray on the table and a pack of Lucky Strikes next to it. He could still remember every blessed detail of the encounter, because it had damn near been his last! The place had only a couple of lights left on. Colt had caught the two of them cleaning up, and after a little bit of small talk, he made his speech. It was one of his better ones, pure and simple and, in honor of Jack's reputation, marked with a respectfully conservative request for payment. Jack didn't say one way or the other if any of Colt's suspicions were true. He just listened with those dead, cold eyes holding Colt. Colt told him he would take two-hundred dollars on the first of each month, or he would turn what he had over to the FBI and see what they could make of it. If Jack was innocent, he had nothing to fear. If maybe he knew something about those jobs, maybe he ought to pay Colt a "security consultant fee." Jack had Colt's word as a gentleman it would always stay the same price and would always stay just between the three of them, Jack, Josie, and Colt. A damn fair offer, taken all around.

When he had finished, the three of them were silent. Pretty soon Josie Fortune reached for Jack's cigarettes and said something about wanting filters. She swung herself up and went over behind the bar and began getting change for the machine. Not a good idea to study a jealous man's wife as she did a walk-away, Colt just took a quick peek, then didn't really pay that much attention to her. Besides, he was on a tightrope with Jack Hazard, for God's sake. Jack was staring off somewhere between the middle of that table and murder. The next thing Colt knew, Josie Fortune had come around the end of the bar with a sawed-off double-barreled 12-gauge Purdey shotgun in her hand. She hitched the butt of it against her thigh, laid both hammers back, and leveled its hollow pipes at Colt's eyes, about three feet distant.

Josie Fortune was a beautiful woman, just like her kid. She had a perfect oval face, the features regular and delicate, and green eyes so cool and thoughtful you could almost fall in love just looking at her. The most striking thing about the woman was her hair. She wore it longer than her kid, and it glistened like burnished bronze. None of that had quite mattered at the time, though. Nor did anything ever again quite seem the same about her, from Colt's point of view. With her Purdey pointed at Colt's eyes, Josie Fortune had looked like death itself.

"I listened to what you had to say," she told him, "and I didn't interrupt you, so I expect you'll give me the same courtesy."

Colt remembered Jack just sitting there, staring at the table, smoking a Lucky, a bit of a grin on his lips like he was wondering what Colt was going to do now. Curious, nothing more. Other than that little grin, Jack was acting like nothing at all appeared to be out of order. Hell, Jack didn't give a damn! He was probably trying to remember where he kept the shovel. Since it was closing time, the mop and bucket were already set out. That's how he was! Just take a body out and bury it! Then wash up the floorboards! And *her!* Josie Fortune positively looked like she was itching to pull those triggers!

"There's no one going to arrest me for those bank robberies," she told him. "I didn't live here in those days, and I'd never heard of Jack or Hazy or any of them back then, so I want you to know if anyone comes around even asking Jack questions about those days, I'll vanish from the face of this earth and when I come back, and I will, Mister, I'll be carrying this shotgun and it will be the last thing you see before I turn your head inside out. Are we clear on that?"

Colt had shed no tears the night they pulled that old gal out of a body bag!

The Cabbie

As Josie trotted through the fairly steady drizzle of rain and slipped into the taxicab, she found herself unaccountably depressed. She was safe suddenly or would be after two o'clock that afternoon. She had the promise of the chief of police that Jack Hazard would be locked away until summer. She ought to feel relief. Instead, she kept imagining that she had betrayed the man who had been harassing her. The meeting they had arranged was suddenly a setup for his arrest.

Maybe it was just too easy. With Dan Scholari, it had been different.

Arrested, then released, her husband had been free to make trouble. When she returned to school, he was there waiting. Every day, she had faced the prospect of running into him. They were working in the same building. They had the same friends. She would show up sometimes at the office she shared with a half dozen other TAs, and Dan would be there, or just down the hall. She had no choice but to endure him. His friends had interceded, imploring her to drop the charges. The phone had rung late at night and no one had answered. It had taken courage to follow through with it, and she had paid a terrible price for that courage. This was different. Filing charges against Jack Hazard had required no courage at all. It felt, in fact, like she had done a favor for the chief of police. Josie could not get rid of her feeling of dirtiness. She tried to tell herself it was only the sudden lack of pressure. After all, ever since her arrival in Lues, she had been under siege. She had imagined things culminating in violence or at least the threat of it. Nothing had seemed more certain or necessary, in fact. Now suddenly, her troubles were over with a few strokes of an ink pen.

As Josie's cab turned into campus, she checked her watch. She had originally intended to stop by her apartment and pick up her nickel, since she had not taken it to the police station at the civic center. It felt strange to be without it. She wanted the gun, but it was 9:43, and there was no time to stop. She would barely make her ten o'clock as it was. She directed the cabbie along Willow, then saw the cluster of high rises among the trees and a wet, gray sky beyond. A moment later, they were in the open, the cab pulling up against the curb in front of the Liberal Arts Plaza.

The cabbie announced in a perfunctory manner, "Six dollars."

The meter showed that she owed four dollars, fifty cents. "The meter says four-fifty."

"Six dollars."

The cabbie did not even look at her as he said this. He was a big man, with greasy, yellow flesh and long, greasy hair and a pathetically thin, greasy beard. Boorish and oozing a low grade stink, he was robbing her of a few pennies, just because he knew he could get away with it. He would not treat a man this way, she decided, but she wasn't up to a fight. She shook her head with resignation. *Slews*. Like Jack and his brother Virgil, like all the men she had seen the day before. God, but she hated them! Holding out dollar bills and watching a naked woman doing backbends to pick them up off the floor with her tongue. Even Officer Crouch this morning peeking under her skirt with all the cunning of a demented thirteen year old. She was sick to death of it! Sick of Lues. Come May, when her contract was up, she was going back to civilization. Reaching into the outside pocket of her briefcase, where she kept her cash, driver's license, and one of her credit cards, Josie found three twenties. She brought one of them out.

"Have you got something smaller?" the cabbie grumbled.

First he stole from her, now he wanted exact change. Quietly, she waited the man out. Rolling his body over like some kind of overwrought sea lion, he pulled money from his pocket with a terrible huff. Now turning painfully about in the seat, he reached back and gave her a five, five ones, and then eight quarters, all counted out with dim-witted care. He had more coins in his hand and another five dollar bill flapping loosely between his fingers, but he wasn't letting go of any more money.

"That's eight dollars for the ride," Josie complained. "You said it was six."

"I don't got no change." He rolled around, so that his back was turned to her now, dismissing the argument, and with it his passenger.

"You don't have *any* change."

He didn't answer at first. His eyes simply burned into his rearview mirror. Josie met the gaze. "That's what I said," he told her finally.

"Here!" Josie snarled, handing the man his quarters back. "I don't want your quarters." Turning partially to get the quarters, the cabbie still held the five dollar bill in his fingers. Josie hadn't intended to grab the bill. She had meant only to show the man up for what he was, a damn slew, but the five dollar bill was there, flapping loosely in his fingers, as she dumped the quarters into his cupped hands, and she grabbed it out of spite.

"Hey!" the man shouted. "That's my money!"

Josie pushed the door open and got out of the back of the car on the driver's side. "Not anymore."

He rolled his window down halfway, shouting as he did, "Hey, I want my money, bitch!"

Josie reached in with the hand that still held the five dollar bill and took the man's scraggly beard and pulled it until his head came up against the window and doorpost. He screeched and swore in surprise, trying futilely to get hold of Josie's wrist. "Do you want to apologize?" Josie asked him coolly. "Or would you like for me to rip the hair off your face?"

"Fuck you!" he hissed.

Keeping her fingers in his beard, Josie eased the pressure off, so that his head pulled back slightly, then she jerked his big head back toward her. His head cracked sweetly against glass and metal. Immediately she let him go. Some of his facial hairs still clung to her fingers, and she wiped her hand clean as she walked away with her precious five dollars. When Josie heard the cabbie getting out of the cab, she stopped and turned toward him. They were standing in the rain facing each other, both furious, both insanely intent upon taking this utter absurdity to some kind of showdown. Is this how people crack up? she wondered. Her brain buzzed with odd, old voices, primeval shouts of pain, and she wished—God, did she wish!—she had her nickel. She felt the strength leave her as she realized she had no way of protecting herself. A cold coil of fear shot into her throat as she noticed the man's enormity. No. She would not back down. Not here, not from this . . . slew!

She thought, consciously, about dealing with the man. He was huge, but it was all fat. She could run, or scream if someone wanted to help . . . or she could she drop under him and snap his ankle with a hard kick at the right spot.

She liked that idea best. Just . . . wait for the chance. Drop, kick, and roll up to her feet again. She would not be afraid, as simple as that. So simple, in fact, she almost wasn't, and she settled herself to wait for him. The idea of fighting such a man should have terrified her, she knew that, and yet, something had risen up in her that was foreign and beautiful and wild. And she knew, as she had known nothing else since her return, that in this moment she was her mother's daughter. He actually seemed to hesitate as she came to her decision to fight. "Come on!" she told him. "You want to steal my money, come on and take it!"

That put him off somehow. "You owe me a dollar!" He wasn't coming toward her. His voice plaintive suddenly, he seemed almost to back off. Like a dog in its yard barking at strangers, she thought.

A boy walking across the plaza peeled off from his group and came next to Josie. The kid was one of her students, Josie realized. *Great!* she thought, *a witness.* Her next image was of her standing before her dean, explaining herself. What was wrong with her? She was not her mother's child. She was . . . civilized! Give him the money! she told herself. It was just money. Why stand here and dare him to take it away? Her eyes slipped from the cabbie to the boy next to her. Josie was his composition teacher. In class, he was meek, polite, well-groomed. She knew where he sat and to which class he belonged, her ten o'clock as it happened. She couldn't remember the papers he had written, but she knew the kinds of mistakes he made. One thing was certain. This was the worst mistake he had ever made. "Are you okay, Miss Darling?" he asked. These were the first words he had spoken. The crackling innocence of the voice surprised Josie and tugged at the last threads of her sanity.

The cabbie took a step toward them now, pointing his big finger, "Butt out of it, sonny!" It was a high, tight voice. He was more scared than Josie at this point, but he wasn't backing down.

"It's okay," Josie told the boy. "I'll handle this. Just go. Get out of the way." Drop, kick, roll. Then stand up and get beyond his reach. He wouldn't be looking for it, would expect her to run or at least try to dodge him. That was why it would work.

"If you want to help," the cabbie shouted, "why don't you give me my damn dollar! The lady ripped me off!" Soaked from the rain, dancing from foot to foot, fighting for his illicit dollar, the cabbie looked like a ridiculous oaf. Maybe they all looked ridiculous. For the sake of a dollar.

The boy still didn't answer him. The rain poured over all three of them, so that they all scrunched their faces up. They were all miserable and angry. The boy was quivering, Josie realized, but he still wasn't backing down. Behind her, Josie heard a deep voice, faintly Southern, blessedly familiar. It was Henry Valentine. Val walked past Josie and the boy calmly and went directly to the man, his tall, lean figure standing so close that he almost touched the cabbie. Val said something, and the cabbie turned and got back into his cab. A moment later, he was driving off, his middle finger giving them all the slew salute. Val came toward Josie and the boy. He looked at the boy and extended his hand. "Henry Valentine. My friends call me Val."

The boy took his hand, "I know. I'm Nelson Rush, Dr. Valentine."

"Val. And listen, Nelson . . . you need help with anything, anything at all, you find me. I like what you did here. There were a hundred kids out here and no one else stood up to that filthy slew." Val looked at the kids passing hurriedly through the rain, a surprising expression of contempt for all of them. "You showed some real courage, Nelson. I admire that."

Josie looked at the kids walking by them. She had hardly been conscious of so many kids. She had sensed movement around her, but that was all. They had left her to fend for herself. It was not their fight. But not Nelson.

"What did you say to that guy?" Nelson asked Val. Val had taken over as the hero in all this, and that irked Josie to an unreasonable degree.

Val's wrinkled face hinted at a smile. Water splashed over his bald head and hung from the craggy edges of his face. "Nelson, all of life is about knowing the right thing to say at the right time."

"And you're not telling me what it was?" Nelson was utterly in awe of Dr. Henry Valentine, having forgotten, it seemed, that it was Josie who had actually stood up to the slew.

Val shook his head, a magician with his trade secrets. "I'll tell you this much. It was a single word." He held up a lone finger dramatically.

Touching his arm and meaning to send him on his way, Josie told the boy, "Thanks, Nelson. I'll see you in class." The boy turned to leave, dissolving from Josie's consciousness. She looked at Val with neither awe nor gratitude. They were both soaked in the cold Lues drizzle. Their eyes met in a brief testing of fortitude, then Josie looked away. She saw Nelson Rush slipping into a crowd of students.

"So what was the magic word, Val?"

"I said, 'Here!' and gave him the dollar he was screaming you owed him."

Josie flushed, "He was stiffing me, Val. Damn it, I wish you hadn't done that!"

Val grinned, "Would you risk your life for dollar, Josie?"

There was in this the proper dosage of chastisement, but Josie resisted all temptation to explain: "It was the principle of thing."

These were magic words for Val, and he smiled with nearly as much respect as amusement. "A woman after my own heart. What do you say we get out of this rain?" Josie looked up at the sky angrily. She was totally soaked and still ready for a fight—with God himself if no one else showed up for the honors. She felt like a savage denied her birthright, a slew among slews. She still had a knot in her stomach and all she really wanted was to go home and get her revolver.

Together they walked in an uncomfortable silence. There were hundreds of kids moving toward the buildings for their ten o'clock classes, but Josie felt that she and Val were by themselves. "You know, I could have handled that," Josie said finally.

Val glanced at her with an inscrutable expression of amusement, respect, and solemnity. Finally, deadpan, he answered her, "I know that, Josie. I only meant to save the poor cabbie."

Promises

By the time she got to her office, she had only a minute to get upstairs to her classroom. She picked up a thick folder with 10:00 TR written on its cover and headed back into the hallways of Brand. She had to pass the main office, so she stepped in quickly to check the mail. There were several memos and the department newsletter with a picture of Henry Valentine prominently displayed on the front page. Val was receiving a plaque from the university president. She read the caption, Teacher of the Year Award, 2001–2002. He had gotten it last May. This was the official report of it to the department.

Before she had come to the end of the stack, Josie saw a red envelope with the name Josie Fortune typed on it, nothing else, so she knew it could not have come through the campus mail and certainly not through the post office. She looked about. The student helper at the secretary's desk was reading *Plato's Republic*. "Did you see anyone drop this off, Marilyn?"

The girl looked up, blinking. "What?"

"Did anyone unusual come in this morning and put this in my box?"

"What do you mean *unusual?*"

"An older man, in his fifties, kind of short and skinny?" *A filthy little slew named Jack Hazard.*

The girl shook her head, "I don't think so."

Josie opened the envelope and found one of the standard university bookstore offerings inside. It showed a photograph of Lues Creek Canyon, the ubiquitous symbol of campus, and across the front of it was "The Campus of Lues State University."

Inside, she found the familiar psychotic script Jack Hazard had used before, the crazy spelling like a signature:

u R Heer in mY dReEms

There was no signature, no other mark of any kind. Angrily, she shoved the thing in her briefcase and headed for class.

Josie had no time to check in the mirror, and only belatedly thought about how she must look when she felt the prickles of damp cloth against her skin. She was wet and rumpled. The kids had on the faces they always wore, so it probably wasn't too bad. Nelson—whatever his last name was—sat placidly in the front, watching Josie with that private look kids get when they know something personal about their teacher, even if it's that she's a lunatic. She met his gaze briefly. Only now did she realize the courage he had shown to stand next to her. She gave him a flickering smile, and he understood. She set her briefcase and purse on the table where the lectern sat, then reached in to get her class folder, intending to call roll. When she opened the folder, Josie saw another message.

Across her computer-generated class roster in large red letters, she found these words printed with a crayon:

sooon, JosIe, i promiss

Josie read the message twice. She tried to breathe normally, but instead, she found herself swaying, close to collapse. Then something happened, the salvation of rage, the knowledge that he was done! Today, two o'clock, and then it was over. She shut the folder quickly and looked up at her class. A gentle, contented movement somewhere at the edges of her vision. They were not part of this. They were waiting for class to start. "Forget the roll," she announced with a strained effort at humor. She took a long, deep breath, and stepped around the table feeling drunk or tired, thinking, *knowing*, it was behind her. "I think everyone's here," she said softly. "Speak up if you're absent." She heard a couple of giggles. Stepping away from her lectern and Jack Hazard's latest composition, Josie struggled to talk about revision. "The *second* look," she announced, "is often the *first* time we see a thing!" Straight from Annie that was, as all her best ideas were. She went on. She preached the dogma with passion. It was old-time Boston religion, but every once in a while Josie's eyes would fall to the folder and she would think about Jack's message inside. She only prayed to God Colt Fellows would keep his word.

At two o'clock, as she graded a set of papers, Josie thought about Jack walking into the McDonald's looking for her. She felt like Judas, but she knew it had to be done. At 2:15, she looked at her watch again and realized it must be over, prayed it was, at least. She set aside her grading and began copying out a new class roster for her ten o'clock class. All the while, she stared bravely at Jack's "promiss." Finished with that, Josie dropped the old class roster into her briefcase beside the card she had pulled from her department mailbox. Out of sight, just not quite out of mind. Then, after staring at her telephone for nearly a minute, she turned back to grading.

The phone rang at 3:30, startling her. She looked at the receiver. It's over, she told herself, picking up the handset. "Josie Darling."

"This is Colt Fellows. Just wanted you to know we got him."

She closed her eyes, let her breath go, and knew finally that she had done the right thing. She felt . . . *free!*

"You talked to him?"

"I sure did. He admitted everything."

"He say why?"

"Yeah, he did. Said you looked something like your mother. He thought it might be fun to do you. That's just the way he put it."

Josie felt weak, dizzy, cold. *Fun.* "He's in jail now?" Her voice wavered uncontrollably.

"Jack's in and he won't be out before summer, I guarantee it. I've already taken care of everything."

She thanked Fellows for his help, then hung up. For a minute, she tried to enjoy the triumph, but her stomach felt sour. She took several, slow, deep breaths, then opened her briefcase to look at Jack's card and the class roster he had ruined. She studied both just to remind herself of the kind of man she was dealing with. She thought she should have told Colt about the notes, considered calling him, then let it go. What was the point? Colt wasn't building a case for trial. He had just used her complaint to get Jack's parole revoked. It was over. *Fun.*

To hell with Jack Hazard!

Clarissa Holt

Josie had drinks at five with the Girl Scouts. She caught a ride off campus with Cheryl Fischer. An apologetic creature but as sweet as apple turnovers, Dr. Fischer was an overweight middle-aged woman with a tepid spirit, the meekest of revolutionaries, but trying. She had kind of a *Damn the patri-*

archy, if you don't think they'll be too upset about it attitude. They talked about a recipe for lasagna on the way out to the bar. The key to it, Cheryl Fischer explained passionately, was the cottage cheese. Josie loathed cottage cheese on principle.

Once at the bar, with plenty of alcohol to stir the revolution, the more courageous feminists of the group pursued a sexual harassment case that was making its way through the grapevine. Someone very high up, it was thought. This brought out a number of personal encounters with sexist behavior. As one story produced another, Josie struggled not to tell them about pulling a revolver on Virgil Hazard during her "job interview." She drank thirstily and smiled vacantly around the table. She was pretty sure Virgil Hazard would be a bit more considerate of the women he interviewed after his experience with D. J. Darling. As if that really helped. She looked around the table again. Bad as they imagined things were for them, her friends were isolated from the real thing. They couldn't imagine the humiliation Josie had seen the day before. Being educated, they didn't have to pick up dollar bills with their tongues or let men stuff them into their panties. Neither were they visiting the police or calling a garage to get the broken glass in their car taken care of. Had any of them really seen hatred, the kind of violence Jack Hazard had delivered to her mother? They were talking about jokes that made them feel uncomfortable. She wanted to tell them about a woman, on this campus twenty years ago, who was hanged, strangled, and finally raped with a knife. Or a more pedestrian story about lying in a library parking lot last winter in Boston, while a stranger screamed for someone to get an ambulance. All because she stood up in court and spoke the truth. Now that was a joke that made you feel uncomfortable!

Instead, Josie kept her own counsel. She drank deeply and watched their faces, as they shared anecdotes and commiserated about the general failure of the movement that had once promised so much more. At least they had that part right.

Josie hitched a ride home with Clarissa Holt. She could hardly stand another recipe, and besides, she liked Clar. Clar was the real thing, not just hot talk after a couple of drinks. If anything, Clar got nicer after a couple of drinks. Bright, aggressive, politically astute, she was a take-no-prisoners-kind of feminist, cut from the same cloth as Annie Wilde.

When they got into her Civic, she asked, "So what happened to your car?"

Josie looked out at the darkness, knowing she had nothing at all to fear but struggling to calm herself anyway. "Vandalism." Clarissa Holt stared at her until Josie had to meet her gaze and explain. "Someone smashed out all the glass."

"Nice. Just in time for the rain."

"I haven't decided if rain was part of the plan or just my bad luck."

Clar pulled into traffic without seeming to look. "You seemed a little tense tonight. I guess I understand why now."

"I don't know. The car is part of it. It's Lues mostly. Too close to what I grew up with and too far from what I need."

"Tell me about it. I got my degree from Berkeley but I grew up in Ashland, Kentucky, for God's sake." They talked comfortably for a while about small towns and big cities. The trade-offs. The different kinds of isolation. "I left home and I swore I'd never go back. I never did, either, but then I ended up here, which is about the same, except I don't have deal with my family and the people I went to high school with. Thirteen years in Lues and, I swear, sometimes I think I should have stayed working at the Ashland Dairy Queen. Financially, I'd probably be money ahead, plus no papers to grade."

She turned into campus and accelerated into a group of three students cutting diagonally across the street in front of her. She hit the horn, then her brakes with a dramatic squeal before they looked up with drugged gazes. Only a thin smile let Josie know this was sport. The intellect's version of cow tipping.

"Tell me it's not that bad, Clar."

"Not really. We do some good sometimes, get a student or two every semester who makes everything worth the effort. It's just sometimes I listen to my colleagues and I want to scream."

"The men?"

"Men have always made me want to scream, Josie, especially when they try to be cute. After thirteen years at Lues State, I'm not sure anymore about women This group . . . the Girl Scouts . . . originally . . . well, originally we had an agenda. I mean we were going to do some damage! Now . . . it's like . . . a New Age sewing circle!"

"Just so we still have a good reason to get drunk."

Clarissa's anger wilted into a smile. She slowed the Civic down as she approached Willow Circle, the road that lead to Josie's apartment, then, as she turned in, she hit the gas and the car roared up the hill. A bit over the line, Josie decided, but not sloppy or dangerous drunk. When she parked behind Josie's VW, Clar's face went hard and brittle as she glared at the broken windows.

"They do that to you on campus?"

"I was at a bar."

"Which one?" Warnings were coming. There were campus bars and bars for the locals, and never the two shall mix. Slews and Losers, oil and water. She had gotten the first warnings in her orientation and plenty of them afterwards. It was a fact of life in every small town with a university attached to it, as old as the riots in Oxford during the Middle Ages.

"The wrong one," Josie answered simply.

"The wrong one. That's good. You made someone mad, did you?"

"Turned a guy down for a drink."

"You went to the police about this, I hope?"

"First thing this morning."

Bandolier

The day was over, and Josie still had a hundred pages to read in James Fenimore Cooper's *Last of the Mohicans* before her nine o'clock class the following morning. Before she gave herself over to it, she called Annie.

"You talked to the police?" Annie asked her.

"They got him on a parole violation, Annie. Picked him up this afternoon."

"What are they charging him with?"

"Nothing. They're just revoking his parole. I filed an assault and battery complaint, and they picked him up. Jack goes back to prison until sometime this summer, by which time I'm back in Boston."

"But he didn't *assault* or *batter* you, Josie. I mean it sounds to me like he did everything but that. How could they arrest him for that?"

"Technically, he did." She looked at the tiny bruises on her arm. "Look, it's over. Jack admitted he was the one leaving the messages. You know what he said? Said I reminded him of my mother. He thought it would be *fun* to do me. Can you believe it? The creep."

"Weird notion of fun."

"He's a psycho, but at least he's in jail, and he's going to stay there. That's all that matters. I talked to the detective who ran the case twenty years ago, Annie. He's chief of police now. What Jack did to my mother was unbelievable. I had no idea."

"Meaning?"

She told Annie about the letters Jack carved into her flesh, the fact that Jack had tortured her mother by hanging her, then carried her into the canyon to finish it with his hands. Even then, he wasn't finished, she said, and told her about Jack raping her mother's corpse with a knife. Her narrative brought an understandably shocked reaction from Annie. They had always imagined something more typical of domestic violence. They had assumed a long affair with abuse preceding the murder, but this was violence of a different sort, horrific precisely because it was not done in the heat of passion.

"And he admitted he wanted to do the same thing to you?"

"If that's what *doing me* means."

"He's a monster, Josie."

"Definitely."

"You're okay?"

"Yeah," she lied. "I'm feeling great. I'm feeling so great I'm thinking about going down to the jail and doing some target practice."

"Speaking of creeps, I got the latest on Dan this afternoon."

"How's he doing?"

"He's supposed to undergo a psychiatric evaluation before the school takes any kind of disciplinary action. If he's sane, they'll fire him. If they decide he didn't know what he was doing, he could be back in the classroom as early as next week."

"Wonderful. I'm sure the kids will all feel safe."

"Safer than the dean, anyway. Oh, and the best part! We got a scheduling 'adjustment' in our mailboxes this afternoon. Nothing is different except that Professor Scholari is going to teach the seminar he asked for the other day. I'm talking the dean tomorrow, Josie. I have a few scheduling changes of my own to propose. I was just loading my pistola for the interview when you called."

There was something hypnotic and nostalgic about listening to Annie, and Josie encouraged her, if only for the pleasure of imagining herself somewhere else besides Lues. She saw the familiar halls of Bandolier. She remembered Annie's office, the books stacked weirdly, even dangerously high, thousands of them it seemed, and the pictures of women, some cut out of newsprint, others from the glossy pages of fashion magazines, some neatly framed, others fresh-cut like wild flowers, *hero-women*, Annie called them. She thought of Annie rolling in her chair back and forth between her bookshelves calling for a book on high or digging into a stack of newsprint and ranting against . . . everything. She thought of Annie's mid-afternoon impromptu lectures, the late night bottle of rye she would pull out of her desk, "Irish 'til I die, Josie!" There were the endless arguments over poetry and psychology, myth and symbol, that whole world where dream and reality are one, the essential human cosmos that universities alone can probe. Even the sudden violence that occasionally disrupted it was never enough to thrust Bandolier University into the real world, and it seemed to Josie that Lues State just didn't give that same feeling.

She wasn't sure if it was Lues itself or her change of position. She wasn't a student anymore, and maybe that was the problem. She was an authority figure without the authority. An unimportant lecturer, a kind of second-tier citizen who, if she behaved, might get to join the ranks of the immortals one day, but at present, she hadn't the freedom to shout her convictions or the punch to stick it to the old bulls. She hadn't even the guts to drop a hand grenade or two in the ladies' New Age sewing circle. And she missed that. She had been swept out of the unpredictable but essentially safe world of study into the calm but dangerous world of work. She wanted to go back and talk about truth with real conviction again! And yet she knew it could never be the same. Truth was eternal, not her youth.

All the same, it was good to listen to Annie's raspy voice, possible for Josie to believe she was back in Boston with the faces she knew and the familiar academic wars. Josie sipped at a cup of mint tea, encouraging Annie's rambles and listening with the dreamy sensation that Lues was faraway, Boston close-by. When Annie ran out of gossip, she pushed Josie for more about her meeting with Colt Fellows. What had happened exactly, how had she handled it?

Josie gave a detailed answer, but she didn't tell her friend how she had felt pushed into making the charge, nor did she mention the sense of dirtiness that came over her after she had left Colt's office. She covered only the facts. The facts gave her comfort. There were, she said, two witnesses who saw Jack in the woods the day her mother died. She had talked to one of them, in fact. No doubt about it. The guy told her he got a clear, unobstructed view. He had seen Jack at the falls. Both witnesses had picked Jack out of the lineup without any problems. There was a wristwatch with Jack's name on it, and what nailed it down, without a doubt, the word Jack had carved into her mother's flesh: "*h-o-r*"—as in "still thinking of you."

"So it *was* him?" Annie answered with a sense of finality.

"Annie the chief of police looked at that note, just that note, he didn't even know who I was, and he said, 'Jack Hazard.' Just like that."

Re-Vision

The next morning, as she was leaving, Josie slipped her gun inside the drawer of the bedside table. History, she told herself, and then she smiled. It was over. She was safe, even if her nerves weren't quite buying it.

Outside, it was still raining, misting really, and she peeked into her car to assess the damage. The upholstery was going to be ruined. Once she was off the hill and walking along Willow Avenue, several cars splashed her. The third time, Josie found herself longing for her nickel. At her office, Josie called a garage to pick up her VW and fix the glass and see if they couldn't save the upholstery. It was going to take a month at the very least, the man told her. In the language of Lues, Josie was certain that meant eight to ten weeks.

It was almost nine when she got off the phone. She opened her briefcase, double-checking on the Cooper novel, then leaned across her desk to grab up the folder marked 9:00 MWF. She stopped suddenly as she did. How exactly had Jack gotten into her office yesterday to write the note that was inside her 10:00 TR folder? She had been so distracted in front of her class, so full of the promise his words gave, and so happy about the prospect of the man being arrested that she hadn't noticed anything peculiar about what she had only assumed was Jack's latest and last message. But for Jack Hazard, it would not have been easy.

He had to have used a key. She was also certain he had used a key to get into her apartment when he left his welcome home message on her bathroom mirror. Dan Scholari, she thought, might be able to bluff his way through something like that. But unless Jack knew a janitor, . . . well that had to be it. Some nobody-janitor with all the keys. Or a secretary-girlfriend from one of the departments or a fluff-head in housing ready to do anything for a friendly smile. So he had gotten a key and come in and shuffled around in her papers and left his "promiss." When she thought about the card in her mailbox, however, it was a bit more complicated. From its placement in the stack, she was sure it had been left sometime after the office had opened at 8:00. And it wasn't campus mail, so someone had gone in and dropped it off. Jack Hazard walking into the department's main office without being noticed? The idea was ludicrous. The guy was a slew. That meant someone else had dropped it off. A secretary, maybe. Maybe a student worker. A janitor. No, not a janitor. Same problem. A janitor would be noticed. A student worker didn't make sense, either. That left the secretaries. She went through the short list of prospects, but there weren't any good ones.

She sat down at her desk and called Colt Fellows. She wanted to know exactly what Jack had told him, but Fellows wasn't in, so she asked for Officer Crouch. When she got Crouch, she explained to him what had happened with the notes at school. Officer Crouch wanted to know what she wanted him to do about it. "I have a problem seeing Jack doing something like that without an accomplice. If someone helped him, I'd like to know who it was."

Crouch didn't seem to pick up on what she was saying, and she interrupted his rambling with a degree of irritation, checking her watch and realizing she had to get to class. "I don't care *why* he did it," she snapped. "I want to know *how*. If someone around here is doing his bidding, I think the university needs to do something about it!"

"I think you probably need to talk to Colt. Colt's handling this."

"He's not in," Josie answered. "And I have to get to class. Will you tell him about this when he gets there?"

Silence. Maybe he is in, she told herself.

"I need to talk to Colt about this myself, don't I?" Josie asked finally.

"I can't do anything until Colt tells me to."

Josie looked at her watch. Six minutes late. She was talking to an idiot, and her class was about to get up and leave. Ten minutes was all they gave you. "Look, forget it! I'll call Colt when I get back from class."

Josie hung up in frustration. What was she doing? One day she was sure Dan Scholari was flying in from Boston, the next it was this hapless old ex-con who had looked genuinely happy to see her. . . . Well, he did do it! He knew someone! A secretary. She got a key for him as a favor, and she dropped the card off in Josie's mailbox the next morning. She broke some rules. She broke some serious rules, and if nothing else, she needed to be confronted about it.

Once outside, Josie broke into a run and made it to class just as her students were rising and shuffling toward the door. They gave the obligatory groans, most of them good-natured. Today, the lecture was about the dying frontier, she announced, discarding her worries with the sudden excitement of knowing what she doing: "The evils of civilization—read *matriarchy,* ladies and gentlemen, as in *mama rules*—and America's *hero-male* on the run, as in, 'I don't want to grow up!'"

Sixteen hands hit the air at once. *God bless Annie Wilde!*

When class finished, Josie went back to her office and called Colt again and once again couldn't get through. She called again after her next class and then throughout the rest of the morning and into lunch hour. Out. Out. Busy. He's on the other line. Can I have him return your call? I'll see he gets the message. Waiting for his call, she grew impatient and tried again. Colt Fellows's office. I'm afraid he's busy. Certainly. Maybe you had better give me that number again. Josie set her phone down and looked tiredly at her watch. It was after one o'clock. Maybe she had better just get a taxi and go down there, but as she started to get her things, her door rumbled. She went around her desk and looked out from behind the curtain. Dick Ferrington, tweed jacket and penny loafers, a touch of gray in the temples, a square jaw set hard with a little angry twitch of the nerve just over the bone. Something was the matter.

She unlocked the door and opened it. "Dick," she said, "come on in." As he walked in, he asked that she keep the door open, all very professional in a paranoid way. He remained standing, scowling, his face bright red. He had a newspaper rolled up in his hand and he slapped it absently against his leg.

"What's the matter?" she asked, looking first at the paper curiously, then into his eyes. He was angry about something, not just perturbed or upset!

"That's what I want to know, Josie."

"What are you talking about?"

"I think you know. I mean we can both read the newspaper, can't we!" He shook the thing at her.

"The paper?"

Dread coursed through her as Ferrington tossed the thing on her desk. "You mean to tell me you didn't see this? You're the talk of campus, Josie!"

She unrolled the baton and saw on the lower right quadrant of the front page the headline, "Local Professor Assaulted in Topless Bar."

"Oh, God!"

What followed was a rather extensive and complete, if not entirely accurate, narrative of Josie's complaint against Jack Hazard, identified as her stepfather. *Colt Fellows.* Damn him! She would kill him!

"You think the university condones this kind of behavior, Josie?"

Josie's anger with Fellows and the anonymous author of the article faded briefly as she tried to absorb what Dick was saying. "What *behavior?* What are you talking about, Dick? Being *assaulted?*"

"That bar, Josie! It's nothing but a whorehouse. According to this, you were trying to get work out there!"

She started to protest, wanted to explain, but stopped herself. She didn't need to give Dick Ferrington an explanation. "I don't think I quite understand what your role is in this, Dick."

"I'm trying to find out what's going on with these charges and this 'audition.' What's it mean? What are you doing? Are you stripping?" He asked this with an incredulous bit of a laugh tagged on, as if he thought there might be some better explanation but he couldn't imagine what it was. She saw all the faces of that morning again, felt the cool breeze of gossip at her back, and it all made sense. The silence before her office door, the complete lack of visitors, even the excess of absences in her two classes, like a holiday was coming up and she didn't know about it. She was the new department leper, and just hadn't realized it until Dick Ferrington came by to let her know about the quarantine.

"Is this an official visit, Dick?"

"If I don't get some answers, I imagine the dean will want some. You don't have tenure here, Josie. You're on thin ice with this stuff."

"I've got a contract, Dick, and I don't remember any passages in it about having to ask your permission before I go to a bar!"

"We do have a morality clause. You think about that."

"I think I'd like for you to leave, that's what I think."

"Fine." He looked around the office. "Oh, and by the way, if I were you, I wouldn't carry that gun on campus. Permit to carry or not, and I seriously doubt you have one of those, there's a weapons ban on campus unless you're law enforcement. The way you're going, someone might just tip off security. That will get you fired, even if stripping won't."

"I don't know what you're talking about." ·

Dick shook his head, his smile as ugly as anything she had ever seen. "You're messing up big-time, Josie. This stuff will follow you through your whole career." He smiled wickedly. "Or maybe I should say *non*career."

He was out in the hall as he finished this observation, and Josie followed him. She caught herself before she responded. She thought about explanations, then profanities. Damn him, anyway! What right did he have saying anything to her? The man had murdered his own wife!

Wisely, she said nothing. Instead, she slammed her door as she walked back into her office. It sounded like a gunshot, and it took some of the edge off her sudden rage. Dick had left the paper, apparently so she could read it at her leisure. She picked it up and forced her way through it. It took several attempts before she could get all the way through, her fury reigniting at every statement, her eyes swimming out of focus. Finally, she shook off the confusion and steeled herself to read all of what lay on the page:

LOCAL PROFESSOR ASSAULTED IN TOPLESS BAR

Lues State University lecturer Josie Darling filed charges of assault against John Christian Hazard yesterday, after an incident at the Bust of Country in Codswallop late Wednesday afternoon. According to Darling's complaint, Hazard, who is Darling's stepfather, grabbed her and dragged her toward the club's exit with malicious intent. Patrons who witnessed the event, however, said the trouble began when Darling, 27, attempted to audition in the nude and Hazard, 53, dragged her from the dance stage and expelled her from the club, only partially clothed. Police Chief Colt Fellows commented that his department became involved because Hazard appeared at a local restaurant. "We knew the sheriff had a warrant out on Mr. Hazard, and we apprehended him."

Josie slapped the paper down. She checked her watch and stepped out into the hallway. Val was listening to a woman talking about her abortion. Josie sighed and looked for a friendly face, but the halls were empty. She thought about Clarissa Holt, but Val would be the one to handle this. Ferrington's enemy, if she had read the signs correctly, and perfectly willing to step into the arena against him.

Impatiently she peeked into Val's office again. Val glanced up, and the girl sitting before him turned to look at Josie, her face red, streaming with tears.

"Yes, Josie?" Val called. He seemed faintly irritated at the intrusion, nothing more.

"Can we talk when you're free, Val?" Josie asked. She was sick at interrupting such a scene.

"I'll leave," the girl announced.

"No! I didn't mean to interrupt!" The girl ducked her head and left the office. Josie watched her guiltily until Val told her to come in. Like one of the penitents, Josie took a seat before him. The chair was actually hot. Josie said nothing for a moment. She simply looked at Val and tried to collect herself. Finally, feeling her world crumbling and unable to stop it, Josie announced, "I need your help."

Short Skirts

Josie spent nearly an hour talking to Henry Valentine about what had happened to her since she had arrived in Lues and most of the things that had gone on before. She told him everything about her past in Lues, even the parts that weren't published for the world to read. She described her fears about Dan when she had arrived, the threats she had received, the fact that Dan hadn't been involved, her visit to Codswallop to find Jack's brother, the broken glass in her car, the note she'd found, the visit to the police and the subsequent assault charges against Jack Hazard.

There were no more secrets, no more shades of truth. She finished her narrative with the latest bump in the road, Dick Ferrington in the incredible role of the university's moral guardian. She needed someone she could trust, someone close to things at the university who could tell her what she ought to do. That was what she said. What she wanted, the reason she went to Valentine, was help from someone with real power, someone whom the others feared. It seemed to her the only way to survive this mess. If Valentine stood with her, even Ferrington might hesitate. The more she talked, the more certain she was that Val was the right person to go to. Val listened with a kind of genius. He caught the nuances of an event at once. He grew excited as she became excited, he was full of pity or outrage or sympathy, according to the story's turns. He didn't intrude on her telling, never stopped the flow, never gave the look that so many do almost unconsciously: *What do you want me to do about it?* Val listened as we imagine, in our weaker moments, God must listen. His patience was beyond measure. She realized that he didn't force her to eclipse the details. When he spoke, his observations were incisive but always with empathy.

When she had finished her story, and he had asked a certain number of questions and seemed to understand all that had happened, Val raised his eyebrows with the resignation of a man who knows the shallowness of human emotion and announced: "This Chief Fellows set you up, Josie."

"But why?" Josie revolted at the naivete of her own protest, but could hardly help herself. She had trusted Colt Fellows, even if she had not especially liked him. They had had an understanding. They had made a deal!

"You're *college*, Josie. He's a *slew*. Slews hate anything to do with us. It wasn't even personal. It was just a cheap shot, and he took it because he could." Val's big loose lips gave a smile of condolence. He knew it wasn't right or fair. Only a fact of life.

Josie felt the air running out of her. She was beat up again. Only this time, the bruises wouldn't show for a while. "I'll sue the bastards," Josie murmured, meaning Fellows as well as the newspaper.

Val studied Josie calmly. "You could sue," he offered, "but from what you say, you might not get any satisfaction."

"But it's a lie!" There was that naive kid screaming again. Josie fought to get a handle on it. She hadn't the luxury of idealism. She was in the middle of a dirty fight, and she needed to think like a survivor, not the perennial victim!

"From what you tell me, it's a matter of perspective," Val said. "Eighty men, as you say, saw the thing one way, you saw it another."

Josie thought about the men and the voice of the disc jockey. She thought about what she had done to Jack. She saw how others could perceive her actions. An objective view of the facts would not include the necessary subtleties of this case. Objectivity, like any other perspective, had its limitations. Objectively, Josie Darling had entered the Bust of Country for the purpose of getting work. She had had her job interview, then faced the crowd and lost her courage. Now she was filing charges of assault for the sake of her bruised arm and lost dignity. Had the paper really taken it much farther than that? Couldn't Colt Fellows tell the story of their interview any way he wanted?

"Even if you prove maliciousness on the part of the paper or this Chief Fellows," Val told her, "you won't get any sympathy from the slews, and they're the ones sitting on the juries, not the professors or the students. The hard truth is," he went on, "anyone who reads about this incident, and everyone will, is going to believe it. What you may want to think about," Val offered, "is how you want to handle our dean when he approaches you about it."

"The dean?" The dean seemed like one more absurdity tossed into the stew, but Val was serious.

"Here's the fix," he said. "If he comes after you for this, you're vulnerable to an investigation."

"Why? I don't understand." Josie felt a mild pressure screwing down into the middle of her chest.

"He could use the morality clause in your contract, as Dick mentioned, or he could be particularly devious and invoke the 'no moonlighting' clause." Val had a faint, perverse glee in this thought. And why not? Universities are merely asylums without warders. Josie swore dully at her diminishing prospects.

Val considered matters for a moment, then shook his head. "I doubt he's smart enough to try the moonlighting issue. That might even work. If he does anything, he'll jump for the morality clause. Moral high ground and all that. Eventually, of course, you'll win your case in court, assuming you fight it long enough, but the point is, professionally, you'll be washed up."

Pistolas in thirty minutes or less? Not so funny anymore.

"If you refuse to take legal action, they work you over, humiliate you for a while, then leave you wearing the stigmata of scandal. Even after they discover you did nothing wrong. You'll get work, maybe. But the recommendations will always have a shadow."

"So how do I stop it? I mean I don't like either of my choices here, Val." Josie was smiling, but the look was all teeth and grit.

"Dick Ferrington has Dean Meyers's confidence. Dick is the one who can help you."

"I think I blew that angle." Josie's smile stayed locked in place. She was having trouble breathing and the pain in her chest had sharpened. She kept thinking this was all absurdly funny, and no one was laughing. Why weren't they laughing? Audition. For God's sake, it was just a stupid joke!

"Mend the fence, Josie. Tell Dick what you told me. Throw yourself on his mercy. He'll come through for you. Deep down, I know he still has a lot of respect for you."

"I'm not so sure. After what just happened, I don't think he wants to hear anything I have to say."

Val considered this briefly. "Dick's problem with you," he explained, "is that he supported your candidacy. He told everyone on his committee what a great scholar you are. Then you arrived and you weren't what people expected. You weren't what Dick expected, for that matter."

"What do you mean?" Josie was genuinely confused by this. Things had been going well! What was the problem? What exactly had people expected?

Val had the look of letting something out that he shouldn't have. He was faintly embarrassed, but he pushed on, now that it was started. "I've heard several things, Josie. Much of it from Dick . . . indirectly. I'm afraid we haven't shared confidences for a number of years."

"Like what? What's he not happy about, Val?"

"Provocative outfits, aggressive language in the classroom."

"*Provocative outfits? Aggressive language*? What the hell are you talking about?"

Val lifted his eyebrows and broad shoulders in an expression of infinite weariness. He was only too familiar with Richard Ferrington's methods, it seemed. "Dick isn't happy with creativity, Josie. To be honest, I think you intimidate him with your . . . abilities. In the abstract, of course, he admires good teaching. In practice, it shows him up as a plodder. He can't very well say that, of course, so he and his new girlfriend make hay with the short skirts and the things they hear from students. The odd remark, the quirky theories. The sentence out of context. The occasional profanity. It's an old trick, but still a good one."

Josie tried to defend herself. There was nothing wrong with the way she dressed. In Boston, it would have been stodgy! As for aggressive language, she had never . . . well, once! But wasn't it the academic's right—even duty!—to be outrageous?

Valentine gave her sentiment the respect it deserved, but then, like a gentleman of the Old South, suggested the wisdom of conformity. More conservative outfits, perhaps. Less enthusiasm in the classroom, certainly. Above all, a bit more care about her friendships.

"*Friendships?*" She had no friends! What was he talking about?

"There's some loose talk about your relationship with the lesbian in communications, Josie."

For a moment, Josie could not speak. She simply stared at the old professor in confusion. "You mean Clarissa Holt? I don't understand? I didn't know she was . . . I mean, who the hell has the *right*—?" She stopped herself, felt her chest pounding with outrage. "This is unbelievable, Val!"

"You didn't know?"

"No." She meant to say she didn't care, that no one in this day and age should care, but at the moment, she was feeling a bit punch-drunk, and the words just wouldn't come.

"You caught a ride home with her last night?"

"How did you know that, Val?"

"Tongues are clucking, Josie."

"Nell McGraw?"

"I don't want to name names. I just thought you should know there's speculation."

Thought you would be in line for those honors, Josie. She didn't sleep with Ferrington, ergo she must be a lesbian!

"It's fine with me whatever orientation you have, Josie, but again, you might want to think about the impression you make with . . . the more conservative members of our faculty, at least until you have a tenured position. They *are* the majority, after all, and they *are* the ones who vote for your tenure."

Josie stood up angrily. Then she sat down again. She didn't care what anyone thought! In the next instant, she was trying to tell Valentine that she was not attracted to women. She had been married, for God's sake. Val nodded agreeably. Marriage was no defense, though he was polite enough not to say it. Conformity coursing through her like a Mickey, she counted the number of slacks she owned, the possible male faculty members she could date, and more traditional approaches to the classroom. Long lectures on Henry James might help. Then hating herself for even considering it, she decided the best thing to do was to resign. Even if it meant never teaching again!

And then? Then nothing. Her whole life she had wanted to teach, and now it was as good as lost.

Val smiled benignly as her life unraveled before him. "People have to have something to talk about, Josie. You just happen to be the flavor of the month. My advice is keep your head down, mind your manners, and ask Dick Ferrington for his help with the dean. I'll try to say something scandalous next week and take the pressure off."

This was a joke, of sorts, but Josie was still struggling with the concept of passive obedience and kissing up to Dr. Ferrington. "So I have to go to Dick Ferrington or this whole thing trails after me for the rest of my life? That's what you're saying, isn't it? That and wear slacks and give duller lectures and make sure everyone knows I'm a healthy, happy, totally nonfunctioning heterosexual? Is that it, Val?"

It seemed almost to hurt him, but Val told her that about covered it.

Margaret Bennet

Colt Fellows dodged people so routinely that he hardly ever returned calls without at least four or five messages. He had been seasoned under the old system of message taking and had fired three secretaries who had urged him toward the new technology of voice mail. If he wanted to hear the bastards talking, he would answer the damn phone! Or so he said. Margaret Bennet was perfectly comfortable with Colt's methods and idiosyncrasies, all of them, thank you. She took phone messages so routinely that, as a rule, she didn't even bother calling in to see if Colt might be interested in talking to the caller. She said things like he wasn't in or he wasn't available or he was in conference or he was in the field, and she didn't mind doing it because that was the job. Colt was an important person and everybody wanted to talk to important people. His wife Betty got through. Two of Colt's three kids got through. Department players calling from outside got through, and that was it. Inside, of course, the policemen could ring him directly, at their peril. The mayor left messages, the state's attorney needed six or seven calls, the sheriff had to explain to Margaret his business before Colt would return his call, and if the governor ever called, Colt's very words, "I ain't in, and I ain't coming back."

It was, in a managerial sense, a very insulated administration. Josie Darling—with the legs and aren't I proud of them—made several attempts to get Colt that Friday, the day after Jack Hazard's arrest. Margaret Bennet had written, "important, something about keys." The next half-dozen she took down whatever the woman told her to, and that was it. She left Colt alone. She had no expectation of moving Colt to returning her calls. Margaret understood that her job was to be eagerly concerned, passionately ignorant, and forthrightly protective of the boss. For that service, she received good ratings on her quarter-annual reviews, regular pay increases each of her three years as an administrative secretary, and a sweet little bonus of one hundred dollars every now and then, directly from Colt's pocket to her purse, and not even her kids knew about that money, let alone the IRS. The money wasn't all that important. Margaret was hopelessly poor, and it mattered, but what mattered even more was that Colt appreciated her. Colt Fellows had a number of shortcomings, among them an inability to speak without profanity, but the one thing that he possessed to the point of genius was the ability to create private alliances. He had stepped in, for instance, when Margaret's ex-husband two years back was making noise about getting custody of their four children. Bertrand had never wanted to be around them when they were married! It was nonsense, purely a nuisance because the man was a hopeless drunk and hated the kids, but he did it because he had the money to do it and because Margaret couldn't afford even a bad attorney, and without one, she was bullied and scared and could hardly sleep for the worry of it all. Margaret had gone to Colt finally, and within a matter of days, her ex-husband had ended up in the hospital. When he got out, he left town, the way he should have before he got his limp.

There were other alliances as well. Margaret hadn't gotten to be the boss's secretary by being ignorant. Every player in the department had some private history with Colt. It wasn't that kind of sloppy allegiance that usually happens between administrators and their subordinates, poker players and beer-drinking buddies evolving into professional allies. With Colt, there was always a service and a debt. Everyone knew if you wanted something taken care of, you only had to ask, no promises made and none asked, but when Colt asked a favor in return, you did it without being asked twice. Colt Fellows had a sublimely simple notion of justice in the law and fairness in the work place: everything went his way or everything went to hell in a hurry.

At 4:30 on Friday, on the twentieth of September, Margaret Bennet patched Sheriff Cal Yeager through to her boss per her instructions. The sheriff and Colt spoke amiably, Colt's big voice booming, Yeager's voice equally affable but never possessing the raw rough and tumble of a man like Colt Fellows. Jason Morgan said Yeager was sheriff because of Colt, whatever that meant. Margaret didn't know about that, but Cal Yeager sure was the most agreeable man Margaret ever listened in on. Per her instructions.

As Colt spoke, it became clear that he wanted Yeager's cooperation, and following the lead, Yeager had answered as Colt obviously expected him to. If Colt wanted to bring the prisoner down personally, that was fine with him. Late this evening? No problem. Whatever Colt Fellows wanted was fine. Always had been, always would be.

"You'll want to be on hand when I get there, Cal, and maybe a deputy or two extra. I'm bringing Jack Hazard down. You remember Jack, don't you?"

"I sure do, Colt, and I'll make sure we have a couple of extra men ready to help out."

There was a light exchange about dinner sometime. They had been promising each other a social evening for as long as Margaret had been recording their calls, probably the whole thirty years they had known each other. Then Yeager clicked off, and Colt Fellows punched Margaret Bennet's extension. "You get that, Peg?"

"I got it recorded, Colt."

"It's a keeper. Get a fax out over my signature to Cal and copies to Stackman upstairs. Keep it simple. John Christian Hazard is 'an extremely dangerous prisoner' and I want to make the delivery myself, so there won't be any problems. Time and date stamp on all copies, and a copy in our files, too."

"Do you want to see it before I send it?"

"I got to go get drunk with Corny Callahan and Ham Evans in about twenty minutes, Peg. Am I going to have time to see it?"

"I'll try, Colt."

"You're the greatest, kid."

Well, of course, she was.

Five minutes later, Tobias Crouch walked into Margaret's office. Margaret was busy preparing Colt's fax but immediately intercepted him. Gun at his side and badge on his fat chest or not, Toby Crouch was most definitely not a player. Colt had gotten him a job on the force sometime in the last century, and that was the end of it. Crotch-Sniff was "somebody's dead cousin's orphaned pet rock," that was Colt's description, and his position in Colt's hierarchy had never changed.

"Do you have an appointment, Officer Crouch?"

"He told me to be here . . . now." Crotch-Sniff looked at his watch, then smiled at her. As smiles went, it had all the appeal of curdled milk. Margaret didn't like the man. He never called her by her name, never looked at her, unless Margaret wasn't looking, then, of course, he looked plenty! Margaret was thirty-nine and holding (on for dear life). She watched herself. She didn't let herself go the way some women did. After all, you never knew what fish you might catch, as long as you kept a worm on your hook.

Margaret slid back to her desk without answering, and the thick mahogany door that led to Colt's big office opened as Patrolman Crotch-Sniff pushed through.

"Key-rye-st!" Colt screamed, "you still on that cane?"

Crotch-Sniff stood with the door still open, cane in hand. He mumbled something. He was just inside the room, but Margaret couldn't hear him.

She heard Colt Fellows fine, however. "I forgot about that frigging ankle, Tobias!"

The door closed. Colt had something dirty going on. Something to do with Yeager and Crouch. Now that was an odd pair. What could Colt be planning with Yeager and Crotch-Sniff? That was a mystery.

Margaret finished Colt's memo to Cal Yeager, short but sweet, and hit the print button, stamped them, and scribbled a perfect likeness of Colt Fellows's signature, perfect because Colt's signature was always done in Margaret's hand.

The door opened as she was getting ready to fax the letter. Colt's voice, ". . . tell your mother it's going to be Watch Commander Crouch! See how she likes that!"

Crotch-Sniff came into Margaret's domain, a mean little smile slopping over his fat cheeks. *Watch Commander Crouch?* Well now, that was real interesting, wasn't it?

Shooting a Dog

Having scanned his eyes over Peg and her memo to Yeager, Colt Fellows left his office around five o'clock. He was in a good mood.

In the Civic Center parking lot, the rain still falling, Colt climbed into his LTD. The big eight purred like a well-fed lap cat as he took off.

Five minutes later, he slipped into Pauli's shaking hands, shouting, and buying a couple of rounds of drinks. All the while, Corny sat up on high, watching him like some kind of royalty. When Colt finally climbed the stairs and sat down with the mayor and his city manager, Corny asked him how life was treating him. Colt knew better than to be too happy about things, and said life would be better if he could give some of his people new patrol cars. Corny thought that was a good idea. Over a second round of drinks, the mayor finally got around to business, a new security company was coming into town, he said. As a personal favor, Corny wanted to make sure they didn't have any troubles. Colt said a good security company just made his job easier. Corny thought so too, and that was it, all that he wanted to say.

About half an hour after seven, mellow with his drinks and satisfied Corny and Ham were up to no end of mischief, Colt went on home to his supper. There were a couple of phone calls, which Betty intercepted, then after dinner, Colt asked for some coffee. Betty was afraid he was going to be up half the night, and he told her he hoped so, because he was working late.

About two years before, Colt had gotten something going with Peg Bennet. Peg just loved her boss, that was a blessed fact. It was nothing that was going to break up a marriage, just a little fun now and again. Peg was a good girl and knew that Betty, who for all her faults, was going to stay Colt's wife. Peg wasn't stepping into that kind of game. All's well when you don't get caught. Right? Well, Betty knew. How she knew, he didn't know. But she knew. She knew the first time it happened, and she'd given him a look damn near every time it happened since. So now, when he said he was working late, she didn't believe it, though she didn't say anything. Still, it was written all over her face what she really wanted to say, *It's Peg Bennet, isn't it?* How the hell was Colt going to tell Betty that she had it all wrong this time, that tonight he was going to have himself some real fun?

At 8:30, Colt arrived at the civic center and ordered the prisoner's hands and feet cuffed, his hands behind his back, and a chain to shackle his wrist and ankle cuffs. Since his incarceration, Jack Hazard had been an agreeable prisoner, except for demanding a lawyer, but for this occasion, at Colt's instruction, three men showed up, one with a shotgun. He wanted nothing at all to go wrong. After Colt's call to the cell block, he ordered his Ford LTD gassed and vacuumed. He said he wanted his Remington pump shotgun, fully loaded, and he wanted a box of shells in the trunk. When he finished with his orders, Colt went to one of his cabinets and pulled out his old .44, a flat black piece with a six-inch barrel and an ugly bore that spit a slug big enough to take out a fist-sized chunk of flesh. The first gun he ever wore as a police officer, it was damn near an antique, but it was still the best weapon he owned, the gun he wanted when there was serious business waiting. After cleaning and loading it, Colt tucked it in his pants at the small of his back, then slipped on his shoulder holster with his service revolver, a .38 Smith & Wesson. As an afterthought, he cached a box of .38 hollow points in his sports jacket's pocket. A man claiming to expect trouble had, by God, better look ready for it!

At nine o'clock, Colt heard someone stepping into Peg's office. He called out Crouch's name, and the old boy limped in. Crouch was in uniform, but he had his foot wrapped and he was still on that frigging cane. Colt considered him a moment, then told him to get the ankle unwrapped and ditch the cane.

He watched the fat man bending over to take off his shoe, then went on out. "You aren't down to lock up in six minutes," Colt announced pleasantly, "I'm going to forget all about what I said this afternoon. You're back on the streets, Tobias. You understand me?" Leaving Crouch, Fellows skipped on down the stairs instead of taking the elevator, stopping twice to adjust his .44, the second time tightening his belt, so that it would stay in place. At lock up, Colt entered the holding cell to check his jailer's work. Jack Hazard's face was blue and puffy, with several abrasions. There were still some open cuts on his cheeks, and his lips were torn up some. Colt's answer to Jack's request to see a lawyer.

Jack looked up when Colt entered the holding area. "Any trouble with the prisoner?" Colt asked, meeting the little maggot's gaze dead-on.

"No sir," his jailer answered.

"Must mean he learned his lesson. You learn your lesson, Jack?"

Jack answered with his eyes, a blank, contented animal look, not even a blink. Twenty years in prison, Jack Hazard hadn't learned a damn thing, except to wait for his chances. Jack was wearing city colors, a bright orange, one-piece jumpsuit. He had his boots on for the transfer, his civilian clothes in a little pile beside him. Jack was sitting on a bench, uncomfortably twisted off to the side with his weight on one haunch. He was forced to sit like this, since his hands were pulled tightly down to his ass and the chain running behind his legs to his ankle cuffs cut into the seat of the bench.

"You don't look so comfortable, Jack. Let me know if them chains are a little too tight."

Colt's jailer, Fig Newton, handed Colt a small ring with two keys. "Here's the keys to unlock him."

The door jarred behind them, and Colt turned to see Crouch through the bars. Newton pulled his keys out and opened the steel door. With a show of irritation, Colt looked at his watch, then slipped the keys Fig had given him into his right front pants pocket. Jack watched him do this with studied indifference. Colt didn't like the look at all. Too damn calm about everything, too certain of himself. Maybe he didn't get it. Or maybe he had something lined up.

"Fig, you take the prisoner out the back and put him in the LTD."

When he was alone with Crouch, Colt asked the fat man, "You up to this, Tobias?"

"Looking forward to it, Colt. Him or us, right?"

Colt grinned. His very words back at him. "Him or us, buddy. And don't you worry about anything going wrong afterwards. Cal Yeager will be there personally. Cal owes me. We make our report just like I told you, and that's it. Not a worry in the world. You understand?"

"What about the professor?"

"She's nothing. I'll handle the professor."

"Woman like that might hire a lawyer if she thinks we lied."

"Woman like that might just end up a corpse in Lues Creek Canyon like her mamma, Tobias."

Crouch smiled, and it was a damn happy look, all things considered. "No problem with that, Colt. Might even be more fun than tonight."

Colt put both hands on the patrolman's broad shoulders and leveled his gaze on the man. "Tobias, it don't get more fun than tonight."

Jack was waiting when Colt and Crouch came out. He followed their movements, noticed Crouch limping. Colt was pretty sure Jack had the thing figured out when he looked up and met Colt's gaze. In Colt's LTD, there was a screen between the back seat and the front. Once he was settled, Colt studied Jack's bruised face through the steel mesh. A thin string of blood ran out from his nose and curled into his swollen, cracked lips. "A little ride in the country, Jack. How does that sound?"

Jack smiled with one side of his mouth, his eyes slipping out toward the darkness. He knew. This night had been coming for years, ever since Josie Fortune had leveled that Purdey on Colt. It was funny how things had finally come together. Proved the wisdom of patience. By God, ever since he had been out, Jack Hazard had been skirting the city limits like he knew Colt was there waiting for him. Then Josie Fortune's kid walks into his office and delivers the son of a bitch!

"I've got a question for you, Jack." Colt saw Jack shifting his attention from the dark woods to the mirror. The two men were suddenly looking at each other in the mirror, time draining out, and Colt felt a chill of apprehension despite everything. "You been writing notes to Josie's little girl?"

Nothing but silence. "I didn't think so. Not quite your style, is it?" Still nothing. Colt looked at Crouch. "Like taking a dog out to shoot it, eh, Tobias?"

"Lot more fun, Colt."

Colt laughed. "Got that right!"

The rain hadn't let up, not for two days, but it hadn't gotten worse either, just a Lues mist, the kind of stuff that could settle in for weeks. As Colt drove, he used the wiper for a while, then got tired of hearing it and turned it off for a half minute at a time. The radio crackled until they were well south of the city limits, at which point Colt reached down and shut it off. The highway cut back west after a couple of miles, but Pauper Bluff was southeast. There was no direct way to get there—if you took the highway it was fifteen, twenty miles out of your way. And no woods. Of course, most people avoided the gravel roads and took the long way, especially at night. At night, the road to Pauper Bluff was damn near as lonely as poor Jack Hazard sitting in Colt's backseat!

"Here's another question for you, Jack! Maybe you can answer this one. What do you suppose you'd do if you knew who dropped that watch with your name on it in the canyon? You let a man get away with that?" Nothing more than a hard look.

"Ever since you've been out, I've been waiting for you, buddy. For a while there, I was damned sure you were just too stupid to put it together, but you know what? I think prison broke you, Jack. I think you're just flat scared of me."

Jack Hazard's smile was a cold, crooked piece of work. "To tell you the truth, Colt, I couldn't see you doing it. Looked to me like way too much effort for a fat ass like you."

Colt smiled, even though he hated being called a fat ass. Crotch-Sniff was a fat ass. Colt was . . . big. "Remember how we talked the night Two-Bit pulled Josie out of the canyon, Jack? You gave me everything I needed, buddy. Times, alibis . . . everything! Hell, it was *too* easy! I couldn't resist! I had you off in the woods all afternoon. Not a soul besides your brother Louis to say you didn't go into that canyon. Now, normally, you're right. I wouldn't take the trouble to get someone to engrave that watch, but I had a friend who owed me one. And what the hell, you and Josie crossed me a good one, so we had unfinished business."

"You ever get the stink of piss out of those pants, Colt?"

Colt's face flushed red, but his eyes caught Jack's. "Watch yourself, buddy."

Jack's eyes cut toward Crouch. "What are you going to do to me if I don't?"

"You know Josie's little girl is all grown-up these days, Jack. Looks a lot like her mother, but I'll bet she's a whole lot easier to handle."

"You leave her alone."

"What are you going to do to me if I don't? Toby here tells me he wants to take her into the canyon and give her what her mamma had. Thinks it'd be a hell of a good time."

Nothing. Absolutely nothing.

"You got anything more you want to say to me, Jack?"

Nothing again.

Colt saw Lues Creek cutting over the road in front of him and pulled his cruiser to a halt in the middle of the road. He looked in the mirror, saw Jack watching him. "You remember Hazy Mundy, don't you, Jack? What was it, three or four slugs of a .22 he put in your belly before you got that little gun out of his hands?" Jack's eyes were cold, flat, and disinterested. "I always said Hazy Mundy had the right idea, just the wrong fucking caliber. If the old boy'd had a .44 like I'm packing tonight, this world would be a better place!"

Colt pulled his cell phone out and called the sheriff's dispatcher. Identifying himself, Colt asked for Yeager, who came on a couple of seconds later.

Colt told him they were at Lues Creek Crossing. Their prisoner was begging for a rest stop. Then he laughed, "Just like a dog, Cal. Sees a tree, got to lift his leg!" Cal answered with an amiable bark of static, and Colt told him he would give them a call when they were on the road again.

Colt slung himself around and pulled himself out of the big car, leaving his door open and the engine running. They hadn't seen a car since they had gotten off the highway. Up ahead, just in sight of Colt's headlights was Lues Creek Crossing. At the moment, it was a forty foot spread of water interrupting the road. A few inches under the surface, at least it was a few inches most times of the year, the ground was hunched up to form a mole to drive across. "Rest stop, gentlemen," Colt announced amiably. He slapped the roof of his car, meaning to startle Jack, then leaned in and told Crouch to get out of the car and take care of business if he had to. Colt walked off the road into the woods a few steps. Standing in the shadows and unzipping his pants, he watched Toby Crouch get out of the car and head into the woods.

With its driver's door open and the headlights on, Colt's Ford was lit up, and he could see Jack clearly in the backseat waiting for them, knowing his life was over. Be interesting to see if Jack held out like that to the bitter end. Just stare back at Colt while he aimed a gun at Jack's heart. Colt shook his head. Long time coming, but he was about to find out. A damn shame about Tobias, though. Pretty much trust him to keep his mouth shut, but damn stupid to put yourself that deep in anyone's pocket. Colt zipped up his pants, then reached back and checked his grip on the .44. Besides, with a cop down, nobody would dare look at Colt Fellows, not even Jason Morgan. That was the beauty of it.

Beyond the car maybe ten or fifteen feet, Crouch was out in the trees taking his last whiz. He was supposed to pull Jack out, then step away. Just like that. After Colt shot Jack, they would get the cuffs off, and then take Crouch's revolver and wrap Jack's hands around it, while they put a round in the fender of the LTD. That was the script that Crouch was following, at least. Just that much better turning the gun on him at the last second and hitting him point-blank. Simple, easy, and best of all, no bullet hole in Colt's new Ford!

Colt checked the road in either direction, then walked back to the car. Crouch was already there waiting for him. "Get him out of the car, Tobias."

Colt stood directly behind his car. His right hand hung to his side, his left hand rested lightly on the trunk. Crouch had some trouble after he opened the door. Jack wasn't coming. He had turned himself into dead weight and rolled back to the other side of the car, putting his chest to the seat, like a whining kid refusing to come out. So he was human, after all. Colt grinned. He was hoping the little son of a bitch would beg at the end, but hell, this was even better. It looked like he might even cry!

Crouch reached in farther, taking the chain and pulling Jack toward him, Jack's face dragging across the seat. Once Jack's legs came out of the car, Crouch leaned forward to get him by the shoulders before he could crawl back into the car again. Colt called out to be careful, but he was too late. At just that moment, Jack bucked back hard into Crouch. The force of his body knocked Crouch off him. Then, instead crawling back into the car again, Jack slipped off the seat and fell out into the road. Crouch screamed out, and Colt realized Jack had just stomped on his injured ankle. So he was going to make a fight out of it! As Crouch staggered back across the road, Jack Hazard sprang to his feet and followed him. With his feet chained and his hands bound tight behind his back, it was curious the way he had to move, but he was faster than Colt could have imagined, faster than a damn rattle snake! He was right on top of Crouch suddenly, and when Crouch finally stopped reeling back, Jack was face-to-face with him. Then he ducked down and turned, going for the holstered revolver on Crouch's hip.

Colt peeled his sports jacket back out of the way and got hold of the .44 as soon as Jack made his move. It hadn't really surprised him. Other than a slight bump of adrenaline, he was perfectly at ease, even smiling. He stepped out from behind his car while they danced across the road. Then, as Jack swept around to grab the revolver, Colt let off a round that kicked Crouch off his feet and sent him down flat and hard on his back. That left Jack Hazard standing by himself, his fingers catching nothing but air. Colt brought his thumb over the hammer of his big gun and cocked it without hesitating. As he fired it, Jack fell to the ground beside Crouch. Hit? Not waiting to be sure, Colt brought the hammer back once more and stepped one stride closer for his last shot. He saw Jack slide his back beside Crouch's holster, then wiggle slightly. Colt fired the third round at Jack's chest. He was positive this one got him, especially when he saw Jack's legs kick up and his body twist. At the same time, though, something hit Colt's shoulder, slamming him back off his feet. The shots were fired simultaneously, or nearly so, causing Colt's .44 to obliterate the bark of the .38, but the echo of both guns came back out of the trees, and Colt thought at first a Hazard had picked him off from the woods.

He couldn't seem to take his thoughts beyond that during the next second or two, then found himself focusing only when he realized that he was sitting in a puddle of water beside the rear bumper of his car. His .44 was just out of reach, close to his feet. He looked across at Crouch's prone body and expected to see Jack there too, but Jack was standing. Eighteen feet separated them. Jack held Crouch's .38. His hands were still bound tightly to his buttocks by the cuffs and chain. Jack's body was hunched up strangely, and his head was twisted about slightly, so he could look at his target. From eighteen feet, Jack's chances of a kill shot were slim, and Colt reached confidently for his holstered .38. The action was smooth and quick. Colt was a thirty-year veteran, by God! He could sure as hell handle an old man bundled up in chains with his hands cuffed behind his back!

Two shots hit him before he could pull the gun. He knew it was bad. He could feel the fire turn his guts liquid, and even though his fist was locked around his .38, he couldn't move his arm to get the thing out of the holster, even though his life depended on it. He heard the gunshots and the first echo crackling out of the trees, but that was the last conscious moment he had. When the third bullet slammed between his eyes, Colt Fellows was dead before his head kicked back into the puddle.

The Last Man Standing

Jack Hazard glanced down at Crouch and dropped the .38 well out of his reach, then hopped toward Colt. At the foot of the big man's corpse, he threw himself to his knees and rolled up against Colt's body with his hands close to the man's hips and thighs. He got hold of the right front trouser pocket and ripped the cloth with two mild jerks, Jack's body convulsing in order to leverage the tear. He felt about in the gravel and mud, touching coins and then the ring with the keys. It took nearly a minute of fumbling before the tiny key fit into the keyhole and the cuffs slipped off. As they did, the chain between his ankle cuffs and wrist cuffs went slack. He reached down and unfastened the ankle cuffs next, leaving the padlock on the chain unopened.

Dropping the keys in the gravel, Jack stood up, moving his limbs in odd, pleasant jerks.

He studied Colt Fellows closely now. He lay with both arms stretched to either side. The right forearm was wounded. There were blood stains on his shirt, one from a wound in his chest, the other just under the collarbone. That was Jack's first shot, fired from a prone position. It had gone high on him. Colt's shot had been a little high, too. The .44's slug had whizzed by Jack's face close enough that he had felt the hot air behind it. Rocks had kicked against his skull. By the time Jack had come to his feet and taken aim, Colt had recovered. The three shots Jack had then fired had all struck. One slug had hit low in the belly. The second had pierced his arm as Colt had reached across to grab his .38. It should have been the kill shot, but it wasn't. The third bullet had finished it. It had broken the ridge of Colt's nose at eye level, then had blown out the back of his head. Jack left him as he was but checked his coat pockets and found a soaked box of .38 hollow points. He pulled the other pocket of Colt's trousers inside out without ripping it. As the big body stirred slightly, a line of blood tipped out of the left eye and ran over his cheek to his ear. Jack found a wad of bills in this pocket, sixteen dollars. He took the money, then reached under and lifted Colt's soaked wallet. He did a little better here. Three-hundred dollars and a wet badge proclaiming Chief of Police, City of Lues. Jack knew people who would pay a lot of money for that badge, just because Colt Fellows had carried it.

Next Jack slipped into the front seat of Colt's LTD and retrieved the cell phone and shotgun. He turned the engine off and pulled the keys out. Against the console, he saw a large police issue flashlight. It was heavy and cast a good beam. He could use it. In the trunk, Jack found a strand of clothesline, some thirty feet in length, a government-issue blanket, a fishing pole and tackle box, a box of shells for the 12-gauge, a striking flint, matches, flares, a pocket knife, a first-aid kit, and the clothes he had been wearing when he was arrested. Packing the blanket, he made a bedroll of it, then tied it off and slung it over his shoulder. He grabbed up the flashlight, the shotgun, and finally Crouch's .38, then without closing the trunk or looking back at Fellows or Crouch, Jack trotted across the road toward the dark trees.

Inside the forest, he snapped the flashlight on and headed northwest, the direction of Lues.

Part Four

Jason Morgan

T HE SILVER Bronco beat over the washboard roads relentlessly. Leaping and skidding, it threw its headlights first somersaulting over the treetops, then straight down into the puddles. It rocked and shook. Even on the flat the Bronco shivered under the stress. The wipers raced to clear the water off. The engine whined. Chief of Detectives, Lieutenant Jason Morgan gripped the wheel tightly, his pale blue eyes searing the darkness. When he had time, he remembered to swear.

Coming to Lues Creek Crossing, Morgan passed six county-issue sedans and pulled up behind the coroner's van. The lights of the county cars and his own Bronco illuminated the area. Seeing two figures carrying a body bag, Morgan jumped out and hurried forward. He knew the men with the body. They stopped when they saw Morgan. There is little room for the customary pleasantries at such sites, but Morgan spoke each man's name and met their gazes respectfully. They answered in the same fashion. Unzipping the body bag, Morgan looked down into Colt's broken face. The skin was gray and cool, the muscles slack.

"How long?" Morgan asked them.

Ira Gammon shrugged, "They said a couple of hours."

Colt Fellows looked dead for days. "This the only wound?"

Gammon shook his head. "Four others. Stomach, chest, left shoulder, and right forearm."

As Morgan considered Colt, he tried not to think about facing Betty or looking at Colt's kids. He heard his wife Charli telling him, *What goes around comes around, Jason.* She had been predicting this night for years.

Nodding, he thanked the men, then stepped past them and ran squarely into Cal Yeager. Standing here in the rain, Yeager looked every bit the lawman in his yellow slicker and plastic-covered, snow-white Stetson. Now past

173

sixty, Yeager hadn't changed much in the twenty years Morgan had known him. He still had the vibrant, white hair and pale skin, a prominent bulb of a red nose, and a quick smile. It was an affable, intelligent face, all the better in photographs. The eyes possessed a wonderful innocence, even after a lifetime of law enforcement, and every time Jason Morgan confronted the face, he had to remember the essential lie of it. Yeager's competencies were limited. His corruption was fundamental. His loyalties extended only as far as his fear.

"He went down fighting," Yeager observed.

Jason ignored this and looked past Yeager to what appeared to be the wrap-up. They were supposed to be gone by the time he arrived, Morgan realized. "What's going on!" he shouted.

Yeager was soothing. "Now I know you're upset."

"You're damn straight I'm upset." Morgan's pale blue eyes danced in anger. "I get a call twenty-two minutes ago, I get my ass out here, and you're done! How long have you been here?"

"Well, now Jason, it's our case. We're taking care of it, but if you want copies of our reports, photographs of the scene, whatever, all you have to do is ask. We're prepared to cooperate!"

"You'd better be ready to cooperate, and I don't mean pictures, Cal. I want to see what happened!" He looked past Yeager to where Colt's big Ford was parked. The doors were shut. One of the deputies had started the car.

"Stop that car, now!"

"Calm down, Jason."

Morgan pushed the sheriff out of his way and went to the driver's side of Colt's car. "Turn it off, Billy," he told the deputy.

The driver considered Morgan briefly, then turned the engine off. Morgan looked across at four other deputies, all standing beside the front passenger door.

"Where was the body?" he asked them.

One of them answered. "Colt was around here, somewhere, the other, I don't know." The speaker was looking at the ground. Finally, he looked back at Yeager for some help.

"You had *two* shot?" Jason asked in surprise. Yeager's senior deputy had told Jason on the telephone that Colt had been shot while taking Jack Hazard to the county jail, and that Hazard had escaped.

Yeager answered, stepping toward his deputies, "Toby Crouch was assisting in the transfer. He's still alive, but they don't think for long. We got him out first thing, for all the good it'll do."

"Was he conscious?"

Yeager shook his head.

Morgan looked at the collection of county officers, which now included their sheriff, "Gentlemen, do you suppose it would be too much trouble to move out of the area of the shooting until I look around?"

They glanced at one another. They murmured and shrugged and sauntered away. Only Yeager remained. He was playing tough on this one, no doubt thinking to win a little respect with his own men and maybe test the waters against the heir apparent to Colt's crown. If, for the moment, Jason let it go, he had no intention of letting it go for long. Billy Highsmith got out of Colt's LTD. "Is this the way it sat?" Jason asked him.

"Three of the doors were open, and the trunk was up. Oh, yeah, and the lights were on."

"Where were the keys?"

"In the trunk."

"Like it was, please. Exactly!"

Morgan walked around to the other side of the car. Nothing was on the ground, of course. He looked at Yeager angrily. "Where were the bodies, Cal?"

"My people have already worked this scene, Jason."

"You're going to take me through what you have, Cal. You're going to put everything where it was, and you're going to put down a couple of body-outlines as close to perfect as you can, because if you don't, I'm coming after you with both fists right now, and I think you know I mean it." Jason Morgan was a simple and direct man, purely Lues. When he spoke of fists, he was not talking in metaphors. Cal Yeager had five armed men with him. It was silent testimony to Jason Morgan's broad shoulders that no one thought to take a head count.

Cal nodded at his men, and Morgan shouted a warning to keep out of the area as much as possible. It was too late, of course. The gravel road was soft at the edges. He could have read every step each man had taken if he had made it to the scene before Yeager. While the deputies taped in the rough outlines, Jason went back to his Bronco and pulled out a slicker and a beat-up Stetson. He changed into a pair of old leather boots that he kept in the vehicle and he fished out a fresh notepad. In the back of the Bronco, Jason reached for his old Coleman lantern.

Yeager came up to him while he was tying his boots, "They've got a couple of outlines down for you. We'll fax a preliminary report to your office tomorrow and get photographs to you in a few days. I'm taking off, Jason."

"You're not going anywhere, Cal."

"Now just a minute!"

"You botched this scene up, and you're going to stick around and tell me what you found. I want keys, shell casings, positions of guns, every last blessed detail."

There was no love lost between the two men. Nineteen-and-a-half years ago, Cal Yeager had declared his candidacy against Morgan's old boss in the early spring of an election year, then proceeded to steal the election. Morgan had stayed on as deputy to Yeager for nearly a year, not wanting to join up with Colt Fellows, but finally he had made his choice. Hard as it was to work for Colt, anything was better than this man. Yeager tried to stare at Jason threateningly but failed. He always had. In the end, he mumbled that he could spare a few minutes. Morgan took it as a complete acquiescence, because it was. He turned his collar up and tightened down the belt of his slicker. "We'll start at the beginning," he answered.

Brick Walls

On Saturday morning, Josie came up toward consciousness through a series of dense, flashing images. She was driving at night, she realized. The streets were wet. Mansions everywhere. She was driving an old boyfriend's Corvette. She had never been allowed to drive the car. The facts were murky even in her conscious memory—it was nearly ten years ago that she had dated Steve Graham—but Josie always believed she had broken up with him because he wouldn't let her drive his car. She was driving it now and doing it without his permission. Annie was running beside the car, and Josie was explaining to her that in heaven there are no monsters, because we all have tenure. Annie ran ahead of her as Josie said this, her head thrown back, her short gray hair suddenly a floating reddish gold mane. "Yes, there are!" The voice was her mother's. The figure had become equine. When the wall in the middle of the road appeared, Josie realized she was trapped. To either side, the forest edged in against the road. Where were the houses? She hit the brakes but nothing happened. The Corvette floated silently toward the wall, as if on ice. *Ask me anything but don't ask to drive my 'vet.* Steve wasn't going to like this. The horse that Annie had become leapt over the wall and flew away. Josie was inside her VW. The windows were unbroken, but she was sitting on shards of glass. The tires squalled. She was too close. She was going to hit the wall.

At the moment of impact, Josie saw a canyon of bloodred stone. She floated through the air, falling. At the same instant, she sat up in her bed gasping for air. Her mother's voice shouted something, the words lost as the dream ended. Josie's heart was beating violently. She looked at the room and thought herself a stranger. She did not know this place.

In fact, she realized, she knew nothing at all.

Confessions

"Annie Wilde." Josie had caught her friend at her office, even though it was Saturday.

"Annie, something's wrong."

"To whom am I speaking, please?"

"It's Josie."

"Josie? I didn't recognize you! What is it?"

Josie hesitated as she summoned her courage. "I didn't tell you everything that happened at the Bust of Country, Annie." Over the next half hour, Josie explained about the "audition," then admitted to feeling pressured in her interview with Colt. Finally, she explained what had happened after Colt gave the story to the press, effectively ruining her career. It wasn't good, Annie answered, but it wasn't the end of the world either. The important thing, professionally speaking, was to try to be patient and get a perspective on things. Because the audition was nothing more than a joke, she was certain cooler heads would eventually prevail. Josie needed to concentrate on school, and maybe now, with Jack going back to prison, she could. But that was the thing, Josie answered. She wasn't sure Jack was really involved. She spent a lot of time talking about Jack, especially her feeling that he hadn't meant her any harm. She'd spoken to him for only a minute, she said. She hadn't been particularly impressed with the man, but when he had thought she was going to be dancing for Virgil, she'd seen a frightening rage in his eyes. "It wasn't an act, Annie. He thought Virgil had hired his little girl to dance, and he was going to kill him! Why would he abuse me and then get upset because I was going to dance?"

"It could be a con, Josie. Psychopaths are notoriously good actors."

That could be, she admitted, but there had been something about the man when she had seen him that had brought back the certainty that she had loved him. Annie warned her against trusting her emotions. She had been seven years old!

"I'm not *trusting* my feelings. I'm *listening* to them."

"What are you saying, Josie?"

"I'm saying I have a lot of questions about Jack Hazard, and suddenly I can't talk to the police. I feel like they set me up. They *wanted* Jack. They didn't give a damn about *me*."

"Fellows thought you were going to be screaming about the newspaper report. How was he suppose to know you don't bother reading the newspaper?"

"Maybe," Josie answered. That made a lot of sense, but still, something about the whole thing bothered her. "The first time I mentioned Jack's name to Officer Crouch, I saw something, Annie. He knew the name, and it wasn't just recognition. He got interested suddenly."

"Josie, I've said it all along. You don't have enough information."

"I don't know where to start, Annie! I mean this isn't exactly my field. There aren't any good bibliographies on this!" An academic's joke, and getting no laughs.

"Josie, I was in women's studies before there was women's studies. If you can't find a good bibliography, kiddo, you make your own. You have some names. That's where you start. Find this witness who saw Jack at the falls. Talk to that Sheriff Bitts. Take him a bottle of rye and talk about old times in Lues. Maybe you don't know the truth at this point, but it's always there if you're smart enough to coax it out of hiding. This is just three-dimensional research, Josie. Same steps, same processes."

"I guess I've just been afraid of what I was going to find."

"I think at this point you'd better be more afraid of what you haven't found."

The Text of a Nightmare

Where is the place of monsters, Annie? Josie had asked the old professor once. They had been deep in their cups, deep into metaphysics.

Annie had answered in that strange whisper of hers, strange at least when she was fabulously drunk, a voice from another world, "There are no roads to that place, Josie."

The truth of that day had finally hit. Josie needed to go to the place with no roads. She needed finally to look truth in the eye without blinking. No fear, no apology, no embarrassment. She needed to pretend her life was no different from the literary puzzles she had learned to solve. She would start over. She would start this time with hypotheses, and not jump to conclusions. Nothing was an absolute at this point. Everything needed the test of reason, and if a thing were possible, she would face it. Because if she was wrong about Jack Hazard, there was still someone out there who meant her a great deal of harm. Her career was lost, no matter what Annie said. Nothing she could do about it either, but she had no intention of giving her life away as well.

She knew she had let Colt Fellows manipulate her. Every instinct had been screaming at her to wait, to reflect, to get away from Colt Fellows before she signed anything. She had failed to listen to her own instincts. That would not happen again. If the man after her was not Jack Hazard, she was in danger. More than she had even imagined when she thought Dan Scholari had found her. Not a violent man with the heart of a jackal, but a sadist who moved with great care and toyed mercilessly with his victim. If she wanted to live through this, she had to give up the panic, she had to listen to her inner voice. She had to make this world—history itself—her own private domain and let no one and nothing master her again. Right now, mastery meant gathering information, and when Josie wanted to, no one could amass more information faster. No one. It was her genius, really, if she had one, and right now, she needed all the genius she possessed. It was nearly impossible almost twenty years after a crime to learn the truth, but not entirely so. Not this crime, at least. Whoever it was, he was close to things, watching her. He knew from the beginning she was coming back. She had been a fool to think only her adoptive parents and Annie and Dan Scholari knew that Lues was her first home. A lot of people had known her mother, and anyone who had known her mother could also have known about her mother's child. Assumptions were killing her. Fear was robbing her of her best weapon. *Oops!* It was a hell of an epitaph. She smiled bitterly at the thought. Miss Darling blushed at scandal and blanched at threats. Real life was a little too much for her nerves, but Josie Fortune was a slew and that might just get her through this. Gunpowder in the blood. She needed to find Josie Fortune, the younger and the elder, because if she didn't change fast, she wasn't going to chase the nightmare. She wasn't even going to be able to outrun it.

Josie took a cab out to the edge of town and rented a black Mustang because it was fast. Afterwards, she purchased another parking sticker at Harrison, then went to the undergraduate area of Worley Hall. She needed some telephone numbers. One of these was going to be especially difficult to find, but it was manageable. Everything was manageable with a little bit of imagination. Afterwards, she scoured the undergraduate library for sources of Lues's history. There were several books about the area, but the most comprehensive was *The Lues Scrapbook: A Pictorial History.* There was plenty here to interest her, but the most important thing, she realized happily, was the index. With it, she found photographs of Sheriff Pat Bitts. He had been a tall, beautiful man a half century ago. His life read like a hero's saga. Fires, floods, brawls, gunfights, armed robberies, kidnappings, even the occasional speech with a good punch line or two: Two-Bit, as everyone called him, was the man for the job. She needed to talk to this man.

To her astonishment, Josie found her mother's picture in the *Lues State University Yearbook 1983* on the memory page. She felt a jolt of recognition at the image and the ache of sorrow. She knew this woman. She remembered her, and the strangest thing of all was that she had been looking at her in the mirror each morning for years. In the picture, the hair was longer, and there was more reddish gold in it. The features were finer. The nose was straighter. Still, the essential character, the delicate shape of her forehead and eyes lived on in Josie's face. Even the qualities Josie disliked in herself were there, the bushy eyebrows and round lips. When she read the account of her mother's murder in the campus paper, she learned that Josie Fortune had made the dean's list. The dean's list! It was far cry from what she had read in the *Rapids* that first weekend she had chased the nightmare and lost heart, and it left Josie wondering about the lies that might not yet be exposed. Not *mistakes* either, but *lies.* Insults passing as facts. Colt Fellows? She thought it very likely and wondered why.

When the lights flickered, Josie looked up and realized the library was closing. Saturdays, it was four o'clock. Inside a rest room stall, Josie shifted her .357 to the waistband at the back of her jeans, then went through the bag check and out of the building. There was a faint drizzle, and the lot was busy for a late Saturday afternoon. Josie stayed alert.

That evening after dinner, Josie consulted her notes and dialed a Ms. Grimes, of rural Belleville. "Hello?" The voice was that of a modestly educated, middle-aged, Midwestern white woman.

"I'm trying to reach Melody Grimes."

"This is her." The woman was suspicious, though her tone expressed an unconscious vulnerability. Josie probably sounded like a salesperson. Before she said no, she wanted to know what Josie was selling.

"Ms. Grimes, is your maiden name Mason?"

"Who is this?" Real wariness now, as well as panting curiosity.

"My name is Josie Darling. I'm a professor at Lues State."

"Oh, God! You don't want to take my diploma back, do you?"

Josie smiled. Melody Grimes was serious. "I'm doing some research on my mother's death. Her name was Josie Fortune. The police here gave me your name. They said you were the first to find her body."

There was a heavy silence. Josie was sure Melody Grimes was going to hang up.

Finally, reluctantly, the voice answered, "That was a long time ago."

"It'll be twenty years this April."

"That was your mom?"

"I'd like to talk to you about it. Is there any way you could see me if I came up to Belleville tomorrow afternoon?"

"I don't know what you think I could tell you."

"Anything you remember."

"You're in Lues? That's a long trip. I think you'd just be wasting your time."

"My mother died when I was seven. I don't remember anything about it. I can't even remember much about her. Before I came to Lues this fall, I couldn't remember anything at all. I guess what I'm trying to say is I'm grabbing at straws, and I need your help."

A slight pause. Was she wondering how to get rid of this pest or clearing her schedule? "Sure," Melody answered. "My husband's just watching football tomorrow afternoon. It'll be fun. What do you drink?"

Melody Grimes

Melody Grimes was a heavyset woman with a reckless teenager's giggle. Josie liked her immediately. Her voice had a certain lilt to it, an engaging inclusiveness about it. Melody might have known that no one ever had a university diploma jerked, but she still believed that kind of thing could happen to her. In fact, it was the sort of thing that could only happen to her.

Josie made one quick assumption about Melody Grimes. She had survived the incident in Lues Creek Canyon without any of it ever affecting her. Her shallowness was rock hard but genial. Nothing much got through and so life had never really wrecked her. Neither had it been especially sweet or thrilling or dramatic. Melody saw herself as someone locked inside a situation comedy, maybe as the likable neighbor to the star. The niche she had carved for herself was a safe place to hide, as long as she kept laughing. Melody's discomfort with Josie, if she had any, was that she wasn't tragic enough about the discovery of a body twenty years ago. It embarrassed her slightly that she had survived it without a legion of nightmares trailing her.

Mr. Grimes didn't get off the couch when Josie entered the house. He was a blubbery, balding man, not even energetic enough to bother with drinking beer on a Sunday afternoon. When Melody pointed at him and said, "That's my husband, not a pillow," he studied Josie with brief but pointed curiosity, then turned back to the football game. Melody noticed the effect Josie had on him and made a joke out of it. "It's a real person, honey. See, there's no box around her head, that's how you can tell." She seemed to enjoy her own joke without the bile that usually goes with such marital jousting. As they walked to the kitchen, Melody confided to Josie, "A few years ago, we had a suicide watch for him when the baseball players went on strike."

The place was rundown and shabby, but no apologies for it. The Sunday dinner dishes were still out, greasy and crusted. The kitchen table, where they had eaten, was cleared but not cleaned. A couple of kids, one boy, one girl, moved about occasionally, but there were no introductions. Melody handed Josie a can of Miller Lite, and they sat across from each other at the kitchen table.

"I got your name almost by chance," Josie confessed. "The police didn't show me their file on the case, but they gave me your name. Your maiden name, actually."

"That's weird."

"Why is that?"

"Why me? There were five of us."

"Do you remember their names?"

"Sure! Well, . . . most of them." As it happened, Melody remembered Bob Tanner, Susie Hill, and Cat Sommerville. The other guy's name, she said she couldn't remember.

"Tell me about the day, why you were out there, anything you remember."

Smiling, embarrassed, she looked at Josie for a long time before she responded. "This is tough," she said finally. "I mean she was your mom. I don't really feel comfortable talking about it. If someone told me about my mom, you know, it would freak me out!"

"I've had almost twenty years to get used to the idea that someone killed my mother. But you're right. It still freaks me out."

Hearing her own sentiments and language echoed in Josie's response, Melody seemed suddenly to relax. She was a girl again, the girl she had been. "We didn't know her. We just found her." She shrugged. "I feel bad about your driving up here just for that. But it's all I know."

"Was it a sunny day?"

"No. Cloudy, cool. We were skipping this class in history, drinking beer."

"What kind of beer?"

Melody laughed and held up her can, "Miller Lite!"

There was no sense of a moving narrative, but there were random images, strands of conversation, the number of beers they drank, the brands of cigarettes they smoked, even the color of the clothing they wore. She described the day with incredible precision, at times, and Josie played like Henry Valentine, letting her go where she wanted, bumping and urging when necessary, simply watching and listening otherwise. She didn't even take notes, afraid it might disrupt the flow of memory. Melody's was a mind without order, but it was a mind of brilliant capacity.

"It was my first time in the woods," Melody explained. "We were all drunk, like that was something new." She laughed at herself and launched parenthetically into a description of her life as a debauched college student. It was a long detour, but Josie listened and smiled and even probed a little, because she liked the woman and because she saw that memory builds from context, that the more Melody talked, the more she recalled. Melody went back to the canyon now. She told about almost going off the ledge, a rotted board breaking, Bob Tanner pushing her out over the edge as a joke, then losing control of her. That kind of thing just always seemed to happen to her, she said. She started to tell about a couple of things that had happened more recently to make her point, and Josie nudged her back to the canyon. Melody said when she was safe, she thought she was going to be sick. "That was when I saw her."

About the body, Melody said she didn't remember anything. This time, Josie could get nothing more. She thought she understood why. It was not that Melody had suppressed the image. She was lying to protect the victim's child, because a convenient bit of memory loss was far better than describing the effects of a knife used as an instrument of rape. She said she remembered the canyon, the huge boulders, and the high waters. She knew they had telephoned someone afterwards. The rest was gone. "Listen," she said with a friendly smile. "I'm worthless. I don't remember anything that could help you."

Her eyes grew distant, as she tried in vain to go back into the canyon, then she laughed. "Must be all the liquor and dope I did back then: *fried* those brain cells! I was always getting trashed. I probably had sex with forty guys in college. I mean it didn't seem that bad at the time, but after a while, they just kind of added up, you know? Forty and I couldn't name three of them now. Well, maybe three, but first names only." She looked toward the living room, the direction of her husband. "I forgot his name about twelve years ago and he won't tell me what it is. Hey honey, hey you in front of the TV! What's your name?" There was no answer. She shrugged prettily. "He won't tell me." She giggled, then caught herself and grew solemn. "I wish I could help. We saw her. We called someone. Then we all ran away." Melody considered for a moment, pretending once more to try to remember, then lit a cigarette, Merits, these days, Lucky Strikes in the bad old days. "I wish I could tell you more."

"How did they find you if you ran away?" Josie asked her. Melody frowned, confused. "The police?" Josie asked. "If you ran away, how did they know you'd been there?"

"I don't know. Just my luck, I guess. The sheriff came to our sorority house. Scared me to death! God! I thought I was going to jail!"

"Why? Because you left?"

"Yeah. He took us into this room and talked to each of us for like two hours apiece. 'Where were you?' 'Why didn't you stick around?' 'Did you kill her?' It was terrible. He was so mean."

"The sheriff?"

"Some guy. I mean I thought he was the sheriff. Had a tan uniform. Tall, old. I don't know what he was really."

"Did he actually think you were involved somehow?"

"I don't know. I never understood what it was all about. I mean, I just assumed we were in trouble because we called and then ran away."

Josie wrote a quick note to herself. That had the effect of closing down Melody's concentration, so Josie went ahead and jotted down several other curiosities. As she finished, Melody got them both another beer.

"Have you been there?" Melody asked her. When Josie looked up in confusion, she added, "Into the canyon, I mean?"

Josie shook her head, smiling uncomfortably. "To tell you the truth, I've been afraid to go look." Josie gave an amiable shrug, Melody-style.

"It was your dad who killed her?" Melody was excited by this fact, maybe imagining something like it happening in her own family or maybe just remembering things suddenly, the blood and wounds she would not describe, perhaps.

"My stepfather."

"We thought there was going to be a big trial, but then, he liked confessed or something, and we all went home for the summer."

"He confessed to second-degree murder. They sent him away for twenty years."

"Why did he do it?"

"I don't know. He's saying now that he didn't."

"Do you believe him?" Melody was skeptical but kind. She would take what Josie offered at face value. She took all of life at face value.

"I don't know. I thought maybe you could help me figure it out."

"Me?"

"The detective in charge of the case gave me your name because you picked him out of a lineup."

"Your stepdad? News to me."

Josie's brow knitted furiously, "You didn't identify anyone?"

"Oh! Right! I saw somebody at the falls. I completely forgot about that!

I was the only one who saw this guy. I thought maybe he was the killer, but I didn't get a good look at him. Some cop brought me some pictures and I couldn't identify anyone, and that was it. I was in the hospital, okay?"

"The hospital?"

"Poison sumac all over my legs and *everywhere,* you know what I mean? I squatted in it to pee, and oh, baby! Talk about an itch needing to be scratched, let me tell you! I thought I was going to die! I never itched like that in my whole life. It started that evening. It was burning and itching, and I didn't say anything because, you know, I thought I had the clap, and then the sheriff came by, and I was wiggling and almost crying. Anyway, about midnight, I finally got a good look at it, and then I showed it to Susie. She thought it was some kind of Asian clap. And man! I was scared to death. Susie took me to the university hospital after that sheriff left. I was there, I don't know, a night or two. Something like that. Oh! It was bad though. Anyway, this cop shows up in my hospital room. He's got a handful of pictures. He shows them to me and I can't recognize anybody. I think he pointed at one of them and goes, 'Could this be him?' and I'm like, 'Yeah, maybe.' I always agree with people. It's easier, you know? Look, it's been a long time. The cop probably just doesn't remember it any better than me."

Josie nodded at this assessment, as if she accepted it as fact. Melody was the kind of person who didn't put blame on other people. She was too easy, too ready to take blame. And she certainly didn't want to cause problems, even if her reluctance cost a man twenty years in prison.

"Do you know where any of the others are, the people you were with? I need to talk to all of them."

"Bob was from around there, one of those little towns. Susie was from upstate, Vandalia, I think, or Effingham or . . . I don't know. I'd love to see her again. God! We were best friends, and now nothing. I should have gone to the ten-year reunion, but I didn't. I don't even know if she ever got married."

"I've got a best friend from high school like that," Josie admitted. "I don't know where she is or what's she's doing. I heard she got married, but I don't know his name or if they stayed in the area."

"It's a bummer. I've been here, in Belleville, ten years with," Melody pointed toward the television, "what's his name. We have like zero friends. When I was at Lues State, I knew everyone." She giggled. "If there was a party,

I was there!" This was especially funny, and Melody's eyes danced. She missed those times. Even at almost forty, she missed them.

"I'm going to find the rest of the people who were there," Josie offered. "I'll get you the information, if you want."

"If you can get Susie's number, that would be great. The little slut still owes me a trip to Florida." Josie asked her what she meant. "When we graduated, we were going to go to Florida. We were all set, then one of us didn't get the money or the folks said no way, I don't remember exactly what it was. We were broken up about it, but you know, we went home and that was it. I haven't seen her since."

The boy came into the kitchen. Melody told him to get a shirt on. "It's cold!" she told him. He shrugged, got a can of pop, and left. "Where are your shoes?" she called to him as he left. Nothing.

"Do you have kids?" she asked. Josie shook her head. Melody rolled her eyes, "Life's great blessing."

"Did the others graduate?" Josie had found Melody through the alumni association records. Graduation was the way one got on that list.

"Susie and I graduated. Bob stuck around, but I don't know if he ever graduated. The other guy . . ." she shrugged. "He saved my life, right? And now, I can't remember his name. Go figure! Oh, and Cat. She dropped out. Well, I mean she got pregnant and just didn't come back to school. I mean, it's great! She's this 'virgin 'til I die,' Young Christian League, or whatever, and she finds this guy, I guess it must have been right after we found . . . you know . . . and, I mean, she must have spread them legs right away and said give me a baby, DADDY!"

Melody's daughter walked into the kitchen on this note. She looked to be thirteen, cute and cherubic, like her mom, and maybe, Josie decided, a girl with a few secrets. "Who spread her legs?"

"Nobody. Go to your room."

"I want to know who you're talking about!"

"A girl I knew in college."

"God! I thought you were talking about someone in this century!" She spun on her naked heel and walked away.

"Get some shoes on! It's cold out!"

"You didn't know the guy?" Josie asked.

Melody's face screwed up thoughtfully, "He wasn't a frat. All the frats had already tried. Not so much as a hand job, that's what I heard. Susie and I hated her, you know, because she wouldn't and we always got drunk and did, but God was she a boy magnet, let me tell you! I got the best sex hanging around that girl at parties. Anyway, he must have been *something* to get Cat going!" Melody raised her eyebrows expressively. She knew about *something.*

Josie took the offer of a third beer and heard about the mating habits of another generation. She got nothing now about her mother's murder, but that didn't bother her. She had more than she had anticipated. She had caught Colt Fellows in a lie, for one thing, a critical one, as it turned out.

Josie stayed simply because she liked the woman and because she had seen her circle and return to the canyon, and each time she went back, mentally, there was something else. Josie wasn't leaving until they were both exhausted. That seemed to happen just as the football game ended. The husband walked in and got a sandwich. He looked at Josie as he leaned against a kitchen counter and ate. It was raw lust, but he knew better than to think she might see anything in him. Josie might as well have been a beer-commercial-babe. He was barefoot like the kids. Melody said something about this, and Josie realized they were done, even a little drunk.

"I'd better go," she said.

"Good luck," Melody told her at the car. "And I hope you remember, you know, what you want to."

Josie thought about the words, *remember what you want to.* That was the memory of Melody Grimes. Josie wanted the rest. She wanted to remember the things that weren't so pleasant. According to Annie Wilde, that was the secret to revising the soul.

A Late-Night Interview

That evening, two uniformed police officers from the city of Lues stood framed in Josie's peephole. Lieutenant Morgan would like to see her at the civic center, the older one told her when she opened the door. What about? The officer couldn't say. They had orders to drive Josie there. And if she didn't chose to cooperate? Neither cop answered, and Josie decided it was maybe better not to test them. She insisted, however, that she drive her own car.

Jason Morgan met Josie in a small, cluttered office. The place was all business: folders stacked on shelves, a bank of file cabinets, twenty-some years of FBI journals, a large chalk board (covered, she noticed), a wall full of meritorious service awards, and a coffee pot that was working overtime. Morgan was a short, broad man with plenty of gray hair and the look of a man who was all cop—one of Colt's own, she decided. He wore a sports jacket and a mismatched tie. His eyes were tired, and she guessed he had been living on short rations of sleep for a day or two. Without so much as an introduction, the man studied her with undisguised suspicion. Josie found herself unable to hold the man's gaze and looked back at the officers who had brought her to him.

"Do you know why I asked you come in here, Miss Darling?"

Josie focused on Morgan again. "I assume it has something to do with the complaint I filed last week."

The man laughed. It was almost pleasant sounding, "I think you can do better than that."

"I don't understand." Josie was nervous suddenly. There was something in the man's look, the heavy exhaustion in his eyes, that bothered her.

"You mean to say you haven't heard about Jack Hazard's escape?"

"Escape?" Josie felt the blood drain from her face.

"Jack was being transferred to the county jail Friday night. Somehow he got free. In the process, he killed two of our people, Chief Fellows and Officer Crouch." Josie's mind reeled in confusion. Colt Fellows and Toby Crouch . . . *dead?*

She had talked to them Thursday. And Friday night, Jack Hazard had killed them. Loose two days, she realized with a tremor of fear, and she hadn't known. They hadn't told her!

"Since you were the one who filed charges against Jack, I thought we'd better talk. I've been trying to get you all day." He studied her briefly, a skeptical look crossing his face, "You really hadn't heard?"

"No." She thought to compose herself, but it felt like she was doing a miserable job. "I went upstate today. I worked in the library and at home yesterday. How did he kill them? How did it happen, exactly?" She meant how was such a thing possible.

"I don't know what happened, *exactly.* They were both shot to death. That's all that I can say at the moment." There was a cold reckoning in the man's pale blue eyes, and Josie looked away again. "You didn't pick up a newspaper or turn on the TV?" Morgan acted as if missing the news for a day or two was incredible.

"I told you I hadn't heard. I've had other things on my mind."

"I want to know how serious Jack's assault on you was, Miss Darling."

Still not looking at him, Josie answered, "The assault charge was Colt's idea. Colt said it was the only way to get Jack back in prison."

"Why did you want him in prison?"

"Colt thought . . . well, I thought, at the time anyway, that Jack had been leaving me threatening messages." She went through the basics, everything she had told Crouch and Fellows, finishing with her car being vandalized at the Bust of Country.

"And you thought Jack did it?"

"He was there. He could have done it. He . . . or someone left a note. When I came here last week, I showed it to Officer Crouch. You should have it somewhere. It's the only evidence I gave him."

"All I have is a copy of the complaint you filed with the sheriff."

She explained about the note, the spelling of whore, and what Colt had told her about her mother's body, the letters carved into her flesh.

"So you thought Jack had to have written the note?"

"At the time, it was the only thing that made sense, and Colt said once they had Jack in custody for assault, he would get the rest out of him: find out if he had really been leaving messages. If he was, he would turn Jack over to his parole officer."

"Jack doesn't have a parole officer, Professor."

"He's not on parole? Colt said he was."

"No."

"Colt said I wouldn't have any more problems if I filed charges, because they could just send Jack back to prison on a parole violation."

"He said that? You're sure?"

She nodded. "When I got back to school, I found two more messages. Whoever left them had gotten into my office to leave one of them, and suddenly, I wasn't so sure Jack was behind any of it. I mean, I just didn't know. If he was, I thought he had someone at school helping him."

"Which is why you called Colt several times on Friday? Or were you calling because of the newspaper article?"

"I didn't see the paper until one of my colleague showed it to me that afternoon. I called Colt, in the beginning, about these." Josie reached down into her briefcase and tried to hand the card and her class roster to Morgan.

Lieutenant Morgan asked her to pull the card out of the envelope for him. He didn't want to touch the evidence. He studied the material earnestly. He was a quiet, thoughtful man, Josie decided, not so eager to help or take sides. For some reason, the man's neutrality appealed to her. In the end, Colt's sympathy had been self-serving. A setup. They had just wanted a reason to arrest Jack, and she was stupid enough to give it to them.

"You found these after Jack was arrested?"

"No. After I had signed the complaint. It was before the arrest. The envelope was left in my department office. The class roster was inside my office in Brand Hall, which was locked. That bothered me. I mean it's possible to get a master key, but it didn't make any sense."

"How is it possible?"

"You get the right slip of paper with some initials on it and take it to building and grounds, or you steal a master key from someone, or you know a janitor. The janitor seemed more likely, but the card was left in the main office during the day, while I was here filing charges, actually. Someone dropped it off personally. It couldn't have gotten to me through campus mail with that name and no address. I thought an older man not connected to the university would be noticed walking into the department. I asked the girl facing the mailboxes if she had seen anything, and she hadn't. I mean they let student workers in that area and faculty, of course, but otherwise, it's not really permitted for anyone to just go into the those boxes and leave papers or notes. A lot of people could do it, I guess. There's really no special security, but I just thought Jack would be noticed."

Morgan consider this for nearly a minute before he answered. "I'll make sure what you've told me goes into my report."

"I know that Colt Fellows lied about something."

A thin smile she could not quite read answered. "I'm listening."

"Colt said one of the kids who found my mother's body identified Jack Hazard in a lineup. She told me it was a photo spread, and she couldn't identify anyone."

Morgan asked for some information about Melody, and Josie told him what she knew. He looked up after scribbling the information on a little notepad. "If she was a witness, she signed off on the identification," he answered finally. "The state's attorney wouldn't consider any sort of ID until he saw a written affidavit."

"I think she'd sign anything she was told to sign."

Morgan's eyes twinkled. "A lot of people do, especially when a cop is asking."

Josie bristled at the implicit insult and tried to go on the offensive "I'd like see the file on my mother's murder. I want to know exactly what went on."

"I can't help you. The case was pulled out of storage Thursday morning by one of our detectives. I talked to her and she tells me Toby Crouch wanted it ASAP. Colt's orders. She got it and dropped it off with Crouch. That's the last anyone saw of the file."

"You think Colt destroyed it?"

"I don't know the answer to that, Miss Darling. All I know is the thing is missing."

"You don't seem very upset about this!"

"It's gone. There's nothing I can do about it."

"I need the information in that file."

Morgan's smile was suddenly condescending. "If you think you can sleuth this thing, I'm afraid you're in over your head."

"Someone out there is leaving some nasty messages for me to find. He's broken into my apartment, my car, and my office. Now I don't know for a fact it's connected to my mother's case, but if the letters *h-o-r* were carved into her flesh, like Colt says—."

"They were."

"Excuse me?"

"I saw them myself."

"You saw them?

Morgan considered something for a moment, then told her, "Look, I don't know what good it will do you, but if you want to know what happened to your mother, that's your right, I guess. I can't help you with the case file, but I know a man you need to talk to."

"Pat Bitts?"

The detective allowed himself a friendly smile, the first she'd seen. "Two-Bit still has his notes on Noah's flood, Miss Darling. You go out and talk to him. He'll give you an earful. I promise you that."

An Old Soldier

Don Stackman, leaning back in a leather chair, faced Jason Morgan, who had just finished a narrative of the events of Friday evening. It was early Monday morning, just past eight o'clock. The funeral services for Toby Crouch and Colt Fellows were to take place within the hour, and this had been the best time to get Morgan's report. Morgan's version of the shooting was an impressive piece of police work, as usual. Cal Yeager's theory that the Hazards had sprung Jack during the transfer was already grist for the newspaper, but it was entirely without an evidentiary foundation. Yeager's people had turned up no unexplained footprints in the woods and no shell casings or slugs that were unaccounted for, no evidence of any kind, in fact. Besides Hazard's departing trail, there had been only two other trails leading into the woods and then back to Colt's Ford, yet the sheriff wanted him to believe that Fellows had been stopped by some kind of roadblock and that those tracks proved it. He furthered argued that once Jack had been released, Jack had summarily executed Crouch and Fellows, Crouch with Colt's .44, Colt with a .38, most likely Toby Crouch's .38. It was the way of cold-blooded killers like Hazard, Yeager argued, though he hadn't bothered to explain why Jack Hazard changed guns or shot Chief Fellows from two different angles.

Morgan held a rather more ingenious opinion about the events but one that accorded perfectly with the facts. It was the sort of narrative of events that could get a man convicted, even executed, and Lues County's longtime state's attorney liked that about the theory. "Let me get it straight," Stackman said. "Fellows stops the car, and he and Crouch walk to the woods. Rest stop." Morgan nodded. "They come back, and there's some kind of scuffle at the back passenger door. You're saying they pulled Jack out?"

"Crouch pulled him out. I've got a beautiful set of Colt's fingerprints on the lid of the trunk and a nice trail into the woods and then back to the rear of the car. So I know where Colt was. There was a good deal of damage done to the footprints where Jack and Toby were, but it was still obvious there was a struggle. I found some sharp heel indentations, some clear signs of a foot turning. I've got a couple of good plasters of them downstairs, Don."

"They stumbled back together about eight feet from the car?"

"I found some deep marks in the mud at the side of the road. Toby's body was right behind them."

"You're saying Colt fired the shot that killed Crouch?"

Morgan nodded. "He's aiming at Jack, who, I figure, is going for Toby's gun."

"With his hands still cuffed behind his back?"

Morgan nodded, "*And* his feet shackled."

Stackman shook his head. He had heard stories all his life about how fast Jack Hazard was, some of them probably even true, but this was something else. He just hoped the newspapers didn't get hold of it. "Why do you think Jack's still in shackles? If he needs a rest stop, they're going to take the shackles off."

"Colt's pants pocket was ripped open."

"Meaning?"

"The only explanation that makes sense is Jack's still in the chains after the shooting and needs the key. He went into the other pocket but didn't rip it. So I figure his hands were free by that point."

"Okay. Jack makes his move. Colt gets three rounds off."

"We lose two rounds somewhere in the woods, but one of them hits Toby square in the chest. Meanwhile, Jack fires at least four rounds. The first shot hits below the collar bone."

"You know it's the first?"

"The angle of entry indicates that Jack was on the ground when he fired that shot. The next three, he's standing, and Colt is sitting in a mud puddle."

Stackman nodded as he worked through the choreography. "So then he gets free and goes to the front seat, takes the shotgun and Colt's cell phone, then goes to the trunk?"

"He gets Toby's service revolver, a box of shells, some fishing gear, the flashlight, his clothes, and he takes off."

"Any chance Colt hit him?"

"No blood anywhere inside the car or trunk, Don. The way he moved around the car, we'd have found something if he had been hit."

"Okay. It sounds good. You've done a great job, Jason, especially given the questions left unanswered in the sheriff's report."

"You're not buying the theory?"

"I buy the *evidence*. I don't like the *theory*."

"Colt meant to execute him, Don. He set this thing up from the start."

Don Stackman put his hands up, palms out, as if to stop him physically. "Jason, you have hard evidence for everything you say, except that. We have plaster prints, a detailed picture of the scene, and a convincing sequence of action: all of it difficult, if not impossible, to question. It's just great police work. Then you come in with the part about Colt trying to kill Jack Hazard, and I'm not buying it."

"What's wrong with it?"

"Plenty, but let's start with the fact that nothing you've given me puts Colt in the role of executioner, and frankly, I don't want to believe it."

"Everything Josie Darling tells me indicates Colt was using the arrest to take care of some old business."

"I don't want to bring the specter of scandal over the department and this office on theory, Jason. Speculation ruins careers, and nothing brings back a good name once it's lost."

"The arrest is suspect, Don. Colt told Josie Darling that Jack was on parole, for God's sake! He said he was going to get him sent back to finish out his sentence, and that's just bullshit!"

"The sheriff ran the complaint by my office. We were the ones who went to the judge for a warrant! As far as Jack being on parole, that doesn't mean much. She was upset. Maybe she heard the word and misunderstood, maybe she made it up. Who knows?"

"I'm telling you Colt pulled a fast one. He brought a deputy in to take the complaint after he convinced Miss Darling it was the only way to get Jack to stop harassing her."

"But now she's saying it wasn't Jack who was harassing her?" Jason Morgan's face twitched in frustration. "The woman changes her story to suit the occasion, Jason."

"The only thing that's going to push Jack Hazard to try to go for a gun the way he was chained up is pure necessity, Don. It's an assault charge! All things considered, he could probably count on getting his stepdaughter to drop the charges before the thing ever went to a judge. What the hell is he looking at? A couple of nights in jail? He's not going to try to get out of that by killing two cops! The guy's not afraid of a little jail time. He's not going to panic."

"Now you're telling me Jack Hazard is a reasonable man. I don't buy it, Jason. Jack's record tells us what kind of man he is. He decides he's got a chance and takes Crouch's gun. That's how his mind works. If Jack Hazard worried about consequences, Jason, he wouldn't have spent more than half of his life in prison!"

"The transfer to county jail is suspect." Morgan pushed stolidly. "What was Colt doing out there?"

"He expected trouble. He didn't want anything to go wrong."

"If he didn't want trouble, he could have moved Jack on the highway with an escort on Friday afternoon. They ran a routine transfer from the court-house to the jail at four o'clock. Why not put Jack in the van with the rest of the county prisoners? Don, Colt's *never* run a prisoner transfer. Think about it! Why now, why the middle of the night, why in the middle of the damn woods?"

"Jack's threatening a young woman, Jason. The guy has a history of be-ing violent with women—right? So Colt wants a little time alone with the guy. Call it the personal touch. Call it whatever you want. To tell you the truth, that was one of the things I liked about Colt. He had a way of mak-ing sure domestic problems didn't escalate. You know that as well as I do."

"Colt's secretary tells me Toby and Colt were suddenly into it thick. Colt can't stand the guy, and suddenly, he's talking about making Toby a watch commander. Promised it, according to her."

"Give me a motive, Jason."

"Okay. Colt sent Jack Hazard to prison more than nineteen years ago. Toby Crouch was working security for the college back then. He was the one who identified Jack in a lineup. What if they framed Jack for the murder and now they're afraid Jack's onto them?"

Stackman shook his head, "You just gave Jack Hazard one hell of a mo-tive, Lieutenant! Look, we've had our fights about that murder when we were all younger and handsomer men. That murder is history. And thank God for it. There were problems, serious discrepancies, but the truth is you get contradictions in almost every homicide. You know that! And Hazard con-fessed. If he was an innocent man, he wouldn't have confessed."

Morgan looked away angrily. "Where's the case file on it, Don?"

Stackman flushed. He wasn't happy about losing files, but that wasn't the only reason he was irritated. "Let me give you some advice, Jason. Mr. Jack Hazard isn't worth it. You've given me a pristine crime scene, every movement choreographed, every shot that was fired explained. I mean, this is great police work. Then you come up with a decent motive, but you're tagging it to the wrong guy. I know you're Two-Bit's friend. I know you want to vindicate him by proving Jack's an innocent man, but that's in the past, Jason. This is a different homicide, and you're just not looking at the evidence objectively."

"The evidence suggests Colt meant to take Jack out into the woods and kill him."

"The evidence indicates that Colt was transferring a prisoner who needed a rest stop. They stopped and Jack made his move. Given his reputation and his history with Colt and Toby Crouch, I can understand that motive."

"Colt would tell him to piss in his pants, Don. They're ten, fifteen minutes from the county jail."

"Maybe Colt had to stop. You think he'd tell Yeager the truth if he was the one who needed the rest stop?"

"So why get Jack out?"

"I don't know, Jason! Maybe he was feeling generous! Maybe he liked his damn car and didn't want the smell of piss in it! What do you really want? Do you want the Lues Police Department to look like a gang of murderous thugs, and Jack Hazard to be some kind of folk hero? That's what you're giving me, and frankly, I'm not buying it! The guy's a psychopath! Prison tests confirm it. No anxiety, no feelings of guilt, none of the normal reactions human beings have! You know what that means? He's got no soul, no fear, and God damn it, no brains! This is not my opinion. This is medical fact!"

"I wouldn't trust some doctor's test on a guy like that."

"Jason, look at the record, for God's sake."

"I can't. It's missing, and Colt Fellows was the last man to have it."

"You remember the case, Jason. Think about what Jack Hazard did to that poor woman."

"You remember the problems about the time of time of death, don't you?"

"HERE WE GO AGAIN! I had the best medical examiner in five states tell me it was *absolutely impossible* that Josie Fortune was dead at the time Two-Bit told us his 'witnesses' spotted her! Come on, Jason! Forget everything else. Do you think Marcel Waldis is going to perjure himself for the likes of Colt Fellows?"

"People saw the body."

"I read all kinds of claims about when they saw what. They were all over the place! Nobody I can trust saw that body until late, including, I might add, Two-Bit himself!"

"I'm just saying the guy behind the confusion was Colt Fellows, and he knew Jack would figure it out sooner or later and come looking for him. He got Crouch to help him because Crouch was involved in the case. He was one of the reasons Jack had to make a deal!"

"The guy behind the confusion was your old boss, but we'll let that go. Your loyalty is commendable. Believe what you want, Jason, but here's how it plays until you give me some real evidence. Fellows returns to the car after a walk, and he tells Crouch to get Jack out and let him have his turn. Crouch brings him out of the car. Jack makes a move, and the shooting starts. When the smoke clears, we've got two cops dead and one psychopath loose in Lues County."

"I'll keep working on it."

"Jason, don't let your emotions get in the way of your police work. This one's finished until we get an arrest. Besides, you're going to be too busy to keep working on it. Word is Corny has asked Ham to submit your name to the city council. You're about to become the acting chief of police. I can't think of a better man for the job, and maybe in the big chair, you'll start seeing things with a little different perspective. Everyone I talk to wants the 'acting' dropped as soon as possible. In other words, you've got a lifetime of good service to this community, and they all want to reward it. Wrecking the entire department for the sake of a hunch can only hurt you, Jason, believe me."

"You're not telling me there's a condition to this promotion, are you?"

Stackman hesitated. "That's not what I'm saying, Jason. What I'm saying is ancient history proves nothing. If I don't get hard, irrefutable evidence Colt meant to kill Jack Hazard, I'm going the other way. Jack made a move. Colt reacted. And you'll keep your mouth shut unless you can prove it didn't go down that way."

Morgan nodded. "I'll get a full report to you by early next week. You don't care if I put my theories in writing, I take it?"

"For my eyes only, I wouldn't expect anything else. Just see that you act responsibly. No news release. No loose talk in the department or to anyone in the public. You want a difference of opinion, fine. You want war, I'm the best there is when it comes to that. If you don't think so, go talk to Two-Bit again."

"I just want the truth, Don."

"Truth, my friend, is an old soldier who knows to keep his mouth shut."

Miss Fortune Comes Calling

The phone rang ten times a day, or never at all. Pat Bitts had been up to Lues to Dempsey's Auto Fair to see if maybe he could swap cars, that was three months back, and Dempsey was still calling. Anyone wanted his business that much, he might go back and see what they could do. Then there were the siding people. Didn't want siding, didn't like it, didn't need it. Polly would come up out of her grave if he let them near her house. Like Bitts was afraid to get a paint brush out now and then! Taking it easy was like taking poison. Like that remote control! If he got one of them, he'd never get out of the chair. He'd heard there were men who had died in their re- cliners and could still channel surf. A fact! Seventeen no-thank-yous didn't seem to get the message across. Next time they called, he'd tell them to come on out, then he'd just take a few shots at them, while they were coming up the drive. That would stop the calls. And get him Cal Yeager to deal with in the process.

The old man smiled. Cal and what army? Wouldn't mind squaring off against that lying—. "Hello!" he called.

There was a long silence. Bitts decided he had missed them, whoever they were. He was still plenty fast coming across the yard, but he had been slow- ing down off the starting blocks for the past fifty years. Well, old age beat the alternative. Someone was on the other end. "Hello!"

A woman's voice. "I'm trying to locate Pat Bitts. He was the county sheriff of Lues about twenty years ago."

"What are you selling, missy, storm windows?"

"I teach at the university."

"I'm sorry to hear that. I'm too old to learn anything. Fact is, I'm older than that dog that's too old for anyone to teach."

"Excuse me?"

Give a person two or three doctor degrees and they traded off their common sense every time. "I'm not crazy you know, I'm just mean."

"That's what I hear."

Bitts liked that. He liked the voice suddenly. Youngish, quick. Touch of the East and a little of Lues in it too, if that was possible.

"Where did you hear that, Professor?"

"I'm doing research on a murder that happened here twenty years ago. Your name's come up a couple of times."

"You writing a book then?"

"It was my mother who was killed."

"Josie Fortune?"

Stunned silence, then: "That's pretty good. I mean, yes. It was."

Bitts smiled. That made this one Josie Fortune, as well, though she was going by some other name according to the paper. Polly had fallen in love with the girl. Bitts, too, if truth were told. "Last I saw you, young lady, you were no bigger than a pumpkin seed. You grow up any?"

More than a touch of a Lues now, "I grew up a little. Mr. Bitts, may I come out and see you?"

"Everybody calls me Two-Bit. That's twenty-five cents better than nothing. You don't have a jealous husband, do you?"

No answer.

"I'm kidding you. Sure. Come on out. I go to church on Sunday mornings. I get drunk Tuesdays, Wednesdays, and Thursdays from two to five, religiously. The rest of the time, it's just me and my fishing pole."

"How about this afternoon? I can be there around three. Is that good?"

"Sure, that's fine. You been this way lately?"

"No, sir. Why do you ask?"

"They changed the road back about fifteen years ago. Of course, in the middle of it, they ran out of money. What the county has got now is just a disappointed bridge. It's a mess. What I mean is you can go about thirty miles out of your way on a decent two lane or you can come through the woods and save some time. Just don't be scared when you see the river in the middle of the road. That turns a lot of folks back."

She laughed. "I bet it does, but I don't turn back for much, Mr. Bitts."

"Let me give you directions."

After he hung up, Bitts stretched and ambled back through the house to his office. Between his desk and file cabinet, he had a stack of shoe boxes. Each box was filled with notepads. Every suspicious death Bitts or his uncle had ever investigated had a single notepad to describe the investigation. He could hold the whole of a case in the palm of his hand. That was the theory, at least. The first box was dated 1932, the year his uncle took the oath to become sheriff of Lues County. The last box included the years 1979–1983, Bitts's final term in office. Bitts opened this box and dug around for the pad marked Josie Fortune, April 7, 1983, and opened it. It was filled almost entirely with ruminations, odd marks, cryptic words, times, dates, names, questions. He still remembered the case, but he just wanted to get a few things nailed down before Miss Fortune came calling. On the first page he saw his initial estimates. TIME OF DEATH—2:20–4:15. At the bottom of the page, he saw the notation: *Clothes!* They hadn't found any that night, never did as it turned out. Bitts let his chin pump up and down thoughtfully as he studied his first ideas. Carries body in? It still didn't make sense. He began flipping the pages. Now he turned back to the first page. He looked at the scratching of a rectangle with two *X*s, the time 3:40 written beside the drawing. The phone call from the kids: 4:41.

Bitts flipped forward several pages to the medical evidence. Doc Waldis's autopsy. "Here it is," he mumbled, shaking his head. Twenty years and it still made the old man's blood boil: TIME OF DEATH, 6:00–7:00.

Pauper Bluff

Before she left school to meet Lues County's former sheriff, Josie called Virgil Hazard at his home and got no answer. When she tried the bar, she got no further than giving her name. Virgil hadn't answered earlier that morning or the night before. She wanted to talk to him, to explain what had happened with the charges against Jack. For all the good it would do. After meeting with Jason Morgan on Sunday evening, she had gone to Worley Hall and read the newspaper accounts for the last two days. It was immediately apparent to her that Jack was in it too deep to ever find his way out, and she wondered why he had done it. Despite what Colt had told her, he would not have gone back to prison over it. It was crazy to run when a decent lawyer probably could have made him a millionaire. The worst of it was that if he didn't come in soon, someone was going to shoot him. One account said that more than a hundred special deputies were looking for him, and there was talk of offering a reward.

In the parking lot, Josie saw Dick Ferrington talking with Deb Rainy. At her Mustang, Josie looked back in their direction and saw them both staring at her. She wondered what Ferrington was telling her. She suddenly hated the man passionately. *Morality clause.* And with his history. The hypocrite. Josie let the engine rumble briefly, then left the lot with a squall. Like a slew.

Pauper Bluff was forty miles southeast, a straight shot on the gravel road, and Josie had thought she had left in plenty of time to make her appointment with Bitts, but by the time she came to Lues Creek Crossing, she was running late and still had five miles to go. Bitts had been right. There was a lonesome, rusted sign telling you to proceed with caution and a long stretch of nothing but water telling you to go back. Josie pushed on. She listened to the water rushing across the underside of the Mustang. Realizing that one chuckhole in the middle of all this might sink her, she kept it slow and steady. The water was about eight inches deep, but it felt worse in places, and the current was strong from several days of steady rain. Sometimes it seemed the car was shifting about. Downstream, there were two old rusted vehicles almost entirely submerged. They looked to be victims of a spring flood that no one had bothered to fish out.

In Pauper Bluff, the land turned wildly hilly, but none of it was familiar until she saw the general store in the village. The place was nothing more than an Ozark-style tourist trap, but Josie was sure she had been here before. She shook her head at such strange quirks of memory and followed the road out of the village. She slipped alongside the big Ohio, watching the barges and boats with a strange sense of nostalgia, and then she came to a long quiet lane and a front yard the size of a couple of football fields, perfectly manicured. This too, she recognized but could not place. High up on a hillside at the end of the field, she saw a quaint two-story painted brick farmhouse that looked like it had been built in the middle of the nineteenth century. It was a pale cream color with bright vermillion trim. It commanded a view of the bend in the river and looked out toward the Kentucky shore.

As she was staring at the house, a pack of dogs, all shapes and sizes, all of them barking, came up from the river. Behind them came a tall man in a cowboy hat with a tackle box and a fishing pole. He carried no fish. Josie stopped her Mustang in the middle of the drive and got out. The dogs circled and bayed, but there was no meanness in any of them. As the old man came toward her, she called out, "Mr. Bitts?"

Bitts's Stetson was pure poetry, the white felt was wrinkled and stained into a weathered motley. His face was the kind that could get a man reelected to the office of sheriff just by posting his picture on a few trees. It was a flinty, intelligent face, and old as he was, he seemed fully capable of staring down a gang of outlaws.

"Josie Fortune?" His gruff voice was like an accusation.

"It's Darling," she responded. "I haven't gone by Fortune for almost twenty years."

Bitts shifted the tackle box he carried, and reached to shake hands with Josie. It was a strong hand, but his grip was gentle. "Well, you growed some."

Josie released Bitts's hand and looked down at the dogs. They were quieter now that he had come up to her, eager and friendly. She counted seven.

"Get away from her! Get, now!" Bitts's voice was mean, but the dogs stayed close, sniffing at Josie's jeans and watching her for treats.

"Is my car okay there?"

"Sure. What is that? A Mustang?" Josie saw a look of genuine interest and answered affirmatively. "You get that at Dempsey's?"

"No. It's a rental."

"It's a nice one! Dempsey wants me to come swap. I got taken in by one of those Japanese tin cans. I never liked it. It don't *fit!* Fifteen years I been complaining about it, but it just won't die! Of course, now it's not worth more than ten thousand dollars—at least that's what I tell Dempsey." Bitts winked at her, "He wants too much for his, too. How much is that one? You know? That one there looks like it *fits!*"

"It's nice, real fast, but it costs more than what I make in a year."

"For a car that pretty, I'd change jobs."

"Maybe I will," Josie answered, thinking she might have to if Dick Ferrington had a say in matters.

Bitts opened the front door, which was not locked, and kicked at the dogs to keep them out. He made sure not to connect, and the beagle, who seemed to understand his technique better than the rest, got in despite the old man's efforts. Josie stepped into a large kitchen, which was pure country, right down to the black potbelly stove with a stack of wood waiting beside it. While Bitts wrestled with the beagle, she walked to the windows. She could see the river stretching below them. A barge was floating along, and she saw some recreational boats too. In the hills, the trees were starting to turn.

"You recognize it?" he asked.

"No, sir. Should I?"

Bitts slipped off his hat and jacket. Inside, he looked like a man close to eighty, his movements tender and careful. "You stayed here a week with Polly and me. Polly wanted to keep you. Well, we both did."

"I don't remember. I'm sorry."

"State thought we were too old and sent you to live in some foster home that had about a dozen kids, all from different families. Terrible! Polly raised Cain! And she was the woman to do it, too! Well, we never got you back, but we saw to it you got your chance in life. You get a good family, finally? We tried to see you did."

"Yes, sir. They gave me everything. They're good people."

Bitts took this for what it was and nodded. Josie wished she remembered the place. She wished she remembered Pat Bitts. She looked around the kitchen and she knew his wife—Polly?—was dead. People like Pat Bitts didn't divorce, and he lived here alone. The place was scrubbed clean, real clean, but there was nothing here of a woman's touch.

"Polly died ten years ago this March. I was out . . . ah, you don't want to hear this."

"Tell me."

Bitts studied Josie with a solemn, frightening aspect. He looked around the kitchen angrily, then walked over, opened a cabinet, and retrieved a can of coffee. As he worked, Josie studied the river. His emotions were too over-powering to contemplate directly.

"She choked to death!"

She looked back at the man. He was busy dumping coffee grounds into a filter. She turned her eyes again to the Kentucky shoreline.

"I was down by the river, cleaning some trash out. These weekend boaters seem to think their trash improves the scenery. Anyway, I come back up, and there she was. I've seen bodies all my life! It comes with the territory, came with it, anyway. I saw Polly right here!" He pointed at the floor between them as Josie answered his volatile hesitation by turning to see where, " . . . and my whole life ended." Bitts finished with the scoops of coffee and put the can back neatly in its place. "You never know," he said finally, and that was it. Nothing more.

She watched him draw some water and pour it into the machine. His gestures were part habit and part rage. "Come on in the sitting room," he commanded and set the machine to brewing with a flip of the switch.

Josie took a plush couch that didn't fit the antiques scattered throughout most of the house. Bitts was a sucker for a good salesperson, she decided. He fell into a recliner that looked to have his signature in its padding. In the kitchen, the coffee gurgled. "Now tell me what I can do for you?"

"Jason Morgan tells me you know more about my mother's murder than anyone in Lues County."

"You know Jason?"

"I met him last night. When I asked about my mother's death, he said the file on it was missing, but that you could tell me anything I wanted to know."

"I remember the case, all right, and I'll tell you something else. It doesn't surprise me a bit the file's lost. There wasn't anything about that investigation that was done right. The whole thing, everything about your mother's case was . . . off. And I mean off a hundred-and-eighty degrees!"

"Can you give me an example?"

Bitts studied Josie solemnly. "What do you know about it? What have you found out?"

"I read the newspaper accounts of it."

"Lies."

"I talked to Melody Mason."

"Why is that name familiar?"

"She's one of the kids who found the body."

"Right! She's the one that got the poison ivy! No! Poison sumac, it was! I remember Miss Mason. She squatted in the stuff! Smart as that crooked-tail beagle I got out there, not a lick more."

"I talked to Colt Fellows and Tobias Crouch, too."

Bitts grumbled, "What about your stepfather? Did you get his side of things?"

"Do you read the paper, Mr. Bitts?"

"I catch the front page now and then," the old man offered.

"You know what happened then?"

"I know Colt Fellows." He gave Josie a curiously wry smile, "I bet you're worried that Jack is looking for you."

"It crossed my mind."

"Let me tell you something about your stepfather, Professor. When he was a boy, just after his father was killed, Jack's mother and him and his two brothers and his sister moved in with his mother's sister. She was married to a man named Vern Shake. Now that man was the meanest son of a Missouri mule that ever lived. Back then, I was the only law in Lues County, so I got acquainted with Mr. Shake on a number of occasions, and I was sure I was going to have to shoot him or he was going to shoot me, assuming I ever gave him a chance at my back. There was no play in that man. When Jack and his family moved in with him, Vern took to beating the boys regular. He'd come home drunk, and he'd catch one of them, and he'd tan that boy until he bled. No favoritism, he beat his own boys too. The only salvation for any of them was there were so many they could share the burden.

"Now what I mean to tell you is this: one day, a few months after they had all moved in, Vern slapped Jack's mamma. I don't know why he hadn't done it before, but he hadn't. I don't think Vern thought much about it, just a cuff across her cheek. Nothing more than that, but it was the first and last he ever touched her. The next morning, Jack shot him while he was sitting at the breakfast table. Shot him three times, and then he sat down and waited until I showed up to arrest him. That boy was ten years old, but he was man enough to know that nobody, absolutely nobody, was going to hurt his mamma."

Josie blinked in wonder. "So it was justified?"

With this, Josie saw a lawman's smile, the careful and somewhat bitter distinction between law and justice. "It was in Jack's mind." After a moment, he added, "Jack Hazard never touched your mother, Professor. I could have proved it, too, if I had had a fair call on the time of death and Jack hadn't been in such an all-fired-hurry to cut a deal with Don Stackman."

"What was the problem with the time of death?"

"The sheriff's office got a call about a body at 4:40 in the afternoon. It was the city's jurisdiction, but since we knew we would get involved anyway if there actually was a body, I decided to have the call verified by campus security. It sounded like it might be a prank call, you understand. So I called head of security up at the college, Cal Yeager, *Sheriff* Cal Yeager these days. This was a quarter to five. He called me back around seven o'clock. Turned out the call was legitimate, and his people were holding the scene until we could get there. A half dozen or so of us went into the canyon. This was a few minutes before eight. You following this?"

Josie nodded.

"A couple of days later, Cal Yeager tells the state's attorney he called me at seven and told me about a body! Said he had gotten the call. The security officer he sent in to verify the report was suddenly saying he had started into the canyon well after six. I got my dispatcher, and Cal Yeager got his people, and it was a dead heat of liar's poker."

"That doesn't make any sense. Didn't you have the call recorded?"

"I did, but then it got mysteriously *un*recorded."

"Why?"

"Colt Fellows is *why*, not that I could prove it. He had Jack good for it as long as it happened well after four o'clock, so he moved the time of death to fit his theory! Jack had opened the bar with his brother Virgil at two, you see. Around three, he and his brother Louis took off to look for your mother again. That meant he had no alibi to speak of, and Colt jumped all over him with that. The only trouble was after I brought your mother's body out of the canyon, I found the kids that made the call. According to them, they saw her body from the top of the falls at three in the afternoon. They were standing next to her at just after four and called me as soon as they got out of the canyon, at 4:40. I just couldn't prove it. I expect Stackman might have been more inclined to believe me if the autopsy hadn't put the time of death after six o'clock. The way it turned out, with both city police and university security standing together on the time, the medical examiner's call turned it. I went for my tape of the call from the kids, . . . and it wasn't there. I proved I called Yeager from the phone records, but I had nothing to show what we talked about. He said I asked him not run for sheriff! Begged him to let me have one more term."

"So Jack was innocent?"

"For all the good it did him. Colt Fellows found the same witnesses I had. I don't know about the rest, but I saw Miss Melody Mason's signature. She was saying it was well after 6:30 when they saw the body. Two other kids had signed off, saying the same thing. The others just didn't know. Of course, nobody asked them what they did know, because when I went back to talk to them and get signed statements, the university wouldn't let me on campus! Orders from the president of that misbegotten outfit. If I wanted on campus, I need a court order! All of a sudden, a court order was a hard thing for me to get hold of. Now I worked that case as the county coroner, you understand! But the more I tried to get to the bottom of things, the more trouble I got for myself."

The coffee pot finished gurgling, and Bitts went to the kitchen to get two cups. "You take cream?" he called.

"No, sir."

"I put half the cow in mine!"

When he returned with a cup for each of them, Bitts sat down comfortably and continued, "The kids were scared of me. They had instructions not to talk to me by phone or in person, and I didn't see the point of getting them all tied up in the thing at that point. If the case had ever gone to trial, they'd have thrown it out, that was a natural-born fact. Of course, it never did. Don Stackman knew exactly what he had, and he played Jack and his lawyer with a bluff. Got a plea bargain out of it. Stackman liked your stepfather for it, and there was no need to get confused by the facts. I told him that, too!"

"There was something about a watch they found."

"Jack Hazard's name on it? I tracked that watch all over Lues County. Not a soul ever saw Jack Hazard wearing any kind of watch, not his best friend or his worst enemy. It was a plant, whether by the killer or Colt Fellows or one of his cronies, I don't know. I liked Colt for it, but I couldn't prove it any more than I could prove he got one my people to sabotage my 911 tape."

"So you're saying Colt Fellows was lying, not just making a mistake?"

"Him and Cal Yeager. They were both lying. Same as Toby Crouch. But I haven't told you the *good* part!"

"There's more?"

"There's more. The kids all told me your mother was on this rock when they found her. There was some bruising on her neck and a rope burn like she had been hanged and something just scratched across her chest, letters."

"What were they?"

He studied her a moment, "*h-o-r.* Like her killer was too dumb to spell it right."

Josie nodded. "Go on."

"That was it. Her wrists and ankles were swolled-up, but according to them, there wasn't another mark on her. By the time I got to her, four hours later, the body was in a whirlpool and the whole thorax had been ripped open with a knife."

Josie set her coffee on the table, her thoughts struggling to grasp what the old man was telling her.

"Now wait a minute," she said finally. "Her corpse had been moved . . . and cut open? Eviscerated?"

The old man nodded his head in slow deliberate agreement. "It takes just under thirty minutes from the base of the falls to reach the first telephone," he explained, "so I know what time they saw her. Now I had five people describe your mother as she was at four o'clock. They didn't all see the same thing, but it was close enough. What they saw or what they claimed they saw at four o'clock wasn't anything at all like what I found at 8:20."

Josie struggled to calm herself. She fought for some kind of saving skepticism. An old man's stories. Fable and fact can get confused with time, she told herself, and yet she couldn't believe it. Not this old man.

"Were there any other . . . wounds or marks?"

"There were. He raped her with a knife. That was postmortem, like the evisceration."

Josie leaned back and tried to breathe for a long tense moment. Finally, she stepped into the silence of the old man's gaze. "How do you explain it?" she asked.

"Just two reasonable possibilities. The kids were lying, or the killer was still in the canyon when they left and he went back to the body."

"Why would he do that?"

"Maybe they interrupted him. Maybe he got scared and wanted to make sure we wouldn't find any evidence from an examination of the body. I don't know what else to make of it."

"But you think the kids were lying because they changed their story later?"

"Possible. Confused as that case got, maybe they did it! I don't know. None of it makes any sense."

"Toby Crouch found the body in the same condition as you did?"
Bitts answered affirmatively.

"Why would he lie about the time he went into the canyon?"

"Simple. His boss Cal Yeager told him to. Then there's the fact that Crouch got a job with the city right after all this. He wanted that real bad, and Colt probably made a deal with him. As long as he happened to see Jack Hazard lurking around the scene and went into the canyon at the time his boss told him he did, he could become a police officer."

"And the director of campus security, Yeager? Why would he lie?"

"That one's easy, too. He declared himself a candidate for sheriff within days of your mother's murder. Smelled blood . . . *mine!*"

"Did you ask him not to run against you?"

"Sure, in his dreams!"

"So it was politics and self-interest? They all lied, so they could get what they wanted?"

"It was for Cal Yeager and Toby Crouch. I figured Colt just liked the case the way he could understand it, so he made all the pieces fit. He did that plenty. They say Colt wrecked his kindergarten, putting square pegs in round holes."

"What about the doctor who performed the autopsy?"

"Waldis made a mistake. He got some misdirection from Colt and made a bad call. When I caught him in it, he wouldn't back off and admit he was wrong. Said if there was misinformation, it came from my office, because a time of death before three in the afternoon was just not possible. 'Not possible.' That's just what he said. We almost had a dead professor, now that's the truth. All the good it did me to get mad! Your mother officially died after six o'clock, and I was without the proof or witnesses to do anything about it. Even Jack went against me."

"What was the cause of death? Was it strangulation, like the paper said?"

"Manual strangulation. The hanging was a good twelve to fifteen hours prior to death."

"I want to know what happened after you found the body and talked to the kids. Who arrested Jack? All of it, if you remember."

"Well, I never got to talk to Jack. Colt was barking about Jack Hazard killing his wife, even though she was his ex-wife. Now the funny thing was, Colt claimed he didn't know your mamma, but I found plenty of men who said he did. But that was later, and there was nothing I could do about it. I went to Colt, and he told me I had just misunderstood him. Anyway, Colt was putting Jack in the middle of the thing, and I knew Jack couldn't have done it. I wonder now if I had spoken up if it would have made a difference. My plan at the time was to let Colt blow hot air until he got his feet pulled out from under him. Most fools just end up confirming public opinion, and I was looking forward to it, I can tell you that. My mistake was failing to understand that Colt Fellows had a knack for changing reality. Once he got into the case far enough, I think he had to make it come out the way it did, if only to save himself. I should have seen it coming, maybe. At least, I should've pointed him in the right direction before he committed himself. I knew the time of death was about three or four hours earlier than he had figured it. I even warned him to be careful, at least wait for an autopsy before he went for an arrest warrant. He was convinced Jack was guilty, and when he found out you weren't a blood relation to Jack, he got worried Jack might be holding you hostage and called the state police in. I was at the autopsy at the time. By the time I heard about the arrest, all I could do was take care of getting you somewhere safe, out here with Polly and me, and then go to war with Don Stackman and Colt Fellows.

"I started off pretty good, too! I got our state's attorney plenty curious about the anomalies of the case, especially when I told him about my witnesses and what I'd gotten, at least until he read the statements Colt had gotten from them. When Yeager and Crouch came into the middle of it, it turned bad, but I still had a chance until Crouch took a lie detector test. After he passed and your stepfather failed his, no one took me seriously. A couple of days later, I was still nosing around, and I heard Jack confessed to it for a reduced sentence. All I could do then was fold up the tents and go home."

"Colt let Jack go to prison, knowing he couldn't have done it?"

"That's the long and the short of it, but Colt wasn't involved in the murder, if that's your next question. Not directly anyway. I checked him out before I gave up. He was working a case that afternoon."

"What about the day she disappeared?"

"I don't know about that. I had a little trouble getting anything directly, you understand. There's something else. Colt let another detective take lead on the case when it first broke. Next morning, he was running things."

"I don't understand."

"If Colt knew anything about that murder before we got a call about the body, he would have taken the lead on it from the start. Better control."

"Why would he take the case from another detective?"

"High profile case. Colt was still angling for the big chair and needed to build his reputation."

"Or he wanted to frame Jack Hazard," Josie offered simply.

"That's possible, too."

"Who was the original detective?"

"A cop named Kyle Raider, ex-CID with the state police."

Josie raised her eyebrow.

"Criminal Investigation Division. They only keep one man down here in the eleven counties we call southern Illinois. Anything the locals can't handle or need help on, CID comes into it. Once Kyle had enough time in for a pension with the state, he joined the city and worked another nine, ten years. Top-notch investigator, but Colt broke him down, took the fight right out of him. He passed on maybe a dozen or so years ago. Still a young man, sixty-five or so. Cancer got him, though I've always blamed it on Colt. Now there was another detective on the case, Happy Harpin. In the department they call him Mr. Fix-It. He runs Colt's—he used to run Colt's—errands, the kind no one was supposed to know about. Harpin was the man who found Jack's watch in the canyon. Doesn't take much imagination to see how it got there."

"Did Harpin have an alibi?"

"Sitting at a detective's desk all that afternoon. He does a lot of that still."

"What about the others? Did all the liars have good alibis?"

Bitts took a deep, angry breath and exhaled slowly. "Doc Waldis did. He wasn't the sort to get mixed up in the dirt, but I checked him out anyway. No motive, no connection, real good alibi. Believe it, I'd have stuck to him if I'd thought I had something. SIX O'CLOCK! I never heard the like of it!

"Now Don Stackman was a big problem in that case, too. He was the state's attorney back then. Still is, for that matter. He was in court when the kids found your mother. Out of town, the day your mother disappeared. Had a bit of a problem with Cal Yeager, though. I never could lock him down tight. I got it on good authority he was talking to K. V. Rogers that afternoon, that was the university president back then. This Rogers was fighting me every step of the way though, and he could've had that story spoon-fed to me without much trouble. They all loved Cal, especially when they thought he'd take the sheriff's office from me. Rogers' secretary gave me the information, but it was the only proof I could get. Of course, I talked to Cal myself three different times the day we found your mother. First time was at his office at quarter to five, then again around seven o'clock when he called me, and the last time at about nine, I called him at his house. From about half an hour after nine to midnight, he and I went around together trying to find our witnesses. He was a suspect, but I could never rustle up anything else on him. I spent quite a bit of time trying, too! Far as I know, he never met your mother or Jack.

"Not so Toby Crouch. Mr. Crouch had been out to the Hurry On Up plenty of times for the girls, and there were some people said he'd been there when your mother worked the bar before that. Been a while though, and nobody was sure. I tell you, Officer Crouch looked very good 'til I found out why he couldn't account for his afternoon the day your mother's body turned up."

"Why?"

"Doing a long liquid lunch with his buddies. That lasted until almost three o'clock in the afternoon, on the clock, mind you. Then he went out and wrote some parking tickets drunk as a skunk, and that's what he was doing when the kids called in about finding a body."

"What about Jack's lawyer? I got the feeling he wasn't exactly doing Jack any favors."

"R. K. Manley. Jack loved him because Manley got him off on a killing some years earlier."

"The black man in Pilatesburg?"

"Jack was in a card game with a man the name of Hazy Mundy. Some piece of work he was! The closest thing we had to organized crime back then. Jack was just a kid, twenty, twenty-one, and he to went work for Hazy as his bodyguard. Now Hazy was seven feet tall and carried guns all the time, but he had a lot of enemies and always kept a couple three people around like Jack, just to make sure he was covered front and back. He liked to pay his people pretty well for not doing very much, but mostly, it was so he could win it back in a Sunday afternoon poker game. You see, Hazy could deal you any card he liked anytime he wanted, or so people said. The way I hear it, he was doing what came natural-like when Jack caught him at it. Put his finger on that card before it hit the table is the way they told it to me afterward, and then, he said to Hazy, 'Why don't you deal mine from top?' Hazy took a lot of pride in himself and he pulled out a little .22 pistol and put it right in Jack's belly and asked for an apology. That was all he wanted, but Jack wouldn't give him the satisfaction. He took three slugs in the stomach before he got the gun away from Hazy and shot him with his own gun.

"The issue of self-defense turned on the fact that Jack had fired three bullets into the man's mouth. Manley was worried about it, and so he was ready to plea-bargain for a charge of manslaughter. Since Jack was wounded and wasn't armed and had come over the table to get Hazy's gun, I didn't see a problem and went to the state's attorney and said we ought to just drop the charges. There wasn't anything to it. Jack hadn't done anything but defend himself. Wounded the way he was, he had to kill the man, that or be killed. The state's attorney in those days would listen to me, and he did as I suggested. All the same, Jack's lawyer took the credit."

"You think Colt could have bought him off?"

"Why bother? The only evidence R. K. ever wanted to chase down was the kind that was in a barroom. Colt told him how it was and Manley bought it. Watch, witnesses, time of death, the only thing Manley ever worried about was making happy hour at the opening bell!"

"Is Manley still around?"

"He passed on, I guess, four or five years back."

"Anyone else?"

"That's the list I worked, none of it very promising."

"What about Virgil Hazard? Did he have an alibi?"

"Serving drinks with Jack. Started at two o'clock and kept on serving all night."

"You had no other suspects?"

"Your mother didn't have many friends on campus. Still just a freshman, plus she was a single mother, quite a few years older than the rest of them. That took her out of the social life. I take it she and Jack were seeing each other again by that spring, too, trying to mend some broken fences. Jack didn't quite fit into the university crowd, so with him around, she wouldn't have been involved much with any of her classmates or any of the professors. The long and the short of it, I couldn't turn up a decent suspect anywhere."

"I have the names of four of the five kids who found the body," Josie said.

"When I talked to Melody Mason, she couldn't remember the fifth kid. Is there any chance you have the names?" Josie realized that the fifth kid was into ripe middle age by now.

Bitts pulled a little notepad from his shirt and smiled like a man with a gold nugget, "My own personal field records, and they're good, Professor, the whole of a murder in the palm of my hand. Every homicide or suspicious death I ever investigated, I recorded in a little notepad like this, then copied it out later to be put in the official reports. It's mostly just names, times, questions, details. In the case of your mother's death, I got a lot of question marks. But I've got the names of the kids." Bitts flipped through the first few pages, "Melody Mason. Cat Sommerville. Jim Burkeshire—."

"That's the one. Do you have anything else? Parents, home addresses? Melody's lost touch with everyone."

Bitts nodded, "Got it all. Got your mother's professors, too."

"Her professors?"

"I thought they might have some information. An older woman is sometimes more likely to confide in a professor rather than one of her eighteen-year-old classmates. I talked with all of them eventually."

"May I have that notebook to make a copy?"

"I'll copy the names of people you might want to talk to, times, that sort of thing." Bitts stood, "You want more, you call me or come on back out. I don't mind missing a chance to catch a fish or two, not for this, I don't. Tell you the truth, I never quite put this thing to bed. Twenty years I been mulling it over. I just could never figure it all out so that it made sense."

Josie finished her coffee. She wanted everything, not just what he thought she could use, but she understood the old man. He wanted a degree of control, wanted to hang on to the thing even now. "Do you care if I get some more coffee?"

"Help yourself." Bitts had risen from his recliner with a couple of strange catches in the effort. Now he hobbled a bit, before walking gingerly back toward the hallway.

In the kitchen with a fresh cup of coffee, Josie stood alone and looked out across Bitts's lawn.

She liked the old man and wanted to believe him. But what he said was incredible. Had everyone conspired against Jack Hazard? No. That wasn't what he said. They had lied. There was a difference. A conspiracy would mean they all agreed to an action, then proceeded. This was more like they had just piled on, the way of a feeding frenzy. Guilt by accusation and no room for the facts. But if Bitts was right, Jack was an innocent man, and her mother's killer had gotten away. No, not away. He had probably stayed in Lues. And somehow found out Josie was coming to Lues. *WilcuM HoM Josie.*

Her thoughts drifting, Josie continued staring out toward the river. She was thinking about Colt Fellows and Toby Crouch, the way they had worked her, Jack Hazard's smile when he asked her if she was really a professor. She remembered the notes left for her to find and thought about all the liars. She sipped her coffee, losing track of time as she wondered why she had become a target. When Bitts returned, Josie spun around. Before she could stop herself, she had almost reached into her purse. Bitts didn't seem to notice. He was in the middle of a twenty-year-old case, the same as she was.

"This is about everything."

"They all knew Jack was innocent, didn't they? Stackman, Crouch, Fellows, Yeager. They knew and they didn't care?"

Bitts's smile creased his haggard face, "I don't know about that, Professor. Colt knew, and so did Crouch and Yeager. Stackman . . . no. He wanted a conviction, but a fair one. He looked at what he got from all of us, and he figured I was trying to get reelected. I fault him for not trusting me, but you have to remember he was looking at a bad case and a man with two killings behind him. That made Jack the easy man to blame."

"Not for you."

"I knew something about Jack Hazard that Don Stackman didn't."

"What's that?"

"I knew Jack Hazard was the kind of man they don't make anymore. I knew it the first time I met that boy."

Lues Creek Crossing

Bitts came out with Josie to look at her car again. Josie humored him but soon found herself staring at the late afternoon light reflecting off the river.

"It's pretty here," Josie said. She thought her whole life she'd been trying to find this place again and now she probably wouldn't be coming back.

Bitts looked away from the car and out toward the river. "I was born here seventy-six years ago," he answered. "Right on this hill."

Josie looked at him briefly, wondering what she might have been if this man had adopted her, as he had wanted. Then she looked back at the house. Her home for a week. Something in the shape of the hill and the forest beyond the house reminded Josie of her childhood, but that was all. She couldn't even be sure if this was a real memory or only a happy delusion.

"Pull on up to the house and turn around," Bitts told her when she had started the Mustang. "The yard's too wet to pull out on!" The engine of the Mustang rumbled and Josie nodded. She let the car kick forward with a brief surge of its power, then watched Bitts shake his head and grin. He was a sweet old man, and lonely, she decided. She coasted through the tight circle beside his rusted-out Toyota and a fairly new Ford pickup truck, full-size. A moment later, she passed Bitts, waved, and headed down the long hill toward the road.

At Lues Creek Crossing, Josie slowed the car and rolled carefully into the water. The mole quickened the current. Nearly a week of constant rain had swollen the creek, as well, but it had been this bad a couple of hours earlier, and Josie pushed out into the waters with the faith of an old-time Christian. She didn't like the sound of water pushing up under her floorboards. Downstream, she glanced toward the abandoned wrecks. At the midpoint in her crossing, Josie looked upstream. The water seemed to come right toward the passenger door of the Mustang. It was simply an illusion, but creeks and rivers create powerful illusions, she realized.

After she had crossed the center, something happened. Somewhere back across the creek and upstream a bit, Josie thought she heard a faint popping sound. She looked back into the dull light of the woods and saw nothing. The car felt different. She turned the steering wheel and felt it kick and quarrel in response. The gravel was sliding under her wheels? She tried to move the car left. It jumped some, then pulled back right. She turned slightly to the right and felt it pulling hard.

She had a flat tire.

Josie rolled on through the creek, then stopped the car close to the edge of the road. It was just past five o'clock in the evening. There was still plenty of light, but the forest was close around her. It wouldn't be too long before it was dark. The road was empty. She looked out toward the woods, swore briskly, and got out of the car. She walked around to the front of the vehicle and looked at the tire.

Contemplating the obvious, she shook her head in frustration. What else could go wrong?

She heard rustling behind her. Her hands reached for her purse, left hand rising, right hand crossing, but there was nothing there. Her purse was in the car. She turned in time to see the man. He was thin and tall. He had a red beard. He hit her at the waist and pushed her back across the hood of the Mustang. Josie curled her leg up and kneed him hard in the ribs. He grunted at the impact. She pushed against him and felt his weight give. *Fight!* she screamed to herself and hit him twice in the face with the heel of her hand. His strength seemed to fade, and she wrestled herself nearly off the car. That was when she saw the others. They were coming toward her on the run. The man who had tackled her grabbed at her again, and Josie hit him once more, this time with her elbow across his jaw. He fell back, and she tried to crawl across the hood of the car toward the driver's side. She wanted to get to her purse. She heard a sickening cry of country glee and felt the next man hit her with the length of his body, knocking the wind out of her. She felt another take her legs. She pulled back, but the hands stayed on each ankle. She kicked twice with her right leg, putting her foot into his chest, but couldn't free herself. Then, lifting her left leg, she took aim at the tiny man's filthy grin. The move surprised him, and his smile turned bloody. He fell back out of sight. Josie's first attacker had rolled off the front of the car also, but another one came scrambling over the hood to take her free arm. Two more of them grabbed for her legs now. Held by four men, Josie jerked with the last spasms of her strength. They had her.

"Tie her up!" the one still in the woods commanded. Her first attacker, his red beard bloody, stood dumbly looking down at Josie from the front of the car. His nose was bleeding heavily. He reached into his deep pockets, bringing out a dangerous-looking pocketknife and several strands of bailing twine. Josie ceased fighting as she watched the knife. The small man she had kicked came up now, his lips and chin bright red. He swore with a peculiar reverence. The others ignored him.

Seven. Her mind moved quickly. One of them had seen her passing through on the way to Pauper Bluff. He got the others, and they had waited for her to come back. The popping sound was from a rifle. They had shot out her tire. One more of them across the creek, or was that just an echo? The man in the woods held a rifle and one of the others had a gun also. It could have been one of them. As her feet were bound tightly, Josie looked up into their faces.

What they wanted was pretty clear. But not here, apparently. She looked down the road. Still no one coming. Maybe just the car. Maybe the car, but that wasn't all. Josie felt the clawing fear of rape deep in her gut. She tried to shut that thought away. She heard something that was not quite a voice telling her to survive, to simply hang on. It was the primal self. There were no words with the thought. It was simply the impassioned scream of life itself that could drown out even the terrible and sometimes debilitating fear of pain. She studied their faces, so she could remember them. Three of them had beards. Two were fat-cheeked, flushed, excited, middle-aged. They had light brown hair and flannel shirts with quilted jackets. Muscular, both were average height. The others were physically a mixed bag. Her first attacker was the only one with red hair. He was the tallest and thinnest. The second to come at her was a big, powerful man with dark hair and dark eyes. The one she had kicked in the face was short and wiry, his chin and cheekbones nearly flat against his face. He'd had bad teeth to begin with. They were a lot worse after Josie's efforts. The other two were short, powerful men, both with salt-and-pepper hair, their eyes dark, intensely disturbing. The leaders. The killers, when that time came.

Her ankles bound, they tied her wrists quickly, taking a length of the twine around her waist to keep her hands close to her body. A bandanna came out now, wadded into a ball. A second fluttered, wrapped into a gag. "Take it!" Josie resisted. "Hold her nose!" Josie opened her mouth slightly to breathe and tasted the filthy cloth shoved into her mouth. She looked mournfully down the road again. Still nothing. The second bandanna was wrapped tightly across her mouth. She fought with the cloth in her mouth, pushing it forward in a tight knot toward her teeth. She nearly vomited. She breathed desperately through her nose. She felt the cloth softening with saliva. The reflex of nausea passed.

The strongest of them, the one with the dark hair and thoughtful, sharp, black eyes, slid Josie toward him over the hood of the car now and heaved her over his shoulder. Josie saw two of them moving toward her car as the others carried her into the woods. She saw them open the driver's side door. She saw them getting her keys, then her purse. They found the .357 immediately. One of them stuck the revolver into his jeans. A moment afterwards, they opened the Mustang's trunk. She saw nothing else as the heavy brush now obliterated her view of the road. Lying over the man's shoulder and feeling his powerful strides, Josie looked at their legs. All wore jeans and leather boots. They were clear of the road now. She heard the distant clank of metal and realized they were changing the tire. Maybe just the car. This was simply a prayer. The forest would give them cover. One spot as good as another. Still, they were going deeper into the woods. Josie tried to look back in the direction of the creek. They were angling away from it, taking a small incline. They passed over the ridge finally. Behind them, the hills blocked out the road and creek. She twisted around to see to either side. Nothing but the September forest and the men. Five of them. Several minutes passed silently. Their feet trampled the damp leaves of the forest floor. Josie's stomach rolled against the man's shoulder. Her nerves were merciless.

Josie forced herself to lift her shoulders and look at the men. She fixed their faces a second and third time in her memory. They were solemn, angry faces, but they were walking easily. No grins, no winks, no lust. Would they just leave her? Was this to buy some time to get the car out of the county? The next thoughts were so cruelly skeptical they might have been funny in another context. Josie was coming to terms with her own death, slowly, bitterly, sorrowfully. This was what had happened to her mother.

From the hill that ran between them and Lues Creek, a young man came running to join them. He came up quickly, and the others stopped to wait for him. Six now. And the other two with the Mustang. The new arrival carried a rifle with a scope and a wet pair of waders. *The shooter.* He was a kid, maybe twenty-five. He had a beautiful face, a wild, unconscious beauty in his step, and lustrous dark hair. Had she seen him before? she wondered. His teeth were white and square. He was smiling like a boy as he looked expectantly toward the men.

One of them finally rewarded him. "Nice shot, Cy."

"Good work, Cyrus," the oldest added.

"Want me to take her?" another asked.

The man carrying Josie set her down.

"Maybe we can let her walk?" Cy offered. Josie looked at him. His voice was as bashful and country as Lues Creek. Dark, bright eyes. If there was any kindness in any of them, it was here. Josie tried to catch his attention, but he didn't react.

"Keep her tied up, she kicked my tooth loose." The speaker moved toward Josie's face, staring at her weirdly. She thought he would hit her, but he only opened his bloodied lips for her to see. "It hurts."

Did he want sympathy?

One of the shorter men in the group slipped under Josie and took her up on his shoulder. The momentary relief of being able to stand passed quickly, and Josie felt her stomach now pushed into the lump of another man's shoulder. The pressure was slightly different because of the change in position and the shape of him, but soon enough, the ache of being carried simply became more universal. This one walked with different rhythms, his step heavier, shorter. Josie's body flopped painfully so that the wind was knocked out of her in a series of shots that hit just below her diaphragm. She struggled to twist her body away from the repetitious jolts. She wanted the first man to carry her again. Or better yet, she wanted to walk. She wiggled slightly, managing to take her shoulders and head down. For a minute or so that was some relief, but the discomfort gradually returned, along with the horrible sense of not being able to breathe.

The men moved silently. The shooter, Cy, and another man ran ahead now. Josie tried to drop her shoulders lower still and look forward. The world upside down, she couldn't quite focus. They were coming to a dirt road. She heard a shout of encouragement, then another. They crossed the road at a trot, then fell back to their original pace. The wet leaves whispered under their boots. The forest swallowed them again.

They meant to keep her, she realized. She looked at their bodies, pulling up to catch the expressions in their faces. She was too weak to hold herself like this long and fell heavily back, so that her focus remained on the back of her carrier's legs and the boots of the men closest to him. They didn't care that she could recognize them. That was bad, real bad.

They started up a hill, and Josie twisted off to the side. A cabin. Well, here it was. She felt a surge of regret. Maybe an hour or two, maybe a day or two, then one of them takes her out and finishes it. She felt tears. She swore silently, bitterly. At least not that! No tears. She looked at them again. The shooter might be able to catch her, but if she could get a few seconds on him, she would test him. She could outrun the others, she was sure of it. Play along, they loosen the ropes for their fun, and go. She glanced up at the leaders. They probably owned these woods, had claimed their rights in this fashion for years. So it was nothing new for them. Only Josie was new. All else was part of a ritual too macabre to understand. Silently, Josie decided she would have to be patient. And that meant shutting off her mind, while they. . .

. . . Don't fight, don't struggle, wait for their mistake, wait for your chance. One chance only. If that.

Nobody was going to come looking for her. Nobody knew where she was. Bitts would never know she had been taken. They had the car. Nobody would find it and know she was missing. The first they would know of this would be tomorrow morning, when she didn't show up for class.

Maybe they'll let you go when they're finished? No, she told herself. It would not do to lie to herself. Her only chance was to face her death, un-blinking. If she did that, she had a chance. She was going to have wait until that moment when they didn't expect her to do anything, and then she was going to have to run. And keep running. Five miles or so back to Pauper Bluff. Thirty-some to Lues. Thirty miles of woods. Eight of them coming after her, knowing the woods and roads. They would have trucks and cars, spotlights after dark, maybe even dogs to track her.

She heard their boots thumping on the boards of the porch. She saw the rough-hewn logs of the cabin. The door opened. She was carried through. Inside, the room was dark and chilly. No light, no fire. There was a damp here like a cave. She lifted herself to look. Two dark, nondescript figures in the shadows under a lone window. Ten.

She found herself standing again and tried to focus on the two men in front of her. They sat at a small table. One of the men in the shadows said, "Cut her loose." Josie studied the darkened face of the speaker. She felt her feet freed. She looked at the knife, as it slipped between her wrists and sawed briefly at the twine. The handkerchief was jerked down around her neck, and she reached into her mouth to spit out the wad of cloth they had forced into her mouth.

Clothes next? Cut them off. Then the men in succession. That's how it goes, isn't it? She looked across the room to a corner, a single bed, filthy sheets, a couple of blankets.

We all die somewhere, Josie.

"Any trouble?" This time the voice was familiar.

Her eyes adjusting finally, Josie saw it was Jack Hazard. Beside him, still quiet, Virgil Hazard sat contemplating her coldly.

"She kicked my tooth loose. And I think she broke Blake's nose."

Josie stared at the two brothers, ignoring the men around her. Virgil stood up now and walked toward her.

"Hello, D. J." His voice was full of bile.

The Cabin

Virgil was standing within range. Josie could take his knee out, for all the good it would do her. If he touched her, she would do it. When he made no move toward her, Josie stared defiantly back at him, an implicit dare. In the dim light of the cabin, Virgil's face seemed peculiarly ugly, as if he were looking at one of his uncooperative girls. Finally he announced, still looking at her eyes, "Come on! Let's go."

They all moved toward the door behind her, and Josie realized they meant to leave her with Jack. She looked at the window just behind the table where he was still sitting. It provided a small opening high up on the wall. She could crawl out of it once she broke the glass, but to run for it and jump through it was impossible, even if she had the courage to go face-first into glass. She looked at Jack's dark features as she watched him stand up. He was in jeans and a flannel shirt. He had on a pair of leather boots and an old Cardinals baseball cap. A shotgun leaned against the wall. A revolver was stuck in his belt. As he stepped toward her, she thought maybe to get the revolver from him. With the others outside, it didn't promise much, but it was something, better maybe than dying without a fight. *See what he wants. You get one chance. Make it a good one.*

She expected he would hit her before he did anything else.

"Hey! it's not McDonald's, but it's going to have to do."

Josie came out of her reveries and remembered their plans to meet at the Lues McDonald's. He was smiling, making a joke of it. His whole body slouching in a posture of feigned ease, but in his eyes, Jack looked ready to pull his gun and shoot her.

"Colt set me up," she said. "He lied, and I fell for it." Josie announced this as fact, her voice emotionless. She didn't expect it would have any effect, but she wanted it for the record.

"Colt?" Jack was dubious but still putting on a humorous face. "I thought you were the one who said let's meet at McDonald's."

Jack was nearly a step from her. Josie thought about trying for his gun now, but she realized Jack knew what she meant to do even as she thought it. His face almost dared her to try it. She looked squarely into his eyes, concentrating on her words, not the gun.

"Someone smashed up my car the day I met you. Colt convinced me it was you and that you meant to kill me. He said if I charged you with assault, he could protect me from you."

"He didn't do a very good job, did he?" No remorse for killing Colt. And no remorse for this.

"Look, he talked me into doing something stupid. If anyone could understand that, it ought to be you."

Jack's eyes flashed angrily, "What are you talking about?"

"I seem to recall a certain damn fool confessing to a murder he didn't commit."

His eyes cut away, and he mumbled. "That was different."

"So what now, Jack? Are you going to kill me?"

"Did those guys threaten you?" Worried, irritated.

"They didn't say anything at all."

"They hurt you? Any of them hit you?"

"They hurt my pride a little."

"We've been watching you for the past two days," he admitted with a grin, "looking for a chance to get you. You're pretty careful, and I didn't want anyone shot." An appreciative appraisal of her, maybe.

"Why?"

"You and I need to talk, Josie."

"You ever hear of a telephone?"

"This is better."

"Who are these people helping you, Jack?"

"Family. Cousins mostly. A few in-laws. Don't get them in trouble, Josie. They were just doing what I asked them to."

"Did you set that up at the creek? Was that your doing?"

He pointed toward the door vaguely, "My brother Louis did that. Nice job, huh? Except for what you did to Lincoln and Blake."

"I got a couple of them pretty good," Josie answered, proud of herself suddenly. She had fought, hadn't she? "God, Jack, I'm so sorry!" she admitted suddenly. She felt the exhaustion that comes of folly. "It was so stupid to trust that bastard! I just got pushed around!"

"Look, I know I scared you."

"You didn't scare me."

"I just wanted out of the bar," he answered. "I didn't want to talk to you there."

"It wasn't that. It was—." She stopped herself. It was utterly stupid, what she had done. "I've ruined it for you, Jack. If I hadn't gone out to find you, you'd still be a free man. They're saying, now, when they catch you, they'll ask for the death penalty."

Jack smiled. Smiled! "People say a lot of things, Josie. First thing they have to do is catch me, and they're not going to do that."

"So did you kill Colt like they say or did someone in the family do it?"

"I killed him."

"You want to tell me about it?"

"Don't worry about it, okay? I can't prove anything, so it doesn't matter what I say."

"So just tell me the truth. I don't care. I mean it's not like I can turn you in or anything."

"You want the truth? Colt had his man pull me out of the car. They had me chained hand and foot, Josie. They were going to shoot me, and I made a move."

"You know he meant to shoot you? You're sure of it?"

"Forget it. It doesn't matter."

"I'm asking."

"They said it was like shooting a dog. Only more fun."

"Fun? Colt said that?"

"Yeah."

"That son of a bitch."

"What?"

"I want you to write out what happened. Everything he said, everything you did. I'll take it in to . . . to somebody. . . ."

Jack smiled at her. "Somebody? Who are you going to take it to, Josie?"

"I'll get a lawyer. We'll get the best lawyer in the country, Jack, and we'll straighten this out!"

"Leave it. I can stay out here forever, and they won't find me. Hell, it beats what I had. This here is the first time in years I've felt alive."

"You can't stay out here. They have a hundred special deputies looking for you."

"Those boys answered the sheriff's ad, so they could get the free beer and hot dogs, Josie. It's just a big party in the woods! But I'll tell you something, there's not a mother's son in Lues County wants to get off the pavement and come in and *look* for me."

"It's not a joke. Okay? They'll find you eventually. You know they will."

"What are you doing here, Josie? You got out of Lues once. What did you come back for?"

She looked away. She looked to the little window that five minutes before she had thought about trying to dive through. "I didn't like what I'd become, Jack. I thought I better find out who I had been."

"Virgil says you don't remember any of it."

"I guess I should have kept it that way." She stared into his eyes. The man who didn't murder her mother. The man she had betrayed and who didn't care, didn't hit her, didn't yell. The man who made light of an army of men hunting for him.

"Hey, what happened between me and Colt was a piece of old business. To tell you the truth, I'm glad it did. That man stole twenty years of my life, and I didn't have the guts to go make it right. If I had done the right thing when I got out, you never would have been involved, and no one would have ever known what the hell happened to Colt Fellows."

"You can't just murder a man because you don't like what he did to you!"

Jack laughed. "Someone should have told Colt that."

Josie shook her head and walked back toward the table and window. "I want to know what happened between you and my mother. I want to know why you two got a divorce?"

She turned now and saw him looking at the planks of the floor. Maybe ashamed, or maybe just a man with no good answers.

"What's it matter, anyway?"

"It matters," she said, walking toward him, wanting to reach out and touch him the way a girl does her father when they've disappointed each other. "I want to know."

"Josie wanted to do better than just owning a bar. Going to the university was just part of it."

"You were afraid she wanted to get a degree and move away?" Jack tried to look like he didn't understand. "She wanted to leave Lues, and you didn't want to?" Josie asked.

He shook his head. "It's complicated."

"Complicated is what you tell a seven year old, Jack."

The man growled, turned and walked away. "I thought it was me, so I gave her a good reason. It was dumbest thing I ever did."

"Did you cheat on her? Is that what you're saying?"

Jack looked at the floor, "I got real drunk at the bar one night. Told myself I didn't need her and she didn't need me." He shook his head, smiling a bit, "she hit me with divorce papers before I could even lie to her about what happened. Which was fine with me, at least until I woke up and realized that you and your mother were the best part of my life, the only part of it I couldn't stand to lose. That spring we were seeing each other again. We were talking about the future. I don't think we'd ever talked about the future before. We were just kids and got married, bought a bar, had a good time making money. The whole thing . . . it was just fun. You know? We finally got talking about things after the divorce. Turned out we wanted the same things, we just had different ideas about how to get them. She wanted to finish school. That was something she had set out to do. It had nothing to do with me or even wanting to leave. She just wanted . . . to know things."

"Why did you work for Virgil after you sold him the bar?"

"I didn't, not really. Not as an employee anyway. We sold the place to him outright, as far as the county was concerned anyway, but he was paying as he went. Same way we bought it from Louis. Only they were having fights in the bar, and some of his dancers were hustling tricks in the parking lot. I mean Virgil's worth diddle now as a manager. Back then he was really bad. I had to get to the place under control or the city would have shut us down, and we'd have all lost our shirts. I didn't like it, and neither did Josie, but we didn't really have any choice. We both stood to lose a lot of money if I didn't get the place straightened out."

"Did my mother ever work there after you sold the place? Bartending?"

"Where did you get an idea like that? She hated what Virgil did to the place. She wouldn't talk to him after he brought the dancers in. Well . . . not for a long time. She sure never got over it."

"The newspaper said she was dancer."

"That was Colt. He fed them . . . crap. You see, he and your mother ran crossways of one another. What it was, he came out to the bar one night and wanted to shake us down for some money. Josie put her sawed-off Purdey in his ugly face, and he pissed his pants." He shook his head miserably. "Wet himself just like a little boy. I knew then he wouldn't ever let it rest. Trouble was Colt didn't have the guts to come at either one of us straight on. I think your mother scared him more than I did. So, he just waited his chance."

"You think he killed her?"

"I don't know, Josie. I expect it's possible, but I just don't know."

"Tell me about the day she disappeared. Do you remember it?"

"You called me up at the bar. You said your mom wasn't home. I came to get you. We started looking. I mean everyone in the family. We found her car on a parking lot up at the college. . . . I guess it was the next day. At that point, we went to the sheriff. I don't know what they did with it, but the following evening, one of Colt's people called me, said I better come to the medical center."

Jack fished out a Lucky and struck a match. He kicked across the small room and squatted on the corner of the bed, just letting the cigarette burn. "Colt was there, waiting for me as I was leaving. He said we needed to talk about where I had been, so he could eliminate me as a suspect. What he did, he used what I gave him and then he went out and got that watch and put my name on it. Told me so the other night. I knew he had pushed things around, but I never really . . . I didn't want to believe it. I kept thinking he made a mistake. I couldn't accept that he would take my life away just because . . . he could."

Josie remembered the image of Jack in the state police sedan, face bloody, head bent down. Ashamed or just beaten senseless? *JAAAACK!*

You don't want to talk to him, honey. That man there is the one that killed your mamma. But it wasn't so. She hadn't wanted to believe it. She had loved him, the only father she had ever known. But everyone had told her Jack was a monster. The man who held her child's world together. Everyone had lied. Colt and Yeager and Crouch. They had taken Jack's life almost as completely as they had taken her mother's. But there was something else, as well, and it finally dawned on her. Jack was not the only one who had lost a chunk of his life for no other reason than pure meanness. They were her twenty years lost, too.

Cyrus Hazard

They talked about other things eventually, pulling relentlessly at a past Josie could not quite recall. Finally, she promised to get him out of these woods, and he swore to her that it would never happen. A cop killing, he said, could never be excused. They would string Don Stackman up by his thumbs if he didn't go for a conviction and get one. Nothing would convince the police that Colt had simply taken him out to execute him. Even if Stackman wanted it otherwise, there would be a cop somewhere waiting to even the score. But it didn't matter, he said. For the first time since her mother's death, he was actually free. Or so he insisted. She could almost believe it from the look on his face. When he asked if she was safe, Josie said she could take care of herself. To her astonishment, Jack took her at her boast, and that was how they left it. Lying to each other because neither of them could do anything to help the other.

Outside, the others were all gone except for the young man named Cyrus. Cy was waiting up the trail. When he saw them coming out of the cabin, he walked back down the path toward them, a flashlight's bright beam bouncing in front of his steps. Josie turned to say goodbye to Jack, but he was already gone, a ghost among the dark leaves fading into the dusk, and she was alone suddenly with a stranger who carried a scoped rifle and smiled bashfully when she looked at him.

"I'll take you to your car," he said softly, ducking his head and walking beside her.

As they followed the light at their feet, Cyrus was preternaturally quiet, and Josie thought to say something, if only to take her fear of the dark away.

"So you're related to Jack?"

"Nephew." The voice came like a whisper, then the silence between them returned.

Finally, she asked him, "Where do you work, Cy?"

"I do some carpentry for Virgil, sometimes. Run errands for Louis. Whatever they need."

Josie studied the darkness, then the light at their feet, the deep carpet of wet leaves. "I saw you that day working on the roof across from Virgil's bar?"

"Yes, ma'am." Ma'am?

She studied him furtively as they continued walking. He was hardly more than a shadow against the dark woods, but he was so handsome, so quiet and gentle and confident.

"Have you ever been out of Lues County, Cy?"

"I was over in Vienna a couple of years." He pronounced it *Vy-anna,* like everyone in southern Illinois.

"Vienna . . . as in, you robbed a bank?"

"It was a misunderstanding."

A long silence followed with only the sound of their footfalls in the leaves. "So tell me about the misunderstanding," Josie said at last. The men Josie knew rarely stopped talking, even when they had nothing to say. With Cy, she had to pull the words out, and yet the sound of his voice was hypnotic.

"Not much to it really. This guy was hurting his girlfriend out in Huree at some bar. He was twisting her arm, pushing her face into her beer and calling her names. That kind of thing."

Josie nodded, waiting for the rest.

Cy shrugged, his narrative finished, "I stopped it."

"They sent you to prison for stopping it?"

"Yes, ma'am."

"Did you know the man?"

"No, ma'am."

"The woman?"

Cy shook his head.

Josie thought about this before she remembered the point of his story. "So what was the misunderstanding?"

"I said he'd better stop, or I'd kill him. He didn't understand I was serious."

At the Mustang, Cy handed Josie her .357, and pointed the way back to Lues. She could hardly follow his directions for thinking about his story. Had he really killed a man, or was that just what he had said to him? She was afraid to ask, afraid she already knew, and even so she didn't mind. Not at all.

When he stood back to let her drive off, Josie told him, "Take good care of Jack for me."

Cy smiled, his white teeth flashing beautifully. "Jack can pretty much take care of himself, if you ask me."

"He's in a lot more trouble than I think he realizes. I just don't want to lose him before we get this straightened out."

"You want to know the truth?" Cy asked her.

"Sure. I'm a great one for the truth."

"Ever since I was little, people talked about Uncle Jack like he was something special. Well I saw him in Vienna, and I worked with him some after he got out. There wasn't nothing special about him. He was just some old guy, you know? Nice enough, straight talker ... but I mean he wasn't someone you really noticed. People talked about him in the old days, told stories about him, but that's all they were. Stories. Then this weekend he got loose out here. I got out to help him get things together, and I could see it right away, what everyone said about him. It was in his eyes, the way he moved. I don't know how to explain it any better, but he's different. He's got the woods in him or something."

Josie knew what he meant. She had seen it too, without quite realizing it, a kind of animal grace that had been missing in the bar. The man she had met in the cabin was laughing about a hundred special deputies chasing him. Laughing and meant it. These were his woods. Here even the law hesitated.

"This thing happening to him," Cyrus finished, "it made him a man again."

Josie had no answer for this. She thought he was probably right, but mostly, she was thinking that her mother had met and married a young man such as this a quarter of a century before. Something wild and dangerous, a man with the woods in his soul but as gentle as a summer breeze to those he loved.

Definitely the sort of man they didn't make anymore.

The Huree Hideaway

It was completely dark when Josie pulled into the parking lot at her apartment complex on campus. By chance, no one was moving around outside, and only a few windows showed light. The place had an eerie aspect. A wind was kicking in the treetops. Clouds were racing toward the crescent moon. At the door, her key already into the lock, Josie stopped. She backed away quickly and pulled the revolver from her purse. She looked out at the darkened forms of the cars and trucks, then looked at the door again. A terrible instinct warned her against going inside. She had been giving away too many chances. She knew he could get past a locked door, and yet she was letting herself believe home was *safe* just because she had changed her locks. Home was anything but safe! Home would be where he was most likely to strike. Here, late at night, she could walk right into his hands and no one would know it for days. If not tonight, tomorrow or the day after. One evening, she would return home, tired and thinking about something else, and it would be the last mistake of her life.

Josie gunned the Mustang hard as she left. She came off Willow Circle and down the hill quickly. On Willow Drive, she raced through campus at nearly sixty. It was time to think like the hunter, time to settle in a new blind. That afternoon, Josie had fought two Hazards to a standstill, and if she could have gotten to her gun, she would have stopped them all. She had stared Jack Hazard himself down in that awkward moment of ignorance and accusation. She wasn't the obedient wife anymore, Mrs. Scholari, sucker punched because she couldn't believe someone might actually resort to violence. Nor was she little Miss Darling hiding from the ex, the fight all kicked out of her. She could claw and kick and shoot. More than that, she knew she could find this man, whoever he was. She needed time. That was all. Nothing said she had to sit and wait and hope he wouldn't strike before she had found him out. No rules required that she submit to the whims of a madman. This was a country fight. There were no rules at all. The first thing she needed to do was to stay out of easy reach. That meant she wasn't going to let him know where to find her, not after dark, at any rate.

Josie made a fairly lengthy stop at the twenty-four-hour grocery store, getting everything she would need for the next day or so, including cash. Once back in the Mustang, she headed west through the hills until she joined with a spur of highway that would eventually take her to Huree. There were a couple hotels out that way because of the interstate, and that was her destination. A few miles before she reached the town, however, Josie found the perfect motel along a winding stretch of two-lane highway. She turned into the narrow drive on impulse and dropped down a steep incline, and she was no longer visible from the highway. The Huree Hideaway was a place just made for illicit love affairs: it was cheap, quiet, and relatively clean. Best of

all, it was discreet. One registered at the front of the building in a little office, but the motel guests entered their rooms and parked their cars at the
back, close-up against the woods.

The motel rented rooms for the night and efficiencies by the week, Bea,
the old lady at the registration desk, told her. Behind the woman, in a little
apartment where she stayed when she wasn't watching the desk, a television
was playing. A beer can and pack of cigarettes rested close-by on a little table
next to the easy chair. Bea was close to sixty. Her face was a bit bloated, her
eyes quick and small and full of an old fire that wasn't quite out. She was
the sort who believed people are going to do what they want to do and no
sense worrying about it, though it was kind of fun knowing. She took one
look at Josie and decided she knew the game. "We don't allow parties, hon,
but a quiet friend or two is perfectly okay. "Don't worry," she added with a
wink, "I keep an eye on things, but I say nothing."

Filling out the register, Josie used a fictitious Beacon Hill address, then
signed the register, Josie Fortune.

Bea looked at the name thoughtfully, then at Josie.

"That's a pretty name you have," the old woman offered.

"It was my mother's name," Josie answered.

The efficiency was small and a bit musty. The bed was cheap, the mattress soft, the covers worn and thin. There was a tiny desk that could barely
support Josie's elbows, a rickety straight-backed chair before it, and a broken-down couch pulled up close to an old Sony television set. The flooring
was linoleum, the paneling dark. In the kitchenette, she found some cook-
ware and started boiling water. She tried the phone, but Annie Wilde didn't
answer. Josie had no one else she could call. She ate the fruit and bread she
had picked up at the store, then dropped a couple of tea bags in the boiling
water. A couple of minutes later, she began pouring herself small measures
of black tea into a tiny yellow mug, while she wrote out on motel stationery
all she knew about her mother's death. She had thought to spend only a few
minutes on the project but wrote for nearly three hours. When she had finished, she discovered she knew a good deal more than she might have imagined, and it was with some satisfaction she turned to the thin mattress of
her bed.

That night, Josie slept naked. A .357 magnum lay on top of the bedside
table, a Gideon Bible in the drawer.

Assassination

Josie bribed a mechanic with an awful gee-whiz routine and had her tire patched before her first class the next morning. Later, she slipped out to Willow Circle and with her revolver drawn entered the apartment. As quickly as she could, Josie cleared out only the most necessary clothes and files and books, then headed out to see old Bowers for another lesson with the .357. The old man swore she'd been practicing. Josie was back at Brand Hall for her office hours with a few minutes to spare. Having missed all of her Monday afternoon office hours, Josie was hardly surprised to see so many students waiting for her. They were stacked up outside, and she had to force herself to slow down, to give each of them her full attention. It was easier than she had imagined, actually. The routine was comforting. The way was well lit, the answers within easy reach. She read with excitement some new lines in the football epic. The young man was bright and creative. She told him he was finding his voice, then nudged him toward the idea of prose, epics being, she said, a little stilted and out-of-date. The boy wore overalls and carried Homer in his backpack, like some kind of misplaced Alexander. At Josie's suggestion, he blinked with a slew's thoughtfulness. Epics, he told her in all sincerity, were bound to make a comeback.

A few minutes later Josie was looking at a sonnet about "... a young man's eyes / An older woman's urgent, silent past." Splendid! Beautiful! Josie shouted. She hugged the woman impulsively and saw her eyes fill with proud, sad tears. "Now this is poetry, Harriet!" Josie told her, and the smile that answered tore away, if only for the moment, a lot of the woman's aching. A lot of Josie's too.

At three, Josie sat down for an unscheduled departmental meeting and what victories the day had given her came crashing down. The talk was about hiring standards for the department's lecturers. Scandal lingered in the air, though all the words were about academic credentials. At some point in all this, Josie realized she was sitting utterly alone in the center of the room. She had taken her chair and watched the others file in. She had thought nothing of the fact that the sides and back and front had filled with her colleagues and that not even Henry Valentine had gotten within ten feet of her. The meeting culminated when Dick Ferrington finally spoke. He suggested that the department ought "to do away with all the lecturers."

Dr. Case, chairing the meeting, cleared his throat nervously. He certainly hoped Dick meant eliminate *the positions* and not the lecturers themselves. There was some laugher at this, and Ferrington answered with good natured coyness, "Whatever."

The talk turned into a motion, duly seconded, and with no further need for discussion, the question was called. Now Henry Valentine stood up. He took his time and looked each professor in the eye. "I should like remind my learned colleagues of the scholar's enemy...." Another long pause with a certain theatrical satisfaction in his crocodile grin, then in a stage whisper: "... the sin of haste, people. The ruin of many, the savior of none!" The professor, having said all that needed saying, sat down again, and with only a little grumbling, the rest decided to kill the lecturers at their next meeting instead.

As they filed out, Josie noticed quite a few furtive looks cast in her direction, and in the hallway outside, there were several cliques locked in animated conversation. All grew deathly silent when Josie passed.

Yep. Assassination was on the agenda.

At just past six o'clock, an hour later than she had intended to leave, Josie finished grading a stack of compositions and checked the halls. Seeing no one, she slipped on her jacket, slung her purse over her shoulder, took her briefcase in hand and started away. Josie was only a few steps down the hall when she heard Henry Valentine, his voice hollow and cold like a stranger's. "I forgot to tell you, Dean Meyers was here yesterday afternoon. He was asking if I had seen you."

Looking back, Josie saw Val almost thirty feet away. His hands stuffed deeply into his pockets, his shoulder leaning gracefully against Gerty Dowell's office door, he seemed to have appeared out of thin air. All the offices were closed and darkened, and despite the fact that it was only Val, Josie felt a hard punch of adrenaline.

"He didn't leave a message?" Josie hoped her voice was calm, but she couldn't be sure. He had scared her. He was still scaring her.

"I think he wants to bump into you," Val answered pleasantly. There was a faint irony in Valentine's tone and smile, but the eyes belonged to a different man.

"Thanks for the tip, Val." Josie started on. "Wish I could talk, but I'm running late for a meeting."

"Another meeting at this hour?"

It was a stupid lie, and Josie scrambled to make it sound plausible. "I'm meeting some kids at Williams Hall in ten minutes."

"I take it you didn't talk to Dick, as I suggested, Josie?" Valentine's look was nothing so much as an I-told-you-so.

"They can pass all the resolutions they want, Val. I'm under contract to the end of the year. What happened in that meeting was nonsense. We both know that."

The old eyebrows lifted sadly, "All Dick really wants is to hear an apology."

"I can't do it, Val."

They were still standing some distance from one another, but there was a kind of intimacy in the narrow hall.

Val pursed his big, loose lips kindly, "My mother told me once that all of life is perfectly easy to understand. 'If it feels good, it isn't. If it hurts, it must be the right thing to do.'"

Josie hesitated.

"Dick has a lot of pull with people around here, Josie. All he really wants is to be your mentor. Instead, he feels like you've ignored him, that you've plowed around here like some kind of equal. This scandal is just an excuse to make trouble, but if you ask him for his help, he'll give it to you. It's just ego, Josie. Swallow a little pride, and let him know how much you respect him and need him, and all this will be forgotten in a couple of weeks. It won't hurt too much to do it. Besides, if you play tough on this, he'll destroy you. He has quite a temper, our Dr. Ferrington." The old man shrugged in a kindly manner. "That's my read on it, at any rate."

"I'll think about it, Val. I really will."

Val made good sense. He was telling her how to get around her problem. She had gone to him for just such advice, after all.

"I wouldn't wait too long. Rumor is the lynch mob has already formed."

Josie smiled wryly, nodding. That was about right, she said.

In the main hallway, Dick Ferrington was coming out of the department office as Josie passed. The placed was closed, the lights off. Ferrington had been inside getting something, apparently, and he had a bounce in his step, a crooked little smile. Then she recognized what he was carrying: the department's *Policies and Procedures*. One finger was even jammed inside it, as if he had just found some precious page he wanted to study at his leisure. Seeing her, Ferrington's stride caught slightly in surprise. He recovered at once, his face composing into perfect sincerity.

Josie started to speak. She meant to apologize or at least to arrange a meeting where she could, but the man cut her off.

"About what I said in the meeting today, Josie, I want you to know there was nothing personal."

All thoughts of apology fled as Josie's face flushed crimson. "What happened in that meeting this afternoon, Dr. Ferrington, was nothing but personal, and you know it."

Meditations

After a hurried meal and a couple of phone calls, Josie forced herself back to Worley. Once in the library, she forgot about Ferrington's maneuvers against her and Valentine's kindly advice, plunging instead into the past. Josie worked with focus and excitement, convinced she could reach into history and pull her man out of it by his very neck! Gone was the sense of embarrassment about her mother's slewness. Gone too was any kind of outrage she might have felt about men like Colt Fellows, Toby Crouch, and Cal Yeager using the murder for their own ends. Outrage, numbed shock, even thoughts of revenge were simply emotions that would dilute her vision of things. She was looking for one man. Right now, nothing else counted so much. It was coming, too. She was closing in on some ideas, building the scenes up slowly, each possibility in turn. She ran through motives, guessed at passions and payoffs, and still pondered a few enduring enigmas. Josie worked late, worked until her eyes burned, then went a bit longer. This wasn't school work, nor was it some kind of academic exercise. This was how she lived or died.

At 10:30, Josie headed back into the dark country. There were cars behind her as she approached her first turn, so she drove until they passed her. Once they were out of sight, she made a quick U-turn and went back. She stepped into the accelerator and the dark woods flashed by. She hit a hundred, then asked for a little more. At her motel, certain she was alone, Josie emptied her car quickly and set up her computer and books on the floor just inside the door. After that, she called Bea at the front desk and asked if anyone had been looking for her. "I've got a man trying to sell me a car," she lied. "I thought he might come by, and I really don't want to see him."

Bea told her there had been no one, but she'd keep an eye out for him. "What's he look like?"

"He's a man, Bea. They're all the same, right?"

Bea laughed, the phlegm in her chest crackling like gunshots. God, wasn't that the truth!

When she had made a mug of tea at the stove, Josie called Annie. It was past midnight in Boston, but Annie was up.

Between Annie's news about Dan Scholari's imminent return to the classroom and Josie's encounters with the Hazards, Pat Bitts, and Dr. Richard Ferrington, it took the better part of an hour for the women to bring each other up-to-date. What surprised Josie was the calm she felt as she detailed her interview with Bitts and her subsequent research. Panic was no longer a luxury she could afford, and she talked about murder and the threats against her with scholarly detachment. It was the way she worked best, everything a riddle, herself the woman in possession of the facts and piecing together the jigsaw puzzle of history. No longer was there a feeling of overpowering despair or even the frustration of not knowing. She was on the trail of something now, really chasing it. She was no longer the victim of some invisible force. She spoke of details that left her curious. She wondered, for instance, if Colt Fellows's alibi could really hold up under close scrutiny. Now that she understood he might have had a motive against Jack and her mother, especially her mother, she told Annie, all of Colt's actions twenty years ago took on a diabolical aspect. Not just a frame for murder, but murder itself. The wristwatch was not even the worst of it, she said. Colt had been eager to confuse everyone about the time of death, which meant, perhaps, that he didn't have as good of an alibi as Bitts had thought.

On the other hand, there was the issue of character. She had spent the evening tracking the man through news articles on the Internet. Colt Fellows didn't seem like the kind of man who would've have been really interested in creating the situations Josie had been subjected to since arriving in Lues. She could see it in a deranged ex-husband or an obsessed loner—someone like Toby Crouch, for instance, but it wasn't quite what she thought someone like Colt Fellows was all about. He was the sort to get in your face and growl a bit, she said. "Give him a spotlight," she said, "and he would grab it. Those kind of men don't work back doors very effectively." Annie was skeptical. Violence was violence. If the man had motive, and the humiliation of pissing in his pants was motive for a man of that cut, especially if it was at the hands of a woman, there wasn't much he wouldn't do to get even.

"But the man I'm looking for has put me right in the middle. I'm not just looking for a violent or dangerous man, Annie. My guess is the guy has a peculiar bent toward women. He gets his kicks making women suffer in all kinds of ways. Colt Fellows was the kind of guy who ran the show. He wanted power and prestige. When he needed dirty tricks, he had others who could handle things for him. The brotherhood of cops and all that. But he wouldn't delegate something like this, especially if it was payback for my mother embarrassing him. I mean face it, you don't share the things that make you ashamed. Men don't, at least."

"But he went after Jack and apparently didn't have any trouble getting a lot of people to help him!"

"A crime had been committed. A terrible crime. A fellow cop might cooperate to see justice done, even if some rules had to be broken. Harassing an innocent woman the first week she's in town? That's not quite the same thing. If Colt wanted to do something like that, I expect he would pretty much be on his own."

"What about the newspaper reports? He did the same thing to you and your mother, Josie. What was his motive for that?" That was why he was still at the top of the list, she answered.

She had a similar problem with Cal Yeager. To all outward appearances, the man's passions were transparent. His lies were all for the sake of political gain. Once Colt Fellows had manipulated the situation, Yeager responded. He saw the chance to discredit Bitts and become sheriff. Until Colt made his move, Yeager had seemed to sit quietly on the sidelines. Yeager's campaign for the office of sheriff that summer and fall verified Josie's theory. He made Bitts look incompetent, outdated, old-fashioned. He talked about the misplaced tapes, lost evidence, contradictory witness statements, and competition rather than cooperation between the county and the city. "He used the murder to prove Bitts was too old for the job and had lost control of his department. This whole notion about turf battles between law enforcement agencies got a lot of play back then. He said it wasn't about ego, it was about solving crimes. He looked good, Annie, and Bitts look exhausted, confused, and out of step."

"But he's still a liar, and he could've had reasons commit the murder. An affair with your mother, maybe."

"What about reasons to threaten me?"

"What if you had seen him, remembered him? You come to town twenty years later and all he can think is to scare you off before you put two and two together."

"Possible," Josie answered thoughtfully.

"That's the problem with this whole thing, Josie. Anything is possible. Nothing makes sense."

"That's where Napoleon comes in, Annie."

"Napoleon did it?"

"Napoleon said it: geography explains history."

"Okay." Sixteen flavors of irony, this.

"I'm working from the theory that the man who killed my mother is the one who's stalking me."

"That's always been the assumption. Just remember, it's not a fact."

"It's a premise, Annie, and a good one, especially since it's the only reasonable way I can track this bastard down."

"So where does geography take you?"

"If it is the same man, he has to occupy a given space at a given time, meaning he has to have been in Lues twenty years ago and he has to be here now."

"Great. You just eliminated most of the human race, but you still have a few thousand viable suspects, kiddo."

"I can put him in certain places at fairly precise times, Annie."

"How many places?"

"Quite a few, actually. In fact, that's my biggest problem at the moment. I've got the perfect suspect, but he has an ironclad alibi."

"Who is it?"

"Toby Crouch. He was on his own a good part of the afternoon my mother was taken into the canyon. Drinking with friends the rest of the time. Lot of leeway there. Plus, he's a pervert, Annie."

"Three beers and they're all perverts. God bless 'em."

"This one's different. I'm telling you, he's a total creep. The kind who peeks up your skirt and then licks his lips."

"I knew a German shepherd like that!"

"This guy gives dogs a bad name. I've started reading a few profiles on these kinds of murderers, Annie, and this guy fits. He's there to find the body, he helps the police, he stays close to the investigation. He's a loner, he's fascinated with police work. And look at the rest of it. He was in a good position the last twenty years to follow my career. A simple check with no suspicions, he can know everything about me, right down to the fact I've taken a job at Lues State."

"Did he know your mother?"

"Bitts said he had been out to the Hurry On Up quite a few times when they had dancers. If he had gone there before my mother sold the place, he could have watched her for a year or so with all kinds of fantasies. When she shows up on campus, he maybe decides it's some kind of sign for him to actually do something about his fantasies. He's a campus cop, Annie. He wants to talk to her, he wants her to get in his car, what's she going to do? She gets in the car. And then he's got her."

"Why come after you? What's the connection?"

"I look just like her. I saw a picture the other day. If we're dealing with someone who's gone over the edge, that could be the trigger."

"You're right. He's perfect. So what's his ironclad alibi?"

"Toby Crouch was at the police station talking to me when I got the card in my mailbox." Simple geography, Annie: he can't be two places at once."

"You're sure about the time the card was slipped into your mailbox?"

"I can't find any way around it, Annie. Toby Crouch didn't leave that note, and I don't think he could ask someone else to leave it for him."

"Napoleon had his problems, too, Josie!"

Delbert

When Josie entered the department office the next day, she found a handwritten note from Dean Meyers.

See me as son as possible.

Del

Josie assumed Meyers meant *soon* and called his office to arrange a meeting. She made a second call immediately afterwards, then went on about her business, even catching an hour and a half at Worley. She was scanning the intervening years between her mother's death and her return to Lues. If there was no real motive for the murder of her mother, and if the man was still here, as it seemed, Josie thought it possible there could be other murders, but the first three years turned up nothing even vaguely similar, and before she changed reels to look at the next couple of years, she had to go.

Shortly before noon, Josie met Clarissa Holt outside the dean's office, as they had arranged. Clarissa's face was ashen with anger, her dark eyes smoldering. "How are you doing?" she asked.

Her career in a free fall, and that the least of her problems, there didn't seem to be a reasonable answer to the question, so Josie shrugged and smiled sheepishly. "Nervous. Mad. Numb."

"I'll handle it, Josie. Say as little as possible. Del and I have . . ." she hesitated for emphasis, ". . . a history."

"This whole thing is—."

Clarissa touched her arm. "Don't apologize. Don't even think about apologizing. You did nothing wrong. Okay?"

Josie nodded.

"This is about what happened to your car, right?" Again Josie nodded. Clarissa smiled grimly. "Well, you were right about one thing. It was the wrong bar."

"You don't know the half of it."

"No, I guess I don't, but on the other hand, it's not my business any more than it's Del's. Are you ready?" she asked.

"My gun's loaded, if that's what you mean."

Clarissa smiled. She thought it was a joke.

A man who had come to the university some fifteen years before as a professor of philosophy, Dean Delbert Meyers was in his mid-forties but looked older. He was average height, slightly overweight. His hair was dull and thinning, his eyes narrow, cautious, and calculating. Josie knew Meyers solely from the faculty meeting in August. He had introduced himself to her briefly, asked a couple of inane questions, then moved on to more interesting quarry. The speech he had given lacked both courage and vision. Whatever else Josie knew about Dean Meyers she had picked up from shoptalk. There were contradictory reports about his method. Josie had heard he was capable of any savagery, so long as one's back was turned. Others claimed he was confrontational, that he was something of a hothead, ready to shoot from the hip at the first sign of trouble. That didn't bode well in the present circumstances. Josie was sure Clarissa meant to antagonize him. Still, Josie had little choice, unless she wanted to crawl to Dick "nothing personal" Ferrington.

Starting for the door, Clarissa whispered, "We're dealing here with an extremely big dog. If you let him smell fear, he'll hurt you. On the other hand, if you get him off his own porch, he's just a dog."

Josie saw immediately that Clarissa's presence had somehow gotten Meyers off his porch. The moment Josie and Clarissa entered his outer office, his eyes widened in surprise. "Clarissa?"

Meyers looked like a man with a mouthful of cottage cheese.

"Delbert." Clarissa Holt's tone was something of the schoolmarm's with the class troublemaker.

Meyers looked at Josie in confusion. "I'm afraid I had a meeting with Ms. Darling." This was purely wishful thinking. Dean Meyers had already read the scenario perfectly.

"We'll have a meeting together," Clarissa told him.

Meyers considered this, his big white face seeming to retract, as if from a series of punches, his shoulders wilting. Anything but a happy man, Meyers managed a smile and let his voice boom as he asked rhetorically, "Why not?"

The three of them met in the dean's large conference room, sitting at one corner of the long table. Meyers had probably intended to get right to the point, since meetings before a dean's lunch hour usually lack the amenities of a proper foreplay, but with Clarissa's presence, his battle plans were in shambles, and he was forced to start with a query about things in communications. Clarissa gave a detailed answer. After this, they sparred with cold smiles and tepid praise, names dropping like so much Lues rainfall. As the conversation continued, Clarissa leaned forward like a big cat on the stalk, while Dean Meyers began crossing and uncrossing his legs, finally tucking his hands between them in a gesture that was entirely unconscious. It seemed to Josie the two of them had slipped into the time-honored roles of castrating lesbian mother-goddess and sacrificial old bull.

When the conversation finally turned to Josie's situation, Josie readied herself.

"I think you know why I wanted to see Ms. Darling," Dean Meyers offered. A patient, nurturing expression had come over his big, plain features.

Neither woman answered him, Josie because she was not addressed, Clarissa because she was waiting, Josie assumed, for the opening salvo.

"This thing in the newspaper," Meyers continued, "is very upsetting."

"The assault on Josie?" Clarissa's voice cooled the room.

"Exactly." Meyers looked suddenly at Josie, almost as if he expected her to sympathize with his position. "My real concern, Josie, is that you're okay. Something like this can be emotionally difficult, and I just wanted to let you know I'm here for you if I can help."

Thunderstruck, Josie stammered her appreciation.

Dean Meyers smiled at Clarissa, "Josie is one of our best teachers, and I'd hate to see the vitality she brings to the classroom compromised in any way."

Clarissa agreed. She spoke briefly about unfeeling systems and insensitive administrators, the implication being, anywhere but Lues State this thing could have turned ugly.

"I'm sorry we couldn't have had more time to talk about it," Meyers said to them, as he stood to signal the conference was over, "but unfortunately, I have a twelve o'clock meeting with Case and Ferrington." He looked at Josie with a mock-scolding expression. "That department of yours always wants more money!"

Outside, Clarissa announced, "I think Del got the message."

"What happened in there, Clar?"

Clarissa raised her eyebrows, like a big cat licking her chops after a good meal. "You remember the reference to Phyllis Morales?"

Josie shook her head. *Phyllis Morales* she had heard. The reference she had missed.

"Interesting case. College of Education. She sued these bastards three years ago to the tune of $1.7 mil. Before it was over, her dean found himself scrambling for his golden parachute."

A name among other names, a casual query about what Phyllis was doing, nothing more. Velvet threats, Josie realized. As they stood together, they watched Josie's department chair and Dick Ferrington approach. Case nodded nervously toward Clarissa and Josie, then hurried inside. Ferrington had a cool smile for the two women. He was still under the impression he was winning. A moment later, the three men ensconced themselves in the dean's cubbyhole office.

"That's about me, isn't it?"

"Not anymore. Now it's about how to calm down whoever stirred this mess up in the first place."

"Ferrington."

"Ferrington?" she asked. "That's interesting. In your department, I would have guessed Gerty Dowell was making all the noise."

"Gerty? The old lady in sweats?"

"Henry Valentine winds her up and lets her do his dirty work."

"Val's on my side in this, if you can believe it."

Clarissa laughed. It was a dry, spiritless sound, "The only time Henry Valentine ever took sides in something was to get his own way."

"Not this time. Ferrington's the one who's turned me into a cause. Last week, he was waving the newspaper at me and saying how he had backed me with the hiring committee and how I'd embarrassed him."

Clarissa's mouth twitched. "Who was on the hiring committee?" she asked.

"Dick chaired it, that's all I know. In fact, he was my only contact until I got to campus."

"Has he asked you out?"

"Not really. No. I mean . . . with the department, but not like on a date. He has no interest in me that way, Clar. The guy is seeing Deb Rainy, remember?"

"If marriage didn't slow the guy down, a girlfriend certainly isn't going to."

"The guy turns me off. I mean we did fine on the telephone before I got here, but the first time we sat down and talked, there was just something about him I didn't care for. He reminded me of my ex-husband, if you want to know the truth. A bit of a stuffed shirt, on top of that. I mean Dan was a wild time, a lot of fun when he wanted to be. But arrogant. As far as I can see, Ferrington is just arrogant. He has to have the last word, he has to be the authority on everything, and he's way too political for my tastes. Plus, I don't like the fact that he pretty much has any woman he wants. It's like I'm supposed to fall down when he smiles at me."

"A lot of women do."

"Men like that know what to *say*, Clar, but they never *feel* anything."

"Well, we've blocked him, at least for the moment, whatever his problem is, but he will definitely do everything in his power to destroy you inside the department. Come next year, I wouldn't be surprised if they told you the funding for your position has dried up. You can fight it, of course, and claim it all goes back to this, but it might not be worth it in the long run. Much as I hate to say it, probably the best thing you can do is finish out the year and offer your resignation before they have a chance to do anything. It stinks, I know, but it's about the only reasonable thing you can do."

"I had pretty much decided to leave before all of this got out of hand. I can go back and finish my degree, or maybe I'll just move upstate and get a job at a Dairy Queen."

Clar laughed, the tension leaving her. "If they have a couple positions open, I might join you!" But then the laughed faded, and Clarissa Holt looked back toward the dean's office. She seemed, Josie thought, to be calculating the imponderables of Dick Ferrington's character, as if something about the man's behavior was not quite to form.

James Burkeshire

Late that afternoon, Josie drove north almost three hours to a suburb on the outskirts of Bloomington. She arrived at the Burkeshire residence shortly after eight, as she had promised on the telephone. Jim and Mandy Burkeshire lived in affluence. They had a large house, a couple of nice cars, all the electronic gadgets. The moment Josie saw him, she could see Jim Burkeshire was a serious, reflective man and had probably been the same as a college kid. Her first impression was that he kept his emotions capped. Burkeshire tried to make Josie feel comfortable with her intrusion into his life. He introduced Josie to his wife and three small kids, then took her into a well appointed den, where they sat down opposite one another over cups of coffee. He talked about his business when Josie showed some interest in it. An engineer by training, he owned a small manufacturing company outside the city and supplied his former employer and other customers with components for their production lines. He seemed satisfied with what he had done with his professional life but did not seem especially excited about it. His passions, she thought, lay elsewhere. The wife and kids, perhaps, but she wasn't sure. There was something about Mr. Burkeshire that didn't quite tally.

Josie spent some time explaining what had happened to her after her mother's death. She said nothing about Jack Hazard's innocence or the fact that someone was harassing her with threatening messages. She wanted to know about the murder, she said. She had never been allowed that knowledge and had gone back to Lues to face the crime and somehow come to terms with it. Burkeshire seemed to understand. He said he would tell her what he knew. Like Melody Mason, however, he claimed to have forgotten quite a bit. At first, the conversation moved in fits and starts. He had not especially enjoyed life as a college student, so he had forgotten most of it, he said. Sometimes, he added with a wry smile, he wished he could forget all of it. He had done well in his classes, really well, actually. He just hadn't particularly gotten on well socially. He was there, the day they had found Josie's mother, because Bob Tanner had talked him into it. Tanner had convinced him that he should get to know Melody Mason. Like most things in his social life back then, nothing had come of it. Melody had ignored him from the start. In fact, she had seemed more interested in Tanner.

"What can you tell me about Cat?" Josie asked.

Burkeshire seemed surprised by the question. "I didn't really know her," he said after a moment. We were in that one class together. I mean all of us were. She was beautiful, way out of my league." A slight, sly smile. "That was what I figured anyway. I was a geek. Engineering, computers . . . I probably could have won the contest for dullest guy on campus. She could have been anyone's homecoming queen, if she had wanted."

"Things change, don't they?" Josie asked pleasantly.

He liked this and smiled. He was really very handsome, she thought, but his virtues were all the quiet sort. Easy for kids to miss.

"They were all friends, Bob and Susie and Melody and Cat. I was like . . . odd man out."

"You don't know what happened to Cat after college? I've located everyone but her, and I'd like to talk with her if I could."

He thought about it for a moment and shook his head. "I don't know that I ever saw her after that day, let along after college. I mean I know we must have run into each other a few times, we were in the same class! I just don't remember."

He said he had forgotten what class it was they had skipped, had forgotten if any of them had any kind of social contact after that day. He and Bob had lived together in the same fraternity house for the next two years, and yet he couldn't remember ever really talking to Bob again after that afternoon. "Different lifestyles is the easy way of putting it," he said with an uncomfortable grin. "He was a jock, a football player. I . . . wasn't. But the truth is, I don't think either of us felt comfortable with each other after that day in the canyon."

"Why is that?"

"I don't know really. For me, it was. . . ." He gave Josie an embarrassed smile. "I used to have nightmares about it. I'm talking years. Not every night or anything, but I had them. I ended up going into therapy for it after I got out of school."

"I'm sorry to bring it all back."

"It's okay. Part of the therapy was learning to face that day objectively. The fact that I didn't do anything with my feelings at the time was most of the problem. A lot of the therapy was dealing with this misplaced guilt I had. We would spend a lot of sessions going through what I saw, what I did exactly, what people said. Probably as a result of that, I remember quite a bit about what I saw in the canyon and practically nothing about afterwards."

"You remember seeing the body then?"

"Oh, yeah." Burkeshire closed his dark brown eyes, and two fine, tense lines formed between his eyebrows. "She was on this huge rock. Just to the side of the falls. It would have been right of the falls as you faced her. We'd had trouble seeing her from the ledge because of the angle and because she was so close to the falls. The water was hitting her indirectly, so she was right in the middle of this mist. She was on her back. The rock slanted down toward us, so her head was just touching the water. If any of us had wanted to, we could have reached out and touched her, we were that close."

"Did you?"

"No. We didn't dare. We left everything the way we found it. We just stared at her. Her eyes were open, the pupils rolled back. It was eerie because you could only see the whites of her eyes. Her arms were spread out to either side. They were at about the level of her head. Her left hand and her hair were in the water. Her hair was thick and long, a red-gold color. The water in front of the rock was churning and foaming slightly, so the hair was floating on the surface of the water. It looked liked she had been placed there. Like a sacrifice, I guess. That's kind of what came to mind, anyway."

Burkeshire opened his eyes, blinked several times and then focused on Josie.

"Were there any marks on her?" Josie asked, feeling almost like hypnotist.

Burkeshire closed his eyes again. His face grew pale. "Her killer had cut the letters *h-o-r* above her heart. The *R* was capitalized." He opened his eyes.

"Anything else?" she asked.

Burkeshire studied Josie with a frightening intensity, then closed his eyes again. "Both her wrists," he answered, "and her ankles had deep indentations where she had been tied up, and around her neck, here," Burkeshire pointed just under the jaw, "there was a thin, red mark, about a quarter of an inch wide. It curled up behind her ears."

Burkeshire opened his eyes, raising his eyebrows as he said this last part. He stared at Josie now, almost shaking off the trance but not quite free of it. "I thought at the time she had been hanged, because of the angle of the ligature mark. I think later they said she was strangled. I suppose they meant garroted. I don't see how from the angle of it, unless maybe the guy didn't know what he was doing and put his hands above her head, you know, and hanged her with his hands." The man shrugged. He didn't understand anything any better than Josie.

In the next room, Burkeshire's wife moved about, picking up toys and adjusting pillows. She was checking on Josie, or seeing if her Jim was still okay.

"Do you remember what time it was when you saw her?"

He thought for a moment, then answered simply, "Daylight."

"Do you remember anything about leaving the canyon?"

"Nothing."

"And nothing about going in?" They had covered this point. He shook his head. "You talked to someone about it. Do you remember when that was?"

He smiled weakly. He wanted to help, but he had told her all he could remember. "It was a long time ago, Professor."

"You talked to Sheriff Bitts that night, I think?" He shrugged. He wasn't sure. "And to someone else later?"

"I don't know." Mandy Burkeshire came over and sat next to her husband. It was a consoling, protective gesture.

"Do you remember the bruises on her neck?"

Burkeshire frowned and shook his head, "Just the ligature mark."

"You're sure?"

James Burkeshire gave a look as if to say, *This is my nightmare, Professor, I know what I saw.* "Positive," he answered.

Library Hours

Tiredly, Josie cranked the handle of the microfilm machine until the next headline came into view: "Body Found." Josie scanned the account, as she had every murder reported in Lues County in the previous seven years. This one was different. A nude body had been suspended by its feet from a log that stretched over a narrow ravine near Clems Hollow. Police had identified the victim as Shelley Kruger, twenty-four, a Lues State coed.

Josie picked up her pen.

The Farm

Josie called Virgil Hazard at his bar in Codswallop Friday afternoon. She wanted to know about her mother's belongings. "Who took them?"

"They sent most everything with you. The rest, I took. There wasn't much," he said.

"You still have it?"

"Sure. At the farm."

"I want you take me there. I'll be at the bar in an hour. Meet me in the parking lot."

"I'm working, D. J.! I got a hundred lunatics in here. I got to keep things under control!"

"They'll do fine without you. This is important."

Snidely, "You going to get me arrested if I don't cooperate?"

"I might. Just don't make me come inside, Virgil." Josie hung up and started north through the countryside. Virgil was waiting when she got there and took her along several twisting back roads toward his farm. A few minutes later, they found a long narrow lane and went back along it slowly because of the potholes. At the end of the road, they parked next to a couple of antique hearses and got out of their vehicles.

Cut out of the forest years before, Virgil Hazard's farm was not much more than a couple of hills and a creek. With a few broken down outbuildings and a roofless barn, the place was a portrait of Virgil's whole life. Virgil kept a couple of swaybacked horses in the field behind his barn and nothing else, except a dog and a couple of outdoor cats.

The farmhouse was a little shack, one room set behind the other. Josie stepped into it as far as the front door and then decided she didn't want to go any farther. A wood stove, a couch, and a decrepit reading chair were in the middle of the room. Beyond that was the dark cave of a bedroom.

"Nice, Virgil!" This was pure sarcasm.

"Yeah, well, it's just me and Buster and the sheriff's phonetap, D. J."

Buster was Virgil's dog. He was a big Labrador male. He moved slowly through the mess of the house and nuzzled Josie with an affection she felt compelled to return.

"So how's Jack doing?" she asked.

"Still alive, no thanks to you."

"I called a couple of lawyers."

"Good for you."

"If he comes in, they'll work with him."

"Sure they will. Same as the last one *worked* with him. I'll tell something right now, D. J. The only way Jack is coming out of the woods is dead."

Josie dropped her eyes. "It doesn't need to be like that."

"Sure it does. You got two dead cops. Nobody wants to hear the truth. Look, forget it," he said. "It wasn't your fault. Colt was working the thing and you just got played."

"I'm glad he's dead. What he did to Jack . . . the bastard deserved it. Both of them did."

Virgil's eyebrows rose appreciatively, but he didn't answer.

"What?" she asked.

"Nothing. You reminded me of your mother, just then. When she got mad. It was just a little weird is all."

"So where did you put her things?"

Taking a ring of keys from the clutter, Virgil answered gruffly, "Come on! Josie's stuff is out here." As he led her to a paint-peeled shed next to his barn, he told her, "A couple of times, I thought about throwing it out, but I figured that was Jack's call, maybe yours if you ever showed up. After a while, you just forget about stuff. You know?" Virgil opened the door to the shed, and they were both overcome with the damp rot of the room. Virgil had forgotten about this stuff at least a decade ago. "The roof went to hell about five years back."

"And you didn't fix it?"

"I meant to. Just . . ."

Virgil left his lie unfinished, and the two of them kicked through the furniture briefly. A brown sofa with the unmistakable traces of mice filled most of the central room. The stuffing was chewed out and exposed, and it was anybody's guess how many warm fuzzies the thing housed. On the bare dirt just next to the couch, there were some boxes of kitchen goods. The cardboard was bowed and waterlogged. What utensils Josie saw were rusted. The whole room stank so badly that Josie was about to tell him she had seen enough when he pushed through some tables and chairs in front of the couch and reached bravely back into a pile of clutter. "The pictures are over here." Virgil presented three soggy albums, and Josie stepped carefully through the trash to take the top album. The thing was damp, soiled, and broken. Josie opened it with dread.

The first page contained a tiny newspaper clipping centered on a stained sheet of thick paper. Something from the vital statistics section of the *Rapids,* the clipping described the stark facts of a civil wedding between John Christian Hazard and Josephine Fortune. On the next page, she saw Jack and her mother together, his arm around her. With their pose and exaggerated solemnity, they looked like nineteenth-century pioneers on their new homestead. Jack had said they were just kids, not a worry in the world. Looking at them, Josie could almost believe it.

"That was taken out here on their wedding day."

Virgil seemed almost sentimental. On the next page, a small child stood with Jack. It was apparently taken the same day. Josie felt like she was looking at someone else's memory.

"I don't remember being out here," she said.

"I kept it up a little better back then. I mean I had girlfriend who kept it, you know."

"I think I get the picture, Virgil."

"What?"

"You exploit women. No big deal. You're a pig."

Virgil shook his head, "I'm a businessman. I give women jobs. Around here, people kill for jobs."

"So women love you?"

"Let me tell you something, D. J. Not everyone gets to go to Harvard or wherever the hell you got all your degrees. Some of us have to do things we don't necessarily like."

"Now you're telling me you don't like running your bar."

"It's a lot of work."

Josie nodded, not even bothering to give Virgil mock sympathy. On the next page, she saw Josie Fortune holding her daughter, this also on Virgil's farm. She was standing with her hip thrust out so the child could straddle her.

"You were a good kid, D. J."

"You liked my mother, didn't you?"

He reached down and turned the page. A woman with a shotgun sat on top of a bar. She wore a plaid shirt and jeans. Her hair was pulled into one long braid and lay over her left shoulder. Her feet were hanging in the air. The shotgun was propped up, so that the butt of it was resting on her thigh and the twin barrels came to about the level of the top of her head. The face was solemn, playfully reminiscent of the early photographs of outlaws in the Old West. The gun looked to be a piece of deadly business. The wall behind the bar was made of barn wood, something of the effect of a hillbilly cabin. Out of focus and partially cutoff, a sign read: Hurry On . . .

"That's the Josie Fortune I remember," Virgil whispered. It was a voice full of awe. "If God made any woman better, Josie, He kept her for Hisself."

"She looks like a slew, Virgil."

Josie shook her head and started to turn the page, but Virgil put his finger on the paper, stopping her.

"Look at her! Look at that picture, D. J.! That's your mother! That's Josie Fortune! Huh? You see that? Let me tell you something, you should be half the woman she was!"

Josie wanted another image of her mother, something less like a slew, but she was moved by Virgil's passion.

Virgil smiled fondly. "Jack told me one time she put both them barrels right in Colt Fellows's face and kicked his sorry ass out of the bar."

"Jack told me about that, too."

"You know, Colt was the guy everyone wanted to do something like that to, but Josie Fortune, your mamma, she was the only person in Lues County ever had the guts to do it."

"Kind of gives him a motive, doesn't it?"

Virgil shrugged, "I don't think Colt could have got within fifty yards of Josie without her blowing his head off. Your mother wasn't a woman to cross, D. J. Colt knew it, too. You ask me, Colt was scared to death of her."

"So who killed her, Virgil?"

"I told Jack it was someone she trusted, someone she knew. No one else could have gotten close to her. I saw her in a couple of fights at the bar, D. J. Let me tell you something, she was faster than Jack, and whole lot meaner. And scared of by-God nothing!"

"You think someone from the bar might have done it?"

"Someone from the college," he answered. "I always thought it was college. You and her are just alike about that. You think those people at the college are special. Like they aren't just as mean and crazy as the rest of us. That's what got her killed. Trusting some fancy talk."

"Maybe whoever it was just surprised her."

"The Devil himself couldn't sneak up on Josie Fortune! Listen, Jack married his match! I guarantee it! No, her killer walked up to her face smiling and telling her some line of bullshit, and Josie trusted him because he was college. That's the only way I can see it going down."

"Do you know where she came from, Virgil? Anything about my father?"

Virgil's fat gray face creased fondly, "Your mamma blew in on the wind, you and her together."

"Was she on the run from something?"

"We're all of us running, D. J. It's just that most of us never get anywhere."

Josie shut the album. "I want the albums. The rest . . . well, I don't have the guts to reach in and see what's here. This place is a sty, Virgil."

"Her books are over on this wall." He pointed to a waterlogged cardboard box.

"That's it?"

"What do you mean?"

A single box of books. Josie smiled. "I'll take the books too," she answered, then seeing the damp box coming off the wall, added, "I guess."

"Clothes are back there." His arms around the wet cardboard, Virgil rocked his head in the direction of the corner. Under some broken ceiling tiles, a stained pile of clothes answered.

"I'll pass on the clothes."

"That's it then."

Outside, after they loaded the Mustang's trunk, Josie asked, "What happened to the shotgun?"

"I keep it under my bed. It's illegal as hell, but who gives a damn? So's cocaine."

"I don't want it, Virgil, but I'd like to see it."

"I'll get it." He started toward the house and stopped. "Speaking of coke, you want to get high?"

"How did you stay out of prison all these years, Virgil?"

Virgil shrugged affably, "Too quick for the law, D. J. Just too damn quick!"

When Virgil returned, he held the shotgun up before him. It was a well-cared-for prize. The twin barrels were half their original length. "I want to fire it," he said. "Come on!" Josie followed him as he carried it out into his yard. There were a couple metal drums, a fence post, a sheet of plywood, the two hearses, and a suspicious cat. Virgil considered each in turn. Finally, he walked over to the plywood and stood it up against the rusted barbed-wire fence, then walked back four paces. In one motion he turned, while setting the stock of the gun against his right thigh. Both barrels roared. The fire and smoke and wadding leapt out three of the twelve feet between him and the plywood. Quickening her pulse, the sound hit Josie deep in her chest and left her momentarily gasping in surprise. The sheet jumped in response, and a gaping hole about eight inches in diameter appeared dead center. Its edges were ragged.

Virgil straightened up and swore fabulously. "OH, MAMMA!" He turned to her, still grinning. "You want to try it?" He reached into his pocket and pulled out two shells. Popping the spent ones, Virgil loaded the twin barrels and closed the gun with a crisp snap. "What do you say?"

Josie took the gun carefully, inhaling the intoxicating residue of gun smoke. Virgil had taken care of it, even if the rest of his life was in ruins. Josie held the gun with both hands at waist level, looking for a target. The cat, she noticed, was long gone.

"I know this gun, Virgil," she said quietly. "I remember that sound."

"You ought to. Your mother loved that gun. You and her and Jack would come out here all the time. They'd spend half the day shooting different guns, but that was the one she always went back to."

"Did I ever shoot it?"

"She let you dry-fire it, but you were just a kid. It would have knocked you over. You had this little .38 caliber you shot all the time. It was about as big as you were, but I mean you were pretty handy with it!"

"You're kidding me! I don't remember ever touching a gun when I was a kid."

"You loved guns, D. J. Josie said you were going to be a better shot and quicker than either Jack or her."

"So what happened to all guns she had?"

"Jack traded a couple of them for the attorney fee, gave the rest to different cousins. They're mostly still around if you need one. I kept the Purdey, but it's yours when you want it."

Josie studied the gun, tried to remember the feel.

. . . *in the grass, the trooper's shotgun.* She had known how to use it. She had been looking at it because she had wanted to get her hands on it.

"Go ahead! Fire it! I mean damn! With that shotgun, you look just like her!"

Josie settled on the plywood Virgil had shot. She brought the shotgun down to her thigh as Virgil had done and aimed at the very top portion of the board. The gun kicked hard into her leg as the fire from the twin barrels blew out in wild sparks, but this was nothing to the noise the thing made. Coming as it did up from her thighs, it sounded like the end of the world—or the beginning.

It was only an afterthought that caused Josie to consider the effect on her target. Across the top of the plywood, the charge had cut a crescent of jagged space.

"Nice, huh?" Virgil asked.

"Virgil," she answered, "there's nothing nice about it."

The List

When Josie returned to her efficiency, she called Pat Bitts. She had missed him earlier but heard him answer now. "I'm sorry to bother you again, Mr. Bitts," she began after her introductions, "but I've found some things in the newspaper I'm curious about, and I thought you might be able to help me."

"I'll do what I can, Professor."

"I need some information on four women. They were all abducted, all of them murdered."

"From around here?"

"Yes, sir. Lues County. The first was June, 1990. The name's Shelley Kruger." She waited, while the old man wrote it down. "Next was Anita Paget. She was found south of Carbine Ridge, October, 1992. Two more: Melissa Bates and Cathy Ferrington." The old man repeated the names as he wrote them out. "Bates will be seven years this coming April. Ferrington died three years ago, last June or July, they aren't exactly sure of the date of death."

"I remember both of those last two. The Ferrington woman was the wife of one your professors up at the college."

"I want to see the police reports on those cases. Everything they have. Can you get that for me?"

There was a long pause, then, "I guess I could talk to Jason about it. He could get them without much trouble, if I promised him they'd never leave the farm."

The old man wasn't letting go, but that was fine with Josie. "You up for a partnership, Mr. Bitts?"

"What exactly did you have in mind?"

"I thought we might find a killer."

"You think these might be tied to your mother's death?"

"The first thing I want to find out is what other people thought."

"Fair enough, I guess. Give me your number, and I'll call you next week."

"Call me at school when you have something, and I'll get back to you. I'm kind of hard to catch these days. It's safer that way."

"You need a hideout, you're welcome out here!"

"If I need hideout, Mr. Bitts, I'll have a pretty mean man on my tail."

"I'm a pretty mean man, myself, young lady. You need help, all you have to do is ask."

Susan Wallace

Susan Wallace, who had been Susie Hill in college, was a vibrant, thin, attractive middle-aged woman. A manager of a small temporary-employment agency, Wallace lived alone in Memphis in an upscale apartment complex.

She came across with that kind of Southern openness that startles outsiders, a woman proud of her checkered past and amused at the habits which used to hold her hostage: "I'm an ex-bulimic, ex-smoker, ex-drunk, ex-nymphomaniac, ex-druggie, and now a full-time aerobic monster." Her apartment had a certain sterility about it. What Josie could see of Wallace's life she found on a couple of shelves in the living room. There had been a family: three boys and a tall, thin, bald husband. They looked from the clothing and her own age in the photograph to be about ten years behind her. Her hair was longer then, and she was heavier, cherubic, a lot like Melody Grimes. There was another ex-husband pictured as well. He had the look of a man well acquainted with his vices. Susie Wallace, in that picture, was scarecrow thin, apparently on medication, almost certainly self-prescribed. Wallace saw Josie examining this picture and commented: "That's Norman. Norman Wallace. We were doing the group-sex thing and Norm ended up finding out he liked men better than women." She shrugged, "Last I heard, he was in rehab with his lover. I just hope when he gets clean and sober, he still likes men, you know?"

Josie walked away. Something in the easiness of Susan Wallace's manner about her past bothered her. She was certain it was bravado, a mask to hide the pain. Behind everything that Wallace admitted to was the fact that she had lost her children, a matter about which she said nothing.

"How did you get my name?" Wallace asked her when they had settled down to talk.

Josie smiled. "I talked to Melody Mason."

Susie screamed like a young girl suddenly. "Oh my God!" she laughed, "I haven't seen that little whore since we graduated! How is she?"

Josie described what she had seen of Melody Grimes, happily married, funny, cute. About the relative poverty, or at least the stifling sterility of Melody's life, Josie kept her opinions to herself.

"She says the two of you were going to go to Florida after you graduated. I think she would still like to go."

"Florida! Listen, we had the tickets and everything, and Melody comes down with the clap. I mean serious stuff. Give that girl a six pack and she'd do anyone!" She considered this with a genial expression, then added, "Of course, so would I."

Susie, like Melody, talked for a while about college, friendships, sorority life, parties, and then finally, almost reluctantly, made a feeble sketch of the afternoon they had found Josie Fortune.

"... I don't remember very much. What I remember the most is freezing my butt off. It was so cold, and we just kept going deeper into this frigging canyon! Water up to our asses! Have you been inside there?"

"I've seen pictures."

"It's a lot colder when you actually go in!"

"Do you remember seeing the body?"

"I could hardly look at her, you know? I think Bill started to touch her."

"Who's Bill?"

"Uh, one of the guys."

"Bob Tanner or Jim Burkeshire?"

"Bob Tanner! That's right. Goofy guy! Don't even bother talking to him. Have you talked to him?"

"No."

"Save yourself the trouble. He's the stupidest guy that ever went to college. I mean Melody wanted in his pants so bad and he didn't have a clue! And Melody was about as subtle as . . . me! Right? I mean like, "Hey! You wanna fuck?" But he doesn't catch on. I told Melody, 'You're crazy, the guy's an oaf,' and she goes, 'I don't care, he's cute, and I think he's got a really big one,' so I tell this buffalo, 'I think Melody wants to go out with you.' Subtle, right? The guy spends a month asking me out." Susie considered for a moment before adding, "He wasn't that big, let me tell you."

"You said he started to touch the body."

"Right! The other guy . . ."

"Jim Burkeshire."

"Jim screams, 'Don't touch her!' So we didn't. And we left. That's it."

"Jim said he stayed behind when the rest of you left," Josie lied. "Why did he do that?"

"No. He led us out. Melody thought this slew had followed us in, you know, so we went out in a line. Stupid, right? No, Jim led. And Bill—."

"Bob."

"Why do I keep calling him Bill? Oh, well, that's another story. I won't get into it, but a really dumb guy, too, but he was packing, if you know what I mean?"

"What happened when you left the canyon?"

"God, I'm just going on! Let's see. We left the canyon. We called someone, and then, we went to the room and Cat went off. Okay, Cat went off to get a shower, and Melody and I talked about running away. She thought this slew she saw—you know about him?"

Josie shook her head and tried to summon a reasonably confused expression for Susan Wallace.

"Up at the falls, she saw this guy or said she did. Anyway, she was sure he'd killed this woman—I'm sorry." A look of pure embarrassment. "This woman" was Josie's mother.

"Go on. I want to know what happened."

"She'd seen him kind of, like he was watching us or something, and she thought he was going to come after us or her or something. Right? And I told her, hey, 'Look, maybe you're overreacting. If it was the killer, he's probably so scared he can't remember what you look like, or any of us, except Cat.' See, like everyone remembered Cat. God did we hate that girl! So, Melody goes, 'I don't know, Susie!' She's crying and almost laughing, you know, and we're all crazy about . . . you know, what we just found. Anyway, she goes, 'God damn slews! I hate slews!'

"And I'm like, 'What if he wasn't the killer?' What if he was just some slew walking around in the woods?'

"'He looked at me,' she says. Then she goes, 'I think he was trying to remember what I looked like.'

"So then I'm like, 'He thought you were hot. I mean guys think we're hot. Some guys.' You got to remember we had the self-confidence of a couple of slugs. I'm like, 'He's a slew. He hasn't seen anything but a cow's hind-end for six months. He sees us, and he gets hot.'

"She goes, 'He killed that lady, Susie.'

"And I'm like, 'Look, he was probably following us to get a look at Cat. Right?' That's pretty typical, see. 'So anyway,' I'm like, 'he can't remember us, but he remembers Cat and kills the bitch! Our prayers are answered!'"

Susie Wallace sat back, laughing at herself, her narrative finished. "God, we hated that girl. We had all these jokes about her getting killed or having some terrible disfiguring accident. That was my favorite. I just wanted her to be as ugly as I felt! Not very funny really, but you know, we were nineteen. It seemed funny at the time. Anyway, Mel didn't run away, and no slew ever came looking for us. And we all lived miserably-ever-after."

"What time of day was this?" Josie asked. "When you got back from the canyon?"

"Dinner was always at 5:15. These days I have lunch at 5:15, but for some reason, the sorority served dinner at 5:15, like clockwork. Melody and I didn't go. We didn't have time to get showers. I think we got high and ate cookies or got high on the cookies, and we talked about this slew killing Cat. Cat never missed a meal. I don't know how she kept so thin. Her mom paid for it, she said, and she didn't want to cheat her mom, something like that." Susie rolled her eyes. "It wasn't the money. Believe me. She was just re-pressed! She used to get these boys worked up and then walk away. It was wild. She was the queen of tease, saving herself for marriage. Of course she only ended up teasing herself, and her only outlet was food. Food as sex. Believe me, I've been there! Of course *I* got fat."

Josie asked if Susie knew what had happened to Cat.

"I remember one thing, right? It's finals week and she comes up to me all upset. And she goes, 'How do you know if you're pregnant?' And I'm like, 'If you have to ask, girl, it's probably too late.' Anyway, she wasn't back at school the next year, and no one ever heard from her again."

"Any idea who the father was?"

"I figured it was what's his name . . . Jim."

"Jim Burkeshire?"

"Cat wasn't out there because of us. She had this thing for Jim. Not that he noticed. The guy was like oblivious, but you know, she was only out there so he'd maybe get a clue. I mean, I don't know if it was the nerd or not, but it had to be right after that day in the canyon, because she wasn't seeing anyone before that."

Josie nodded, wondering if Burkeshire had lied because of his wife or because he didn't care to talk about Cat's pregnancy.

"Do you remember anything about what you saw in the canyon. Anything about the body at all? Any marks? Cuts, abrasions, . . . something like that?"

"I wish I could help you. I was so freaked out. I thought she had fallen, you know, but then, you know, when I saw her, I realized someone had . . . you know! I mean, God damn it! I'm standing there up to my ass in freezing water, and I'm scared to death!"

There was anger in this—something Josie hadn't seen in her before.

"So when you realized she hadn't fallen, how did you think she had died?" Josie asked.

"I didn't *think* anything. I could *see* it. This . . . this *fuck* did her with a rope! You know what I mean? Like up behind her, like that!" Susie Wallace raised and crossed her hands as if garroting a victim.

Out of Memphis

From Memphis to Cairo, Josie drove toward heavy purple thunderheads. The rain started at Cairo. The road seemed to empty out as most of the cars pulled over to the shoulder of the road. Josie pushed on stolidly. The sky and countryside were washed in a dull gray.

Josie was tired. She had been tired for weeks now, and she was afraid of her intuitive leaps, but something was wrong, something at the base of the falls had happened that she wasn't quite seeing. And her interviews with the people who had found her mother's body hadn't straightened out the confusion. In fact, no one had reported the same thing as anyone else. Garroted. Hanged. Strangled. Eviscerated. Dead at three. Dead at six. Cover ups, lies, polygraphs, signed statements, lost files . . . and the worst of it: everyone was sincere, helpful, sympathetic, and . . . just so damn nice! Nothing fit. Nothing worked. Nothing made sense.

Well, that wasn't quite right. Both Crouch and Fellows were still possible suspects, and there was one more scenario that made sense. In fact, it was the silence that argued the theory best. It was now two weeks since the deaths of Colt Fellows and Toby Crouch. She didn't want to get her hopes up. She could hardly bare to believe it was over, but the silence was arguing profoundly that her troubles were past. The wildcard theory was this: her mother had been the victim of a killer who had long ago vanished into history. Finding her mother's corpse, Colt Fellows had sought to have his vengeance on Jack and get him committed to life in prison. That had been spoiled by the necessity of a plea bargain, and ever since Jack's release from prison, Colt Fellows had been worried that Jack might just find out how Colt's enthusiasm for a conviction had actually been a setup. As it happened, Jack's release from prison had been at about the same time that Josie had committed to come teach at Lues State for a year. On learning that she was coming to campus, not an entirely improbable occurrence, she thought, Colt had seen his opportunity and immediately began to arrange a rather ingenious trap to get Jack out of the way. It was a bit complicated, she thought, but not entirely out of character. This was how she saw it, anyway. By leaving a series of threats, Colt could effectively guarantee that Josie would eventually show up at police headquarters. When she did, he would let everyone know that he was to be called. Once that happened, Colt trusted his abilities to persuade Josie to press charges against Jack.

From there, it was simply a matter of an arrest and then a transfer to the county jail and a thwarted prisoner escape. Even the almost silly little detail of a card addressed to Josie Fortune could be explained if Colt had been behind the break-ins and messages and calls. Colt would almost certainly not have left it personally, but as the chief of police, he had any number of undercover people who could drop a note off without needing to know what he was up to. Keys, no problem. A man like Colt would have had all kinds of contacts at the university and everywhere else in town for that matter. He had pushed after the attack at the Bust of Country with two messages on the following day, because at that point, he had made several moves against her and still wasn't getting a reaction. Interestingly enough, the moment she had gone to the police, everything stopped. Now, it seemed obvious to her why. Colt had finally gotten her to file her complaint. He had everything he wanted from her! It made sense, too, that he would discredit her after she had filed charges against Jack. Colt didn't want anyone taking her seriously if she started asking questions about Jack's arrest and subsequent death.

Information, opportunity, motive. It was all there. Colt was perfect, and even his motive made sense. None of this was about Josie Fortune's kid twenty years later. It was about getting Jack! With a warrant, Colt could pick Jack up using all the manpower he needed. Classic bully that he was, Colt Fellows was a coward underneath all that bluster. Her mother had proven that. He would never go after Jack one on one. He had arranged it so that Jack ended up as his prisoner.

That was all it was. History, or so the theory went, was not repeating itself. Colt Fellows had been the source of Josie's problems, with or without the full assistance of Toby Crouch, and Colt's game had blown up in his face.

Blood

Josie pulled off the interstate at Huree. Ten minutes later, she parked her Mustang before her door at the Huree Hideaway, its nose out toward the woods. In spite of her optimism, she scanned the tree line, then looked down the well-lit walkway in either direction. The Huree Hideaway, as usual, was blessedly quiet. The place had been a perfect choice. This evening, there were three cars, Saturday night lovers inside and quietly going about their pleasure. She opened the car door, her purse in easy reach, with the room key ready. Though she wore a jacket, she was drenched in the three quick steps she took before she opened the door to her efficiency. Inside, she saw at once the room had been disturbed. Something—the stack of papers on her desk, she thought—was different. She shut the door behind her out of impulse and slid down on the floor. In the same motion, she brought her revolver out and threw aside her purse and briefcase. The door locked automatically behind her. From where she had positioned herself, she could see the whole room, even look under the bed. If he was still here, he was in the bathroom. Standing slowly, Josie felt herself shaking and tried to steady herself with several deep breaths. It did no good at all, and angrily, hoping he was waiting, she marched toward the closed bathroom door, the point of her nickel leading. The door was flimsy, and Josie kicked it open with a single blow. Shower, toilet, sink. She could see the entire room at a glance. He was gone, but he had been here.

The words on the mirror over the sink proved it.

MIsS mE?

In blood. Josie walked back to the front door, then into the rain. She had her keys and her gun. She checked along the wall and out across the small lot to the trees. She climbed into the car and started the engine. Spraying gravel, she pulled around to the front of the building and stopped. She looked for someone, anyone, then climbed out and went into the registration area, her gun hanging in her hand.

"BEA!" she called, walking into the room. Bea kept an eye on things. Maybe she had given Josie's "boyfriend" a key. At the very least, she might have seen him drive around to the back of the building.

"BEA!" Josie saw the woman sitting in her chair watching television. A beer can and a pack of cigarettes were set on the table next to her arm, as usual, but Bea was not getting up out of her chair.

"BEA!" Josie stepped into the little apartment and smelled it, the diapery stench of sudden death. She came forward more cautiously now, calling Bea's name one last time.

The woman wasn't answering, and never would again. She had been shot twice in the heart. Her sweater was soaked in her own dark blood.

Part Five

Midnight

JOSIE WAS waiting in the Mustang, her revolver in her lap, when the first deputy's car came off the highway twelve minutes after her call. Slipping her gun under her seat, she got out of the car to meet the man. Once he had surveyed the crime, the deputy made a call on the motel phone. While he waited for assistance, he took information from Josie. Who was she? What was she doing here? What did she know about any of this? Josie answered his questions honestly but with care. She was numb, maybe in shock, but hardly ready to trust anyone, especially the law in Lues County. Thankfully, before the interview had gone very far, two more cars arrived, and Josie had time to make a few decisions about how to handle the questions. Both of the new arrivals checked out the apartment where Bea's corpse sat. Afterwards, they interviewed Josie separately. Why was she using an alias? Why had she given a Boston address if she lived on campus in faculty housing. Did she know the woman? Did she see anything? Did she hear gunshots?

Josie explained that she had been in Memphis and had just gotten inside her apartment when she remembered she wanted to tell Bea she would be checking out soon. "I wanted to tell her personally. So I drove around."

"You drove?"

Josie nodded. The rain. The second deputy covered most of the same things, but he wanted to know about the other guests. How long had they been around? What kind of people were they? Josie hadn't seen them, she said. She usually came in late, and she left early. She was doing research here and hadn't had any interest in seeing the other guests. The place was quiet, she said. "That's why I liked it."

Her answers satisfied them, and both men eventually wandered away, their interest in her finished. The sheriff's crime scene unit arrived and began processing Bea's apartment. They opened a room off the main office and kept Josie there. One of them asked Josie if she would be willing to give her prints. She said that would be fine, even though she knew she would be a suspect in the investigation. People who found bodies always were. Another deputy arrived, then a huge brown county van pulled into the lot. Finally, the news vans and reporters began trickling in. They stayed outside, huddled inside their vehicles until the detectives arrived.

As everyone waited on the detectives, Josie stared out into the rain and darkness. Bitterly, she wondered if he was still there? Was he watching her even now? Laughing? *MIsS mE?* An old woman dead so he could leave his taunts in blood, playing his deadly game of hide-and-seek! She wondered how long he had known where to find her, if it had humored him to imagine she thought herself *safe,* knowing he could take her just by walking into the front office and grabbing the key. She wondered how long he would wait before he struck again and if the next time would be to finish it.

When the detectives arrived, they went into Bea's apartment together. A couple of minutes later, they stepped out and joined the other officers. Finally, they made for Josie with grim determination. Who was she? What was she doing here? What did she know about any of this? Did she know the victim? Did she hear a car? Gunshots?

As she tried to answer them, Josie heard the deputy in charge say to the others, ". . . the sheriff won't get out of bed for this old crone, you know what I mean? I mean, who cares? Am I right?"

"You don't think . . ."

Josie missed the rest.

"You went to your room?" the taller of the two detectives asked.

Josie focused on his face and nodded. "Yes. I went to my room, then came here."

"Where had you been?"

She gave the name and address of Susan Wallace. Her alibi.

"Did you see any strange cars when you drove up?" the other detective asked.

Josie shook her head.

"So you didn't see anyone at all?"

"I didn't see anybody."

"Hear anything?"

"I'm sorry, nothing." They thanked her for her help, and Josie said, "I'd like to go to my room now." The two men looked at one another, then at her questioningly. "I want to get out of here," she explained. "I don't want to spend another night in this place. Not after this."

"If you'll wait a bit longer," the taller of the two men answered, "Lues PD is sending a detective out to talk to you." Her face expressionless, Josie nodded, but her legs felt weak suddenly. What was the city doing with this? How did they even know about it?

The wait lasted nearly an hour. It was almost midnight before a city detective finally showed up. He was a short, powerfully built man in his late forties with very little hair and something of a Cupid's bow for lips. Like the deputies and sheriff's detectives, he tracked through the office to Bea's apartment, rainwater dripping from his coat, his footsteps sloshing along the same track as the others, the same as Josie's, and probably the same as the killer's.

He huddled with the detectives when he came back out. Josie heard him ask, "Robbery?" and thought one of the sheriff's detectives said, "She interrupted it." A thumb pointed in the direction of Josie. The men all looked at her. One of the uniforms volunteered, "The shooter left the money in the till."

"How much?"

Josie missed the answer but heard the words *Darling* and *Fortune*. "Says Boston here, but she's got an address on campus."

The detective shook his head and came into the room where Josie waited. He brought an artificial smile to his face at the last minute, the labored look of friendliness as he let her see his badge. "Sergeant Harpin," he growled with a raspy voice. "You're Josie Fortune?"

"It's Josie Darling . . . officially. I'm in the process of changing it." It was close enough to the truth. She was thinking about changing it.

Sergeant Harpin didn't care about the confusion of names. "You're a writer?"

"A professor. A lecturer, actually."

"I thought you were here writing a book."

"I'm doing some research, but it's not for a book."

"And you've been here, what a couple of months?"

"Almost two weeks."

"You got a boyfriend you meet out here?"

"No."

Harpin studied her quizzically. "You doing some moonlighting?"

Josie felt a flush of real anger. "Just what does that mean?"

"You know what it means." His eyes gave her body the once over. It was the same assumption Bea had made, but Harpin's attitude—the dirtiness of his expression—irritated Josie.

"I told you what I'm doing," she answered evenly, looking away from the man.

"You know the lady that was shot?"

"Not really."

"You didn't see the guy that did this?"

"I didn't see anybody at all." She was not looking at the man nor giving him any emotion. The insult of his assumptions burned her.

"How about the last couple of weeks? Anything unusual? Anyone you thought might be casing the place?"

"No."

"Do you know how much money she kept on the premises?"

Josie shook her head.

"She ever tell you she was worried about being out here alone?"

Again, Josie shook her head.

Harpin called to the deputies in the main office, "Anyone check on the other people?"

A sheriff's deputy answered simply, "Tom Hager took some statements, Happy. Saw nothing, heard nothing. Asked to keep their names out of the papers."

Harpin looked back at Josie, who now placed the name. *Happy Harpin.* Colt's man. What was it? *Mr. Fix-It?* Great. Knowing her luck, he'd probably fix her. "You figure this has anything to do with your stepfather, Professor?"

The question took Josie by surprise, but she didn't give herself time to react. "I really wouldn't know, Sergeant."

"Have you seen Jack, since he turned into a cop killer?"

"That has nothing to do with what happened tonight."

"With all due respect, I think that's our business to decide, not yours."

"I'd like to clean my room out and leave—if that's all right with you."

Sergeant Harpin studied her for a moment, then, without shifting his eyes away from her, he called out to the sheriff's people, "Any objection if our witness leaves?"

The detectives looked at each other, shrugging. One of them called back, "We got all we need from her."

"What's this Boston address you gave the victim?" Harpin asked her as she started past him.

"I made it up. I wanted my privacy. I didn't care for her to know I was a lecturer at the college."

"The old lady wasn't too careful about things like that," Harpin told her with a smirk.

Josie's words strained with anger. "She was a good lady. This stinks, what happened to her."

The cop's delicately curled lips flattened into a world-weary grimace, "I've never been to a good murder yet, Professor." He smiled the same friendly smile he had given her at the beginning, "But, then again, I haven't found your stepfather shot to hell either."

Later, standing in her studio apartment, her car packed up, the place clean except for the bathroom mirror, Josie studied the bloody scrawl one more time. *MIsS mE?* Bea's blood had dried on the glass. Josie thought there had been some wetness before, but she couldn't have sworn to it. A thin drip line had run off the first stem of the capital *M*. Had it been there when she had found the words? Had she arrived only a matter of minutes after he had gone? And if the rain hadn't slowed her down, would she have walked into the apartment while he was here? Would she have been ready?

She shook her head, looking through the words into her reflected eyes. Angrily, Josie reached for a wad of tissues, wet them, and began wiping the mirror. The glass turned muddy. Meaning faded, then even the smudges.

Sunday Morning

Late Sunday morning, Josie called Annie from the Huree Motel and told her what had happened. Annie listened to Josie's narrative impatiently. Shock gave way to anger, anger to fear. Even before Josie had finished, Annie was interrupting her to insist she leave Lues at once.

"Find the nearest airport and come home today!" she blurted.

"Lues is home, Annie."

"Josie, listen to me!"

"I've listened to you for years, Annie. Everything you've ever said, I listened to. You're the one who taught me we have to fight if life is going to be worth anything."

"It's too dangerous, Josie. If he found your last hiding place, he'll find the next one."

"Damn it, don't tell me I have to run! I've been running from things all my life, I'm tired of it."

"Josie, we can make it so this semester never happened. I mean it! If you're staying in Lues because of your contract, we can get it worked out. No one's going to blame you for leaving—I promise!"

Josie wondered if Annie recalled saying something to the same effect last winter after Dan's second attack had left her in the hospital. *I won't let this semester count against you. We can work this out. . . .*

"It's not the contract," she answered coolly. Of all people, she had thought Annie would understand, would know she had stay now.

"Then what is it?"

"Annie, I've found my mother."

"What do you mean?"

"I remember things. I know who she was."

"That's all you went there for, Josie."

"Virgil Hazard said she didn't back down from anyone."

"You are not your mother, Josie. You have to be realistic about this. Your life is in danger!"

"No, I'm not my mother. I'm my mother's daughter. For years, I had no idea what that meant! Now, suddenly, it's clear to me, and it's a good thing, Annie! She was this incredible woman, and I didn't understand that!"

"Josie, I know how you feel."

"No, you don't," Josie answered. "You have no idea. My whole life I've felt like I ought to apologize for who I am, and suddenly, I find out I never had any reason to hang my head. It wasn't just that my mother was killed or even that Jack was in prison for it. It was the rest, the idea that I should be ashamed. I was supposed to forget everyone I knew, act like they didn't exist and I hadn't existed here either. Everyone taught me to shut myself off from what I was, Annie!"

"But you found it! You've won, Josie!"

"Annie, my people don't run."

Silence. She had said *people,* as in family. Annie would not have missed that, and yet she didn't answer it either.

Finally, sadly, the old woman answered, "Josie, I don't want to bury you."

"Don't do this to me, Annie!" Josie raged. "This bastard walked in and shot a nice woman who never did anyone any harm, and the cops showed up and called her a crone. They said the sheriff wouldn't get out of bed for an old crone like her, that no one would care about her. Well, I care! Annie, I know who did it! It's the same bastard who sliced the womb out of my mother! The same one that walked free, while the only family I had left went to prison for the next twenty years!"

"Josie . . ."

"One question, Annie. That stuff you teach, about chasing the nightmare and staring down Medusa, is that just b.s. for the undergrads?"

"It's not the same, and you know it! I'm talking about the fears of the psyche, about revising the soul. It's not the same when someone means to do you physical harm."

"It's got to be the same! To hell with the soul if it isn't! It's all just garbage—everything you ever said—if we can't live with it. Is that what it is, just so much garbage to make us all feel better?"

Annie's voice was calm, "People win the battle against their demons the moment they decide to face them. Physical enemies are different. You don't win just because you decide not to run. What happens is you get yourself killed."

"I'm going to find him, Annie."

"How close are you? Realistically, what do you have?"

"I'm working on some things. I've got quite a bit, actually. It just hasn't quite come together."

"Josie, you need to get back to Boston, where it's safe."

"I can't find him in Boston."

"You're all alone there."

"I'm not, though. I've got more here than I've ever had in my whole life."

"Meaning Jack Hazard?" This was pure skepticism. "The man's a fugitive!"

"Annie, all I want is for you to believe in me. Don't tell me I can't do this."

"I'm not going to lie to you. I think this is a mistake."

"You don't think I can find him?"

"Josie, in forty-two years of teaching, I've never seen a mind like yours. You're stubborn, flighty, impulsive, and self-destructive, but I've got to tell you, when you decide to do something, you're unbelievable. I'm not going to say you can't. I just don't think it's smart."

"I know it's not smart, Annie. But life's not always about doing the smart thing, is it?"

"One question." Annie's voice was full of resignation, skepticism, and caution.

"Okay."

"Say you find him, just what do you mean to do then?"

"I'm going to bring all hell down on him, Annie."

Robert Tanner

Before they had finished, Annie asked what she could do to help. Josie answered that she had located her mother's professors and had talked to most of them over the past week, not getting much. Of the witnesses in the canyon, she said she had talked to all but Bob Tanner and Cat Sommerville. Tanner wasn't answering his phone, but she expected to reach him soon. Cat Sommerville was the real problem. Cat had vanished from the face of the earth. Josie had the mother's name and address, but the information was twenty years out-of-date, and she couldn't find her either.

"What's the state and county for the mother?" Annie responded.

"It's in-state, Kankakee County. The mother's name is Catherine Johnson. Or it was twenty years ago."

"*Johnson,* yeah, sure, that won't be too hard."

"*Johnson* is the easy part, Annie. Finding the right one is the trick."

"I just dropped out of the midnight basketball program," Annie answered, "so this will give me something to do to keep me from going back to the gang."

"You're a pal, Annie."

When they had finished, Josie made several more calls. Finally, she got through to a Professor Wright, or thought she had when a woman answered. The voice was pleasant and intelligent, the aging wife of a retired professor. Truth was, Josie had caught the daughter, who was watering the plants for her parents. The professor and his wife Joan were sailing in a sloop for Hawaii. Was there a message?

"Wish them luck," Josie answered.

With a feeling of utter futility, Josie tried Bob Tanner for the third time that morning. She had been trying to reach him for so long she was certain he was out of the country, maybe climbing mountains in Peru, but on the seventh ring, Josie heard a breathless, "Tanner!"

Josie introduced herself and told Mr. Tanner she was doing research on the murder of Josie Fortune.

"Wish I could help. I never heard of the lady!" The voice was loud, friendly, and stupid.

Josie told him more, and it came back to him. "Oh! Oh, that!"

"I'd like to set up an appointment to talk with you."

"I'll talk with you anytime, lady."

"Could you do it today? I know it's Sunday, but—."

"Today, sure. I've been on vacation for a couple of weeks, we just drove in this morning, but today's great. I need to get into the office anyway. What time is good for you?"

"I can be there in an hour and a half."

Bob Tanner had a little office that was part of a large rental house in Carbine Ridge. The place was tiny and disorganized. The guy was a slob. The business was run purely on pluck. Five minutes with Bob Tanner was enough to convince her of that. The man had no skills, no system, and no plan, but he was passionate about insurance. Every instinct was tuned to getting the signature. He talked about his afternoon twenty years ago simply to keep Josie sitting in front of him, a life-annuity insurance contract prepared for her to sign. She was getting older. It was time to start facing the inevitable. Rates go up the older we get!

It was a miserable meeting because Josie was running out of options. A madman was chasing her, and she needed something, some chance to turn the tables. All Bob Tanner could do was remind her she could die at any time. It was a truth too painfully obvious to contemplate, and he forced it on her until she could hardly breathe.

"What did you tell the police, Mr. Tanner?"

"To tell you the truth, I don't remember."

"Did you talk to a Sheriff Bitts?"

"I might have. I think someone came out to the fraternity house. He said we could get in trouble if we weren't careful."

Josie frowned. "What kind of trouble?"

"Perjury. He said if we weren't honest, we could go to jail for perjury."

"Anything else? Did you sign anything? Talk to anyone else?"

"Sorry. That's all I remember. I don't even remember who it was I talked to! Well, no, wait . . . no."

So it went. Hope, then nothing. Life, death, and good insurance policies. They talked about the condition of the body, its placement on the rock.

"What did you see? What was she like?"

"She was naked." Nothing else had registered. Josie tried to walk him into the canyon. She asked who had led the way out, who had trailed. She asked about the people with him. He didn't remember last names. He remembered Susie and Cat, and there was another girl, he was pretty sure, but he wouldn't swear to it. Had Jim Burkeshire ever dated Cat?"

He couldn't remember. He might have. He said he remembered going out with Susie a couple of times, then smiled like the cat that ate the canary.

Josie went back into the canyon with him. "What about letters cut into the flesh of the victim? The fat, shiny face of Bob Tanner was screwed into a tight grimace. Nothing. "Were there bruises on her throat?" The shoulders hunched up in frustration. "A rope burn around her neck?"

"No idea. But you know," he offered, brightly, "it just goes to show you how it can happen anytime, how you need to be ready with a good insurance policy."

The Dead

Monday at midday, Josie picked up a phone message from her faculty mailbox. No name, no number. Simply the words, I have the files you requested.

The girl at the desk was reading Lucretius, *Origins of the Universe*. "Marilyn, did you take this?" Josie asked, holding up the pink slip with the girl's initials. She looked up from her text, blinked, then nodded.

"Some old guy. He said you'd understand."

Pat Bitts was waiting when Josie pulled into his drive. "I put the coffee on!" he told her. "It's a cold one!"

He was right about that, the very first cold day of the fall. Inside, the potbelly stove was going, the coffee was gurgling. The place felt safe. Bitts had put what looked to be his desk chair, a card table, and a lamp in the kitchen. It was set up so that Josie could work close to the fire and the coffee. The gesture seemed more kind than necessary, until she saw the files that Lieutenant Morgan had delivered into the hands of his old boss. It was a large box stuffed with roughly a four thousand sheets of paper. Four cases in all, the files included incident reports, detectives's summaries, crime scene notes, photos, transcripts of interviews, toxicology reports, autopsy protocols, lists of seized items, news clippings, and every exchange between the state, FBI, and local authorities. Josie, who had been suffering from a dearth of it, had been expecting information, but this was overwhelming. "This could take some time," she told him.

"Well, Professor, my uncle used to say, 'Only trouble comes easy.'"

Josie smiled at the man. "What do you say we find a killer, Mr. Bitts?"

"You call me Two-Bit now that we're partners." He gave her a wink, "We called my grandfather *Mister* Bitts!"

"Two-Bit it is, if you'll drop the *Professor* and call me Josie."

The old man smiled, and she realized that it had been *Josie* twenty years ago, when she had lived here for a week, and that he must have wanted to call her Josie from the start.

"Okay, Josie, where do you want to start?"

"With Kruger." She sat down and pulled the first of the big files out, while Bitts pulled up a chair and sat next to her. He answered her questions without a lot of extraneous details, explained certain terms, and talked about procedures when Josie had a question. Otherwise, he simply read the pages she had already gone through. He stayed with her from shortly after three through the dinner hour without a break, except to make them peanut butter and jelly sandwiches. At midnight, he brought out pie and made more coffee. At three in the morning, he wandered off to bed. At seven, Bitts came out to the kitchen again, and Josie was still reading. In his robe, the old man padded over to make a fresh pot of coffee and laid out some stale doughnuts.

"Did you eat?" he asked.

Josie grunted impatiently, her eyes never lifting from the page. She hadn't moved for the past four hours, had hardly moved since the previous afternoon. When the coffee came, she thanked the man and turned another page.

She munched a doughnut. She scribbled a note. At eight, she asked to use the phone. She was going to have to call in sick, she said. At eleven, she closed the last file. Bitts looked at her curiously.

"I'm tired," Josie announced.

"Well, I guess!" As an active participant, Bitts had dropped out sometime after nine or ten the evening before. Josie stood up and walked over to get her jacket and revolver. Bitts's eyebrows lifted at the sight of the gun coming out of her purse, but she tucked it in the waistband of her jeans calmly and asked him, "Take a walk?"

Bitts nodded. "Sounds good."

Above the house there was an old barn and a few acres of pasture. From the peak of the hill, the Ohio River twisted beneath them. The only sign of human life was the Bitts farm and the road. The river was empty. The air was cold, the sky blue. The old man wore his Stetson and an old canvas coat. For several minutes, Josie watched the old man's dogs running ahead of them. She had the feeling of coming out of a dream and wanted to sort things through before she spoke.

Shelley Kruger had been the first, she said finally. A Lues State coed, Kruger had been missing three days when her body was found hanging upside down from a log in a ravine not far from Clems Hollow. The autopsy revealed her captor had apparently not fed her between the time of his abduction and her death. On the night she died, she was bound, gagged, and taken naked into the forest. Already weakened from dehydration and hunger, Kruger had probably endured only a short time before she suffocated, her lungs collapsing under the weight of her own body. She was found late the next afternoon by school-age children.

Kruger's death had received considerably more media attention than that of Josie Fortune. A TV news account of it, in fact, had inspired a kind of mass terror in the region—the possibility of a serial killer at large. It was a murder so bizarre that the local press became obsessed with it. When the investigation had finally stalled, the sheriff's department contacted the FBI, who entered the case on a consulting basis. Because they had no other murders quite like it, the agents had recommended going back over the original investigation. Sheriff's detectives questioned everyone Shelley Kruger had known. Of the cases before Ferrington's murder, it was the most thoroughly investigated. Two men who had had sexual relations with Kruger were questioned repeatedly. Their interviews went on for pages. Every detail they offered was eventually checked out. There were full background checks on both men, interviews of people who worked with them, surveillance reports on them, and three different search warrants issued and executed. Three other men who had dated Kruger but said they had not had sexual relations were scrutinized as well. One of her professors was looked at briefly, Bill Waters in Forestry. He was even put under surveillance for a couple of weeks, but it seemed that he only went into the woods to look at trees. Kruger's family members were asked to provide alibis. A couple of them were also followed for several days. In the end, the reports began to recycle suspects. Nothing connected. Whole lists of her friends were created. More interviews were conducted, many of them redundant. Background checks were made. Nothing came of the efforts. Eventually the case gathered fewer and fewer reports.

Of the nearly two hundred people listed as friends or acquaintances, Anita Moore and Melissa Fry were included, but this fact went unnoticed in the investigations of their deaths, because by the time they were killed they had different names. In fact, Josie could find nothing in their files that showed the police investigators had connected either of them back to Shelley Kruger. But there was a connection, once you went back far enough. They had all started college together in the fall of 1989. They had all joined the Kappa Zeta Sorority. They were in the same pledge class. Kruger, an older student, had been the president of their pledge class. She had spent five years in the navy and had come back home to Lues to take a degree in mechanical engineering. Neither Moore nor Fry had been close friends with her, it seemed, and there was nothing but a coincidence to connect them, but it was a coincidence that Josie had spent twenty straight hours looking for.

Just over two years after Kruger's death Anita Moore-Paget's body was found south of Carbine Ridge. A first-year stockbroker in Pilatesburg, living with her husband, Wayne, in Gallows Hill, Paget had been abducted and held nearly three days. Unlike Kruger, she was given food and water. On the night of her death, she had been stripped naked and shot with a .22. The autopsy revealed a total of four wounds. She had apparently escaped her captor and was chased through roughly a mile of forest before the fatal bullet struck her head, a contact wound. One theory, however, offered a more disturbing scenario—not escape, but set free, then hunted. Like

Kruger, Anita Paget had not been assaulted sexually. The investigation had centered around Wayne Paget from the beginning. A competitor in national shooting contests, Paget was having affairs with three women at the time of his wife's death, and the interviews of Paget's lovers had read like something from a steamy romance novel with the addition of a few bitter references to the wife. In the end, however, no charges were brought against the husband.

Four years later, in a woods east of Gallows Hill, an early morning hiker found Melissa Fry-Bates's naked corpse nailed to a tree in the fashion of a crucifixion. A school teacher in Paducah, Melissa Fry had married Marty Bates two years earlier. It was apparently a good marriage. A woman of remarkable beauty and talent, Bates was the subject of numerous news reports. She was loved by her students and genuinely admired by her fellow teachers. She had centered her life in her community, giving herself to charitable causes and working almost ceaselessly for her church. An FBI agent, assisting the sheriff's investigators, had tried to link the death back to Shelley Kruger's. A comparative study showed the bindings might have been from a similar material and the technique of wrapping the wrists and ankles was similar. The detective failed to discover, however, that both women had pledged the same sorority together. No one, in fact, was looking into ancient history for a motive to such a murder. What they looked for was a religious zealot and, alternatively, anyone and everyone who hated religion. The investigation produced almost as much paper as Kruger's case, but in the end, no arrests were made.

The last murder was that of Cathy Ferrington in June or July of 1999. Like the others, Ferrington had disappeared before her death. Unlike the others, she apparently had disappeared in or around the Chicago area shortly after she had dropped her kids off with their grandparents, but even that was not certain. Unlike the other victims, her corpse remained undiscovered for nearly two months. All that could be concluded was that Ferrington had been bludgeoned to death. There was no evidence of rape, no proof that it hadn't occurred.

As with Paget's case, Ferrington's death was suspected to be the work of the husband, Dr. Richard Ferrington. No one ever looked at her murder as possibly being connected to Kruger's, Paget's, and Bates's because there was plenty in the Ferrington marriage to suggest motive. From the beginning, however, police investigators had had difficulty implicating Dick Ferrington. Certainly there was no physical evidence, and no one had been able to explain how Ferrington could have abducted his wife, while he was at a conference in Madrid, Spain. Jason Morgan, Bitts's former deputy, was the lead investigator on a task force that included two Chicago detectives, a CID investigator for the state police, two FBI agents, and two Lues County sheriff's detectives. Morgan had speculated that Cathy Ferrington was not abducted at all but had taken the kids to Dick's parents in Chicago, then drove off to meet her husband for a private rendezvous upon his return. The problem was Morgan had nearly seven days to explain away, and neither the state's attorney nor any of the other investigators gave the theory any credence. Morgan himself seemed to abandon the idea finally, but the notes suggested he never quite got rid of his conviction that Ferrington had done it. Without any proof, however, Cathy Ferrington's case, like the others, had remained open.

The surprise was that Cathy Ferrington was Cat Sommerville.

"All night," Josie told Bitts in a quiet, reflective tone, "I was looking for some connection, some link between these women and my mother. Then, suddenly, I saw the name Sommerville."

"You sure it's the same woman?"

"Positive. She was at Lues State the year my mother was killed, then transferred to North Carolina that next fall."

"Where she met Dr. Ferrington?"

Josie nodded. For seven years, the Ferringtons had lived at Chapel Hill. When Dick took his doctoral degree in 1989, he joined the faculty of Lues State. A decade later, Cat Sommerville presumably met Josie Fortune's killer.

"What do you make of it?" Bitts asked.

"I don't know," she answered tiredly. "It's like the whole thing just fell in my lap, and I don't know what to do with it."

Bitts studied the river calmly. "I remember Cat Sommerville the best of all of them, Josie. Fact is, she threw me off. I kept wanting to blame the kids for moving the body or lying to me about what they had actually seen, but there was Cat Sommerville staring me down. Bright, honest, and proud." He grinned. "She said to me, 'What's your problem?' I told her what my problem was, and she went pale. I thought, if she's acting, . . . brother, she ought to get an Academy Award."

"None of the investigators made anything of her going to school at Lues State."

"So none of them noticed that she was one of the kids who found your mother?"

"Right. No one looked back that far. The whole case was about Dick Ferrington."

"Maybe it's nothing more than a coincidence. A lot of times people leave a place and come back." He shook his head. "It was sixteen years!"

"Do you think it's a coincidence she came back to Lues the same semester that Melissa Fry, Anita Moore, and Shelley Kruger were pledging Kappa Zeta?"

Bitts stared at Josie in stark wonder.

Josie smiled grimly, "Makes you wonder what we're missing, doesn't it?"

Naomi

There are parts of a university that have a peculiar life of their own. Here one finds university personnel that faculty rarely encounter. These are the people moving the mass of paperwork through the system, a whole network devoted to the dark underbelly of intellectualism: the business of business. The woman Josie spoke to was close to fifty. A generic certificate on the wall thanked Naomi Temple for twenty years of service. The name and number of years were hand-printed. It was signed by a VP. It was Naomi's sole prize, as far as Josie could see, and Josie wondered if Naomi was proud of it or just kept it on the wall in case her VP happened through. Naomi Temple had two kids, very handsome boys close to maturity, and a husband who looked in his portrait like a heart attack survivor or a man about to have one. A school logo for the Pilatesburg Pirates was stuck next to the larger Lues State Lancer sticker. Her office fronted a large file room. A counter separated the area from public access.

"May I help you?" There was courtesy in this without warmth. Mrs. Temple apparently assumed Josie needed to order her transcripts sent to a potential employer.

Josie held her faculty ID out like a badge, "I'm Josie Darling, in English. I wondered if I might look at a few transcripts."

Jaw dropped, eyes stunned, Mrs. Temple made the amateur's mistake of overstatement. "You want to look at someone's transcripts?" The voice seemed positively eager for a laugh track to finish her question.

Josie slipped her ID back into her briefcase, "Five of them, actually. The students are all deceased. I hardly think it's a matter of confidentiality."

"Miss—?"

"Darling."

"Miss Darling, I can show you your transcript, but that's all. Transcripts are confidential."

Josie hesitated. "I just want to see what classes these people took. I don't need the grades. It doesn't even need to be an official transcript."

"Without their permission in writing, I can't do that."

"I told you, they're deceased."

Smiles from both sides of the counter did little to break the ice. Naomi Temple had served twenty-some years in this station, and each year she had guarded her records with the enthusiasm of Cerberus. Unless officially sanctioned, nothing went out. Naomi was probably the sort of woman to read the laws of sexual conduct in her state before submitting to her husband.

Josie looked longingly toward the back room. Midnight and a master key might take care of it. "I need to know what classes and which professors five women took. Where do I go to find that information?"

"They're not currently enrolled?"

"I told you, they're dead."

"But not currently enrolled?"

With amazing restraint, "No."

"You come here for that."

"Great. Can you give me the names of their professors?" Josie had her mother's. She thought if she could cross-reference that list against the others she could find what she needed.

"Our policy makes no exception. Transcripts are only sent out after a student or ex-student, as the case may be, gives us a signed request," she tapped a stack of papers, "on one of these forms."

At this point, the boy who had stepped up to defend Josie from her cabbie appeared in the doorway of the file room and came into Mrs. Temple's office. Thin, studious, alert . . .

. . . *what is his name?*

"Hey, Miss Darling!"

"You work here?"

You. That was good. How could she keep forgetting his name? She was good with names! She knew the name of every student, except for *what's his name,* her white knight.

"Ten hours a week, but don't worry. I still have time to write your papers!"

Mrs. Temple smiled brilliantly now, "Nelson is a dream. I'll have worked in this office twenty-three years this January, and I've had good student workers, don't get me wrong, but Nelson is just the sweetest. . . ."

Nelson blushed as Mrs. Temple told a rather complicated story about a numeric inversion and a lost transcript. Josie found herself straining to hold her smile. When Naomi Temple had finished her narrative, Josie made her exit as gracefully as her frustration allowed. She was thinking a master key to Harrison might not be so easy to get hold of. That left her with hiring a lawyer. A lawyer could get her mother's transcripts but not the others, and she already had the names of her mother's profs from Bitts. Break into Naomi's house and steal her keys? That sounded about right. Or just forget it? What did she really expect to find, after all?

As she turned down a long, blank hall, she discovered Nelson in front of her. He was standing before an open door, which Josie realized led into the back of the transcripts and records files. "There you are," he whispered. He looked back into a dark file room, fearful Naomi would appear, no doubt. "She said you wanted to see some transcripts of people who are deceased."

"It's really important, Nelson," Josie whispered.

"I can get you what you want, if they're dead. I mean, it's not like they'd mind, right?"

In the fashion of a conspirator, Josie looked both ways down the hall and reached into her briefcase. "I need the transcripts for these people," Josie answered.

Nelson looked at the list. "I'll bring them to class tomorrow," he said.

"You won't get in trouble for this, will you?"

"No. There's no way anyone will know. I just pull the master, copy it, and put it back. You don't need it stamped, do you?"

Josie imagined Naomi Temple with THE STAMP locked in her desk drawer. "No, unofficial transcripts will do," she told him.

Nelson's dark eyes flashed wonderfully, a really cute kid, she realized.

"This isn't for a grade. I don't want you to give me a break, because I'm doing this."

"I don't give breaks, Nelson."

He smiled, the epitome of average but honest and a boy very much smitten with his teacher, she thought. "I know. That's what I like about you."

Bookkeeping

It was still daylight, and since she was on campus, Josie drove to her apartment. The mail was overflowing. There were four local billing accounts and two Visa cards boiling over the limits. There was also a card from her adoptive mother. Was Josie coming home for Thanksgiving and Christmas? Maybe some weekend while the weather was still nice? Josie groaned. She had promised she would, but she couldn't deal with the Darlings right now, hadn't been able to deal with them for years. She loved them, but she had long ago learned to turn elsewhere when troubles came. They had been of the opinion that she ought to give Dan a second chance. To be fair, that had been before he attacked her, but Josie had never really gotten over that piece of uninvited advice. These days, with her troubles multiplying, the last thing she needed was an opinion about her decision to move to Lues. She would call them soon, she told herself. Assuming she was still alive.

Before she left the apartment, Josie decided to drop her mother's books off. She had been hauling them around in the trunk of the Mustang and hadn't even bothered to go through them, nor even look at the photographs again. They were taking up trunk space, and the odor of mildew had begun to permeate the car. She set the box of books and the albums on the floor of her living room and considered the pile distastefully. The three albums in ruin, Josie went through them quickly and detached the pictures. Most of the pictures were in terrible condition, but the images themselves were powerful reminders to Josie that she had lived in a world she no longer understood or even properly remembered. A part of herself remained secret, and now, as she studied the image of her mother holding her Purdey and sitting on the bar at the Hurry On Up, she thought about the woman putting the gun in Colt's face. Josie could only hope there was a courage she had inherited from the woman, a hidden strength she could tap. The devil himself could not sneak up on Josie Fortune. As she studied the woman who stared brightly into the camera's eye, Josie wondered if her courage was what had gotten her killed. Did she overestimate her ability, or was it like Virgil said, a friend, someone she trusted? College?

When all the pictures were laid out on the carpet, Josie took the three albums to the trash. That left her with the books. She hadn't really wanted them. She had agreed to take them on impulse, purely the instinct to save books, but they were schoolbooks, all of them outdated as well as ruined by water. There was nothing really to save. No one would ever use them again. They were disgusting even to the touch. After she had peeled the cardboard box away, she stacked them on the floor next to the pictures. They were damp, and they stank. They had no value financially or emotionally, but they might have her mother's handwriting, she decided. She had never seen her mother's writing. It would be nice to see that, a treasure to find some old essay she might have written. Josie reached out and pulled one of the books to her. *Macro Economics*. As she flipped through the text, she noted certain passages were marked with a pen. That was it. The book didn't contain any notes penned to herself or even Josie Fortune's signature. She flipped through two more books, tossing them aside rather quickly. Josie considered quitting, then, resigned to the utter futility of her task, reached for the next book in the stack, *Marketing in Today's World*. There she struck gold. Three loose sheets were stuck together in a tight, damp clump. Thinking they might be notes for a test, maybe cheat sheets, or love letters from Jack … or someone, Josie peeled the sheets apart. When the first sheet came free, Josie read: *sooon, JosIe, i promiss.* On the next was written, *stil tHinkING Of u, hoR.* The last was: *MIsS mE?* Each was written in red crayon.

Numbed, enraged, and certain of her man, certain he could be no other, Josie looked through the rest of the books quickly. She found nothing more nor did her breathing return to normal. She left the notes on the floor, face up, and went to call Annie. She got her answering machine.

"I'm at my campus apartment, but not for long. I'll call you tonight. I've got news."

She set the phone back in the cradle and looked at the notes again. Even sitting close to them made her sick. The terror that had cooled as she had chased through history for some sign of this man came throbbing back hotly. He still wore his mask. He still watched her from the shadows of the woods, but now, she was certain he wasn't counterfeit. The man who had killed Bea and made Josie's life a living hell was most certainly the killer of Josie Fortune. She knew another thing, too: what he promised he performed.

Office Hours

Josie got a motel room in Carbine Ridge. She ate at the town's one diner. She spent the evening writing out key information from her memory of the files of the murdered women. She called Annie again and got nothing more than the old rant about her Uzi and karate class. When sleep came, it came quickly. Her dreams were vivid. She was bound and waiting in an empty room. There was no door to the room, no give to the bindings.

The next morning, pushing it to make it to Brand Hall a few minutes before eight, Josie found an envelope taped to her door. There was no name on it, and she was uncertain if the thing was from one of her students or from him. She pulled it off the door and set her briefcase on her desk as she tore it open. With her heel, she reached back and closed the door, listening to it click shut and lock. She wanted no surprises at her back. Opening the envelope, she saw the obituary of Beatrice Quincy. That was it, the official note of Bea's passing. Family upstate, family in Texas, Bea's husband had preceded her in death. They had had no children. There was nothing else in the envelope, no marks, no threats. Resisting the panic edging up in her, Josie tossed the envelope on her desk. Reaching for her briefcase, she turned to leave. That was when she noticed a bright red happy face had been painted on the inside of her door. She gasped in surprise, felt the blood draining from her face. It was some eighteen inches in diameter, the smile grotesquely sunny. For nearly a minute, she studied it without moving, without even thinking. Finally, seeing it was done in paint, Josie taped several memos over the image. He had been in her office again. He could enter it at will, it seemed. She was certain now he had a key and probably had gotten one to her campus apartment as well. Did he have a key for the new lock? Was he looking through her family pictures even now? Drawing happy faces everywhere on the apartment walls? Josie fought the tears of impotence and ignorance and rage. She cursed the man in the hot silence, then she shivered at the end he had planned for her. She would never find him in time. How was she ever going to know who was doing this until it was too late? How could she see him coming? He was nothing more than a ghost! The truth was there was no answer to this riddle. She would not find him among the shadows of history. That was only the delusion of an angry young woman. There were no answers in obscure texts for this puzzle. There was no help from the police. How long she would live was his decision and his alone. The more she struggled to find out something, the more he laughed at her. He would laugh as long as he was enjoying himself, at any rate. When he grew tired of the game, he would come for her. From the dark? In the daylight? Smiling in her face? Hiding in a shadow?

And then? She knew the rest, assuming she did not get to her nickel in time. No need to ask that. It was written in all his victims' files. He would bind and gag her. Two, maybe three days. Maybe weeks, as he had Cathy Ferrington, if she really excited him. And then? What pain? What death? Maybe he would just leave her someplace, while he went about his business. As in her dream: the empty room without doors. She could almost believe at a certain point you would hope for your killer to return. Anyone would do, so long as it ended the terrible silence of an empty room, the slow death from thirst and hunger. Even now, she felt the urge to give over to him. Waiting was so unbearable.

She could still run, she told herself. She had to! She was never going to find the answer. There was no answer! He came and went at his leisure. He was a nobody. These kind always were. A faceless janitor. A maintenance man who came and went without being noticed. For twenty years, he had been playing this game, crafty and mean and virtually invisible. He left messages behind locked doors. He wrote things in mirrors. He called her in places where no one knew she would be. He was full of mock sympathy, utterly indifferent to the meaning of death. As far as she could see, he didn't even seem to have some kind of rage driving him, except for the killing. Those were uniformly horrible, macabre in their public displays of violence. The chase, though, was pure play. All of it was like a game a child might enjoy! Josie could not hide from him. That was what he wanted her to know. He was telling her she was a fool to hide each night, because he could get past doors, because he could find her when he liked. Was she a fool, then, to run, too? Would he follow? Would he find her?

No. She could run. She could be somewhere new by evening. She could be in Chicago or Atlanta, Cincinnati or Kansas City, in a matter of hours. She could get in her car or on a plane, and he would never know where she had ended up or what name she took to begin life again. Didn't he care? Or did he know she was going to stay? Did he know better than she did that somehow she must stay, that she could not leave?

Josie studied her office angrily. He knew so much about her. Because he was close? Watching? Talking to her each day? One of the older students who come and go? One of the faculty? Or did he know because he had been in her office before, as he had been in her apartment? Touching her things, reading her papers. Had he moved anything here? Were there more notes? Had he bugged the place? Installed some kind of camera? Did he know she carried a gun? He might! He could have seen her going out to Bowers's. She had not been especially careful about that. In fact, he could have been one of the shooters on the range one of those times, watching her practice. She closed her eyes and steadied herself. She had some things he couldn't know about, things not written in her notes. She wasn't fighting in the dark entirely, as he no doubt assumed. Not completely. She had more than the names of his other victims. She had read about his murders, knew his technique. She had the enigma of Cat Sommerville. She had the friendship of Pat Bitts. She had Jack Hazard in her camp and with him a family of men who knew no law but their own. She would wager her soul he knew nothing of them, and that knowledge gave her a sudden comfort.

All she needed was to follow the right trail out of the labyrinth. Not so hard really when she considered it was what she was trained to do. History was whispering to her. She could almost hear it. She looked once more at the obituary he had left for her. He knew she was after him, if he knew anything about her at all. So why the taunt? To distract her?

Did he fear that she was close? Maybe she was closer than she knew? Her visit to transcripts and records?

Transcripts

In the hall outside her office, Josie met Val as he was unlocking his door. He was dressed typically, the work shirt buttoned to the collar, a pair of baggy beige pants, a dark sports jacket, a knapsack caught in his big hand. Head in profile, his eye seemed to roll toward her curiously. She said his name. He answered with hers. He was disappointed that she had not taken his advice, so had been a bit cool since. She pushed on indifferently. Her back to him now, she waited for some word or the sound of his door or even his footsteps. She looked down to the floor, expecting his shadow to explain the silence. Nothing. She turned finally. He was gone. The light of his office was shining over his curtain. The door was shut. So very quiet when he wanted to be.

Josie spent most of a free hour in the library reading a textbook written by Marcel Waldis, the man who had performed the autopsies on her mother, Shelley Kruger, and Anita Paget. It was a slow read, dense with technical information, and before she could finish it, she had to go to class. She almost left the book on the table where she sat, intending to pursue some other line, then remembered Annie's methodology: whatever it takes, even eight hundred pages of metaphysical agonies. This belonged to the puzzle. She just didn't how or why, but she needed to read it.

Josie arrived at her ten o'clock composition class a couple of minutes late but tried not to look hurried, tried in fact to enter her classroom as Henry Valentine entered his. She liked this class. She liked the vigor they brought to their studies. So when she entered, having missed their Tuesday class, she felt a degree of comfort. It was enough to encourage a bit of playfulness, so she stopped with a dramatic gesture. "What? No cheering?"

There was a dumb silence at first.

"Come on, people, I'm as good as Henry Valentine, aren't I?"

Some clapping started, then more. Finally, they all began cheering. Josie smiled the polite, embarrassed smile of the deservedly famous, and bowed Valentine-style. This brought a roar of applause, even a standing ovation. Part of it was just silliness, kids looking for an excuse to have some fun and play to her vanity before she graded their papers. It was no doubt the same with Valentine, but at least a piece of it felt like the genuine article. She saw it in their faces. They had heard the rumors that she might be fired, but they were siding with her, in this moment at least. And this moment, she decided, was all that really mattered, all she really had.

At 11:15, collecting their compositions, Josie noted the large folder Nelson what's his name handed her. Josie gave the boy a sly look, "You've been busy!" she told him.

"Yes ma'am." A sly conspirator's smiled trailed in at the end, and she liked him all the more for his subtlety. Naomi was right. He was something special. Even if Josie couldn't remember his name.

As Josie took the rest of the papers in hand and started for the door, Harriet, her sonnet writer, was waiting to speak to her. "Can you look at some of my stuff?" she asked.

Josie hesitated, then shook her head decisively. "Today's not good. I'm kind of busy with some other things. Next week?"

Nodding, head bent wearily, the rejected poet left as only the rejected poet can. Josie was alone in the classroom now and felt a surge of guilt. It was crazy, but she thought she owed the woman. Well, of course, she did. Annie Wilde would have stopped everything to read a poem, even a bad one. Annie would read a poem in the middle of a gunfight! Outside the classroom, Josie caught up with the woman. "I have some time late this afternoon. Can you come by after three?"

The woman glowed.

In her office, Josie shut the door and left the light off, so she wouldn't be disturbed. Over the top of the curtain, the light from the hall was sufficient. Josie fished out Nelson's folder. *Nelson Rush!* Why couldn't she remember that? His folder was thick, and when she opened it, she found the transcripts of five women—including Josie Fortune.

Virgil had said it was college. Maybe he was right. Maybe here she could find the killer. Clearing her desk, she lay the transcripts out side by side. Then, in the half-light of the room, she began poring over the material. Though it was simply raw data, meaningless to an outsider, she worked through the lists fairly quickly.

Anita Paget, then known as Moore, was a business major and had had three of the same professors as Josie Fortune, also a business major. Cat Sommerville, Melissa Bates, and Shelley Kruger, however, didn't have any discernible relationship with these professors. Bates, then known as Fry, had had an advanced communications class with Clarissa Holt. Kruger had studied in an introductory literature class with Ev Case, Josie's department chair. At different times and in different courses, Anita Paget, aka Anita Moore, and Cat Sommerville had had composition classes with Gerty Dowell, the resident gossip in sweats. This was meaningless, except that she was Valentine's friend. *Wind her up . . .*

Although it connected to none of the others, it surprised Josie that her mother had signed up for Advanced Creative Writing 360 with Henry Valentine. Valentine had not appeared on Bitts's list of Josie Fortune's professors. She saw at once the reason. Her mother had dropped the class eventually, in October of 1982, to be exact. Just such overlooked details had let investigators miss the fact that Paget, Bates, and Kruger were pledge sisters and that Cathy Ferrington, aka Cat Sommerville, had been among the five students to find Josie Fortune. What else had gone unnoticed?

The door shook under a heavy fist, and Josie looked up from the transcripts with a start, her hand reaching out automatically for her purse. Again the door rumbled, and Josie straightened up. Bringing her purse with her, she pulled back her curtain slightly to see who it was. She didn't want to be interrupted, but she wanted to know who was at her door. When she saw it was Clarissa Holt, she smiled and opened her door. Clarissa's tight, dark features brightened with as much enthusiasm as she ever allowed herself. "Your lights are out. I almost didn't knock."

"Come in."

Josie whispered the command and looked back at the opened door of Henry Valentine's office. Val was in and taking confessions from an eighteen-year-old alcoholic. "We were so fucked-up, man!" the young man laughed. Clarissa looked toward the door as well, and Josie actually pulled her into her office.

"What's going on?" she asked quietly, as if she knew Valentine might be the problem.

Without answering, Josie went back to her desk and retrieved the transcripts. She handed all five of them to Clarissa and asked, "Do you know any of these people?"

"Where did you get . . ." Clarissa stopped with the second one. "Melissa Fry." She looked up at Josie, waiting for an explanation.

"Did you ever hear what happened to her?"

"Everybody knows what happened to Melissa Bates, Josie. She was crucified. That was years ago." Clarissa's dark eyes burned with curiosity. She shuffled through the others, considering each in turn, then finally shook her head. "I don't know these other women."

Josie stepped closer and took the transcripts from her and laid them out so that each student's record could be easily compared to the other four. "All five were murdered." She tapped each in sequence, pronouncing the year of death, ". . . all found somewhere in Lues County, except this one."

"Who's she?"

"Cat Sommerville. You know her as Cathy Ferrington."

Clarissa grabbed the transcript and scanned it quickly, "Cathy Ferrington went to school in Lues?"

"Two years. She got pregnant and transferred to North Carolina."

Clar looked at her in surprise. "How do you know that?"

"Research."

"What's this all about, Josie?"

"I'm looking for a professor they're all connected to."

"*Connected?* What do you mean?"

"The operating hypothesis is the same man murdered all five women. Abduction, torture, and finally murder. Right now, I just want a name, someone they all might have known."

Holt's eyebrow cocked fiercely, "You think it was a professor?"

Josie shrugged but didn't answer. She didn't drop her gaze either. In response, Clarissa bent over the table, scanning the transcripts as only someone who has reviewed hundreds of them can. Within a few seconds, her finger fell to the name Henry Valentine on Josie Fortune's transcripts. "Here."

"I saw it, but none of the others took his class."

Clarissa's face darkened with concentration as she continued examining the transcripts. "Why do you have the lights off?"

"I didn't want to be bothered."

"Did it work?" Josie thought she saw the woman smile.

"Until you came along."

Her eyes never lifting from the papers, "So I wanted you to take me to lunch for saving your ass."

"I don't know, Clar. I'm kind of in the middle something."

"You have to eat. Something greasy and a lot of beer to wash it down—it's been that kind of week for me. How about you?"

"Beer's definitely out. I'm living on about two hours sleep a night lately. One sip and I'd be gone."

"Okay, no beer for you. Just grease and coffee. Improve the ulcer." Clarissa still hadn't lifted her eyes from the transcripts. Finally, she rapped her knuckles on one of the sheets and straightened up, "Two business majors, a life science major, a mechanical engineer, and a mathematician. Not one of them taking courses she ought to! Not more than a half-dozen Bs in the whole pack either. And look at the two who graduated. Moore takes her degree in two years and a summer. Fry, three years and a summer. They were in overdrive! I took five years for my undergraduate degree and I thought that was rushing it."

"Do you remember Melissa Bates taking your class?" Josie asked.

"She was Melissa Fry when she took my class. Very special woman, Josie."

"What exactly can you tell me about her?"

"Over lunch?"

Josie looked back at the stack of papers she had meant to try to grade over a missed lunch. They would still be there when she got back, like everything else she had put off. "Sure. To tell you the truth, I'm starved."

In Josie's Mustang, Clarissa told her, "Melissa Fry found Jesus with the help of her boyfriend, then, instead of taking the world by storm, which she could have, she took a job as a high school teacher somewhere down south."

"Paducah."

Holt's eyebrow cocked in surprise as she gave Josie a sideways look. "Right," she answered. "Paducah. Very aggressive young lady, even after she found out about turning the other cheek. Physically strong, very bright, very feminist in a country girl kind of way." She tapped the transcripts. "I had Melissa in a class in the spring of her second year, and of course, I tried to recruit her into communications. I talked about the great combination of a hard science major with a minor in broadcasting. It would have taken another year, but at the rate she was going, that didn't mean anything. She had a perfect television face, Josie. She could have had her pick of jobs in any secondary market after graduation and moved right into a metro area inside three years, assuming CNN or one of the networks didn't snatch her up."

"You said she was aggressive. Is that aggressive like you and me, or was she a bitch?"

Clarissa did a double take. She was aware and proud of her reputation as *the bitch*, and she wasn't sure if Josie was teasing her about it. "Professionally aggressive. In my opinion, she wasn't aggressive enough in her personal life. The boyfriend was the problem. I told her what she could do in communications, and her eyes lit up. A few days later, she didn't think it was such a good idea. She said something about it being too worldly. He was threatened by her intelligence and used religion to control her. If she ever got a taste of success, she would have left him in the dust, and he knew it, so he very quietly, very cleverly moved her priorities around until he and

God were the only ones left. I hated him for it, because she was . . . amazing." Clarissa reached toward Josie's briefcase. "May I?"

Josie nodded, and her friend pulled the rest of the transcripts out. As Josie negotiated the snarling lunchtime traffic on campus, Clarissa kept her face in the transcripts. Without looking away, she asked, "Wright, Donaldson, and Lindermann were professors for two of them. . . ."

"Moore and Fortune," Josie answered. "Professor Donaldson is dead. Lindermann's in Seattle. I called and asked her about Fortune a couple of days ago. I didn't know about Moore at the time. She said some nice things, but nothing I could connect to the rest of this. Wright's somewhere in the Pacific Ocean with his wife."

"May I ask you what your interest is in this?"

Josie took a deep breath. "I guess that's fair."

Cokey's

Their lunch and Josie's story finished simultaneously, Clarissa lit a rare cigarette, took a sip of her second beer, and leaned back in her booth. "It's Valentine, Josie."

"Why do you think so?"

"Mailbox, key to your office, key to your apartment, anonymous notes: the guy's a sneak. I've heard it for years. He's got all the master keys to every building on campus, and he snoops." As Josie pondered this, Clarissa continued, "You remember your little mess with the dean?"

"That was Ferrington, Clar."

"You said he was upset?"

"Livid. He acted like it was a personal affront, said I had embarrassed him."

Clar smiled, an old debater who hadn't forgotten how to go for the finish: "Val yanks Ferrington's chain, probably through the good graces of Gerty Dowell, and Ferrington comes storming to you. And where do you go?"

Seeing the picture for the first time, Josie answered with some irritation, "I spill my guts to Henry Valentine."

"A nice little departmental circle jerk. Believe me, it's got Valentine's signature all over it."

Josie shook her head, smiling coolly, "Okay, Val saw his chance and decided to have some fun with the new girl who gets caught auditioning at the local strip club. Let's say I buy the whole thing, whether I believe it or not. It doesn't make him a killer. Just the opposite. Clar, I'm looking for a man who's killed six women that I know of. This guy *crucified* a woman, for God's sake. He eviscerated my mother. We're not talking about someone who gets his jollies yanking somebody's chain!" She hesitated. "Do you really think Valentine could be the man?"

"Honestly? I don't know. No. Not really. You say you want a professor. I give you the best candidate. Val gives everyone the creeps. He's strange, but face it, a lot of good teachers are a bit off. It comes with the territory. I mean there are people who think I'm a little strange. Can you believe that?"

"Not for a minute."

"You're such a good liar."

"So the guy's a genius with kids, and he's a creep. . . ."

"Right. But that doesn't make him your creep. Realistically, I don't see it, but then I can't imagine anyone doing this kind of stuff. It's just beyond me."

"Someone did it, Clar, and he's promising to do it again."

Holt's look was thoughtful, angry. "You need to go the police. This is way too much to handle on your own."

"I went to the city cops, and they took my stepfather out to the woods and tried to execute him. Plus, I've got at least two suspects inside the city police department."

"What about the state police, the sheriff, the FBI?"

"The sheriff lied about the time of my mother's death. Look, if I go to anyone, the locals are going to hear about it. I've got a couple of things right now that give me some advantage, but if I give them away, I'm done. Believe me, cops are not an option."

"But you can't expect to deal with someone like this?"

"I have two choices, Clar. I can run or I can hunt this bastard down. And you know what? I'm not running."

"I don't know whether I'd rather have you or this maniac chasing me, Josie."

"I'm going to find him, Clar."

"I sure hope you do, for your sake."

"Connections?"

"Okay. Connections. You've got three in a sorority. Pledge sisters for Kappa Zeta. Biggest and best on campus. What about your mother? Was she in a sorority?"

"I doubt it. She was a single mom. Not very likely. I suppose I should check."

"What about you?"

"I missed that rite of passage."

"How about Cathy Ferrington? Was she in one?"

"Cat Sommerville was in a sorority, but I don't know which one. If it was Kappa Zeta, I've got four of his five abductions coming out of a single sorority." Josie flashed an icy smile, "You show me Henry Valentine in the middle of that Kappa Zeta pledge class and he's connected to everyone."

"I'm not so sure he even knew your mother was in his class."

"Val knows all his students. It's his signature, right?"

Clarissa shook her head, studying the transcripts. "She's a freshman signed up for an advanced course. My guess is she got handed the wrong card, which means she might not have even known she was taking the course until she got a notice at midterm that she was flunking it. Look at the date of withdrawal. She sees her F and goes in and straightens the mess out with the registrar's office. Never even meets the prof. Happened all the time in the bad ol' days before computer registration. What's not likely is that she was in the class for eight weeks. She would have been out on her ass the minute Val found out she hadn't taken the prerequisite. And he would."

"So it's just a coincidence?" Josie asked. "Val never met her?"

"I don't know if it's a coincidence or not. I'm just saying your mother either showed up for class once and got sent packing or didn't even know she was in the class until she got notified she was failing it. I think it's a lot more likely that Val is hooked into the Kappa Zetas than with your mother, through this class, anyway."

"Why is that?"

"Val is in with all of the frats, Josie. These guys would offer up a virgin to him if they could find one."

Josie's face screwed up wryly. "What's the attraction between the frats and Val?"

"Frats in his class take a gentleman's C, which is a B these days. They turn in old file papers and never take a test. They just show up and cheer like maniacs. Plus, he gives each house a thousand dollars every year."

"He bribes them?"

"Grades and money. How do you think he gets a standing ovation every time he walks into a class?"

"Well, now, I'm disillusioned, Clar."

Clarissa shrugged, "They love him and they love the tradition, but Val knows enough to keep the well primed. And he's got the money to do it. Val's mommy was a rich heiress. He's got a brother now that runs the family business, some kind of valve factory back East somewhere. Val wouldn't dirty his hands with commerce, but he doesn't mind the loot. He's got a big house out in the woods, a nice van. Travels everywhere in the summer. The good life. He can afford to buy the applause."

"So if he's connected to the frats, that basically means he knows the sorority girls?"

"They all live out at the north end. They go to each other's parties, they date each other, and yeah, sure, Val knows everything about anyone who interests him. Has files on all his kids. At least, that's what I hear. He knows who his boys date, how often they have sex, favorite positions, brand of beer, anything and everything. And when they graduate, he knows where they go."

"Maybe the guy just doesn't have a life. That's possible, too."

"That's probably all it is, but you never know." She considered for a moment, puffing on the last of her cigarette and putting it out, "You want to know if it's Valentine?"

Josie laughed. It was a sound without mirth.

"Find out where he takes his sabbaticals. If Val's your man, you'll find more bodies. That's the proof."

Curriculum Vitae

Josie pulled Henry Valentine's curriculum vitae later that afternoon. A document of prodigious size, it traced Valentine's professional life from his undergraduate days to the latest in a string of Teacher of the Year Awards. Once she had photocopied it, Josie slipped it back into the department files and returned to her office. Three students were waiting in the hall, two for Val and Josie's writer of sonnets. Before she went into her own office, Josie dared to peek into Val's. Val sat as usual, facing a young woman. "My sister was down on her knees in front of my fiancé." Val held a letter opener with both hands. He pressed the handle into one palm. It's fine point rested delicately against a fingertip. His eyes flashed at her when he saw Josie looking in. At the same time, the girl's narrative stopped. Caught, Josie waved genially and cursed herself as she ducked into her office. Had he read her mind? It certainly felt that way.

Her poet followed Josie eagerly. Josie tried to get her head into her work. She sat down and read the latest collection, while the older woman watched her facial expressions for every twitch. The poetry was getting better even if Harriet's life seemed to be stuck in a holding pattern. Josie spent nearly an hour with the woman and found herself crossing the line between poetry and psychology, using the one to talk about the other. She thought herself the last person on earth to be giving advice to a woman almost fifty years old, but once she started, it came easily. Maybe too easily. Harriet's enthusiasm for advice invited it without stint. She said she wanted to be like Josie, ". . . a take-charge kind of woman!"

Embarrassed, Josie imagined her poet saw what she wanted, but the older woman insisted. "This morning when you asked us to applaud, Miss Darling, that was the greatest! You know, I'm going to do that with my kids sometime. It was wonderful! I don't think you know how important you've been to me these past couple of months."

Josie couldn't remember what good she had done. It seemed to her she had been caught up in a running battle for weeks, living without sleep and now moving from one motel to another, night after night. Searching futilely through history for the man who meant to murder her, Josie had hardly been conscious of what had happened in her classes. The woman's praise reminded her that she could be doing more, that she had so much to offer, if she could only survive her present troubles. The woman didn't know someone was promising to kill Josie. Josie wondered if she would have been so certain Josie was a take-charge kind of woman if she knew.

As soon as her student was gone, Josie tried to forget her, the haunting poems of pain and loneliness, the sense of failure her praise instilled. Josie had other matters to worry about. She faced another night, wondering if it was to be her last or if some detail might give way under her terrible scrutiny, some fact come forward that would bring her man into clear focus.

Quickly, not even bothering to close the door, Josie began putting her papers together. As she did, Henry Valentine appeared suddenly. He knocked lightly and pushed the door back, so he was leaning into her office.

"Did you want something, Josie?"

Val's exposed left hand took the doorknob. His right hand was outside the room. Through the opening, Josie noticed that the kids in the hallway were gone. She considered the possibility that Val might be holding a weapon in the hand he was concealing and forced herself not to look at her purse, which was tossed on a stack of papers an arm's length from where she sat.

She tried to smile casually, "I just thought we might get a drink sometime next week, Val."

"What's the occasion?"

"I thought I'd tell you how things went with the dean."

"For that, I'll buy! How about tonight? No time for gossip like the present."

"Tonight, I just don't have any time. I'm sorry."

Josie could hardly breathe with the thought that Valentine was looking at her with the calm of a predator. Every instinct screamed at her to run, to get away from him. Was she doing it again? Jumping to one more wrong conclusion based on too little information?

"I take it the dean treated you fairly?"

"He just wanted to tell me he was behind me one hundred percent."

Val smiled savagely, "Behind you, so he could put a knife in your back, no doubt."

Josie found the expression disconcerting. "Anyway, thanks for the warning. Because of you, I was able to avert trouble. I think I should buy the drinks."

"I know you didn't go to Ferrington as I suggested. Did you face the dean on your own?" Pure innocence, this.

"No, I asked Clarissa Holt to help. She tells me she has a history with Del. She must. She handled him beautifully."

"Yes, Dr. Holt. I did see her lurking about in our halls today. I expect she wants her payback." The man offered a smile full of insinuation and insult. Nothing more.

"I have to go, Val."

As she said this, Val stepped into her office and closed the door. Romance? Murder? Josie had not yet finalized her opinion about Dr. Valentine and thought again about the odd trail of facts she and Clarissa Holt had chased, almost casually, over lunch. Josie had her desk partially between them. Val needed two steps to reach her, unless he came over the desk. Before anything else, he would have to negotiate the desk.

If he steps toward me, . . .

If he stepped toward her, Josie had no idea what she would do.

"Have you had any more calls or threats, Josie? That worries me, you know." Val's voice was low and confidential. His wrinkled face was full of the worry he pronounced.

"I think it's over, Val. The two policemen who were killed a couple of weeks ago were both involved in the investigation of my mother's murder. I think one of them was leaving the notes."

She watched his eyes. Did he know she was lying? Was he thinking about the Huree Hideaway, about Bea? About the obituary he'd left just that morning on her office door? The bloodred happy face? Val tipped his head, his brow wrinkling appreciatively. It was a gesture of mild surprise. It could have been innocence or mockery or a man enjoying the game he had created. She couldn't tell!

"Really?" he said. "The police were behind it?"

Genuine? Sham? How do you know such a thing? "That or it was my stepfather. I take it Jack Hazard has more important things to do now than bother me."

Val liked this. "He hasn't found you, since you charged him with assault?"

"Not a chance." Was this the hour she vanished? Standing by the door, his body seemed coiled, ready to spring. The sheets of paper covering the latest message from the man who would kill her were posted right behind Val's bald head. He hadn't turned to look. If he knew it existed, wouldn't he be curious to see what she had done about it? He could take her, she thought, inside a second or two. She might get to her purse in time. Might not. Josie looked at the pockets of his sports jacket. Maybe a gag, some rope. He could keep her here until late, then take her out to his van.

"Our local paper is very concerned that the sheriff's department look competent, rather a full-time job, and, I might add, a losing proposition, but the Paducah paper has run a couple of columns on your illustrious stepfather, John Christian Hazard, all very keen on his woodsmanship."

"I haven't seen them," Josie answered, taking up her purse and slinging it over her shoulder. Without her jacket on, the gesture was odd. She felt the man could see through her. Didn't he know she was scared? Of course he did.

"I think the last one was 'The Legacy of Jesse James,' or some such nonsense. I dare say you've turned a pathetic old convict into a legend."

"I really have to go, Val."

"I can give you the clippings, if you missed them." This with a bright smile. The genial old professor who collects all manner of trivia. He wasn't leaving. Wasn't budging. He was, in fact, studying her and wondering, she decided, why the purse before the coat. Maybe she should just pull the revolver and push him out the door. And maybe she would look like a fool or, worse, doubt herself and let him take her gun. She looked away from his strange, cold eyes. She looked down at her desk. Valentine's vita was exposed. Josie covered it as smoothly as she could. When she looked up, she knew Val had seen it. His face was placid, as if he had seen nothing at all. He was looking into her eyes without threat or anger. Just . . . what? What did he want? Was he contemplating the pain she would know before he killed her?

"I'd like that," she answered coolly, her knees almost giving way. If he came a step closer, she would reach into her purse. Two steps, she would level the gun into his belly, and then they would both have to decide what they did next.

"Why don't you leave them in my department mailbox?" she asked. *Mailbox?* Valentine's eyebrows rose in mild surprise, then his eyes cooled as Josie leveled her gaze and refused to pull away. Between them lay a heavy silence, a reckoning that had lost all sense of lightness. Time to play poker, "Or you could put them in an envelope and tape it to my door." She shrugged, smiling yet full of terror and rage, "Put a little happy face on it, so I'll know it's from you."

Valentine's face went ashen, and he answered like a lover who's been told it's over, "I'll do that, Josie. Count on it."

Time Line

Leaving, Valentine checked the door. He pretended to read the memos covering the happy face. He looked back at Josie and gave her a big, loose smile.

The eyes were dull with menace. It was a look so void of passion Josie nearly pulled her revolver. Instead, she stared at him without expression and caught the faint scent of the man, the goatish odor she had once been drawn to. Not now. There was nothing charming about this man. His savagery had no principle. She counted the rhythm she used to reach for her revolver: left hand up, right hand across, pull the gun, kill the man: one, two, three, four. She was certain the time was now. Certain her man.

The moment he left, Josie felt a vast disappointment he hadn't made a move for her over the desk. She had wanted him to, had believed she could do it. Now all certainty was gone. Leaving, she saw several of her colleagues in the hallway. She saw Dick Ferrington with a thin blonde girl. She was talking to him eagerly. Rainy's tenure at risk. Ferrington's eye caught Josie's as she passed them. The girl saw nothing but her own fantasies. Ferrington and Josie were in open warfare now. No matter what else happened, he would see Josie didn't come back the next academic year. Well, that was hardly a worry right now. A year was all she had come for. She would just go back to Bandolier. Assuming she survived! Josie went on, pushing the academic nonsense aside. Dick Ferrington wasn't her problem, much as he wanted to be. Valentine was the issue. Valentine was the man!

She brought the Mustang out of the lot quickly and got to her apartment a minute or so later. Her gun drawn, she searched the place to be sure she was safe. Holding the .357 kicked her pulse up. Valentine, Valentine, Valentine! That look, that . . . that . . . that . . . promise! *Count on it.* He was the man she wanted, but the proof! Something more than the gut, something to let her know without the slightest doubt! Wrong so often, leaping to conclusions that had seemed so irrefutable! She couldn't afford to do it again. She had to know! And there was just no way to know for sure until the rope tightened over her wrists. She swore angrily at the thought and went back to her office. She lay her revolver on the desk and set out her research. Over two weeks ago, Josie had begun a time line and had periodically redrawn it with increasing detail. Her latest creation stretched over ten sheets of paper and looked like the family tree of Balzac's *Human Comedy.* She tacked this across her office wall and began to study it. Shelley Kruger, Melissa Fry, and Anita Moore had pledged Kappa Zeta in the fall of their freshman year. Over that same period, she had written: Dick and Cathy Ferrington, new arrivals to Lues, in 1989. Now she added Clarissa Holt's name. She went back to her mother's death, six-and-a-half years earlier. Cat Sommerville at the canyon. She circled the name and wrote, aka Cathy Ferrington. She checked another sheet. This was an hourly schedule of the day her mother died. Cat Sommerville had gone to dinner alone just after five o'clock. Melody Mason and Susan Hill had stayed in their room. Jim Burkeshire and Bob Tanner didn't know what they had done. Jim Burkeshire and Cat Sommerville lovers. Or so Susie Wallace thought. Had they met each other after dinner? The sensible ones, they might have talked about what to do. It could have sparked the romance. No way to know, since Cat was dead and Jim Burkeshire was lying about it. Just one more gap. And one more lie that took Josie nowhere.

She looked back two hours: Toby Crouch drunk with his buddies before returning to work to write some parking tickets. He took the call shortly before five o'clock. He had been at the mouth of the canyon at ten minutes before eight when Bitts and his deputies and the city police had met him that evening. Jack Hazard had been at the Hurry on Up until two. Josie Fortune had been seen dead at three. At 2:55, the killer, or just a man, a slew, had been spotted above the falls, nearly an hour from the body. Dead at two? Waldis said six. She set the man's book out. A little light bedtime reading, confessions of a man who had cut open thousands of skulls to satisfy medical-legal curiosity. No motive to lie, just too proud to admit Colt Fellows had misled him. Josie looked at Cat Sommerville, aka Cathy Ferrington. Why was she was so close to it all? Burkeshire? Had he done it? Was he the piece that didn't fit? He ran his own business. He could come and go as he liked. A good little wife who didn't ask too many questions. Motive for Cathy Ferrington, an old flame. Motive for Josie Fortune? Possible they knew each other, possible they had been in a class together. But the others had come in 1989. Where was Jim Burkeshire in 1989? Back on campus for a little graduate work? Have to check it out. She jotted a note to herself. One more path into the woods and no promise it would take her anywhere.

Josie rubbed her hands over her eyes. She was tired like never before. She had been living the past week with hardly a meal a day, no more than a couple of hours of sleep. She could still vanish. She really needed to think about that, because right now nothing made sense. The murder of Josie Fortune had too many loose ends. She could not see how it fit together, why Cat Sommerville was involved. She fingered Waldis's book, then pushed it aside.

She wanted to see Valentine's vita. First, she thought, she needed to make sure he was on campus or in the area when each of the murders took place.

She hesitated. Could the killer have planned Cat Sommerville's murder on the day of Josie Fortune's death? Sixteen years later? No. It was something else. Purely coincidence. No, not coincidence. There was no coincidence in any of this! Something else? Cathy Ferrington hadn't died like the others. Not exactly. Weeks of captivity, then the body hidden away, found only by accident. Not the same as the others. The other bodies had been found shortly after death, spectacular displays of violence. How had Burkeshire put it? *Like a sacrifice.* The same was true for Bates and Kruger. Paget had escaped or was set free and then was hunted down and left as she fell. But Cathy Ferrington was not found for a long time. And yet, like the others, she had been abducted and held and finally murdered. The other women were all in their twenties. Cathy Ferrington would have been the perfect age when she had arrived with Dick on campus in 1989, but she hadn't been killed for another ten years, a woman almost forty at the time of her death. Only one other woman had had children besides Cathy Ferrington—Josie Fortune. Four of the five, though, were married or had just finished a marriage. She counted the ways of death. One bludgeoned, one shot, one hanged by her feet, one crucified, and Josie Fortune—no one knew. Hanged, strangled, cut. *Strangled.*

The Devil himself couldn't sneak up on Josie Fortune. That was what Virgil had said. Melissa Bates had been a tough, smart girl, pure country, which meant a slew with a brain. Josie Fortune, dean's list. Shelley Kruger, ex-navy, but a local as well, with a major in mechanical engineering. Bates and Paget had had a soft spot in their hearts for a slew. Kruger had dated a local. Josie Fortune had married one. Bates, Kruger, and Paget had been locals. Fortune was a transplant but lived like a native. She owned a bar that was anything but university-friendly. Cat Sommerville, no. Cat Sommerville wasn't the same at all in that respect. For one thing, she had married a professor, a Chicago boy, who was educated . . . in Henry Valentine's neck of the woods. Chapel Hill. Valentine had a degree from Chapel Hill, didn't he? She reached for his vita, but the telephone rang.

Josie resisted the irrational panic it caused. Valentine for a drink? Maybe wants to come over? No one at all? Someone she wasn't expecting? Happy Harpin? Jason Morgan? Some other cop? Bill Waters in forestry? Waters was a suspect in Kruger's death. Why not the others? Or maybe it was Dan Scholari all along! She needed to stop thinking about all this, if only for a few hours. She needed time to let things filter through and settle, but time was the one luxury she didn't have! Josie picked the phone up cautiously. She said nothing.

"Josie?"

"Annie!" Relief coursed through her, and she tucked the gun she was carrying into her jeans. "Did you get my message?"

"I just got home. We had a little crisis on the suicide prevention hot line, and I logged an all-nighter. I tried at school. Thought I might as well try your apartment. Are you safe there?"

"As good as anywhere, I guess. You're back to the volunteer work again?"

"Not to worry! I just sleep less. I found Cat Sommerville for you!"

"She's Cathy Ferrington."

"Oh." Annie's voice was pure disappointment.

"I got the police file on Cathy Ferrington's murder. It included her maiden name. I'm sorry. Did it take much time?"

"No! No! I mean I was reading real estate transactions until my eyes swam, Josie, but that's fun stuff!"

"I should have called you as soon as I found out," Josie apologized.

"Then there were the real estate agents. Those kids are hungry!"

"So how did you find her, a real estate agent?"

"After a fashion! You want me to tell you about it?"

Annie seemed eager. She was proud of her search. "I'd love to hear it," Josie told her, smiling, enjoying her friend's enthusiasm.

"Okay! Cathy Johnson sold her house to a man named Vic Dubois about a year after your mother's death. Dubois then sells it in 1987, but he's a man, so he doesn't keep changing his name every time he thinks he's in love. I followed him through four sales, got his number, and called to ask him if he remembered the agent who sold him Cathy Johnson's house. He didn't, but he looked it up. I called the agent. She gives me the name of an agent in Phoenix, and he tells me he has to call me back, collect, of course. He's checking with Cathy Johnson, who's now Cathy—get this—*Sommerville*."

"No!"

"Yep. She went back to the first for seconds! How about that for chasing the nightmare? You and Dan together again?"

"Don't even joke about it."

"Dan's coming back to class on Monday, by the way. Everyone's real excited to see how his new medication mixes with Jack Daniels."

Josie shook her head. Nothing at Bandolier was ever going to change, Dan Scholari least of all. "So did you talk to Mrs. Sommerville?"

"A wonderful lady, Josie. I got the story of her daughter's life."

"I'm sorry you went to all that trouble. It's a pure fluke I found her. I mean I was reading about Cathy Ferrington and there it was."

"Forget it! What's five hours in the life of a scholar? At least I got the scoop on Dick Ferrington."

"What are you talking about?"

"Your Dr. Ferrington and Cat Sommerville had to get married, not that Mrs. Sommerville confessed it. But I got the info from her and then my assistant got into North Carolina's records and went into Orange County's vital statistics. Their baby was born January 20."

"Okay."

"They were married in June of the previous year. Get your fingers out, kiddo. It doesn't add up to nine! By my count, Cat's pregnant in late April or early May. They're married at the end of June in Kanka-Kanka-Kanka."

"Kankakee."

"Whatever! Seven months later out comes a fully developed premature boy!"

"Wait a minute!" Josie protested. "She married Dick Ferrington in June?"

"That's what she said."

"There's something wrong here, Annie. I knew she was pregnant, but I thought the father was . . . someone else."

"Well, it's possible, but to hear her mother tell it, Dick Ferrington was the culprit."

"Have you got the right year? Were they married in June of 1983?"

"I'm looking at a copy of the vital statistics, Josie. Date of birth, January 20, 1984."

"Annie, that means Dick Ferrington was here, at Lues State, when my mother was murdered!"

Quietly, with a bit of curiosity, "Looks like you'd better add another suspect to your list, Napoleon."

Crazy K-Zs

"Grimes residence."

"Melody! Josie Darling, here. I talked to you a few weeks ago."

"Sure, sure. I remember you. What's up?"

"I got Susie Hill's address for you. She's Susan Wallace these days."

"Oh, great! Let me get a pen!"

A moment later, Josie read off the information. Then, seemingly as an afterthought, "One question, Melody. Do you know what sorority Cat Sommerville was in?"

"Sure! We were all in the same one, Susie and Cat and me: Kappa Zeta. The crazy K-Zs."

Curriculum Vitae

Josie's eye fell to September 10, 4:54 P.M., the call for *Josie Fortune* at Cokey's, while Dick Ferrington sat at the table. June 1999: Cathy Ferrington disappears after she leaves her kids with Dick's parents in Chicago.

No one knows if she went back to Lues that night or not. She and her car just vanished. Dick Ferrington was in Spain at the time. Morgan's idea: they agreed to meet somewhere. Ditch the kids with his folks and have a very private rendezvous. A romantic getaway to save the marriage. Too many problems with it, a week to explain away, for one. Where had she gone? Why was there no trace of her? It was the reason Morgan couldn't get anyone interested in his theory. Dick Ferrington just didn't fit. And yet everyone knew he did it.

Josie's eye fell to the converging point, 1989. Dick and Cathy Ferrington had come to Lues State. A return for Cat. For both, it seemed. That same fall, three future victims pledge a sorority—Kappa Zeta. Had Cat gone back to the old sorority house? The faculty wife looking for a place to fit in. She was living on campus in a miserable little apartment with three small kids. Not likely, but it was possible, especially if she felt isolated. And if she knew Kruger, Fry, and Moore, why wouldn't Dick Ferrington know them as well? Certainly there was the chance of meeting them if his wife was in contact with the sorority. The first to die was Kruger, older, mid-twenties at the time. Had Ferrington had an affair with her? The police had dug up Kruger's lovers, but they might have missed a very quiet affair. Make friends with the wife, take the husband on the odd afternoon, . . . and tell no one, because Cathy Ferrington would find out. Possible.

They had looked into Paget's relationships, the same as they had her husband's. They had looked at Dick Ferrington's affairs. Jason Morgan had dug up fifteen women within a three-year period of his wife's death—all with ages that would win most hands of blackjack. The list hadn't included Kruger or Paget or Bates.

She considered the murder of Cathy Ferrington. He certainly hadn't married her with the idea of killing her some day. No, there had been marital discord driving that murder. Divorce looming, according to Nell McGraw. But if he did it, how had he done it? There was no answer to that.

Josie's attention shifted to Val. The answer was Dick Ferrington wasn't Cathy's murderer nor the man stalking Josie. It was Val. It had to be Val. Quietly watching everyone. Tracking his boys *and* his girls. Was Ferrington one of Val's boys? Sure he was! Off to Chapel Hill, Val's alma mater, then back to Lues State to teach. Ferrington was probably Val's golden boy. Exactly why they hated each other now. Interesting to look at Ferrington's transcripts, she told herself. It would confirm the theory if Dick had taken a number of courses from Valentine. Recommend him to Chapel Hill, a few phone calls, and off he goes to finish his undergraduate work and then plunge into a graduate program. Back to Lues State six years later. Year after year contemplate the man's wife, as he had contemplated the others. What did Val call it? The thing about *haste?* ". . . the scholar's enemy . . . the sin of haste, the ruin of many, the savior of none!"

A man who murdered after much contemplation, after years of contemplation? The *sin* of *haste.* Rather extreme. Like *knife in the back* and *lynch mob forming.* And *stigmata of scandal,* not *stigma.* A slip of the tongue or was he actually thinking about the wounds of the crucifixion? She thought about the night he talked about his idea of hell and asked Josie about hers! Getting a feel for what terrors she cherished, perhaps? Or just professorly chitchat? Had he studied Cat Sommerville all those years, knowing he would have her? A sin to rush it. So, for weeks, he held her, watching Dick Ferrington's confusion, worry, panic? Bringing all the suspicion to bear on Ferrington, the way it had been on Wayne Paget and Jack Hazard. Playing his games. Quite good at them really. Every murder a bit different, except in the essence: the capture and delay, the terrible pain he brought his victims before they died, the suspicion of guilt directed toward the husband or ex-husband or boyfriend. His games and double crosses, his reputation for snooping in faculty offices. That look he had given her when she had said the thing about the happy face. *Count on it.* The look of murder. Murder without haste.

Josie walked back to the old metal desk, her throat dry, and flopped down in her chair. She picked up Valentine's vita. This was the man to look at: UNC–CH, 1969, B.A.; Duke, 1970, M.A.; UNC–CH, 1972, Ph.D.; Lues State, 1972, assistant professor; Lues State, 1974, associate professor. First sabbatical, 1979, Lawrence, Kansas, a grant to study . . .

Hello. "Matricide and the Image of Cultural Ruin," published in *Imago*, 1982. Matricide? Killing mamma, Val? Is that what this is all about? In 1982, the year before Josie Fortune was murdered, he was promoted to full professor. Second sabbatical, 1986, Chapel Hill, to work on a book that never came to fruition: a novel. Josie frowned. Ferrington had said Valentine had written a hell of a novel when the world was young. She had just assumed Val had published it, but she saw here that it was never published. Dick Ferrington and Cat Sommerville were still in Chapel Hill at that point in their history. In touch? Friends? Dick reading Val's novel? Val having another look at his Cat? Lick his big, loose lips at the thought of her under his power? Had he seen her the day Josie Fortune died? Was Valentine the man in the woods? Had he followed her for sixteen years?

Josie scanned down the page to Valentine's last sabbatic leave, a year at Indiana State. "Outreach to the Public Schools."

Maybe Clarissa Holt was right. Maybe it was time to look for more bodies.

A Man with a Badge

With the knocking at her door, Josie looked up from Valentine's curriculum vitae. Her .357 in hand, she walked to the front door and checked the peep hole. She didn't recognize the man at first, but once she did, her thoughts raced uncontrollably. It was Lieutenant Jason Morgan. He had been there to bring her mother's body out of the canyon. He had been in Lues that day, had been a part of the investigation. He had been lead on the Cathy Ferrington case. Had he been Josie Fortune's lover? A friend? The age was right. Handsome. Never a suspect in the investigation, never a look at all in his direction! Sheriff's friend. Colt Fellows's friend, too? Ran Cathy Ferrington's case with wild theories that put Dick Ferrington at the center of the thing. Was it him?

She swore savagely. She looked at her gun. Finally, she pulled the hammer back and opened the door as far as the chain allowed. She held the gun pointed toward the floor, just behind the edge of the door. She peeked out.

"Yes."

Morgan flashed his badge. "Remember me?"

"I remember."

"You care if I come in? We need to talk."

Josie stared at the man in confusion. She didn't want him inside. She didn't want to talk to him at all!

"What's this about?" Josie asked.

"Beatrice Quincy. I'd like to come inside, if I may."

Keys, no problem. Information, easy. Cover-ups, he could have whispered them in Colt's ear. What had happened that sent Morgan from the sheriff's department to the city police department? What kind of deal? Josie studied him carefully. "I don't think so." Her bowels churned. Her breath failed her. "I don't know you, not really, and I don't like your showing up here without calling." Or at least, she thought, bringing another officer. The last time he had sent two officers to get her, which made this time . . . *different*. How different she was about to find out.

"I called your office this afternoon. Either you didn't get my message, or you didn't return my call. I called here tonight, and the line was busy, so I thought I'd come on out and try to catch you."

"Well, you caught me." Nice choice of words, that.

He nodded. "I just have one question, then I'll leave you alone."

"What's the question?"

They were still talking through a crack in the door. He must have thought she was crazy! *Forget what he thinks! He's the man!*

"What didn't you tell Sergeant Harpin?"

"I don't know what you're talking about."

"That wasn't a robbery that got interrupted."

"Tell the sheriff's department that."

"I have."

They stared each other down through the crack in the door. He was smiling a little, but he wasn't happy. Had the badge gotten each woman into his car?

"Do you think I shot Bea?"

"Never crossed my mind. Did you?"

"No, but it crossed my mind that you might have. Where were *you* that night?"

Morgan's smile was tense, bright, indulgent. "Okay. That's fair enough. Saturday night . . . let's see . . . I was at a high school football game. The whole family was there. My son was playing. I saw Corny Callahan there. We talked about a couple of patrol cars Corny told Colt he would order for the department. The mayor will remember that, if you want to call him. Or you can call my wife. Call my kids. I think as busy as he was even my oldest son might have seen me."

"I'm not going to call the mayor or your family and you know it!"

Morgan shrugged. He didn't care. Was he an innocent man? A good man? She wanted to believe it, but Josie Fortune had already trusted the wrong man. The others, too? A cop would be perfect. This cop especially. Cute, in a middle-aged kind of a way. And he just seemed honest! Bitts liked him, trusted him.

"It was him, wasn't it? The man stalking you was the man who shot Bea Quincy?"

"Maybe it was, maybe not. Look, I'm really busy. If you want to talk, I'll come in tomorrow with a lawyer and we can have an interview, but I'm not going anywhere with you tonight, and you're not coming in here."

"He leave a note?"

"Why do you ask?"

"It's evidence in a homicide."

"I left Bea's room just like I found it."

He smiled. "I sent a team out to examine your room, Professor. I'm curious. How did the bathroom door get busted?"

"I was in a hurry."

"I bet. But not so much that you didn't clean your bathroom mirror before you left."

"I'm compulsive. What can I say?"

"The mirror in your bathroom had traces of blood."

Josie felt her face twitch. "Easy enough to explain," she offered.

"Right, but I'd advise you not to try. It's a felony count if it doesn't float. That's on top of the one I've already got you for. We call it obstruction of justice."

"I guess I better call a lawyer, huh?"

"I can have it DNA-tested and prove it was Bea Quincy's blood, but I don't think I want to take the time and trouble to do that, especially since I'd have to share the information with Cal Yeager, and he would arrest you on it, and then Two-Bit would never forgive me. All I really want is the truth. Was it Bea Quincy's blood?"

"You just happened to check the mirror in my room?"

"We went over every square inch of your room, actually. Maid cleaned it, but she missed a bit of the blood. What did he write?"

Josie shook her head, refusing him.

"I can't help you if you won't let me."

"I didn't ask you for help."

"Oh? What about the files you wanted to look at?"

"That's different."

"You really think I would have given you those files if I was the killer?"

"Why not? They were useless."

"I don't know. I liked the way you connected the victims." He shook his head. "Three pledge sisters. That's good."

"Cathy Ferrington was in the same sorority."

"I'll be damned. Four. That's a little too much of a coincidence, isn't it?"

"I wouldn't know about things like that. You're the cop."

The door was still on its chain. They were looking at each other through the crack. Morgan seemed innocent enough. But, of course, he could just be talking his way in. *Praise better than a key.*

"I passed what Two-Bit gave me on to Don Stackman. He's ordered the sheriff to reopen the investigations into the Paget, Kruger, and Bates murders. I guess we can add Cathy Ferrington to the list. I always liked her husband for it, but maybe there's another angle."

"Maybe *he* killed them all."

Morgan smiled. "What was on the mirror, Professor?"

"What does it matter?"

"It matters. I can get this bastard, if I have all the evidence."

"You've had all the evidence for years."

"But now I've got a lead."

"He wrote, 'Miss me?' That's all it said. He killed her and went into my apartment and wrote that with her blood."

"If you want police protection, I can arrange it."

"Why don't you send Happy Harpin around. That would make me feel really safe."

"I've got good people. No one would even know we're there."

"Not interested. I can take of myself."

"I understand your mother could take care of herself, too. And this bastard took her. You think about that before you try to go it alone. Think long and hard. No offense, but I get the feeling you never won a fight in your life."

"You've asked your question, Lieutenant, and you got your answer. Now if you don't mind?"

"Look," he said, "when you decide you can trust me, give me a call. If you're not tied up." Deadpan, this, as cold as any look Valentine had ever given.

Tecumseh

When Morgan was gone, Josie hurried to the Mustang and drove back to Worley. She looked in all directions as she walked the thin ribbon of concrete between Brand and Varner. She half-expected Valentine or Morgan or Ferrington to be waiting, but the shadows were empty this evening. The tormentor rested. The victim, never. On the sixth floor of the library, she surveyed the offerings on microfilm and found the one she wanted. After that, it was simply a matter of threading the machine.

Indiana State University is in Terre Haute. As Josie started through that city's *Tribune Star*, she spotted Val almost at once. Professor Henry Valentine, on an NEH grant, had arrived to teach one course in creative writing at the university and to function as a liaison between the university and the public schools. There was a large picture on the front page of the Sunday local news section: Val and select administrative types, Val looking like the cat who ate the canary. Valentine's duties were described in detail. Poetry to the corn fields. The paper quoted him at length. All academic drivel. Josie fast-forwarded the spool. She hit the jackpot five months later. On January 28, 2001, the nude body of Nora Tolley, age thirty-six, of Farmersburg, was pulled out of the

Wabash River near Tecumseh, Indiana. A leather thong had been tied around her neck in a hangman's knot. The branch that the thong had been tied to had broken off when Tolley's killer had tried to suspend her over the river. The corpse had floated downriver until it got caught on a sandbar. A couple of fishermen found it two days later. Cause of death was ruled hypothermia.

Tolley was an associate professor of chemistry at Indiana State as well as an assistant dean of arts and sciences. Josie tracked back to the first entry she had found, Val's grand arrival as he stood among the happy administrative types. One woman alone stood with the old bulls. In the caption, Josie found her easily, Assistant Dean of Arts and Sciences, Dr. Nora Tolley.

Josie leaned back in her chair contentedly, whispering into the light of the microfilm machine, "I've got you, you bastard!"

A Mother's Keepsake

"Josie, here."

"Hey, D. J."

"I need to borrow my mother's keepsake."

"You want to come get it tomorrow morning?" Virgil Hazard asked. It was midnight. He was slurring slightly, a man at peace with the world.

"I want you to get it now and bring it up to Pilatesburg. I'm at the Sleepy Time."

"I know you don't believe this, D. J., but I work for a living! I don't have time to run all over Lues County delivering your mother's keepsakes!"

"Virgil, I need it, and I need it tonight."

A Late-Night Visitor

Standing just beyond the opened door to Josie's room, his fat figure caught in the light, Virgil Hazard offered Josie a feed sack. "It's loaded. Don't kill yourself."

Josie reached quickly to take the sack from him. The stock of the shotgun was heavy, reassuring. When she looked inside the sack, she found extra shells. "Thanks."

"What's going on, D. J.?" It was now almost two in the morning, and Virgil's face looked it.

"I didn't want to say anything on the phone, but I need to see Jack."

"Yeah, well, Jack's a little busy playing Jesse James these days."

"Set it up, Virgil. I don't care how you do it. I'll go anywhere you say, but I need to talk to him as soon as possible."

Louis

Josie called in sick on Friday, then spent the day reading Waldis's book and looking time and time again at the photocopies of the old yearbook pictures she had gotten from the library. Outside it was raining. The day dragged interminably.

Virgil called at three. "Same place as before, D. J."

"What? Where?"

"No questions. Take off now. Someone will be waiting."

"I don't understand!"

"Family reunion, hotshot. Flat tire, piggyback rides . . . ring a bell?" Without waiting for an answer, Virgil hung up.

Lues Creek Crossing. Josie packed her car quickly. On the highway, she kept to the speed limit, and once she hit the back roads, she watched to be sure she wasn't followed. Nearly an hour later, she came to Lues Creek Crossing and saw a pickup truck at the side of the road. A middle-aged man was standing in the rain, waiting for her. He wore a rubber poncho and stood quietly as Josie drove toward him, his hands empty and in plain view.

Josie stopped her car several feet from him and left it running as she stood up beside the car. The door was open. She held her mother's shotgun, so he could see it. She had ridden on this man's shoulder. She remembered the eyes. They were quiet, thoughtful, dangerous. "Who are you?" she asked.

"I'm Louis, Jack's brother, Josie. I'm the one taking you to Jack." The man studied Josie's face curiously. "You alone?"

"I'm alone."

"Anybody follow you?"

"Nobody followed. I was careful."

"What's this about? Virgil didn't know."

"I know who killed my mother."

Louis considered this for a moment, before he nodded. "Then let's go find Jack!"

The pickup splashed across the creek easily, while Josie nudged the low-slung Mustang through the crossing with more care and difficulty. A few yards beyond the crossing, Louis cut into some brush and took off cross-country. Josie gritted her teeth and followed him. For nearly a hundred yards, they were driving through branches and over saplings with no sign of a road. Then the truck came to a muddy lane, and ten minutes later, they pulled up a narrow lane and stopped in front of a primitive cabin. The rain poured down steadily.

Louis stepped out into the rain and whistled. Her windshield wipers thumping, Josie watched impatiently for Jack, but he didn't respond until Louis whistled again, this time four crisp notes. As soon as he had finished, Jack came out from behind the cabin. He stopped at the sight of Josie's Mustang. He carried a long-barreled pump shotgun. A revolver was tucked in his belt. Unlike Louis, he wore no rain gear, and despite the cold, he didn't bother closing his coat.

The two men talked briefly, then Louis went inside the cabin.

Jack trotted toward the driver's side of Josie's Mustang.

His wet face pushed close as she rolled the window down and felt the rain hitting her. "You find him, did you?"

Josie nodded, "We need to talk, Jack."

The Slew

The knock at his door was heavy, and Nelson Rush looked up from his book in surprise.

"Who is it?" he called.

Nelson looked at the clock. It was ten o'clock. Friday night, ten o'clock, the dorm rooms were always empty, and yet someone was knocking at his door.

"Who is it?"

The knock came again.

"I'm coming, all right!"

Nelson, I just wanted to come by and thank you for your help. . . .

Oh, Miss Darling, you didn't have to.

Call me Josie.

Nelson opened the door and felt his heart contract into a cold knot of fear. Before him stood a man his father's age. A slew. He was average height but had a thick build. His eyes were clear, piercing, cold. He was dripping rain water everywhere and wearing a rubber poncho.

"What do you want?" Nelson asked.

"You Nelson?"

"Who wants to know?"

The man reached inside his wet poncho, and Nelson was sure he meant to pull out a knife or a gun. His bowels nearly gave out. Then he saw a sheet of paper. It was folded twice, a letter without an envelope.

"Read this," the man told him, "then give it back to me."

"What is it?"

"A friend of yours needs some help."

Giving Notice

As usual, Dr. Henry Valentine left his van on the lot northwest of the liberal arts complex and went along a path of his own making toward his office. At five o'clock on a Monday morning, the place was entirely his. Nothing at all was stirring. Val slipped through the halls quietly and approached his office with a feeling of supreme satisfaction. He was thinking of Miss Fortune's Darling—Little Josie! Her hour had come. He had hoped for a longer play, but her words on Thursday demonstrated she had become extremely dangerous. It wouldn't do to give her more time. A very suspicious woman, all of a sudden! He had thought Friday to take her, but she hadn't shown up for her classes, had quite vanished, in fact. Take her sometime today, if possible, then work it slowly. The slowest death the sweetest.

There was still some debate as to the best method for Baby Fortune. One school of thought favored tradition. Hang the bitch as her mother had hanged. The second school favored innovation. No ready-made hell for the next generation. Each girl to her own casket! The innovative school favored a crucifixion. Lues County hadn't had one in years! Nothing had ever quite equalled the scandal of Melissa Bates nailed to a tree. In the Bible Belt, a thing like that played mighty big! Of course, Josie must have her own death, if not her mother's, so the innovative school argued passionately for St. Peter's crucifixion. Hasty old Saint Pete, choosing to go it upside down. Regretting it for hours, one is sure. The exquisite pain of such death! Poor

Darling looking at her world all upside down, the blood of her feet dripping into her eyes.

But tradition had its argument. A couple of the notes replicated for nostalgic flavor, the same manner of death, the same stone in the same canyon for the body, even the same suspect! Hapless old Jack Hazard. One could only wonder if he would confess to it, as well! Henry Valentine laughed quietly to himself, as he pondered the aesthetics of it and reached for his key ring and selected the Brand Hall master key. The trouble with the world was it had lost touch with tradition. Everything always new was indicative of an uneasy spirit. Some things bear repeating. And nice to see if the daughter had the spit of her old *maaaaaa*. Clever of her to find that word. Shame to kill a real scholar. Well, well, another loss to the academy, and who gives a fuck anyway?

Valentine's contemplative smile froze suddenly. His step caught. Something was on his door! He hurried forward and saw it clearly now. A hangman's noose! Looped over his doorknob, it was tied to a small leafy branch. Printed boldly in red paint—paint!—on his office door were the words:

Henry VAlentino
mUddered N. Tolley
iN tecum-see-me
ufuk

For a long, terrible moment, Valentine glared at the words. Then he smiled. The little riddle-solver knew a secret. Well, she didn't know them all, did she? And certainly not for long.

Inside his office, Valentine set his backpack on his desk and considered his options. She had been exceedingly hard to track lately, hardly worth the effort, when one considered that she *usually* came to school. On the other hand, this kind of outrage against his property was a matter he knew he had better take seriously. Urgent business, this. He could hardly countenance the idea that someone might see the little whore's graffito. That wouldn't do at all. He was going to have to clean up the mess presently and take care of Josie Fortune's bastard by-and-by.

Curious, really, that Josie should mention Dr. Tolley. The vita, of course. One of his least favorite girls, really. He had liked Dr. Tolley very much at the start of it, her irritating twang, her corn-fed flanks, that tough as nails look, until she had seen the noose. Then: *ohGod ohGod ohGod.* Give Josie Fortune her due. Never once the magic *please.* Dr. Tolley had been pathetic. She would have done *anything.* As if *anything* could equal the perfect bliss of watching her choke to death. Or would have, if the branch hadn't broken.

Valentine took his key and went down to Gerty Dowell's office. Gerty kept paint on her shelves. It went back to the time she had painted her bookshelves. She was set on doing the whole department's until Case had requisitioned new ones. Simply have to block it out. Maybe Josie imagined he didn't know about her .357? Talk of the department, the armed and dangerous stripper. Would she be in her apartment tonight waiting for him *tecum-see* her? Every rat to its corner. And probably very sorry she'd made her stepfather a mortal enemy.

Valentine whistled as he took a can of black paint and a clean brush and went back to his office door. Opening the new can with his pocket knife, he considered dreamily the surprise waiting the woman.

Josie, we have to talk. . . .

Why, certainly . . .

Not bothering to stir, Val splashed huge gobs of the stuff on his door and considered the effect. He didn't like it. It was obvious he didn't care for the graffito someone had left and had covered it up. That wouldn't do. Need the random violence effect. Patiently, Val duplicated his efforts on three other office doors, including Gerty's. Then he smashed the window beside Gerty's door, so it would look like someone had entered the office by reaching in through the broken glass and turning the doorknob from the inside. Using his key, so as not to risk cutting himself, perish the thought, Val stepped in and decided a bit more might do the trick and spent a minute or so storming the office, dumping books and throwing stacks of papers across the floor, and writing Gerty's favorite word on the wall. *CockCockCockCock.* Enough to keep the withered old virgin hopping and quivering for months. When he had done with it, Valentine went out and broke more windows and then finished the melee by throwing the paint can and brush down the hall in the direction of Ferrington's office, a wild wet black spray of it on the wall and floor and just a bit of a pathway left so he could get through without ruining his boots.

Henry checked his hands for paint. Clean as ever. A good boy. He grinned happily. Before going again into his own office, he used his key to enter Josie's office. Nothing out of the ordinary. He checked the drawers, the papers. Rummaging with a light touch, he thought he could smell the woman as he moved about. Lovely smell she had. This morning he would leave no message. No threats, no retribution. Let her wait it out, let her wonder if she's even right. He peeked under the memos taped to her door. Happy face. Important to keep things light. Madness is a laughing man, that kind of thing. The obituary had formed such a nice balance to it. The artist in Henry had resisted the straight journalistic approach, that legal notice thing, but he had to admit, in the end, it was just better. The two masks of theater: happy face, obituary. Fortune's little Darling was going to be sweet to take. Child hastening to her mother's end. Act mystified when you talk to her today. No implied threats, no subtextual messages. Doubt is a terrible demon!

Valentine closed the woman's office door gently and started for the department office. Dodging pools of black paint as he went, Val told himself once more how much he loved this place in the mornings. The quiet. The power he felt! A low whistle broke over his lips. The trouble with hanging was it went too quickly. Even if one avoided snapping the spine, there was a better than average chance it would be over in a matter of seconds. Assuming one's branch didn't break! Lord! Life is absurd! Never more so than when your assistant dean of arts and sciences goes floating down river, tied, gagged, and bobbing like a fisherman's cork! Val laughed outright and shook his head.

Inside the department office, Valentine saw his mailbox contained a single sheet of paper. Picking it up, he read the childish scrawl:

Melissa Bates crucified
Cathy Ferrington bludgeoned
Shelley Kruger hanged
victims of H. vaLenTINY

Valentine looked at the next box and the next. The bitch had copied her scrawl on the Xerox and put a sheet in every box. Every damn box! He began pulling the sheets out rapidly. This time he forgot to smile.

For the rest of the morning, Valentine sat in his office, taking no visitors. Meeting at three. We have called this meeting for the purpose of eliminating all the lecturers. Dick Ferrington. Kill half the girls he climbs on, fill a graveyard.

Cathy Ferrington, so surprised. Val! What are you doing here?

I thought since Dick's out of town, we could start an affair, Cat.

Don't tease a girl if you aren't serious, Val.

Do I look like a tease? Come on, let's take a drive. I'll show you something you haven't seen before.

Oh, you've got me curious.

Curiosity killed the cat.

Killed that Cat anyway.

Josie would be a bit more difficult now that she was making accusations. Perhaps work off it somehow. Something, some secret to take to her. Have reasons for approach. Long held suspicions. Oh yes, for years.

Val kept his head in his stack of papers, sublimely removed from any thoughts other than the occasional fantasy of Josie-oh my-Darling with a look of surprise all over her face. So proud of her riddles! Oh but you missed the footnotes, Josie! We live in modern times, child. The riddles nowadays all have footnotes!

Damn it to hell with tradition! Crucify her! She's a beauty, lovely smell she has too, and her tree was already picked out. Palms pierced, feet curled together and spiked, the blood running down her upended legs. Val had seen nothing in his life to match the expression of Melissa Bates as she found herself dying the death of her Lord Jesus while the Gospels were read to her. Val had asked her if she could appreciate the different styles of the four sainted scribes of God. A shame really to gag her, but a girl's scream, once you put a couple of spikes through her feet, could carry a long way down the holler. Expressive eyes, though. Don't get that in a hanging. All scrunched up. Hadn't really bothered to check religious convictions for Josie Darling. The whole point of Bates's death. Truth was, hangings had never been lucky. Had nearly broken his leg at Shelley Kruger's execution. Dean Tolley, the broken branch. And the near-catastrophe of Josie Fortune. Some things are like that. Don't push against karma, Henry.

Shortly before eleven, Val left his office. No sign of Josie today. Stayed home, lest she catch her death. He ambled lazily over to Varner Hall, dreaming of Fortune's Darling naked and in his power. Let her think she gets her mother's fate, then pull the hammer and two-pennies out. Beautiful day, blue sky, warm. Indian summer. When he arrived at his customary time, seven minutes past the hour, Val had recovered his tranquility. In fact, he had nearly charmed himself to full tumescence! Like his mood, it collapsed the moment he discovered his classroom was empty. There was a standard class cancellation form posted by the door with an explanatory note appended:

Valentine shot to death
Anita Paget and Bea Quincy

Val ripped the notice from the wall and looked about the halls for the bitch. What was she doing? How did she *know?*

Valentine forced himself to stroll back in the direction of his office, calming himself finally with well-reasoned assurances. She did not know. She could not know. A minor detail was missing: proof! Valentine pushed past two maintenance men cleaning paint from a door.

Filthy slews. Val paid no attention to them. At his office, Val reached into his pocket and pulled out his key ring. He was just ready to open his door when Gerty Dowell called to him. "They got yours too, Val?"

Val stopped and turned toward Miss Dowell. "Slews, Gerty."

"Did they break into your office?"

"Thankfully, no."

"They did mine! Come look!"

"Oh, Gerty not now."

"They painted my walls with the *c-word*, Val! Come see!"

Valentine indulged himself. Stepping into the office, he studied his handy work. The word known to all virgins.

"What kind of animals would do such a thing, Gerty?"

Gerty's eyes had a kind of spin to them when she got in these moods. "I come early sometimes, Val. What if I'd been here alone when they came and they had their way with me?"

Val shook his head at the terrible thought. "None of us is safe anymore, Gerty."

"*She* didn't get it." Gerty pointed to Josie Darling's office door.

"Yes, I noticed that. Curious, don't you think?"

"She just came by a couple of minutes ago and left. *Supposed* to be sick."

"Really? She was here? By herself?"

"I didn't see Clarissa Holt with her, if that's what you mean. Those two . . ."

If eyebrows could speak.

"I'm sorry I missed her," Val answered thoughtfully. "I wanted to have a word with her."

Valentine looked at his watch and made his apologies. Papers to grade. Perhaps pay a call on Miss Darling today. At her apartment, maybe? Come see me . . . but where?

Inside his office, Val felt the blood drain from his face at the sight of the paper taped to the wall over his desk. It was a photocopy of a photograph. She had been in his office! *His office!* He knew the face all too well. Miss Josie Fortune, the little Darling's sainted mother. She was seated on the counter of the bar inside the Hurry On Up. She held a sawed-off shotgun in her right hand, the stock of it balanced on her thigh, the barrels pointing straight up. Across the bottom of the page, written in lipstick, were the words:

MIsS mE?

Taking a Message

Valentine reached for the paper with Josie Fortune's image and tore it in half. He was finally out of patience. Did she have one shred of proof? Did she even know the terror of the death that waited her? He tried to slow his breathing. He sat down and stared at the wall where Josie Fortune's image had taunted him.

Then a knock came at his back. It came from across the hall. For Miss Fortune.

Val got up and opened his door to have a look when the knocking continued, only to discover a slender boy seeming in something of a hurry.

"Dr. Valentine?"

"Mr. Nelson Rush! And how are you, young man?"

The boy tipped his head toward the door behind him. "Have you seen her?"

"No, I haven't." Val offered an affectionate smile. "Much as that disappoints me. Did you have an appointment with her, Nelson?"

"I was supposed to meet her for lunch at Cokey's. She wanted to talk to me about something, and I can't make it."

"Really? What was it she wanted to see you about?"

The boy looked at his watch. "Something to do with my job, but she didn't say. I thought I could catch her before she left." He looked down the hall nervously.

Val looked at his own watch in sympathy. "Were you to meet her at noon, Nelson?"

"Yes, sir, but I have a lab at twelve. I just found out about it, and I can't miss it."

"If she comes by, I'll tell her," Val promised. "And don't worry, if she doesn't show, I can give a call out to Cokey's for you and let her know you can't make it."

Smiling, flush, "You'd do that for me!"

"What's a favor now and then between friends, Nelson?"

"Hey, great! And . . . thanks!"

Nelson started running. Rushing. Valentine smiled. So the little Darling slips.

He wandered back to his desk and reached for his phone, hitting the extension for the department. "Give me the number for work study, please, Marilyn!"

Marilyn gave him the number, and he dialed it. A moment later, a voice came across the line, purely Lues. Val answered, "This is Dr. Valentine in English. I want to know about the scheduling of one of my students. I think he's lying to me about his work study."

"And what is the name, Dr. Valentine?"

"Mr. Nelson Rush."

"And his student identification?"

"I have that information next door. Do I really need it?"

"One moment, please. Here it is: Nelson Rush works in transcripts and records, ten hours a week. A flex schedule."

"That explains it! My mistake entirely. I know Mrs. Temple! She's working that boy overtime! I'll take it up with Naomi. Thank you!" Val hung up.

Well, well, Miss Fortune. A little research, I see. Whose grades? Who's who? Who had whom? Where was I when the lights went out? That kind of thing. And dumb luck your boy couldn't make it for lunch. Using children for your research! Another Ellen Marshall!"

He punched the department number. "This is Valentine! Please cancel my afternoon class."

Such a lovely day, I think I'd like to go hunting.

Valentine set his phone receiver back and looked at his watch again. Probably miss the three o'clock meeting. Phone in the van. Call then. He unlocked his file drawer and picked out his Smith & Wesson 640-1. He checked his ammunition and found he had fired two rounds without reloading afterwards. Nasty old bitch. Had thought he was a car salesman! Val reached into a slightly depleted box of ammunition and loaded the gun fully. He was careful to pocket the empty shells in his pants pocket, then settled the gun in his sports jacket pocket. He picked about the cabinet and found some twine. More in the van. Lovely van, really. A moveable feast. Kidnap a whole sorority someday. Hang them all upside down from the rafters of an old barn!

Outside, the day was still a beauty. Clear and warm, first in a week or so. Leaves gone to gold. Lovely! Cold nights, though. Poor Darling! Valentine headed for his van, smiling at the image of a naked and cold young woman walking toward that old rugged cross! As he stepped onto the pavement, he decided he'd better start thinking pragmatically about the capture. She would be scared and cautious but perfectly vulnerable for the unexpected. Need a convincing scenario to get close to her of course . . .

Suspected him, so the best would be a little secret. Something to tell her. Yes. That would do it. She'll be eager for proof. Something the police would take seriously. Of course, there was nothing like a gun in the face. This afternoon with luck! Straight up and fast. Catch her at Cokey's as she's leaving. Catch her with her panties down. Might be seen, though. Could use the phone to draw her out. Come see me. That sort of thing. Or follow her. See what she does, where she goes. Best is patience, Henry. Nothing is lost here. Just accusations because she's proud she's solved a riddle. Nothing good enough for the police. Just wants to scare you into a mistake perhaps. He had to remember, she was a very clever girl. Not to be underestimated!

Henry Valentine crossed the parking lot, keys in his hand. Nearing his van, Val stopped to consider the thing. It was off center somehow! He stepped closer. Christ! He had a flat tire! A damned flat tire and no time to lose! Hurriedly, he looked at his watch. Worst luck!

A Walk in the Woods

The sky was blue. The colors of the forest at their zenith. Josie waited in Louis Hazard's pickup after her run through Brand Hall with the stolen master key. She kept the engine running. She sat low and wore a baseball cap, so Valentine couldn't pick out her silhouette. She watched Val's black van some thirty yards away and a small grove of trees next to the lot. Valentine showed at 11:50. She gave him a moment to cross to the van, then started rolling toward him before he noticed the flat. The flat was on the driver's side of his van, and predictably, Valentine came to a halt, staring at it dumbly. Josie pushed the accelerator and came up fast on him. By the time he checked his watch, it was too late. He looked around just as Josie brought the truck skidding to a halt beside him. The passenger window was open and when Josie leveled the twin pipes of her shotgun on the man, he looked positively certain she meant to finish it.

His eyebrows were cocked in an expression of confused surprise. His big lips hung open stupidly.

"Drop your keys right there, Val." There was a pleasant clink as his keys fell to the pavement, an expression in his eyes that seemed to brighten with optimism. "Now get in!" she told him. Valentine hesitated, looking around. There were people moving through the lot. Josie kept the shotgun extended just under the line of the back window. The twin pipes pointed over the door into Val's face at a distance sufficient to give Josie a two-foot margin of error. "Get in or die now, Val!"

Val's optimism, which had come after a second or so, faded with Josie's voice, but a pleasant bemused expression replaced it. "Certainly, Josie. Certainly. You won't believe this, but I was hoping to find you just now. With this flat tire, I thought I had missed you."

The big man grinned happily and opened the door. He had the look of a man who has caught his prey. Josie shifted the gun, so that it rested in her left hand, both hammers laid back, the twin triggers wrapped in her tense fingers as Valentine came into the truck beside her. "Easy, Val. We don't want any accidents. Keep your hands in view. One bad move, you're a dead man, I'm a fugitive."

The professor settled into the passenger seat and looked down at the weapon that poked into his side. "Very nice, Josie," he whispered, seeming to admire the gun with genuine affection. "Very nice, indeed. Perhaps I'll fuck you with it before we finish. Might be fun, don't you think?"

His eyes twinkled with a weird, mad kindness. His odor was overpowering.

"You're on the wrong end of the pipes for that fantasy, Val."

Josie accelerated and pulled out of the parking lot fast. She turned onto a side street, went half a block, then turned onto another side street, still bordering the lot. This street was empty. She could have finished it here, wiped off her prints and let Louis Hazard explain how his truck had been stolen. It was tempting, and if she had to, she meant to do it.

"Your mother's gun, isn't it? I seem to recall seeing a picture of it." He hesitated thoughtfully. "Functional, I expect?"

"We could find out right now, if you want."

"Not necessary on my account." Valentine grinned and looked out the window, his eyes casting about with easy indifference. His amusement was disconcerting. Josie's fingers were wet on the triggers. She could feel the barrels pushing comfortably into Valentine's side, but the truth was she didn't know if she could pull the triggers if she got in trouble. If he moved at all, she knew to give him both barrels at once, but right now, all she could do was pray she wouldn't be put to the test.

A truck rolled up behind her, two country boys riding in it. They followed closely.

"Are we going out for that drink you mentioned last week?"

"We're going for a walk in the woods, Val. You said something about showing me the falls. Nice day for it, don't you think?"

"Splendid, Josie! I've been meaning to take you there since I met you! Dreaming of it, actually."

He hardly took her seriously. He took the gun seriously, of course, but once out of the truck, he wasn't going to be so easy to manage, and the plans she had for him might need quick adjustments. Josie checked her speed, then turned right onto a gravel road. The truck that had followed her out of town went on. She crossed a covered bridge shortly afterwards. Alone now, she drove a steady twenty mph. She remembered this road. It came straight up the valley toward a ridge, the road bending just before the property where Jack Hazard's trailer had sat twenty years ago. As the road turned left, Josie drove straight into the field, what had once been the front yard. The truck jostled meanly, and Valentine's face paled. He apparently feared an accident.

"Easy, Josie! There's no rush!"

Josie stopped the truck well below the ridge. It was here that she and her mother and Jack had lived. The place had been nestled up against the woods,

Lues Creek behind the house, West Lues Creek before them. The place afforded a beautiful view, especially on a bright October day like this.

"The old homestead, Josie?"

"Get out, Val."

With some extravagance, Valentine pushed out of the truck cab and stepped clear before Josie followed him.

She slid over the seat, making sure to keep the shotgun pointing at the man. Once standing in the thick leaves and weeds, Josie pointed with her left hand to the woods and ridge, "Campus Falls is this way, Val."

"Are you sure you're up to this, Josie? You look a bit pale to me. Are you thinking about what I could do to you if I were to get the gun? Have you thought how things might go wrong?"

"All I have to do is pull these triggers. Seems easy enough."

"Hard work, Josie! Hard work! Believe me, all these voices that want you to do the *right* thing, the *good* thing. They can be devils at one's first kill. Maybe you fire too quickly, maybe not quickly enough. Killing's a business like anything else. Experience pays dividends. The novice goes through the school of hard knocks."

"I've had the graduate program of hard knocks, Val."

The old man's brow wrinkled in a cavalier acquiescence.

"Well then, I'm sure you'll do fine. Still," Valentine's brow furrowed more deeply as he pretended to be struck by a new thought, "justice is such abstract thing. Hard to get the blood up for old crimes, don't you think?"

He was full of mockery. His eyes had grown calm with the threat of the twin barrels in his gut becoming familiar. He was a man waiting his chance.

"I owe you the pain of my whole life, Valentine. Nothing abstract about it."

"You owe me your life, Josie. If not for me, you would have grown up in these godforsaken woods, a well-fucked whore like your mamma, and nothing more."

Tucking his hands in his pants pocket, Valentine began to saunter in the direction Josie had indicated. He had the air of a man who has come to see a property he might buy. At the rise, just before the woods, he stopped and looked around at the cinders and weeds where the trailer had sat. Now he looked down the hill toward the big bend in the road.

"All alone, Josie. May I tell you a secret?"

"Just keep going."

His big lips spread in a kindly old man's grin. "You were marked to die twenty years ago." He pulled his hand from his pocket and pointed his finger toward her forehead as though he actually saw something. "You're still marked. It's your mother's blood. I see it all over you."

Valentine enjoyed the effect he had for a long, insulting moment, then turned and started along the trail through the small grove of birches. Josie imagined the five cars coming down road behind her. She could see in her memory the dust they threw. As they had in every dream and every fantasy, they came off the road now at the bend and straight across the field until they stopped where she had left the truck. The men took up their positions behind the cars. She saw their guns raised up against the gray sky. They racked their guns at once, as three of the troopers came running toward Jack and her. The end of her world.

"Lovely out here, isn't Josie?"

The trooper hadn't expected her to fight, but she had. She had broken free, and she had run. She had followed this trail back to Lues Creek, and she had run as she had never run before. He had caught her at the water's edge, taken her up by one arm, and she had twisted around and kicked him. When he finally held both of her arms, she stared down at his shotgun. Her mother's daughter, Josie had wanted only the chance to get the gun in her hands. She would have killed to save Jack, because she knew he was innocent. That was the memory Josie had lost, and with it all certainty in herself.

"Is it like you remember?" Val asked her pleasantly. "I know you have such trouble with your memory, but are these woods the same? Or has it all changed?"

"Keep walking, Val."

The creek was the same. The water was broad, shallow, and slow-moving. The October leaves overhanging the water reflected off its surface. In the distance, Josie saw the boulders that marked the entrance to Campus Falls. That too was the same. She remembered it. The trail would end there, and they would have to slip into the creek in order to get to the falls.

Valentine went on as far as the trail took them, then stopped. His hands still in his pants pockets, he turned slowly and studied Josie from the ground up, measuring her determination.

"We seem to have run out of trail."

They were no more than a single step apart. The shortened barrels of Josie's mother's shotgun were pointed right into his stomach. Valentine considered the gun casually.

"Are you scared, Josie? You seem scared."

She nodded, meeting his eye. "Aren't you?"

Henry Valentine gave the barrels of the shotgun a contemplative look and tried to hold his smile, but there was a sudden lonesomeness in his expression. It was the look of a man who thinks he may have miscalculated things quite badly.

"You know I sympathize with what you're trying to do," he said finally. "I really do, but I have to tell you your mother would have scared me with that gun. I'm not sure you're quite the old gal's equal, much as you want to be. A real tough girl, your mamma. What do you think? Do you think mamma would have let a husband of hers put her in the hospital?"

"Do you remember the first time you saw her?" Josie asked.

"Josie Fortune?" The thought seemed to startle him, but after a moment, his smile tightened down grimly. "I certainly do."

"She was in your class, but only for one evening."

"*Very good,* Josie. A real researcher. I'm afraid your mother had no talent for research. She was all fight, that one. All fight and no brains. And you're just the opposite. Have you ever even fired a gun like that, Josie? Research, now that's your forte. I should have thought you'd stick with your talents. Aren't you just a little sorry you didn't?"

"If I had called the police, you and I wouldn't have the chance for this little talk, now would we?"

"Advanced Creative Writing. She was late," Val answered. Her tardiness seemed to explain everything.

"She asked you if she could talk to you. You said she was talking right now, to go ahead with what she wanted to say. She asked if she should be in an advanced course if she hadn't been in an introductory course?"

"What's your source, Josie?" He was curious, nothing more.

"She had been on campus for about twenty-four hours and some adviser had stuck her in the wrong class. And of course, you let her come in so you could spend the next hour humiliating her. Some academic point for the rest of the class, something about writing as a discipline."

"Yes, yes, of course. But how do you know this? I'm really quite fascinated as to how you've put this all together."

"Once I had you, Val, I knew where to look. I got the class list and made a few phone calls. One of the kids in your class knew my mother from the bar. He said she never would have let anyone treat her like that at the bar, but she took it from you, and not a word of complaint, because she thought she was supposed to. She thought humiliation was part of a college education. And you just piled it on. He said you teased her when she said something about wanting to write stories for her little girl. You mocked her accent. You insulted her intelligence and all because someone else had made a mistake and put her in the wrong class."

"No, Josie. I insulted her because she was an ignorant slew!"

"When the break came, she left and didn't come back. A few days later, you got pulled in on the carpet. Of course, you thought she had turned you in, but it was the man I talked to who did it. My mother fought her own fights, Val. If she had had a quarrel with you, she'd have faced you with it. You were so damn sure of yourself you didn't even think someone else might have found your arrogance offensive."

A small, crooked smile. No shame, no regret.

"I'm guessing here, but I don't think you considered killing her at the time, not seriously anyway. Am I right?"

"I'm impressed, Josie. You are right, as it turns out. It was months before I decided to kill Miss Fortune. She was an afterthought, really. Simply, . . . well, the best candidate for the job, one might say."

Josie felt herself giving way to his power. Her strength and anger failing her. Was she afraid to take him off the trail and into the water? Or did she want to talk? Need it? "Tell me how it happened. I want to know how my mother died."

"Do you really want to know, Josie?" The eyes scolded her. He meant to say in his silence she wouldn't like the truth.

"I know you hanged her. I want the rest."

Henry Valentine shrugged one shoulder, a man recalling a long ago conquest, "We were at my house, in the basement. I have a lovely room for select guests. It's not far from here, actually. I'd love to show it you. It was night, a couple of hours before dawn, actually. I tied a strap of leather around her neck and ran it up over a rafter. After I had pulled her up into the air for a few seconds, I gave her a little stool that she could reach once the leather stretched enough. Then I took her gag off and untied her feet. Do you know that woman stood almost twenty minutes? The whole time spitting and cussing. I have to confess I had only one other to compare her against at the time, but later, I saw so many beg and cry in those last moments that I've often thought, 'None like Miss Fortune, no sir, none at all!' For all the good it did her. When I kicked away her little stool, she died like all the others, Josie—pissing and moaning."

Valentine smiled at Josie as he said this last, then turned away and started into the creek. He went forward several steps before Josie followed him. The water was frigid, and soon Josie was into it over her hips. She carried the shotgun off her shoulder now. She thought Val might turn on her here, but he didn't. He moved out at a good pace, going with the current and letting the distance between them widen gradually. There were several heavy boulders to the right of the creek, and while it was possible just before the falls to get out of the water there and climb out to a trail, it was far easier to come out of the water to the left, just after the rocky channel widened somewhat. There was a sandbar that would help him come out of the water and a broad flat table of rock. The rock ran out beside the creek to a precipice just alongside the falls, but if he went toward the woods, he could be free in a matter of seconds. His third option was to find cover behind a small group of rocks midway between the creek, the falls, and the woods.

Valentine was nearly thirty feet beyond Josie when he came out of the water and started over the flat rock. As she watched him moving away, Josie slipped toward the edge of the creek, ducking in behind a rock ledge. Finding cover on the broad flat rock beside the creek, Valentine drew a small revolver from his sports jacket pocket and spun down into a prone position.

He actually pointed his revolver at her, just as Josie slipped down entirely out of sight. At such a distance, her shotgun, practically speaking, was useless. But that was okay. Josie had done her part. She had taken Henry Valentine to the edge of the world.

At the Edge of the World

Jack Hazard watched Valentine turn off the trail's end and step into the water. The professor and Josie had stood there a long time, and he hadn't been sure if the whole thing might not end right there.

But then he was in the water. Soon he was out of Cyrus's range but easily within Jack's sights. Cyrus had had Valentine along the creek and coming out of the woods. Blake and Jeremy had covered Josie from the bridge to the hilltop. Lincoln and Virgil had followed them from campus through to the bridge. Louis had used a scoped rifle to watch Josie take the man in the parking lot on campus. But this was the tight spot. If Valentine had a gun, and they had figured he would, he might try Josie here.

Jack kept the rifle off his shoulder and stood back in the shadows of the big rocks. He didn't want to shoot Valentine. That was the last choice for all of them, but Josie had no cover where she stood, and if he even turned around, he knew he was going to have to do it. Then bury him where no one would ever find him.

Louis had guessed Valentine would be familiar with the area. Once he knew Josie meant to take him to the falls, he would probably make his move here. "Either he fights in the water or he lets the current take him out a little," Louis had told them, "and suddenly he's out of range of Josie's scattergun without Josie realizing it. He'll play on your inexperience. If he does, he'll get some distance between you. Otherwise, you or Jack or Cyrus will to have to take him. If he even starts to turn, you're going to have to pull both triggers, Josie."

Josie did a good job coming into the water a little slow. She let Valentine pull away gradually, so that when he came up out of the creek, she still had a shot if she needed to make it, and Valentine knew it. Now he was up behind the rocks and going to see if he couldn't scare her into blowing off both charges of her mother's gun. If he could do that, he wouldn't care to end it right away. That was Josie's read on it. The only danger was if he got pushed too far too fast and had to kill to save himself. That was what made this part so tricky.

Jack watched patiently, ready for anything. When Valentine pulled some kind of snub-nosed revolver out of his pocket, Jack set his rifle into a crevice of rock and walked out unarmed toward the man's back.

"This one's for Josie," he whispered. His Josie, he meant.

Valentine was flattened down close against the rocks. He held his revolver in one hand pointed up to the sky. Jack was nearly twenty feet behind him and came up softly, quickly. Within four strides he heard the man crowing.

"Josie, I'm afraid you've waited too long!"

Softly, never stopping his advance, Jack answered, "I been waiting twenty years. Is that too long?"

Valentine seemed to freeze for half-a-second before he turned, but when he did turn, he came around fast. He got a shot off just as Jack rolled himself into a ball and somersaulted over the bare rock toward him, coming up face-to-face against him. Valentine didn't get a second chance. Jack took his wrist and nearly snapped it off. Valentine yelled out with the pain, and the revolver fell to the rock like a toy. Valentine was a big man, easily 6'4" and a hundred and ninety-some pounds. He was strong, too. Jack felt that at once. He reached over with his free hand to twist Jack away and nearly did it. Jack bumped him once in the ribs and listened to an animal grunt. Taking Valentine's hand and thumb under his wrist, Jack brought him to his feet and started toward the falls.

As Valentine wheeled back, he managed to get ahead of Jack finally. With the pressure off his wrist and thumb, he was able to take Jack by his coat and lift him off his feet, throwing him toward the canyon. Jack caught Valentine's sleeve as he came down, then getting his feet set, he used the man's own energy to bring him around and put his back to the canyon. Valentine reared up hard to stop himself, but already, he was tilted out, his balance failing. Catching Jack's wrist, he tried to bring himself back, but Jack came with him, giving him no resistance at all. Valentine tipped back, starting to go. The only problem was Jack had lost his balance as well.

They could both see straight down into the spewing water of the cataract. They could see farther. They could see the rocks below. Valentine's eyes grew wide as he tipped out farther. Jack shoved him, while they both still had their feet on the rock. The recoil let Jack drop straight down. He hit the ledge with the back of his thighs and bounced out into the canyon, right between Valentine's spread legs. Hooking his left arm around Valentine's right leg, he broke his momentum slightly and swung himself around to face the rock. Already below the lip, and starting to fall, he grabbed a knob of rock. For a moment, his feet swung precariously. Finally, he dropped a few inches more and took hold of a rock. Scrambling for a better grip, he got his boot on a thick mossy vine neatly embedded in the rock and hugged the face of the rock. Valentine's boot struck his head, then he was gone. The scream started well below Jack. There was bellowing at first.

At the end, only a shriek of terror. The echoes answered in waves long after the fall had ended.

As Jack clawed his way back to the edge, Josie appeared and took his collar and pulled him up.

"I thought you were dead!" she cried as Jack got to his feet. She said something else. He didn't really hear the words. He was still struggling for his balance. Stepping away from the canyon, Jack noticed his fingers bleeding. He had ripped up both hands on the rocks. He looked upstream and saw Cyrus, who had come into the creek and was walking towards them. The boy was grinning. That boy always had a grin.

"Jack, I thought you went over. I thought you'd fallen."

This from Josie. Jack turned to her now. She was looking at him with real fear. He stepped back now to the edge. Some thirty feet straight below, tucked back under the rock, he saw the stone ledge he had walked as a boy long before anyone had thought to put up a railing. He looked beyond to the boulders that littered the floor of the canyon. For a moment, he did not see the body. Then, as the mist cleared, he caught sight of a bit of cloth. It looked to be a piece of refuse, nothing more.

Josie was close by him now and staring down at the rocks as well. She looked scared, her flesh almost white. Jack put his arm around her and nudged her back off the edge. She was shivering with cold, but her eyes were dry. Jack looked upstream for Cyrus. He was coming up out of the water and starting across the rock toward them. Jack put his other arm around Josie, trying to keep his blood off of her as he whispered, "We got him, Josie."

Her eyes still cast into the pit, she told him, "He said she never begged, Jack. Not even at the end."

Jack looked back toward the canyon once more. "I believe it," he said. "Your mother was every bit the woman you are, Josie."

The Visitation

In light of certain facts, the memorial service panned this afternoon for Dr. Henry Valentine has been cancelled.

Del

So read the notice. *Certain facts!* Certain rumors would be more precise, and Dick Ferrington knew the source. *Josie Fortune*—at least that was the name she was using this week! Of course the real problem was Delbert Meyers. Del was bowing to pressure.

When Dick called the vice president of academic affairs, Rosy Elwood told him *the facts* had nothing to do with the police investigation into charges that Henry Valentine was somehow involved in a series of local murders over the past two decades. The cancellation of the memorial service, the good woman told him loftily, was due to a scheduling conflict at the convocation center. Ferrington didn't believe it, but he knew better than to cross a vice president. The university was moving quickly to distance itself from scandal, and Henry Valentine's reputation as a teacher was to be the sacrifice. Dick could throw himself on the funeral pyre, for all the good it would do, or he could drop it for the time being and make his paybacks later. He dropped it.

A public memorial service was hardly necessary. He was certain that the private visitation he had arranged for Val, before the body was shipped back to North Carolina, would draw hundreds of Val's students. That was what counted. They were the people who really loved the man. Val would have his hour of respect and honor, the university willing or not.

Last Rites

When Josie arrived at Lues State's Campus Ministries with Cyrus Hazard, she was mildly surprised that the place was empty except for the minister and Dick Ferrington. She nodded toward the back pew and Cy took a seat. Then going forward past the two men, she came to the photograph of Henry Valentine and a single arrangement of flowers. He was gone and nearly as quickly forgotten, but it wasn't over. She needed for it be over, and that was what this night was all about.

"Where have you been, Josie?"

Ferrington's voice at her back was cold, calculating, and bitter.

Josie turned, giving the man her full attention, and yet she felt off balance, troubled, even uncertain. "I needed a few days off, Dick, if you must know."

"A lot of people have been looking for you. I'd say you have some questions to answer."

"I'd say I'm ready to answer them."

Ferrington's handsome face had a pinch of curiosity. "What does that mean?"

"I had Val figured out last Thursday evening when I saw him pictured with Nora Tolley in a Terre Haute newspaper, but there were still a couple of things that didn't quite make sense, so I kept looking around."

Ferrington's brow twisted itself into some kind of an attempt at confusion. "Who's Nora Tolley?"

"That was when I found a picture of you and Cathy at the Kappa Zeta sorority house in an old yearbook. You were standing with the new pledge class, which happened to include Shelley Kruger, Anita Moore, and Melissa Fry."

"I'm afraid I'm not following you, Josie." Those were the words he spoke, but his sudden pallor told the truth.

"I started thinking about their murders, and I realized a man working alone was going to have trouble, a lot of trouble in some cases. I asked myself how one man could get a woman up in a tree and then drive a nail into her hand. I wanted to know how a man working alone could suspend a woman over a ravine or out over a river. I started thinking about the coincidences around your wife's death, how the kids had been taken up north before she was abducted, how you had been out of the country at the time. A little too perfect, wasn't it? Everyone knew you had killed her. No one knew how. Then I started thinking about my own troubles. That phone call while you were sitting with me at Cokey's. It was just too cute for coincidence.

"Then I started thinking about my mother. If Val had crossed her, tried to make her into a fool, she wasn't going to get trapped by him. From everything I could find out about her, the man who caught her had to be a friend. A nice young guy with a pretty smile would be about right. Someone around nineteen or twenty who could play the kid brother. With someone threatening her with anonymous notes like the ones I got, a phone call to her while you were with her would have been enough to convince her you were okay, proof you were exactly what you seemed. Is that about the way it went, Dick?"

"You're out of your mind, Josie."

"There was a woman found at the side of a road a few months before my mother's death. Nothing special about her, except that she was obviously in trouble. Naked in the woods, running out toward a car, waving it down, only to be run over as she stood in the middle of the road. Someone was chasing her, Dick. Someone else was waiting. It was always a two-man game, wasn't it? One of you got close in order to find out how well the torment was working, the other kept his distance. That way you both got to know what they were thinking, how they were feeling. Fear and trust: exactly the way you worked that woman, and exactly the way you worked me. Was it like that with all of them?"

Ferrington's eyes looked past Josie briefly. He seemed to notice Cyrus Hazard for the first time. "Is that boy supposed to be some kind of body-guard, Josie?"

"Touch me and find out."

"He won't always be around, will he?"

"I had you for eight murders, when I started looking for bodies in North Carolina. I figured if you liked your game so much, you wouldn't sit it out for all those years you were away from Lues. While you were there, you'd want to have your fun. It wasn't long before I found a murder in the Chapel Hill area. Just so happens, it was the same year Valentine was there on his sabbatical writing that unpublished novel you liked so much. A mother and her fifteen-year-old daughter. Locals. They watched each other suffocating with plastic bags over their heads. The police were certain two men had been involved in that one. That's when I knew exactly which two men."

"I think I'm going to have a lot better chance of proving you murdered Henry Valentine than you are of pushing your fanciful theories, Josie."

"I only had one question after it all came together, but think I've got it figured out now."

The campus minister stepped toward them. "Excuse me, Dick, I think we should start the service."

Ferrington looked at his watch, then at Josie and Cyrus Hazard. "Forget it, Duane. No one's here."

"Dick, I know it's a small group—."

"These two are leaving. For that matter, so am I."

The minister took a moment to absorb this information, then nodded uncomfortably.

"I thought some kids would come by," Ferrington explained. "There are a lot of silly rumors on campus. Kids don't know what to believe. Why don't you go on?"

"I need to lock up."

"Give me a minute, then."

The minister nodded and stepped away. When he was gone, Ferrington looked murderously into Josie's eyes. "Tell me what you figured out, Josie. I'm curious."

"I was trying to decide if Val started it all or if you did."

Ferrington smiled. It was neither a confession nor a denial. It looked to Josie to be the grin of a man beyond someone's reach.

"I know you were in Valentine's class the night my mother showed up, and you were both certain my mother had filed a complaint against Val after he had tried to humiliate her, but I don't think that was what it was all about. Val said it was months before he thought about killing her, and I believe him. I think it was talk. He had published a paper about matricide that fall, the whole idea of moral freedom, the loss of law and social structure, and the connection it has to the ritual murder of the mother or a mother image. 'Matricide, or the killing of any prominent, powerful woman, whether mother figure or ruler, is the great transgression, the sin against the holy spirit, as it were, precisely because it takes us outside the moral plane of humanity, so that we can never reenter the old order: and it is because of this that the old order dies away in all the mythic representations of a matricide: it is the beginning of all new and great enterprises. . . .' Sound familiar?"

"You're a typical woman, Josie. Ideas scare you."

"You're a typical man, Ferrington. You can't tell the difference between fact and your own fantasy."

Ferrington's jaw tightened.

"I think Valentine had said it, and that was the end of it as far as he was concerned. Then a certain golden boy reads the essay, and over a beer or two, the two of you start talking about murder, any murder, all in the abstract, of course, and suddenly you find yourselves at the *what-if* stage. You talk about doing it, maybe about higher moral planes, both of you suddenly anxious to give a woman what you've always wanted to give her. But there's that *practical* consideration you both have. There's getting caught. There's prison. Then one of you decides two great minds working in tandem can do virtually anything with impunity. It's a game, after all. Damn the police, let's kill some bitch! And then you went out and tried it for the hell of it. Some woman. Jane Doe. Nobody ever found out who she was. A prostitute? Someone easy, no challenge, just to see what it was like?"

Ferrington's eyes revealed a hint of satisfaction. "Proof, Josie. I haven't heard a single thing out of your mouth that is remotely like proof. If Valentine said anything, it won't stand as evidence, except at your trial. You can't prove I was involved in any of this. But I'll tell something. I'm going to enjoy watching them try you for Val's murder. I'll especially enjoy testifying to everything you've dreamed up and told me. I'm an innocent man, Josie. I'll swear by God to it, and no one will ever prove differently."

"Pray it's quick, Ferrington."

Josie stared brightly into the man's confusion, then she spun on her heel and started back up the aisle of the chapel toward Cyrus Hazard.

"Just what the hell does that mean, Josie?"

Josie stopped herself and faced the man one last time. "It means you crossed the wrong people."

A Full Moon

Dick Ferrington did not see anyone in the parking lot besides the minister, who was going on about the rumors and how incredible it was that Valentine could have been responsible for so many deaths. Of course, he didn't believe a word of it, he said. Ferrington knew he was lying. Like everyone else, he believed everything he heard.

Under different circumstances, Ferrington might have listened, even offered an opinion, but suddenly, it didn't matter what anyone thought. Josie and that kid she had with her and God only knew who else were coming for him. As good as a promise. The wrong people. Exactly the people who had gotten Val. When he was finally alone and standing beside his car, Ferrington took a moment to study the trees, the lustrous harvest moon. He knew he had to get home, if only to get rid of some things in his safe, but what he wanted was simply to run, to get into his Mercedes and just take off! As he started the car, he thought about it again. Why not? There was nothing to keep him from just driving away. Still, if he went home, he would have a better chance. No cops to worry about now or later, just a nice clean disappearance. He shifted the car into gear, still thinking about making a run for it, when he saw headlights turning on in the distance. Then another set of lights behind him. His forehead slick with sweat suddenly, Ferrington struggled to slow his breathing. Two vehicles ... that they were letting him see.

He hesitated at the edge of campus, checking his mirror. They were still well back of him. They stopped instead of coming closer. Both trucks. Looked to have two men inside each truck. Which meant she was out there somewhere watching. If he took off now, he thought, and they followed him, they would simply wait their chance. Track him as long as they wanted, then on some lonely stretch of road or at the first motel he stopped in, any damn place they wanted, they could come for him, and he would have nothing to fight them with.

He hadn't thought he was in trouble. He had thought . . . he was certain she hadn't figured it all out. He had listened to the rumors. Everything was Valentine, only Val. In fact, Ferrington had already planned his revenge against Josie. Very quiet, very patient, the way Val would have done it. And when she was sure it was over, he would go to her apartment with Deb Rainy with a piece offering, a bottle of wine . . . and take them both! But that wasn't the way it was going down now, was it? Better to get home, get rid of his trophies, get the Glock, and some cash, and see if he could slip away from these bastards somehow. Call Deb, maybe. Get a ride out of town. They wouldn't like a witness. Two cars, maybe. Pull a switch or create some kind of diversion. Give them Deb, maybe. Let them stumble into a homicide. They'd have to deal with it. Might be just the diversion he needed.

His mind raced with other possibilities, but he was not good at this sort of thing. Val had always been able to see how people would react, to predict things. As he pulled up to his house and watched his garage door open, Ferrington's sense of panic faded. The headlights were no longer behind him. No strange cars were parked in the neighborhood. He decided he would get his gun, some money, . . . and just take his chances! Face them if that was what it was going to come down to! He swore angrily at his missed opportunities. The moment he heard about Val, he should have slipped out of town. Well, he had thought about leaving. Vaguely, at least. Then he let go of the idea. She had pinned it on Val, called people, fed them her theories. Even Deb! Deb said Josie was feeling terrible, because she had confronted Val with it and told him she was getting ready to go to the police. Rather than face arrest, she said he had gone to Campus Falls to commit suicide. Lying bitch!

And not a word about a partner! She had missed him! Everything was Valentine. The police were all over it, checking out the allegations, and damn it, Ferrington had thought he was in the clear. He and Val had worked it out so beautifully for years! A long standing feud, nothing too obvious, just a careful distance, a coolness, a refusal to talk or pass pleasantries, nothing that would ever connect them, even at their homes. No one should have linked them! He was amazed, in fact, that Josie had found Valentine. Well, ... it didn't matter. The only thing that mattered now was to get in his safe. They had both created separate identities years ago, in case it ever came down to something like this. Val's idea. Once or twice after Cathy, Ferrington had thought he would have to run, but it was like Val had said. They just couldn't get him for it, try as they might. Both he and Val had credit histories and bank accounts and tax reports and deeds for property in Idaho. Two cabins about a hundred miles apart. They would know by now about Val's alias but not his.

Might even go there. But he didn't have to. Just the money and the identity and his Glock. Hell, it wasn't like the law would be coming for him, not if he cleared the safe! All he really had to do was get out of town. Shoot his way out or outrun them or . . . he smiled suddenly. He could actually use the sheriff to get some space. Harassment, threats, . . .

A couple of patrol cars might clear a path! He moved quickly from his garage into the house and down the hallway toward his office. He needed to word it correctly. Then it came to him, the magic words: *Jack Hazard!* He could bring in about twenty patrol cars with that name. Ferrington smiled at the irony of it as he stepped into his office and hurried toward the safe. All he needed was half a chance, and the sheriff was going to give it to him!

He spun the dial, then rolled it toward the first number. That was when he felt cold metal touch the back of his neck.

"You looking for this, Doc?" The voice belonged to a man.

His own Glock against his neck. Christ, they had broken into his safe, and now, they were going to shoot him with his own gun and call it another suicide!

"On the floor," the voice told him. Before he could respond, the man took him down. Three others came at him suddenly. They had been waiting for him! They had been waiting all along!

They used rope to tie his hands and feet, a gag to silence him. They worked quickly and then lifted him up and carried him out to the trunk of his car. The whole thing happened in a matter of seconds, and then Dick

Ferrington found himself in the trunk of his own Mercedes. He heard his garage door roll open, his car start. He felt the movement as they left the garage and backed down his driveway. He had no idea where he was going. He knew only this: he would not be coming back.

It wasn't fair. He wasn't ready to die. They had no proof! It wasn't supposed to happen like this! In the dark, . . . in the middle of woods, . . .

God! It was the way they had . . .

But they were just whores. That's all any of them were. He felt tears burning his eyes. He and Val had worked everything out, every kill a bit different, and no one could ever put it together! Alone at night with them in Val's basement, there was always the stink of their fear. Ferrington had liked that best, the way they smelled. It was different from anything else in the world, the smell they got when they finally knew they were going to die. It was awful and wonderful. Total, perfect power.

But it wasn't supposed to be like this! He didn't want to die like one of them!

They didn't drive long. Maybe twelve or fifteen minutes. When one of them opened the trunk, Ferrington heard water. A creek. He saw the full moon behind a canopy of leaves. As they lifted him out, he saw the lights of the fraternity and sorority houses lit up a few hundred yards away, and then he knew. They were taking him into the canyon. The tallest of them threw Ferrington over his shoulder and began tramping through the stream. The rocks inside the canyon glowed luminously. The reflection of the moon glistened in the black current. As they went, Ferrington twisted about to see how many there were. Four of them walked in procession behind him, two had shotguns. Plus the man carrying him.

How would they do it? He closed his eyes, but he could not stop the tears. He told himself he should have just driven away, tried to outrun them. He thought about that life, which he would never live, making his way by the morning sun, a free man with no responsibilities and all his choices still before him. No money, no weapons, nothing but his life. But it was enough. He should have tried it! A few bucks in his pocket to get him to the next town. He had a credit card! He could have used it! Anywhere but here. Run . . . and take his chances!

It wasn't so hard to imagine the life. Even without the money. Sell the car. Get an old beater in trade. Hit some beaches, maybe, camp out, take a job doing . . . anything! Why the hell did he have to go back to the house? She told him they knew, gave him his chance, . . . and he blew it.

He saw the road. He saw himself driving. The morning sun lighting his way. It would have been perfect!

When they stopped walking, the fantasy crashed. This was it. They settled him on his feet, standing ankle-deep in cold water. He stood, while they cut the ropes and pulled the gag free. The two men with shotguns were pointing their weapons at him. Ferrington looked back at the falls. Did they mean to drown him? Or was it something . . . worse? He looked at the guns again. Maybe they were going to use his Glock, after all.

Five of them total. But suddenly he was free. His bindings loosened. He was bigger than any of them, except the tall one. And definitely stronger than any given man, maybe any two of them. They were going to have to shoot him, because if one of them stepped toward him, he would fight. Get hold of a rock, and smash his brains out! Ferrington flexed his hands, spread his feet. Starting right now, he thought, everything was going to be a fight.

But then oddly, as his courage came, they started away!

All five of them! They went quickly, the way they had come. The men with the guns were the last ones to leave, but when they finally turned and vanished behind the boulders, Ferrington looked around uncertainly. That was it? They cut him free and took off?

What the hell? He smiled stupidly. It was some kind of warning, maybe. They were telling him they knew. Maybe all they wanted was to show him that they could do it whenever they wanted. He shook his head, almost laughing. It didn't matter what they wanted to show him. He was *alive!* That was all that mattered. Alive and free. They would not catch him a second time. He would just walk out of here and over to Greek Circle, to the first frat house he could get to, and get one of the kids to get him down the road. Then, . . . as far from here as he could get! Come tomorrow morning, he would be a new man. Ferrington smiled suddenly at the thought. No money, no car, no weapons, but *alive!* And suddenly, the world had never seemed better or his future brighter! He would be any man he wanted to be. Start his life over!

He took a step, then another, then began plunging through the shallow stream at a run. That was when he saw the man standing on a boulder in the distance. He was standing between Ferrington and the way out of the canyon. Standing there with his hands empty, just . . . waiting.

Dick Ferrington's smile failed. His optimism crashed, and his bowels churned. He understood now why they had brought him here and then left. He knew exactly what his fate was to be.

The man waiting on the rock was Jack Hazard.

Bitts and Pieces

Early Saturday morning, Josie drove out to Pauper Bluff in her refurbished VW to go fishing with the ex-sheriff of Lues County. She found Bitts waiting with a cup of coffee. When she had taken a cup, and after they had talked some about the weather in the solemn way of good country people, Bitts cleared his throat. "I had a call from Jason Morgan," he said. There was caution suddenly on both of their faces. "He got the coroner's ruling." Bitts hesitated, letting Josie ready herself. "They were consistent with his own findings, Josie."

"Meaning?"

"Meaning, Dick Ferrington died of misadventure. He apparently slipped on a rock next to the falls, fell into a pool of water and drowned. Only mystery is what he was doing inside that canyon in the middle of the night."

Ferrington's car had been found near the mouth of Lues Creek Canyon the morning after Josie had spoken to him. A campus security officer had tracked back into the canyon that afternoon and discovered Ferrington's body floating in shallow water just beside the falls. As it happened, it was the very same pool that her mother's corpse had been found in.

"I see," she answered finally. "Any idea how the state's attorney is taking it?"

"According to Jason, Mr. Stackman seems ready enough accept the idea, but he did ask where you were that night."

"Where I was?" She was, she imagined, nearly the picture of innocence.

"The police have the campus minister swearing he saw you talking to Dick Ferrington at Campus Ministries the night Ferrington passed on to his just rewards."

"The night Dick Ferrington died, I did talk to him at the chapel, Two-Bit. I told him I had him linked to Valentine. He didn't seem to like that very much, but that was the last I saw of him. I went to a bar with Cyrus Hazard right after we left, a place called Dion's, out at the edge of town where the

Hurry on Up used to be. Cyrus and I got there at nine o'clock, and we stayed until closing. We made quite a scene. People are sure to remember us."

"Stackman also wanted to know where you were when Valentine jumped."

"I was at a family reunion, Two-Bit. Must be a half-dozen people who can tell the police they saw me there."

"A family reunion? They didn't hold it at Campus Falls did they?"

"Is that what Stackman thinks?"

"Well, the trails into the canyon and up to the falls were closed down last Monday, all afternoon. Everything looked very official. They even had campus cops posted to make sure no one used the trails. Trouble is nobody authorized it, and none of the security people know a thing about it. Seems they were all on the other side of campus, where there was some kind of riot going on between the college kids and a few of the locals. A suspicious mind just might see one too many coincidences to all of it, Josie."

"Probably just a fraternity prank, Two-Bit."

Bitts gave a wry half-smile. "I'll pass that theory along, Josie."

"So has Chief Morgan found anything more to connect Valentine and Ferrington to the murders of those women?"

"Valentine's gun, the one they found at Campus Falls, was used in Bea Quincy's murder. He checked that as soon as I gave him the hint. The police are going through everything those two owned. They've got a novel Valentine apparently wrote years ago. Interesting reading, I take it. The real find though is Valentine's basement. He had a cell where he kept his victims. They've already turned up hair and blood. Ferrington had a little collection of his own in his safe. Lockets of hair, pieces of jewelry, even underwear. They're hoping with all that they can get all of the victims accounted for."

"The families need to know," Josie answered. "They need to know it's finally over."

"They will in due time," Bitts told her. "Jason will take care of all that as soon as they're sure just exactly how much trouble those two made."

"I want you to take something else to him. It's about the Josie Fortune murder."

"What about it?"

"To start with, the man in the woods on the day they found my mother was Dick Ferrington."

"Ferrington? You're sure about that?"

"He and Valentine had taken my mother into the canyon the night before." Josie held up her hand to stop the old man's protest. "Just listen to me. All morning, no one discovered the body, and I expect that by afternoon Ferrington wanted to go out and see what was going on, why no one had seen her. That's when he saw Cat Sommerville. By all accounts, she was a beauty, Two-Bit."

"No argument there."

"Maybe he thought she'd be their next victim. Maybe it was something else, I don't know, but I'm sure he followed her until she went to the sorority house. That was all he needed to arrange to meet her later, which he did in a matter of days. I don't know what he was thinking at the time, but once things went the way they did and Cat was pregnant, and she was within a matter of weeks, they decided to get married."

"And the move to North Carolina? Was that maybe so he could start over? Get his distance from Valentine?"

Josie shook her head. "I don't think so. I think they had killed twice by then. Maybe they thought that was it or maybe they planned to do it again, but universities don't hire their own, not for tenure jobs. If Dick wanted to teach with Val at Lues State, he had to finish school elsewhere. So he went to North Carolina, Val's alma mater, and they kept in touch. The North Carolina murders prove that."

"So you're saying Dick Ferrington was off chasing Cat Sommerville, leaving Henry Valentine inside the canyon to finish what the two of them had started the night before?"

"No. That's not what I'm saying. There was no one inside the canyon after the kids left until Toby Crouch went in."

"Now, wait a minute . . ."

"I started with Waldis's time of death and what you knew to be true. The thing that struck me was the fact that you were both uninvolved in any sort of conspiracy, both objective. At the same time, you were each convinced the other one was up to something. Waldis thought you were in a fight with Colt Fellows, some kind of political thing, so he didn't trust you. Why should he? He had the medical facts to convince him Colt was right. You thought Waldis had been misled by Colt and then wouldn't admit a mistake. Neither one of you ever considered the possibility that you could both be right."

"We couldn't both be right, Josie. Waldis said your mother died after six o'clock in the evening. I had witnesses see her body at three o'clock!"

"And then there's my theory, that the body was put in the canyon the night before."

With an odd, contemplative expression, "I have to tell you, Josie, I think even Doc Waldis and me could have agreed on that one: you're out of your mind!"

"But all three of us are right, Two-Bit. Val and Ferrington took my mother's body into the canyon just before dawn. At three the next afternoon, the kids saw her lying on the rock. At four, they stood within arm's length of her, all of them afraid to touch her. At 4:40, they called your dispatcher. You checked with Yeager, and he sent Toby Crouch in to find out if the call was a prank or legitimate. That puts Crouch at the mouth of the canyon at five o'clock, under the falls at 5:30.

"That was too early to implicate Jack, and I doubt if even Colt could have moved reality around on that. But once he got a time of death that was after six, he went to work on a frame. Once he did that, he was committed. The last thing he expected to hear was that the kids had seen the body at three o'clock. I expect at the beginning he just wanted to create enough confusion that his own actions wouldn't be questioned for what they were, but when Waldis came in with six o'clock on the time of death, Colt convinced his buddy Cal Yeager they could bring you down. That was all Yeager needed to put a story together. Once Jack decided not to fight it, because if he did his brother Louis would be on trial beside him, you were all alone, Two-Bit."

"Josie, there are things that happen when life stops. You can't ignore the signs. I saw your mother's corpse. She couldn't have been dead more than five hours. Fact is, I didn't think—."

"You didn't think she had been dead much more than an hour or two?"

"Well, I guess that's about right, but you see, I had witnesses! They saw your mother's body five hours before I got to her! That's what I could never make Waldis understand!"

"You remember the bruises on her neck?"

"You know I do."

"Cause of death. Jim Burkeshire said that there were no bruises on her neck when he saw the body."

"But the others saw bruises, Josie! I got all that in my notepad. I'll get it and show you!"

"I wouldn't bother, Two-Bit. I have no doubt that a couple of the kids saw those bruises. Melody Mason, Susie Hill, Bob Tanner? Melody tells people whatever they want to hear. Less trouble that way. Susie Hill wasn't much better in the old days, and Bob Tanner, like they say, is just plain stupid."

"If there weren't bruises on her neck, Josie, she wasn't dead when they found her!"

"Exactly. Toby Crouch stumbled into an opportunity, Two-Bit. He saw a woman's naked body, and he saw that he was alone. By your own investigation, you have him taking a long lunch and then getting back to campus to write some tickets around three. He was probably still drunk when he walked into the canyon, and he realized that whatever he wanted to do, someone else was going to take the blame. From his twisted point of view, it was the perfect crime, because he wasn't going to be found out. But then in the middle of raping a corpse, he realized his mistake."

"That's not possible, Josie."

"The ligature mark, Two-Bit. Jim Burkeshire tells me it was red."

"God in heaven . . ."

"It was gray when you saw it, because circulation had stopped, but when the kids found her, it was red. She was comatose, but alive. If they had just touched her, felt for a pulse, checked her breathing, . . . they would have known."

Bitts reflected quietly on this. Both of them did, actually, and Josie waited for some objection, some rage, some senseless denial, but Bitts saw that she was right. It was the only way things could have occurred, the only explanation for the lies that worked and the truths that got discarded.

"There's no telling why Crouch mutilated her body afterwards. Maybe it was fear of getting caught. Maybe he couldn't control himself. Whatever it was, it was so violent that everyone was willing to believe the killer had been interrupted and then came back when the kids left. One crime, not two."

Bitts shook his head. One lie after another, the intricate conspiracies, the petty gains that different men had made by the death of Josie Fortune, the confusion of testimonies from the kids, the quarrels Bitts had had with

Marcel Waldis and Don Stackman, even the mystery of how the body had come into the canyon without anyone seeing the killer coming or going: all of it fell into place now, just as all of it had been obscured by the simple consequence of a pathetic human being's chance encounter with the scene of the crime.

"She made it through, Two-Bit. She survived those bastards. If it hadn't been for Crouch, . . ."

What? How do describe the childhood you didn't get to live? How do you make sense of a woman surviving a hangman's noose, only to be raped and strangled by her rescuer? How do you undo twenty years of prison or tell a man he might have been sheriff another ten or fifteen years if only one lone sociopath had not happened along afterwards. How do you call back the string of victims that never would have been, if Josie Fortune had lived to point her finger?

Fishing

"You going to be all right?" Bitts asked her.

Josie knew she would never be "all right," never forget or forgive or see the world in quite the same way again, but she would make it. In the past few weeks, she had found out that much about herself.

"I'd be better," she answered finally, "if I could get Jack to come in."

"You'll have a better chance once Crouch is implicated in your mother's death."

"The state's attorney won't admit his chief of police meant to execute a prisoner during a transfer, Two-Bit. There was plenty of bad blood between Jack and Colt, but that gives Jack as much motive as it does Colt. As long as it's a stalemate, Stackman pretty much has to get Jack arrested, indict him, and then let a jury decide what happened at Lues Creek Crossing. He sure isn't going to change his strategy if Jack remains a fugitive."

"You've got the new chief of police ready to testify that the evidence points to Colt Fellows taking the first shot."

Josie shook her head. "I'm fairly sure no jury would convict Jack, for a lot of reasons, but Jack won't come in. I talked to him about it, but he says he's where he wants to be. 'To hell with cops and lawyers' is the way he put it."

"Well, Josie, there's no arguing Jack Hazard out of the woods if that's how he feels. If he wants to live that way, he's going to do it, and the good Lord help the man that means to force him out. Maybe it's even for the best. Far as I can see, Jack's never had any luck with lawyers."

"I just wish. . . ."

Josie stopped herself. She wanted to undo things, but wishing it so was never going to change the world.

"I'm not giving up on him," she said finally. "I'll get him out . . . somehow."

Bitts had no answer, and Josie sipped at her coffee, walking closer now to the kitchen's potbelly stove. The wood crackled inside and a steady heat spread over her.

After a time, she announced almost sadly, "I'm going north next weekend to see my adoptive parents."

From behind her, Bitts asked, "You haven't been up to see them since you've been here?"

Josie shook her head, looking through the grates at the fire. "The thing is, I'm afraid I'm going to break their hearts."

"Why is that?"

Josie turned to face the old man. "Because I've filed with the courts to change my name back to *Fortune, Josie Fortune*—the name my mother gave me."

"You doing this for Jack or for your mother?"

"I'm doing it because it's my name. It's who I am. I just didn't know that until I came back home."

"I expect they'll understand then."

"They wanted me to forget Lues. They thought . . ." They had thought the worst of Josie Fortune and Jack Hazard. And maybe of her, as well. At least at first.

"They didn't know the truth, Josie. They were like the rest of us, wanting what was best for you and not knowing quite what that was."

"You think I can make them understand, after all these years?"

"Believe me, the biggest fear they have is losing you. They'll come around."

Josie smiled suddenly, "So what do you say you teach me to fish?"

At the river's edge, Bitts's dogs sniffing about their feet, Josie watched the old man toss his line out to a small pool beyond the reach of the current, then she walked downstream a way. Leaving the worm Two-Bit had given her *off* the hook, she tossed her own line in as well. The weighted line made a quiet plunk. There were small ripples emanating out from it. The river was alive with its own odors. The morning sun was still low in the sky, and the river danced with a thousand sun dogs, shifting and scattering with every movement of the water.

Josie had thought she would leave once she had chased down her last nightmare, and no explanations for it. But the morning after Ferrington's death, after her long night with Cyrus Hazard, she had not written her resignation nor on Friday. She was certain now she wouldn't, not until spring at least.

"They going to fire you for missing your classes this past week, Josie?"

Josie pulled herself from her reveries and looked back toward Bitts. Annie had asked her the same thing when she had called her last night, and Josie told Bitts what she had told Annie, "I've got a contract until May. With their unexpected vacancies, I expect they'll let me finish the year without making too big of a fuss."

"Then what?"

The same question Annie had wanted her to answer. And Jack Hazard. And Cy. "Then, we'll see."

Josie looked back to the river. In the distance, a barge beat its way north against the current. On the Kentucky shoreline, a plume of smoke rose up steadily out of the golden leaves of the forest. Bitts seemed to screw down his concentration and play out his fishing line like a man intent on catching a fish, but Josie was sure she saw a deep and abiding satisfaction in the fierce lines of the old man's frown.

Formerly an assistant professor at Arkansas State University and an assistant professor at the University of Northern Colorado, Craig Smith left teaching and moved to Switzerland to pursue a career as a writer. He received a Ph.D. in English from Southern Illinois University Carbondale in 1988.